THE CLOCKWORK TRILOGY

Book One
CLOCKWORK HEART

Book Two
CLOCKWORK LIES: IRON WIND

Book Three
CLOCKWORK SECRETS: HEAVY FIRE

·✱·

—IRON WIND—
CLOCKWORK LIES

DRU PAGLIASSOTTI

EDGE SCIENCE FICTION AND FANTASY PUBLISHING
AN IMPRINT OF HADES PUBLICATIONS, INC.

CALGARY

Clockwork Lies: Iron Wind
Copyright © 2014 by Dru Pagliassotti

Edge Science Fiction and Fantasy Publishing
An Imprint of Hades Publications Inc.
P.O. Box 1714, Calgary, Alberta, T2P 2L7, Canada

In-house editing by Ella Beaumont
Interior design by Janice Blaine
Cover Illustration by Timothy Lantz

ISBN: 978-1-77053-050-8

EDGE Science Fiction and Fantasy Publishing and Hades Publications, Inc.
acknowledges the ongoing support of the Alberta Foundation for the Arts and
the Canada Council for the Arts for our publishing programme.

Library and Archives Canada Cataloguing in Publication

Pagliassotti, Dru, author
    Clockwork lies : iron wind / Dru Pagliassotti.
Issued in print and electronic formats.
ISBN: 978-1-77053-050-8
(e-book ISBN: 978-1-77053-051-5)

    I. Title.

PS3616.A33775C57 2014   813'.6   C2013-905014-0   C2013-905015-9

FIRST EDITION
(L-20140116)
Printed in Canada
www.edgewebsite.com

DEDICATION

To my sister, Leah.

IRON WIND

CLOCKWORK LIES

CHAPTER ONE

DARK SKIES FORMED an ominous backdrop to the bright silk pavilions and balloons of Mareaux's Festival of Flight. The cool breeze smelled like pending rain.

"I don't like the looks of this," Taya muttered, her eyes fixed on the sky. The breeze ruffled her short auburn hair. Back home in Ondinium, skies this gray would keep an icarus alert and ready to land at the first roll of thunder.

The man walking next to her, one sleeve-hidden hand on her forearm, said nothing. Even when he wasn't required to remain mute under heavy robes and a glass-lensed ivory mask, the Demican lieutenant was a man of few words. Even if he *had* argued for an hour before reluctantly agreeing to this morning's ruse.

But, as Cristof had explained over a glass of bismuth powder, he couldn't possibly maintain his ambassadorial dignity while dangling 1,000 feet in the air with an acute case of food poisoning. Which was why the disgruntled lictor was covered like an exalted while the real exalted hid in Ondinium's pavilion, soothing his roiling stomach with ginger tea and dry toast.

Taya cast another look at the ominous clouds. The Festival was intended to honor and impress Ondinium's ambassador, which meant that she couldn't wear her wings without suggesting, undiplomatically if accurately, that she mistrusted the nation of Mareaux's flight capacity.

Their destination was the queen's personal aerostat, its 55-yard-long silk envelope dyed deep purple— the same hue as the pinot noir wine that was Mareaux's most popular export. A complex network of pale cordage which draped over the dirigible's envelope fastened it to the wicker gondola, which had been painted light blue with gilt highlights. Ondinium's peacetime flag, a speckle of silver stars against a field of black, fluttered next to Mareaux's gold-and-purple banner.

Giant steel cylinders surrounding the dirigible contained, Taya had been informed by her husband's enthusiastic lecture, a rare and expensive buoyant gas. The large hose emerging from one of the cylinders' tops was being fed by crewmembers into an opening within the aerostat's envelope.

Taya thought trusting her life to fabric, wicker, and gas was insane. She'd rather put her faith in well-forged ondium and her own strength and reflexes.

Amcathra squeezed her arm, alerting her that Queen Iancais was approaching. The queen was comfortably plump and round-faced, with cheerful blue eyes and flyaway red hair that kept slipping out of the fancy royal hairstyles in which it was pinned. She was in her fifties, a widow of two years who was being courted by one of Alzana's ambassadors but appeared in no hurry to remarry as her three children came of age. Taya liked the queen but hoped she remained single; Iancais's marriage to an Alzanan would be a diplomatic fiasco for Ondinium.

Taya sank into a deep curtsey as the queen approached. Next to her, Amcathra remained stock-still in his borrowed ivory mask and long, heavy layers of jewel- and embroidery-encrusted robes.

The queen curtseyed to him.

"Good morning, Exalted," she said. She offered Taya a friendly smile. "Icarus."

"Good morning, Your Highness," Taya replied, in Mareaux. "I hope this day finds you well."

"Likewise. You look lovely, Taya. What a charming gown! Whenever you wear one of our styles, your Mareaux ancestry shines through."

"Thank you." Taya's paternal grandparents came from Mareaux, and her inherited auburn hair and fair skin had been a source of great discontent throughout her life. She'd always wanted the black hair and copper skin of a purebred Ondinium. "We were wondering if the festival would still be held. The weather doesn't seem promising."

"My pilot assures me that we'll be safe, although perhaps we will need to move our post-flight picnic indoors," the queen said, addressing Taya's companion, as was proper. "I would be loathe to cancel the flight, Exalted. I know how much you've been looking forward to it."

"The exalted has spoken of little else," Taya said, honestly. She didn't add it had been with more trepidation than enthusiasm. Cristof was fascinated by the *technology* of dirigible flight. He wasn't, however, enthralled by the *experience*.

"Then I'm sure you'll want to meet our pilot," the queen said, still addressing Cristof's blank ivory mask while gesturing to the air crew who stood around them. In moments, a newcomer joined the party. "Exalted Forlore, allow me to introduce Professor Cora Dautry, who is in charge of our flight today."

Dautry's eyes moved uneasily from Taya to the masked figure by her side. Like most women in Mareaux, she wore a dress, although Taya noted with envy that it was plain and utilitarian, with a skirt hemmed high enough to permit easy walking. She wondered if Jayce would be willing to hem her skirts a little higher.

The professor curtseyed even more awkwardly than Taya.

"Professor Dautry will be accompanying you back to Ondinium as part of our exchange agreement," the queen said. "She's taken balloons and dirigibles up over two hundred times for the Mareaux Royal University and has been my personal pilot for two years. We're fortunate to be in her capable hands today."

The professor colored and curtseyed again, muttering something inaudible. She reminded Taya of Cristof, who also fell short when it came to the social graces.

"We're pleased to meet you," Taya said, as warmly as she could. "I hope you'll allow us to ask questions while we're in flight. The exalted has read as much as he can about dirigibles, but of course books are no replacement for experience."

"I will be happy to answer your questions," the professor replied in accented Ondinan. "I hope you will answer mine, too. I am very curious about icarus flight, and little has been written about it."

"There isn't much to say. The principles are the same as bird flight. It's nothing as advanced as this." Taya gestured toward the small, well-insulated steam engine tucked in the back of the gondola. Cristof had told her that it drove the propellers.

"But there's nothing published about ondium," Dautry insisted. "Perhaps if we understood more about it...."

"I'm sure there must be a paper written about it somewhere," Taya said, vaguely. If there were, Professor Dautry would never read it. Ondinium was infamous for keeping its scientific findings secret, although it eagerly welcomed reports about technologies developed in other countries. "I'm afraid I don't understand its physics; I just use it."

"I have read a few speculative papers," Dautry said. "The most provocative theory is that it's aethereally transmissive."

"Ah..." Taya wished Cristof were with her. To her surprise, Amcathra lightly squeezed her arm. He didn't know an exalted's tap code, but... "That's quite possible."

Since when did the lictor know anything about physics? Or was he just signaling her to get a move on?

"Perhaps you will have a chance to exchange thoughts on the matter with Exalted Forlore during your trip to Ondinium," Queen Iancais said, checking the tiny golden pocket watch that had been Cristof's gift to their host.

"Excuse me, your highness," Dautry said quickly, in Mareaux. "Of course. Your highness. Exalted." She curtsied and hurried off.

Distant thunder rumbled. The clouds were moving closer.

"I'm afraid it's the rainy season," the queen said, glancing upward. "Our storms move south from the Corundiel Sea. It must be snowing in Ondinium already."

"I'm sure it is. Enjoying Mareaux's long, warm autumn has been a pleasant change for us," Taya replied. "It will be difficult to return to cold weather."

"What a pity the exalted can't stay through the winter."

"Unfortunately, the High Council insists he return."

"Of course." The queen knew as well as Taya that the decaturs would never let their only exalted ambassador out of the country for more than a few weeks at a time. "Given the weather, I'm afraid this will be a short flight. Perhaps we will can arrange a longer, private flight when the weather is better. I'm sure the exalted would prefer to go aloft in greater seclusion and comfort."

Meaning, without his mask and robes.

"He would enjoy that, if time and the weather permit," Taya lied. With luck, the queen's offer of a second flight was as politely meaningless as her offer to let them remain through the winter.

"Your highness?" Dautry unlocked the small door to the gondola. "If you're ready, we should leave now." She glanced up at the sky, smoothing a strand of hair behind one ear. "The storm is moving in quickly."

Taya took a few minutes to ensure that her robed and masked companion was comfortable, his heavily embroidered and jeweled sleeves and hem tucked in where they wouldn't interfere with

Dautry's piloting. The long wicker gondola could barely contain all four of them, so filled was it with boxes and bundles.

"Experimental equipment," the queen explained with an amused, apologetic smile. "I allow the professor to pursue her research when we're not using the vehicle for a pleasure flight."

Taya made a mental note of the labels. Cristof and the High Council would be interested in their contents, even if they meant nothing to her.

Trumpets rang across the field and the rest of the ambassadors entered the other nine aerostats. The crowds in the field thinned, leaving the ground crews to continue their work.

The queen, Taya, her disguised companion, and the professor stood close while the small steam engine started chugging and the ground crew cast off lines. Taya maneuvered herself between Lieutenant Amcathra and the others to protect him from accidental discovery. He was taller and broader than Cristof, although the stiff formal robes did much to hide his physique and the exalted's ornately coiffed black wig covered his light blond hair.

"Are you looking forward to being in the air again, Icarus?" asked the queen.

"I always enjoy flying. But I don't understand how something as insubstantial as a gas can lift all this weight."

"It's miraculous, isn't it?" Iancais steadied herself as the gondola lurched and the aerostat ascended.

Taya leaned over the edge of the gondola to watch the ground recede.

"I'm surprised Mareaux doesn't use dirigibles for transportation or trade. A vehicle like this would have a lot of practical uses."

Dautry cleared her throat.

"Miss Icarus, if you would please stay inside the gondola...."

"Oh, sorry. Please, call me Taya." She'd finally given up trying to explain that she wasn't "Miss Icarus." Mareaux's naming conventions were different from Ondinium's; not only did they assume her caste title was her last name, they also failed to realize that she and Cristof were married, since she wasn't "Mrs. Forlore." They'd assigned Cristof and Taya separate rooms, although at least they were in the same suite.

The floating aerostats were a cheerful sight, their bright flags and colors glimmering against the dark sky. Someone on the vehicle flying the Samaran flag waved at them, and Taya waved back.

Her companion shifted, squeezing her arm again. Taya dragged her attention away from their surroundings.

"Are dirigibles useful for transportation?" she asked, repeating her earlier question.

"Not really." The queen's tone was amused. She knew why Taya was asking. "They can't carry much weight, especially over a distance. At the moment, they're most useful to us as observation posts during sporting events and field exercises."

Taya nodded. So, Mareaux was prepared to admit that the vehicles had some military utility, although not as much as the High Council had feared. The decaturs would be glad to hear that. They didn't care for any challenge to Ondinium's control of the skies.

"How high have you flown?" she asked Professor Dautry. The pilot was relaxed as she kept an eye on her instruments.

"I've personally gone up to ten thousand feet." She tapped a brass barometer that had been affixed to one of the sides of the gondola, next to a compass, a thermometer, and several instruments Taya didn't recognize.

"Did you get nauseous?" Altitude sickness was a problem for the daredevil icarii who sought to break the record for highest flight.

"No, but I didn't stay up very long. We have to be very careful, with gas." Dautry gestured at the long, cylindrical envelope over their heads. "Several pilots have died in explosions while trying to establish new height records."

Explosions? Taya swallowed. Nobody had warned her about *explosions*. She struggled to remember the other questions she was supposed to ask.

"Have you... uh, have you succeeded in flying against air currents?"

The professor rocked her hand back and forth. "With some effort, yes. Not when the wind is strong. It's the weight problem again. Ondinium manufactures the smallest and most efficient steam engines in the world, but if they're powerful enough to fight strong winds, they're too heavy for an aerostat."

"Couldn't you build a bigger envelope?"

"Then we'd have different problems, such as fuel consumption and envelope folding." Dautry shrugged. "Perhaps the problem will be resolved with Alzana's new electromagnetic engines. I hear they've already had some success using them on their aereonave."

Amcathra shifted. Taya didn't know what *electromagnetic* or *aeronave* meant, but if they alarmed the lictor, they would alarm the Council. Any time the Alzanans invented something new, it alarmed the Council.

"Designing a more efficient aerostat is one of the projects Professor Dautry hopes to address with your Great Engine," the queen interjected.

"I'm sure Ondinium will be eager to assist," Taya said, wondering if the Council would ever let an improved dirigible get off the drawing board.

Wind gusted, jerking the vehicle to one side. Dautry turned her attention back to their progress with an oath that didn't seem quite appropriate to use around a queen.

Next to Taya, Lieutenant Amcathra laid a gloved hand on the edge of the basket. The long ends of his silk sleeve dangled over the edge.

Around them, the other aerostats began falling out of their neatly arranged order as they compensated for the wind.

"What's wrong?" the queen asked.

"There's..." Dautry started to answer when the gondola tilted. Taya instinctively leaned back to counterbalance it. "Damn!"

The gondola lurched again and Taya heard the sickening sound of fabric ripping. Everyone looked up as one of the dirigible's fins plummeted past them, scattering bits of debris behind it.

Dautry struggled with the steering controls.

Amcathra started to say something and Taya elbowed him in the ribs.

"What happened?" she demanded.

"Accident," their pilot snapped. "I'll take us down."

"Well, it seems we won't fly as far as we'd hoped," the queen said, her voice strained. "You have nothing to worry about, Exalted. Professor Dautry is an expert pilot."

"Is there anything I can do?" Taya asked.

Dautry didn't answer, concentrating on her steering controls.

Feeling helpless, Taya leaned over the gondola's edge again. The gusty winds were carrying them out of the palace grounds toward Echelles. Thunder rumbled.

"We need to get down before the lightning gets closer," she said, then mentally chided herself for stating the obvious. Dautry ignored her. The queen smoothed her skirts.

"There may not be any lightning at all, if—" Queen Iancais began. A distant flicker made her swallow the rest of her words. "Professor, please bring us down as quickly and as safely as you can."

The winds were driving the dirigible west. Taya watched, every muscle taut with anxiety, as Dautry fought to compensate for the crippled steering mechanism. The professor wasn't battling the wind so much as attempting to ride it to the ground. Taya wanted to shout at her to go faster, but she grit her teeth and stayed silent.

Thunder cracked, sounding closer. The storm had turned the early dawn back to dusk. They were over the outskirts of the city now, well above its peaked roofs. Beyond Echelles' city walls curled a dull gray line of water, the Pomander River, a distributary from the Corundiel Sea. The river was paralleled by the iron rails of the Grand Mareaux Railway, which stretched south to the coast and north to Mareaux-Ondinium Terminal.

Amcathra grasped her arm. She looked at him, shaking her head. He gestured with a silk-draped hand toward Queen Iancais' feet.

"Your Highness…" Taya said, confused. She wasn't sure what he wanted.

The queen laid a hand on Taya's arm. "I assure you that there's nothing to—"

At last Taya spotted the wisp of smoke rising from the box on the gondola floor. "Fire!"

Professor Dautry swore, glancing away from her instruments. The queen gasped and tried to move as a thin line of flame licked around the lid of the box. She bumped into the professor.

Taya darted forward and grabbed the box. Metal bands around its sides scorched her palms. She yelped, yanking her hands away.

The box tumbled, its lid falling off. Flames licked the gondola's painted wicker floor. Taya started forward as the queen exclaimed about her skirts. Taya looked down. The lace trim on her petticoats was on fire.

Then Amcathra elbowed her aside, grabbing the box with his silk-gloved hands. He turned and heaved it overboard, heedless of his robe's hem dragging through the flames.

Another gust of wind rocked the dirigible, carrying a spray of drizzling rain. Taya crouched and beat on the edges of her skirts with her blistering hands.

"Make sure the fire is out!" Dautry shouted, struggling to control the aerostat.

"I beg your pardon, Exalted," the queen muttered, stamping the hem of Amcathra's robe with one finely tooled leather shoe.

Taya swept the hem aside to make sure the rest of the fire had been put out. Then, with a glance at the queen, she carefully rearranged the layers of fabric to hide Amcathra's heavy boots. They weren't exactly the jeweled silk slippers of an exalted; Amcathra's feet were larger than Cristof's.

"What happened?" she asked, trying to stand and losing her footing. Both Queen Iancais and Lieutenant Amcathra reached out to steady her as the dirigible lurched again in the strengthening winds. Raindrops pelted her face as she glared at Amcathra.

"I don't know," the queen said, sounding angry, "but I promise to find out."

The other aerostats were out of sight behind them. The queen's dirigible made its descent alone in the darkness, pelted by rain. At last Dautry warned them to brace themselves. The gondola scraped and bounced across the ground. Something struck it, and the cylindrical envelope slowly, regally, toppled over, dragging them all through the mud and brambles.

A wet half-hour passed before the queen's soldiers found them trudging wearily out of the muddy orchard. Consternation followed when it became clear that neither Taya nor "the exalted" knew how to ride a horse.

"We don't use horses much at home," Taya said, embarrassed. Almost all of the countries around Ondinium prided themselves on their cavalry, but Ondinium had long since replaced horse transportation with wireferries, trains, and icarii. A few horses were still used to pull carriages, carts, and plows, but riding in a saddle was all but a lost art.

After some discussion, the queen was escorted back to the palace while a nearby farmer's wagon was retrieved for the ambassador and Taya, who asked to be taken back to the festival field.

"Are you sure you don't want to go straight to the palace?" the soldier driving them asked. "We can send a rider to your people to let them know you're safe."

Taya shook her head. Cristof would be waiting in the pavilion; the plan had been that he'd put on his robes again as soon as the flight was over, in case protocol required him to unmask during the feast. Even if it had been canceled, her husband could hardly ride back to the palace with a naked face. Even with a fake lictor's castemark, he might be recognized by one of the other ambassadors.

"Please, if you don't mind," she insisted.

The soldier shrugged, rolling his eyes at his companion as he turned back to the wagon. There were some advantages to having a national reputation for strange behavior, Taya thought.

They reached the airfield an hour and a half after their flight had departed. The other dirigibles had already landed and were in various states of being dismantled. A swarm of laborers descended upon them, filling the wagon with cargo as soon as Taya and the false ambassador slid off. Taya held on to Lieutenant Amcathra's arm, assuring everyone that the exalted was well, until their lictors found them and marched them across muddy carpets to Ondinium's dripping silk pavilion.

As soon as its draperies were drawn shut, Cristof threw his arms around her, lifting her off her feet in his worried embrace.

"What happened? Are you all right?" His gray eyes fastened on her bandaged hands. "Did you get cut?"

"Just some blisters." She stood on her toes to kiss him, feeling a ridiculous sense of relief. Her husband was wearing a borrowed, ill-fitting lictor's uniform and looked every inch an Ondinium exalted pretending to be something he wasn't. "Somebody sabotaged the aerostat. Lieutenant Amcathra saved us."

"Sabotage?" Cristof turned, one hand resting on her back. "Janos, what happened?"

The lictor frowned as his two men lifted away the ivory mask and unpinned the wig. He shook his long sleeves back and ran his hands briskly over his face and crew-cut blond hair.

"I am grateful you were born to wear such garments, and not me, Exalted."

"That makes one of us." Cristof slid his hand off Taya's back and stepped forward. "Here, let me help."

"If you expect me to object to the impropriety, you are mistaken." The lieutenant held out his arms, allowing his men, Taya, and Cristof to begin the lengthy process of releasing him from his sodden layers.

"Jayce isn't going to be happy about this," Taya predicted, draping one of the muddy robes over a chair next to the brazier.

Jayce could work miracles with a needle and thread, but saving these garments would take the Lady's own help.

"Jayce isn't happy about anything," Cristof countered, helping the lieutenant out of his second under-robe and handing it over. "Are those scorch marks?"

"Somebody put an incendiary device on the dirigible," Amcathra said. "I smelled vitriol while I was throwing it overboard."

"An incendiary—" Cristof turned to Taya, grabbing her wrist and turning it over. "These are *burn* blisters?"

"I grabbed it with my bare hands," she admitted. "The metal was hotter than I expected."

"Let me see." He started to unknot the bandages, and she pulled her hand away.

"You can look at my hands when we're back in the palace."

"How bad is it?" he demanded, his grey eyes shadowed with concern.

"They're just blisters." She changed the subject. "Come on, you need to get dressed. The queen will want to talk to you about the sabotage."

"The exalted should appear shaken and outraged," Amcathra instructed, slipping out of his third and final robe and standing in nothing but his uniform trousers and boots. Taya wondered how he could stand the chill. Maybe all that blond hair on his chest and arms kept him warm. The snarling bear's head tattooed on his upper arm seemed an appropriate symbol for the hirsute Demican.

"I *am* shaken and outraged. If I'd known the flight was going to be dangerous, I wouldn't have asked you two to go."

"You couldn't have known," Taya reassured him. "How are you feeling? You look better."

"Well, I'm no longer using two chamberpots at the same time. I suppose that's an improvement."

"I don't understand how you can get so sick eating the same food as the rest of us."

"The exalted possesses the refined constitution that accompanies a thousand fortuitous rebirths," Amcathra observed.

"Don't be snide, Janos," Cristof countered. "Impersonating an exalted is an executable offense."

"As is impersonating a lictor, Exalted."

"Both of you, be quiet," Taya interrupted. "Lieutenant, would you please brief my husband before he talks to the queen? I'll get him dressed."

"In wet, muddy robes," Cristof muttered, tucking his glasses into a pocket and holding out his arms. "I can hardly wait."

"Yes, it *is* pleasant to put on a dry uniform." Amcathra reached for the white shirt and black uniform jacket waiting for him as Cristof gave him a dark look.

By the time the exalted was covered by robes, mask, and wig, the rain was dripping through the pavilion roof so thoroughly that the fabric's presence hardly seemed to make any difference. The queen had sent two carriages for them. Amcathra, Taya, and Cristof took the first, and their two lictors followed in the second.

Cristof reached forward to close the curtains, but Taya stopped him.

"Let yourself be seen," she suggested. "To show you're still alive."

"Yes, it will be much easier for a frustrated assassin to shoot you if he can see where you're sitting," Amcathra added, agreeably.

Taya scowled, then leaned forward and yanked the carriage curtains shut.

"You're awful," she accused. Next to her, Cristof fumbled off his ivory mask.

"So is making me wear this when I don't have to." He wiped his face with one wet sleeve, smearing his fake lictor's stripe. "Do you really think it was an assassination attempt, Janos?"

"Yes."

"But why?" Taya pulled a damp handkerchief out of her rain-ruined reticule. "This isn't an *important* diplomatic mission."

"But it is the first time in nearly two centuries that an exalted in good standing has left Ondinium."

"Not that good a standing," Cristof interjected as Taya rubbed at the black smear on his sleeve.

"Nevertheless, your presence may be a temptation to political factions who disagree with Ondinium's policies. That is why I am accompanying this mission."

"I *asked* you to accompany this mission."

"Your request was serendipitous, as the Council had already ordered me to go."

"I see. If that's the case, I think you should stand in for me more often. I'd be much safer that way. And more comfortable, too."

"Regrettably, impersonating an exalted is an executable offense."

"Lieutenant, did the Council *warn* you that somebody might try to kill Cris?" Taya pressed, giving up on the stained sleeve and wiping the rest of the paint off Cristof's face, instead.

"All official envoys from Ondinium are considered to be at risk when they travel to foreign countries. Ondinium has many enemies. An exalted would be an especially attractive victim for an assassin or kidnapper." Amcathra met Cristof's eyes. "Fortunately, the Council considers you to be one of the more expendable members of your caste. Your loss would be a political embarrassment, but it would not cripple the nation."

"Lieutenant!"

"It's all right, Taya. That was my understanding from the very beginning of this ridiculous charade." Cristof gave her one of his rare, crooked smiles, tugging the handkerchief from her fingers to finish cleaning his face by himself. "If I were a *respectable* exalted, the Council would never have let me leave the city."

"That doesn't make it any better." She scowled and leaned back, plucking with annoyance at her soaking skirts and petticoats. Her bandaged palms hurt. "And you don't have to sound so smug about it, either, Lieutenant."

"I have no intention of allowing your husband to be assassinated. I have seen how much trouble you cause when you investigate murders."

"But why a fire?" Cristof asked, forestalling her retort. "Why *not* a bullet to the head or a bomb in a carriage? They would be much more reliable."

"But more obvious," Taya suggested, unwillingly drawn into his speculation. "Apparently aerostats explode all the time."

"Not all the time," he corrected her. "Only nine percent of aerostat excursions have ended in injury or death in the last ten years. Icarii have a much higher accident rate, statistically speaking."

"But we seldom explode."

"Perhaps the attack was not intended to kill," Amcathra intervened. "Perhaps it was only a warning."

"Which brings us back to this being a relatively unimportant mission," Taya said. She paused and looked from one to the other with a trace of suspicion. "This *is* an unimportant mission, isn't it?"

Cristof leaned over in a rustle of robes to give her an ameliorating kiss. He'd become much better at it since their marriage.

"Yes," he promised. "I'm supposed to report on the status of Mareaux's dirigibles, but everyone knows that. Janos?"

"The same. I am also to report on your behavior during this mission."

"Naturally. Anything else?"

"I have no other clandestine mission to accomplish in Mareaux. Icarus?"

"Me? I'm just here to keep the two of you from starting a war."

"It seems your mission has just become more challenging."

The carriage rattled to a halt and Taya helped her husband back into his mask.

"This isn't going to cause a war, is it?" she asked. Cristof muttered something that was muffled by his mask.

"That will depend on who started the fire," Lieutenant Amcathra replied.

Ambassadors and courtiers milled around the palace's marble entranceway, turning to watch as they stepped inside. A few nodded and murmured greetings, uncomfortable around a peer whose body and face were kept hidden in public. Lord Gaio and Lady Fosca Mazzoletti, the brother-and-sister ambassadors from Alzana, pushed their way forward. They looked dry and well-groomed, in contrast to most of the other guests who'd been on the aerostats. They must have changed their clothes as soon as they'd returned to the palace, Taya thought, disgruntled.

"Oh, Exalted, I'm so glad to see you safe," Lady Fosca exclaimed, hurrying forward and laying a slender, well-manicured hand on Cristof's arm. "We were absolutely horrified when your dirigible broke apart!"

Taya bristled. *Nobody* touched an exalted without his or her permission. Cristof's fingers, hidden by his long sleeve, tapped a message on her arm: *Polite.*

"The exalted appreciates your concern," she said, straining to keep her tone level.

Lady Fosca undoubtedly knew about the taboo. She simply enjoyed showing her disdain for Ondinium's traditions.

"And you, Icarus? What happened to your hands?" Lord Gaio asked with a sympathy that Taya suspected he didn't feel. Before she could answer, he'd taken her free hand and cradled it in his own. "Were you injured?"

"Just some blisters, thank you, Your Excellency." She tugged her hand away. Touching an icarus wasn't taboo, but she didn't like Lord Gaio, who was none too subtly courting the queen. If he wanted his suit to succeed, she thought, he should stop flirting with every other woman in the palace.

"Is it true that somebody set fire to your balloon?" Lady Fosca asked, gazing at Cristof's blank mask with a show of sympathy. Cristof's fingers danced on Taya's arm, spelling out a word: *dirigible*.

"There was a fire on the queen's *dirigible*," Taya corrected.

"Its cause will be investigated," Lieutenant Amcathra added, his voice flat.

"I should certainly hope so," Lord Gaio observed. "And you should punish the negligent pilot. The exalted could have died."

"The risk of death was minimal. Perhaps the person who started the fire was under the impression that Mareaux uses the same inflammable gas as Alzana," Lieutenant Amcathra replied. His blue eyes were cold. The other courtiers fell silent, listening.

"Or perhaps the fire was a well-contained but pointed warning to Mareaux not to pursue its aerostat research," Lord Gaio countered.

"Such as might be given by a nation unsuccessfully competing with Mareaux in aerostat development," Amcathra suggested.

"Or a nation that prefers to maintain its ancient monopoly over flight."

"I'm sure the queen's investigation will provide some answers," Taya said, alarmed. "If you will excuse us, Your Excellencies, the exalted would like to change out of his wet robes."

"Of course." Lady Fosca patted Cristof's arm one last time. "I hope we'll see you at dinner, since the picnic was canceled."

"I'm sure you will," Taya said, stepping forward. The Alzanans reluctantly moved aside, allowing them to continue.

In the ambassadorial suite, a crackling fire had been lit and an invitation to join the queen for a private lunch sat on the mantelpiece.

"Thank the Lady!" Taya helped her husband take off his mask. "I'm going to ask the staff to prepare us some baths before lunchtime."

Amcathra gave Cristof a smart palm-to-the-forehead bow. "I will be back soon, Exalted."

"Where are you going?" Cristof demanded, shaking back his sleeves and pulling on his glasses.

"I intend to search for the box we threw overboard."

"Do you think you'll find proof that it's Alzanan?"

"I doubt we shall be so fortunate."

·✳·

Cristof waited in another room until the servants had brought in the copper tubs, hot water, bathing lotions, and towels. At last Taya unpinned his wig with her fingertips and set it on its stand.

"Ada will have to repair it when we get back," she said, looking at its sad tangle of hair and jewels. "But maybe Jayce can do something to fix it up in the meantime."

"Later." Cristof hugged her from behind, resting his chin in the crook of her neck. "Let's get you out of those wet skirts, my love."

She grinned, putting a hand over his. He gently took her wrist and turned it, moving around from behind her.

"But first, I want to see what's under these bandages. You flinch every time you move your hands." He guided her to a couch and unwrapped the strips of fabric. "I wish I'd brought more household staff, so you wouldn't have to do all my robing and disrobing."

"As if I'd let anybody else undress you!"

"Don't you trust me?"

"I trust *you*." She caressed the wave-shaped caste tattoo on his cheek with the back of her free hand. "But I'm sure any number of foreign spies are ready to seduce Ondinium's secrets out of you."

"Oh, good, an ambassadorial perquisite at last."

Taya raised an eyebrow. "You get plenty of ambassadorial perquisites. Your own suite, all the Mareaux wine you can drink—"

"Do you suppose it would be a faux pas to tell the queen that I prefer beer?"

"Without a doubt." She winced as he pulled away the last of the bandage. "I hope you've been drinking *some* of her wine."

"I choke down a glass every night, and then I toss a few more glasses' worth out the window. I hope I don't kill the roses."

"You'll set back diplomacy a hundred years if the queen finds out."

Cristof pushed his silver-rimmed glasses up to his forehead as he studied her hand. Then he pulled the glasses back over his eyes and unwrapped her other hand.

"I don't think these burns will do more than blister," he said, "but the swelling will make it difficult for you to move your hands for a few days."

"Can't we pop the blisters?"

"Our family physician told us never to pop a blister, back when we were boys," he said, tilting her hand up. "Of course we did it anyway."

We. Taya gazed at him, feeling a familiar pang. Even though Cristof's brother had been outcaste and expelled from Ondinium, he still talked about Alister with affection.

"I'll ask the palace physician what to do," she promised.

"Good." Cristof turned her hand over and kissed the back. "In the meantime, my duty is clear."

"What?"

"I'll need to wash and dress you while you keep your hands dry."

"Is that so?" She cocked her head, pretending she hadn't felt a leap of anticipation at his words. "I thought we'd agreed to respect Mareaux propriety."

"Attempted assassination negates my obligations to Mareaux propriety." He nudged her around and began unfastening the delicate buttons on the back of her dress. "Besides, I need the practice."

"At what?"

"At undressing attractive women. I wouldn't want to embarrass my country when those spies show up."

Taya reached around to punch him in the arm, but not hard enough to make him stop.

CHAPTER TWO

"WE HAVE DETAINED every member of the ground crew and are holding them for questioning," said the queen's chancellor, Lord Pomeroy. "The aerostat's fin was intentionally sabotaged; the struts show marks of cutting."

The servants had been banished and the doors locked so that Cristof could sit at the table without his mask. He wore an exalted's elegant but comfortable day-to-day silk robes over a famulate's black trousers and white shirt. His black hair, which he'd been growing longer, was pulled back in a ponytail held by a silver clasp. Taya thought her husband looked good, even though his mish-mash of caste fashion made their tailor cringe.

"Unfortunately," Pomeroy continued, "the field wasn't being closely guarded and numerous people were present to set up the pavilions and dirigibles, so any number of people could have sabotaged the fin and planted the device."

"However," Queen Iancais added, "your lictors and my soldiers both inspected the aerostat last night."

"I found what was left of the fire-box, but there was little to learn." Amcathra still wore his muddy, rain-soaked uniform. The queen had been surprised when he'd joined them, but she had simply ordered another place set. "The exalted smelled vitriol when he discarded it, which suggests a chemically based incendiary device. If it were timed, as I suspect, the person who left it had access to the vehicle *and* the flight timetable."

"The Festival was arranged last month," Queen Iancais pointed out. "Our flight time was no secret."

Cristof glanced at the queen. "Your Highness, could the attack have been directed at you?"

"It is always possible," she said, after a moment, "but to the best of my knowledge, I've done nothing in the last year to invite an attack."

Except entertain the very first exalted ambassador from the very unpopular Ondinium, Taya thought. She was certain everyone was thinking it. She wished someone would just come out and say it.

"Please," Lord Pomeroy said, forcing a hearty tone. "Let us set this unpleasant business aside and concentrate on our excellent cassoulet."

"Of course." Cristof probed at the dish with a perceptible lack of enthusiasm. Taya pushed over a bowl of peaches. He shot her a grateful look.

She wasn't eating much, either; it was hard to hold utensils in her swollen and bandaged hands. Besides, Cristof had poured her a large glass of wine to "deaden the pain" while she'd been in the bath, and between the unaccustomed early drinking and his attentive care, she was feeling light-headed and more than a little satiated.

"Tell me, Exalted Forlore," the queen asked after a few minutes of silence, "are you still interested in touring the aeronautical instrumentation plant this afternoon?"

"Yes, I'm looking forward to it," Cristof exclaimed, his grey eyes lighting up. "Johannes Bezier's going to be there, isn't he?"

"We have arranged it, but how do you intend to talk to him? He isn't of noble birth...."

Cristof waved the problem away. "Just find us a private room. I *have* to talk to him; I've read all of his articles. I've been hoping to meet him ever since I was given this assignment."

"Won't it be irregular, an exalted unmasking before a simple scientist?"

"Yes," Amcathra replied, cutting Cristof off. "Is Mr. Bezier discreet?"

The queen blinked. "I'm afraid I don't know him personally. Lord Pomeroy?"

"I couldn't say."

"As long as nobody else sees me, propriety will be satisfied," Cristof said, impatiently. "It's not as though—"

"The exalted wishes to make a special exception to honor Mister Bezier," Taya interrupted before her husband could blurt out something offensive. Technically, *every* foreigner was outcaste, which meant that *no* foreigner should ever see an exalted's naked face— royalty or otherwise. It was Cristof's scandalous disregard for his caste taboos that made him a perfect ambassador— but it also kept Taya and Amcathra on their toes ensuring that his diplomatic pretense of "honoring" foreign nobility by unmasking before them was maintained.

"As you know," she added, "engineers and scientists are highly esteemed in Ondinium. Their caste standing is quite high in our country."

"Well, if you're certain it's acceptable...."

"The exalted has the utmost respect for Mareaux's top scientists."

"The exalted can speak for himself when he's not wearing a mask," Cristof muttered.

"Although it's usually better if he doesn't," Taya retorted. The queen lifted a handkerchief to her lips as if hiding a smile.

"Does that mean you've decided to come, after all?" Cristof asked, oblivious to the queen's reaction.

Taya wrinkled her nose. The thought of spending hours gazing at obscure scientific instrumentation and listening to technological doublespeak made her eyes glaze. She *should* accompany him, as his official translator, to ask all the questions he couldn't, but....

She looked at Amcathra, who inclined his head.

"I will attend him this afternoon, Icarus. The tour interests me, as well."

"Oh, Taya, has my physician seen your injuries yet?" Iancais inquired.

"He, ah, knocked on the door while I was bathing, so I asked him to return after lunch," Taya said, looking down at her plate and fighting a blush. Actually, she hadn't been bathing. But she hadn't been clothed, either.

"Be sure to see him," the queen advised. "And, Exalted Forlore, we can provide you and your lictor with a translator, if you like."

"With your leave, Your Highness," Taya ventured, "after I've seen your physician, I'd like to go shopping in Echelles. I promised to pick up some gifts for our friends in Ondinium, and I haven't had any time to get away before now."

"Do you require a guide?" the queen asked, her face lighting up. Taya suspected she was imagining the exalted's representative picking up expensive Mareaux fashions and wine to show off in Ondinium. She wondered what the queen would think if she saw the list her friends had given to her— programming manuals from Cabiel, political tracts from Tizier, and a raunchy romance series that Cassie had ordered her to purchase in Mareaux after Ondinium's censors had determined it unfit for import.

Sometimes Taya wished for friends who'd be happy with a bottle of wine and a new hat.

"I should be fine by myself, your highness."

"Rikard will accompany you," Amcathra stated.

"But—"

"Taya— please." Cristof laid a hand over her wrist. "Take Rikard. Just to be safe."

She sighed. "All right." She supposed if her husband could put up with wearing robes and a mask all day, she could put up with an armed guard for a few hours.

It would be more of a trial for Rikard than for her, anyway.

"I'll give you the names of my favorite shops," the queen said, sounding pleased.

The rain had become a steady, depressing drizzle by the time the palace physician finished inspecting and re-bandaging her hands. Taya decided to leave her wings locked up in the suite. Flying in the rain was no fun, and neither was cleaning, drying, and oiling an armature. She pulled on her warm flight leathers, a heavy wool coat and hat, and headed out into the rain with Rikard.

Amcathra referred to Rikard as his nephew, but Demicans used the terms "niece," "nephew," "aunt," and "uncle" for any consanguineous relation beyond the immediate household, as well as for friends, lovers, friends of family members, and even fellow clan members, so Taya wasn't sure what their real relationship was. But like Amcathra, Rikard was comfortable with silence. After a few attempts to draw him out, Taya gave up, walking through Echelles' narrow cobblestone streets without conversation.

Light glowed through the rain-streaked window of the bookstore she wanted and saw. She stepped inside, setting a bell jangling.

"Good day," the shopkeeper sang out as she looked up from her account-book. Her blue eyes flickered to the lictor behind Taya, then back again, confused. "May I help you?"

"Yes, please," Taya replied in Mareaux, taking off her coat and hat and draping them on the coat rack by the entrance. Water pooled across the tiled floor. "I'm looking for some specialized books, and I may need your help finding them."

"Oh! You're from Ondinium?"

Several of the other customers looked up, their eyes immediately drawn to Rikard's severe black uniform and black lictor's stripe. At least, Taya thought with relief, his long overcoat hid the air pistol holstered at his waist.

"Yes." Taya walked up to the desk, fumbling for the Mareaux-style calling cards she'd had printed for her visit. She handed one over, holding it in her unbandaged fingertips. "I'm Taya Icarus. I'm with the ambassador's party."

"An icarus!" The shopkeeper looked relieved as she set the card down and stood. "I'm so sorry— I recognized your accent, but I didn't see a castemark, so I wasn't sure what to think."

"It can be confusing in Ondinium, too, when we're not wearing our wings." Taya was wearing her icarus-feather lapel pin, of course, but nobody in Mareaux knew what it meant. "I understand you specialize in books on science and technology?"

"I do." The woman seemed more comfortable now that they were on familiar ground. "What are you looking for? I'd better get the books for you— what happened to your hands?"

So, news of the dirigible accident hadn't yet spread to the city.

"I grabbed something hot. It was stupid, but I wasn't thinking."

The shopkeeper tsked, nodding in sympathy.

Together they located most of the books on Taya's list, and the shopkeeper directed her to two stores where she'd be able to find the rest. Taya spent another hour walking from shop to shop placing orders to be delivered.

"Oh, look— tea!" Taya stopped in front of a brightly lit window. "Come on, Rikard. Let's take a break."

He didn't protest, so she headed inside and took a table by the window. Rikard hung his dripping black overcoat over the back of his chair and sat down across from her. His pistol and castemark gathered more stares.

"I think I have enough money left for a pot of tea and some sandwiches," Taya said, spilling what was left of her coins on the table and sorting them out with her fingertips. "Are you hungry?"

"Yes." Rikard pulled out a black leather wallet. "I can pay for my food."

"No, no, that's all right. I have enough." She grinned, stacking the coins and sliding them to one end of the table. "I can hardly make you pay after I've dragged you through the rain for an hour and a half."

"That's my job."

"Still— my treat."

"Thank you, Icarus." He tucked his wallet back into his coat.

"You haven't bought anything?" She paused to order as a server stopped by their table, then turned back to him. "If you want to stop by any stores while we're out...."

"I prefer to save my money."

"For something special?"

"My little sister is ill." Rikard ran a finger over the polished wood of the table. "Uncle Janos and I contribute to her care."

"Oh." Taya squirmed. Lieutenant Amcathra had never revealed anything about his private life to her. "I'm so sorry. What happened?"

"The physicians say she was born with weak lungs."

"You don't agree?"

"My family lives in Tertius. There was a fire at a zinc gal-vanizing plant in our neighborhood a month after she was born. Eleven workers died and everybody coughed for months afterward. Most of us recovered. She didn't."

"Did the company help? Did it pay for her medical bills?"

"No. It went bankrupt."

"That's terrible." She wondered if there was something she and Cristof could do to help. "What kind of treatment does she get?"

"There isn't much the doctors can do. She can't breathe well, so she gets tired easily. And the air's so dirty in Tertius, she never has a chance to recover. On bad days, she can't even walk down the street without feeling faint."

Taya nodded with recognition. She'd grown up in Tertius, too. The air quality depended on the season and where one lived, but the sector was, consistently, polluted by smoke and soot from the manufacturing plants tucked into the foothills.

"Are you saving to move up to Secundus?"

"I'm saving to send her back to Demicus." Rikard glowered at the table. "She needs clean air. She wouldn't have gotten sick if she'd grown up in our homeland."

"I thought you were born in Ondinium."

He shot her a sharp glance.

"I was."

"Then you've visited Demicus?"

"No. But I know there aren't any factories there, except where foreigners have settled. Most of our country is untouched. Just fresh air and clean water."

"Were your parents immigrants?"

"My grandparents. I'm third generation."

"Me, too, on my father's side. My mother's family have been citizens forever— famulate caste."

"My mother and father are lictors."

"Are they related to the lieutenant?"

"My mother is his sister. He's second-generation, like her."

"Oh, then you really *are* the lieutenant's nephew."

"Their parents left Demicus together. Most of our clan lives in Ondinium now."

"Do you have any family left up north?"

"Probably not." He shifted in his seat. "Most of my people move away from Demicus as fast as they can. Why put in all that effort living free and hunting and gathering under an open sky? It's much better to work for foreigners so you can live in a house and buy food from strangers." His voice was bitter.

"If you dislike Ondinium that much, why did you stay in caste? You could have left."

The young man shrugged, not meeting her eyes.

"Seven's too young to really understand the choice you're making. Besides, I can't take my sister back to Demicus without any money." He changed the subject. "What about you? Do you have relatives here in Mareaux?"

"I suppose I must, but I don't know who they are. I think my grandparents wanted a clean break." Taya reached up and ran a hand across her red hair. "But the bloodline still shows."

"If you had blue or green eyes, you could pass as a native."

"I was lucky; I got my mother's eyes. My sister has mother's black hair *and* black eyes; she can almost pass for Ondinium, except for her skin. Her husband's dark, though, so her children will look like citizens."

"We don't look like citizens?"

"You know what I mean."

"You'd rather look like a pureblood?"

"Of course I would. I got teased all the time when I was a girl." Taya glanced at her reflection in the window. "I used to sit on the roof each day, trying to get tan, but mostly I just burned.

Once I even dyed my hair black. It was awful. The color rubbed off on my clothes and my pillow… and of course I'm short and pale, so nobody ever mistook me for Ondinium, anyway."

"I was teased once."

She smiled, examining Rikard's reflection in the glass.

"Let me guess— you beat up the bully and nobody tried it again?"

"Ondiniums may not like Demicans, but most aren't stupid enough to pick a fight with us."

"Oh, come on, nobody hates Demicans! Demicans have been immigrating to Ondinium for so long that they're practically—" Taya's eye was caught by two cloaked and hooded figures standing across the street, looking at the window where she was sitting. The taller person leaned over as the smaller one spoke. She frowned, Amcathra's dire warnings leaping to mind.

"What?" Rikard asked, suddenly alert.

"Do you see those two people out there?"

He glanced outside.

The tall figure straightened, one gloved hand resting on the smaller figure's shoulder. His face was obscured by a scarf, but long black hair hung down to his shoulders. The two began to walk away, the one holding on to the other.

For a moment Taya watched them, trying to figure out why they looked so familiar. Then it dawned on her, and she leaped to her feet.

Long black hair, perfect posture, a hidden face, and the cautious walk of the blind—

"Alister!"

"What?" Rikard drew his pistol. Taya scrambled out from behind the table. She dodged a waiter balancing a heavy tray and threw the teahouse doors open, running into the street.

"Alister! Alister!"

Rain soaked her face and hair and trickled down the open collar of her leather flight suit. She dodged an oncoming coach and ran several yards in the direction the pair had gone.

"Alister? Is that you?"

Everyone around her looked alike in their overcoats and rain cloaks. She shivered, turning in a slow circle.

"Icarus?" Rikard caught up to her, brandishing his gun. "Are you certain you saw Alister Forlore?"

"I— I don't know." She stared down the street, willing the pair to appear again, but they'd vanished. They could have ducked into any number of doorways or alleys, or gotten into a carriage, or could simply still be walking away, unrecognizable in the anonymity of rain gear. "He *looked* like an exalted, and his face was covered with a scarf...."

Rain streamed down her face and her bandages were getting soaked. People skirted around them, eyeing Rikard's gun with alarm.

"Did you see where he went?"

"I thought he went that way, but I don't see him now. There was someone leading him— the way you'd lead a blind man."

"Go back inside. I'll look for him."

She glanced at him. He hadn't paused to grab his coat, and his uniform was getting soaked.

"No. No, don't bother. Come on." She turned, heading back for the teahouse. "If there's a blind Ondinium in town, somebody else will have seen him. I'll tell Lieutenant Amcathra."

"My uncle would insist I search." Rikard holstered the gun. "Give me ten minutes."

"I— all right." She trudged back to the teahouse, ignoring the curious looks she got when she sat back down, and stared out the window. Rikard was nowhere to be seen.

What would he do if he found the stranger and it really was Alister? The exile had a right to live in Echelles, but after the dirigible fire, he'd have to answer some stern questions. And Lieutenant Amcathra would *not* be pleased to see him again.

Rikard returned as their tea was being served.

"I'm sorry," he said, sitting down. Like her, he was dripping wet. "I couldn't find him."

"That's all right. Thank you for looking."

"Are you certain it was him?"

"Not really." She shivered, wrapping her damp, bandaged palms around the porcelain cup. Heat soaked through them, and she took a careful sip of tea. "Take off your wet jacket before you catch a cold."

He hesitated, then stood and stripped it off, draping it over his coat.

"What about you?"

"My flight suit's mostly waterproof." She leaned over the teacup and let steam warm her face.

If the person she'd seen had been Alister, were they in danger? Cristof's younger brother wasn't sane, in her opinion, but she didn't think he was mad enough to kill the man who was maintaining a secret bank account for him in...

...in Mareaux.

"It's been a busy day," she said weakly, unable to meet the young lictor's eyes. "I was probably imagining things."

Oh, Lady, was Cristof meeting Alister on the sly? If he was, she'd strangle him for not telling her. And then she'd strangle him again for taking such a risk.

No... no. He couldn't be meeting Alister today, not with Lieutenant Amcathra. Unless the meeting with Bezier were a ruse? Would the lieutenant let her husband meet the scientist alone?

Of course not. Although that didn't mean that Cristof wasn't meeting Alister at *all* during this trip.

"You should never assume that you are safe, Icarus." Rikard said, frowning. Water dripped from his shirt sleeves onto the table.

"You sound like your uncle now."

He glanced at her, surprised. Then he picked up his tea, took a sip, and set it down.

"I don't always agree with Uncle Janos, but he is a good Demican."

"I agree, although I think he overdoes the whole silent-and-stoic act."

"He and my father are reserved men." Rikard hesitated, turning his cup around in his broad fingers. "It's strange. Demicans rush to leave their country, but once they've left it, they cling to its traditions as if they regretted their decision."

"You speak more like an Ondinium."

"The older generation would criticize me for it."

"Is your tattoo a Demican tradition?" she asked. Rikard gave her a startled look and glanced down at his arm. The dark lines of a snarling bear's head were faintly visible through his damp white sleeve. He plucked at the fabric to hide it.

"I— uh, I'm not supposed—"

"Is it secret?" Taya was intrigued. Lieutenant Amcathra hadn't seemed concerned about anyone seeing his bear tattoo earlier that day.

"My uncle doesn't know I have it," Rikard admitted, his face red as he reached behind him for his damp uniform jacket. "Please don't tell him. It's not—"

"All right, relax!" She grinned. So, Rikard had imitated his uncle by getting a matching tattoo but hadn't been brave enough to tell him? "Don't put on a wet jacket. I won't tell anyone."

"Really?" Rikard asked, his face still red.

"I promise."

"Thank you." He looked down at his tea. "I— I'm sorry."

"Don't be silly. Anyway, I know at least one other Demican who isn't very traditional," Taya said, letting him off the hook by changing the subject. "She's a programmer." She idly wondered if Rikard and Isobel would like each other. Maybe she should introduce them.

"What generation?"

"I never asked. Second-generation, at least, since she's in-caste. A dedicate. Very smart and not at all reserved."

"Sometimes it's hard on us," Rikard said, rotating the teacup in his hands again. "We're told how beautiful Demicus is and how important it is to act like a Demican, but we live in Ondinium. I don't understand why. No matter how hard life may be in Demicus, it has to be better than living in a country where you're a second-class citizen."

"There are a lot of Demicans in Ondinium, especially in the lictate. Nobody considers them second-class citizens."

"But black-haired, dark-skinned lictors are promoted more quickly than blond-haired, light-skinned lictors."

"If someone in your family has been discriminated against, they can take it to the courts."

"It's never anything you can prove. *You* know what it's like."

Taya fell silent. She'd been teased about her coloring as a child, but it had stopped when she'd joined the icarii. Icarii faced a different set of prejudices, but among themselves they were as close as family.

"I'm sorry you've had a difficult time in Ondinium. I hope you'll like Demicus when you get there."

Rikard stared down at his tea.

"I will."

Taya tried to lighten the conversation. "I want to visit Demicus, myself, someday. I'd love to see one of its famous white bears."

"They live in the far north."

"So, I'll go to the far north."

"There aren't any embassies up there."

"I'll fly."

"You'll freeze."

"Stop arguing. I *am* going to see a white bear someday. In the wild, on the ice."

He glanced at her, as if wanting to say something, and then looked away and set down his teacup.

"I hope you do."

"I'll see about getting us both up there someday on an assignment," Taya promised. She drained her cup. He reached for the pot to refill it. She glanced outside as he poured, then resolutely pulled her gaze back to the table.

She wasn't going to mention Alister again until she'd had a chance to talk to Cristof.

CHAPTER THREE

JAYCE WAS SITTING in Cristof's suite, grumbling as he unpieced one of the exalted's waterstained robes.

"Can they be saved?" Taya asked, dropping into one of the large leather chairs by the fireplace. She began unwinding the bandages around her palms.

"No." Jayce spread the stiff, mottled garment over his lap and gestured with disgust at the charred and muddy hem. "I'll unpick the jewels and salvage as much of the gold thread as I can. Your gown, by the way, is also ruined. Why in the world weren't you wearing your flight suit?"

"Aren't you the one who keeps saying I need to dress like a lady?"

"Not on some foreign flying object in the middle of a thunder-storm!"

"Well, I'm wearing my leathers now."

"Precisely. Now that you're in the palace and *should* be dressed like a lady."

She made a rude noise. "Give me one of your needles."

"Large or small?"

"Large enough to pop a blister."

Jayce drew his hand back in disgust.

"Taya. *Please.*"

"The doctor said I could if they started to hurt too much." She stood and looked through Cristof's bar, finding a bottle of gin. She'd never drink the awful stuff, but it would clean her wounds. And as far as drinking went... she picked up the open bottle of pinot noir on Cristof's desk, smiling as she remembered their post-flight interlude. She poured herself a glass and looked at Jayce. "Want one?"

"Good Lady, yes, if the exalted won't mind."

"He'd love it if we finished a bottle for him. He doesn't like wine." She poured a glass for Jayce and settled back into her chair. "I bought those awful novels Cassie wanted."

"Really? Can I read them?"

She laughed. "Sure, but Cassie will kill you if you wrinkle the pages."

"She'll live," he said, waving off his niece's concerns. "I need to do some shopping, myself, before we leave. Maybe I'd have the time, if you and your husband would stop ruining your wardrobes."

"Blame whoever set fire to the dirigible, not me."

"Monstrous."

They sat quietly for a few minutes, Jayce juggling his work and the wine glass and Taya enjoying the fire. At last she reached out a bandaged hand.

"All right; the wine's starting to work. Give me that needle."

"You aren't really going to use my sewing needles to pop your blisters."

"My hands hurt. If I don't pop these blisters, they'll break on their own."

Jayce made a face, selected a heavy tapestry needle, and walked over to sit across from her.

"Here, give me your hand. You can't do it by yourself."

"Thank you." She drained her glass and held out her hand. Her stomach twisted. Maybe she should have taken a shot of gin, instead. The wine and tea weren't mixing well.

"All right, hold still." Jayce grasped her right hand, wiped the needle on his sleeve, and started to work. Taya screwed up her face, then laughed to see Jayce's expression reflecting her own.

"I can't believe I'm doing this," he muttered, reaching down and grabbing one of her bandages. He pressed the edge of the fabric against the punctured blister. She hissed as he released the fluids inside. "I deserve a raise."

"I'll talk to Cristof about it."

"You will talk to your husband about what?" Lieutenant Amcathra inquired.

Both of them started, looking up. The lictor surveyed the scene, then stepped aside. Cristof walked in, fumbling with his mask.

Jayce leaped to his feet and bowed, his palm to his forehead.

"What are you doing in here?" Cristof asked, handing the mask to Amcathra. He squinted, trying to focus without his glasses. "Whatever it is, you look cozy."

"Jayce was lancing a blister for me." Taya held up her hand.

"Is that all?" Her husband shook back his sleeves and fished his silver-rimmed glasses out from under his multiple layers of robe, sliding them over his nose. "Good. Icarii don't get perquisites."

He kissed her as Jayce straightened from his bow and edged away.

"If you insist on popping them, let *me* do it," Cristof added. "I used to get blisters all the time when I was training with the lictors."

"A thousand fortuitous rebirths do not build calluses," Amcathra noted.

"I'll take your robes and finish up in my room, Exalted," Jayce muttered, gathering his sewing kit and the robes he'd been disassembling.

"Thank you," Cristof said, absently. "Lord Pomeroy said something about an opera. I think we'll need to wear something traditional."

"Like my armature?" Taya asked, hopefully.

"I'll see that you both have appropriate clothing for the occasion, Exalted," Jayce promised, hurrying out.

"Rikard met us on the way in," Amcathra said once the door shut behind the couturier. "He told us you thought you saw Alister."

"I may have— I'm not sure." Taya helped her husband out of his wig and robes, picking at pins, knots, clasps, and buttons. "Please tell me you aren't meeting him, Cris."

"I'm not meeting him." Her husband shrugged out of his robes, revealing the wrinkled slacks and white shirt he insisted on wearing beneath them, and raked his hands through his loose hair.

"Okay. Now tell me you're not lying."

He raised an eyebrow.

"I'm not lying. For one thing, I'd be insane to meet Al while the Council is watching." He inclined his head toward Amcathra, who gave him a stern look.

Taya bit back the rest of her questions, reminded that some things shouldn't be discussed in front of the lictor.

"Well, I could have been mistaken." She sat back down in the chair by the fire. "It was raining and he was across the street."

"I will make inquiries," Amcathra said. He paused, giving Cristof a long, meaningful look, and then turned to leave the room.

"I'm *not* meeting him," Cristof protested to his friend's broad back as the door shut.

"Really?" Taya pressed, once they were alone.

"Really. His last message was posted two weeks ago." He walked over to the mantel, sorting through the letters there. "I don't see any invitations to clandestine meetings tucked in today's mail."

"Were we in Echelles when his last letter was delivered?"

"Yes. I told him we'd be here, but I warned him to stay away." Cristof looked troubled as he put the letters back. "I don't *want* to see him again."

Taya gave him a steady look. He pulled off his glasses and pinched the bridge of his nose.

"I *don't*. I know— I shouldn't even be corresponding with him, but for the Lady's sake, he's my little brother. I have an obligation to take care of him."

Taya watched as he put his glasses back on. She didn't think Cristof had any obligation to his murderous brother at all.

"Does he have any reason to attack you?"

"You mean, the fire? No, that's ridiculous. He relies on me for, uh—" He stopped, giving her a stricken look.

"I know you're sending him money."

He cleared his throat, glanced away, and nodded.

"I've known about it ever since we set up the funds for those lictors' families," she continued.

"It's not that much. And he's blind. How else is he supposed to survive?"

He isn't, Taya thought, but she knew better than to say it out loud. Cristof had given up his freedom to keep his brother out of the executioner's hands, despite the fact that Alister had tried to kill him.

Twice.

"I don't mind, Cris. It's your money, not mine."

"That's not true."

Taya shrugged. She preferred to pay for her personal expenses out of her own earnings; that way she didn't feel like the fortune-hunter so many exalteds considered her. And as far as criticizing how Cristof spent his own money— she wouldn't dream of it.

"So, if you die, do the payments stop?" she asked.

"Yes, unless you continued them."

Not likely.

"Then it wouldn't make sense for him to kill you." Unless Alister had known that it wasn't Cristof in the gondola? But how could he? And what would be the point of killing Lieutenant Amcathra? Or her?

Revenge?

She rubbed her temples. She was starting to get a headache, and her hands hurt. She looked for the needle Jayce had set down.

"What's wrong?"

"I was going to get rid of these blisters."

"You're going to be stubborn about it, aren't you?" He sat down and picked up the needle. "Are you certain you want to come to dinner tonight? If your hands hurt that much—"

"I don't want Lady Fosca to have unrestricted access to you."

Her husband glanced up, his grey eyes amused behind their glass lenses.

"Janos will protect me from her wicked machinations, my love."

"I'm certainly paying him enough for it."

"Really?"

"No— should I?"

"Of course not. I have no interest in cheating on you. I'm only thinking of whether I'd best serve Ondinium by wheedling her secrets from her during our pillow talk."

"How selfless of you. Does that mean I should seduce Lord Gaio?"

"Tch. Gaio's such a lecher, *I* could seduce him."

Taya laughed. "I'd pay money to see you try. But you're welcome to deal with him; I'm not up to dealing with his wandering hands tonight."

"Wandering hands?"

Oops.

"It isn't personal, Cris. He gropes all the girls. He's Alzanan aristocracy; it comes with the territory."

"Am I going to have to cause a diplomatic incident?"

"You don't have to sound so eager."

"If he's been treating you disrespectfully—."

"Hush." She leaned over and kissed her husband's forehead. "I can take care of myself."

"It would be nice if you let *me* take care of you, for a change."

"I'll let you thrash Lord Gaio if I can thrash Lady Fosca."

"Lady Fosca didn't grope me."

"Her loss."

The comment startled a laugh out of him. She smiled as his brow smoothed.

"Maybe we should both stay away from the Mazzolettis," he suggested, standing and tilting his gin bottle over a handkerchief. He daubed at her hand with the damp cloth.

"Ow!"

"Give me your other hand. You're lucky you didn't get any vitriol on you."

"I only touched the outside of the box."

"Chemical fires are dangerous." He looked pensive as he began lancing her blisters. "Alister would know how to set a chemical fire."

"We're in Mareaux's capital. I'll bet *lots* of people here know how to set a chemical fire."

"I hope so. No— that wasn't what I meant to say. I mean, I hope it wasn't Alister. I can't imagine why it would be. We're on good terms. As good as one can expect under the circumstances, anyway."

There was nothing she could say to that, so she changed the subject. "How was the tour?"

Her husband's angular face lit up.

"Fascinating! Mareaux's aneroid barometers are state-of-the-art, and they're making incredible progress on marine chronometers that can resist changes in temperature. That's an ongoing problem, you know, because of the elasticity of the balance springs. If the metal expands or contracts with changes in the temperature — it varies by about 5.4 degrees per thousand feet, depending on the amount of moisture in the air — then the reliable calculation of longitude becomes impossible."

"Mmmm."

"Taya! Chronometers manufactured with temperature-resistant alloys are of the utmost importance! Accurate instruments are essential for accurate navigation."

"Why can't dirigible pilots just use their eyes, like icarii?"

"They can navigate by sight at low altitudes, but the challenge is to successfully navigate long distances across unmapped terrain."

Taya shook her head as Cristof picked up his handkerchief and daubed her hand clean. "What's the point? We've already seen how vulnerable dirigibles are in a storm— can you imagine what would happen if one of them tried flying through the passes around Ondinium?"

"Well, we don't want them flying into Ondinium, anyway. But developing more efficient means of navigation is one of the projects Professor Dautry is coming to Ondinium to investigate. She has a new instrument Bezier has invented, an anemometer. It measures wind speed. Wouldn't charting the wind currents around Ondinium Mountain be of inestimable value to icarii?"

"Icarii already have a pretty good idea of the local wind currents from flying in them every day. Why bother mapping them out?"

"Of *course* we need to map them out! How else can society advance, except on a broad scientific foundation of precise, valid, and reliable recordkeeping?"

"Yes, of course. I can't imagine what I was thinking." Taya took her hand from him, inspecting his handiwork. Now her palms were covered with ugly lines of pale, loose skin. "Ugh. Maybe I'll wear gloves to dinner."

Her stomach churned at the thought of eating. She pressed her hand against her belly. It gurgled a warning.

"What's wrong?"

"I'm feeling a little sick."

"Do you have a headache?"

"A small one."

"You didn't eat anything strange while you were out, did you?"

"Just tea and sandwiches."

"Well, a headache and a rumbling belly is how it always starts with me." He stood. "We'd better get you to bed."

"It can't be— I *never* get food poisoning!"

"Then maybe you're coming down with a case of influenza; you *have* been walking around in the rain all day."

Taya stood and took a moment to concentrate on how she was feeling.

Her stomach ached. Her bowels were churning. And her head hurt.

"Maybe you're right. You'd better find Rikard; if I got food poisoning from lunch, he'll have it, too."

Cristof took her arm. "I'll walk you to your room. Rikard can take care of himself."

"No, go find him." She waved him away. "If I'm going to throw up, I'd rather be alone, thank you."

An hour later, Taya was curled up on the bed in her nightgown, her eyes squeezed shut and her arms wrapped around her midsection. The door opened and she ground her teeth together. Cristof had been in and out several times to check on her, and she wished he'd just go away. She was feeling miserable, and this brand of misery didn't want company.

"Icarus."

She pried her eyes open. Lieutenant Amcathra pulled up a chair next to her bed.

"What?" If Cris had sent the stone-faced lieutenant to nurse her through this....

"Mister Webb is also ill. However, Rikard is not."

"Jayce is sick?"

"You drank out of the exalted's bottle of wine together."

She closed her eyes, wincing as another spasm convulsed her stomach muscles.

"Did you share any other food or drink?"

"No."

"Thank you." He stood and left.

Eventually the door opened again.

"I've brought some medicine, Miss Icarus," said the physician she'd seen earlier that day as he took the seat Amcathra had vacated. She heard a metallic clank and opened her eyes. The doctor had a large metal bowl next to him.

That couldn't possibly be good.

"It's an emetic," he said, confirming her fears. "I'm afraid we need to give you a thorough purge."

"Why?" She let him help her into a sitting position and eyed the bowl with loathing. Her stomach gave a sideways lurch, as if gearing up for the inevitable.

"To cleanse your system." He uncorked a bottle and spooned a thick, syrupy liquid out into a small glass.

"The wine was bad?"

"The wine was poisoned." He handed her the glass. "Your lictor forced a large amount of it down the throat of one of the palace cats. It died in convulsions. The queen is mortified. About the poison, not the cat. Although I don't think the lictor has won any friends among the animal-lovers at court."

Taya struggled to make sense of the situation.

"I drank some wine this morning and I wasn't sick."

"Perhaps you didn't drink enough. Or perhaps the effects were delayed. Or perhaps the poison was added later— your lictor determined that the bottle was left open and unguarded all afternoon."

"Cris?" Taya felt a coldness grip her that had nothing to do with her illness. "Is my husband all right?"

"The ambassador is perfectly fine; he hadn't had anything to drink yet. However, this incident raises enough questions about his food poisoning that I've decided to purge him, as well. I'll put all three of you on a closely monitored diet until I'm certain you're past any danger." He held out the bowl. "Now, if you please."

Chapter Four

"THE AMBASSADOR IS leaving with Lieutenant Amcathra," Rikard said, stepping inside after knocking.

Taya looked up from the novel she'd bought for Cassie and registered the young lictor's scarf and gloves.

"Where's he going?" she asked, marking her place and closing the volume.

"A man was murdered the night before the dirigible accident. Uncle Janos told the exalted that he was going to the morgue to inspect the body. The exalted insisted on going with him."

"Insisted?" Taya blew out a resigned breath. Cristof had been itching to escape the palace since yesterday. "I'll bet Amcathra was thrilled by that."

"My uncle asked if perhaps the entire Ondinium delegation would care to join him."

"What did Cris say?"

"The exalted said he believed the mercates were still in conference, but that you might be interested."

"A romantic trip to the morgue with my husband. How could I resist?" Still, Taya threw off her blanket. Two days had passed since her purging. Staying cooped up in the delegation's wing of the palace had been boring her, too. And if Cristof was going out in public, he'd need his icarus.

She padded across the room and opened her wardrobe. She was *not* going to wear a dress to a morgue, no matter what Jayce might say. She pulled out her flight suit and boots.

"I'll be there in a minute."

After Rikard stepped outside, Taya dressed with practiced speed, then paused and laid a hand on the ondium wings that floated next to the wardrobe. Iron chains and fetters had been wrapped around the arm struts and keel bars, locking the armature to the heavy furniture around it.

"Soon," she promised. She grabbed her scarf and gloves and hurried outside, locking the door behind her.

The wind in the courtyard was cold and sharp, but the sky was clear and the sun bright. Cristof waited inside the waiting carriage, masked. Lieutenant Amcathra stood by the open door, a rifle slung over his back, watching with an air of impatience.

Taya slid in next to her husband, and the lieutenant swung in on the opposite seat. Rikard closed the door. The carriage rocked as he climbed up to sit next to the driver.

Taya made sure the curtains were closed before helping Cristof remove his mask.

"I'm glad you decided to come," he exclaimed, leaning over to kiss her. "I don't know if any of the hospital staff speak Ondinan."

Taya gave him a withering look.

"Is *that* why you invited me? I thought you wanted to see me again, after all these days apart."

His copper cheeks flushed.

"That's what I meant, of course, my love." He shot Lieutenant Amcathra a desperate look. The lictor raised an eyebrow. "I mean, it goes without saying."

"Apparently." She tossed his mask in his lap. "Didn't the queen offer you a translator for the times I'm not around?"

"I do not trust the palace staff," Amcathra said as the coach jerked and began moving.

"I don't think the queen's translator wants to kill me," Cristof objected. "I'm keeping him employed."

"It does no harm for the queen to believe these attempts on your life could rupture diplomatic relations between our countries."

"Could they?" Taya looked from one to the other.

Her husband shifted under his heavy robes.

"Technically, they should," he admitted. "Withdrawing our delegation would be the mildest response."

Amcathra nodded. "I am under orders to insist the delegation return to Ondinium at the first sign of danger to the exalted's person."

"Apparently food poisoning wasn't considered a danger," Cristof noted.

"My role is to protect you from external threat, Exalted, not internal frailty. I had, of course, assumed the latter."

"Of course."

"Well, what are we going to do? You haven't said anything to the queen yet, have you?" Taya folded back her husband's long sleeves until she could take his hand. His expression brightened as he curled his gloved fingers around hers.

"No. She was wise enough to stay away while I was vomiting. But she stopped by last night and said everything you'd expect her to say. Very apologetic."

"Did you tell her we were going to leave?"

"No, but...." Cristof hesitated. "Janos is right; somebody wants to kill me. And I don't like the fact that you're endangered by it."

"What about the trade agreement? And the scholar swap?"

"Our professors are already installed in Echelles University. I don't see any reason to pull them out. Besides, if we did, we'd have to leave Professor Dautry behind, and I'd really like her to plot out Ondinium's wind patterns. Science shouldn't suffer because of politics."

Taya squeezed his hand. Cristof was being uncharacteristically optimistic if he thought science and politics could be kept apart. As far as she could tell, they were inextricably entangled in Ondinium, where science justified every political decision.

"As for the trade agreement, Mercate Trichas has already volunteered to close down negotiations," Amcathra reported. "Mercate Corundel advises patience and has moved up the meeting timetable. Mercate Macerain expresses his hope that you two feel better soon."

"I'm surprised Trichas is willing to withdraw," Taya said. "He's a member of North Reach's board. The company won't be happy if this negotiation falls through."

"We were going to leave in another week, anyway," Cristof said. "Maybe this puts him in a stronger bargaining position— the last chance for Mareaux to make a deal before we leave."

"I have no interest in how our departure affects trade," Amcathra said, his voice flat. "My job is not to protect the mercates' interests."

"Anything that's important to the Big Three is important to the Council," Cristof countered.

"So, who are we going to see?" Taya asked, deciding it was time to change the subject. "How is this dead man involved in the sabotage?"

"I do not know if he was involved. However, he was the first man to be murdered in Echelles in five weeks. It seems unduly coincidental that he died the night before the attempt was made on your lives."

"There's only been one murder in the last five weeks?" Taya exclaimed. "In the whole *city*?" Ondinium had five murders in one day, sometimes.

"He came from Grimaucourt. His throat was cut. His room at the inn was torn apart. The constables have no leads. I am suspicious."

"Why was he here?"

"I do not know."

Conversation died until the carriage stopped.

Passers-by paused to stare at the exotically robed and masked stranger, but Amcathra's and Rikard's forbidding glares and ready rifles kept them from venturing too close. Taya remained alert as they worked their way up the stairs and entered the hospital.

Inside, their presence caused just as much of a commotion. Physicians, assistants, patients and visitors all stopped to gawk. Rikard halted in the middle of the corridor.

"I can't read the signs," he said, gesturing to a line of doors.

"Let's start there," Taya said, pointing to the door that said "Director" in Mareaux. The lictor knocked, then stepped back, his rifle not quite aimed at the doorway. "I think we're supposed to walk in."

Rikard swung the door open, revealing a balding, thin-faced clerk standing in front of a filing cabinet. The clerk froze, staring at the lictor's rifle.

Taya led Cristof inside. The clerk's horrified gaze rose from the weapon to Cristof's blank ivory mask.

"His excellency, the exalted Cristof Forlore, ambassador of Ondinium, would like to confer with the hospital director about a body that was brought in here several days ago," Taya said in Mareaux. "Lictor Janos Amcathra and I will speak for the ambassador. I am Taya Icarus."

"I, ah, I've heard of the exalted, of course," the clerk stammered, fumbling with his files a moment before setting them down on top of a desk. "Um, welcome. My lord. Please, um, sit down, and I'll get the director. W-was he expecting you?"

"He is not expecting us." Amcathra slung his rifle over his shoulder.

Taya repeated the lictor's words in Mareaux, her tone considerably more polite.

"I see." The clerk looked on the verge of panic. "Well, I'll go get him, then. Can, I, um, get you anything?"

"No, thank you. Just the director," she said, feeling sorry for him. "And I apologize for the unexpected visit. It's a matter of some urgency, however."

The clerk nodded, hesitated, bobbed an awkward Mareaux bow to Cristof, and then hurried out, avoiding them as well as he could in the confined space until he vanished out the same door they'd come through.

"You should have told them we were coming," Taya chided the lictor.

"This way they have no time to hide the evidence."

"We're visiting a morgue, not a crime scene."

"Every place is a potential crime scene."

Taya started to reply and then thought better of it. She suspected Amcathra made statements like that just to annoy her.

"Are you going to unmask to talk to the physician?" she asked her husband, instead.

No.

"All right."

They stood in an uncomfortable silence for several minutes, by her heavy gold pocket watch, before the clerk returned, followed by a baffled-looking white-haired man in a suit.

"Yes, hello, is there a problem?"

"Are you the director of this hospital?" Amcathra asked. Rikard stepped backward and swung his rifle around, keeping the barrel low enough to avoid blatant threat but high enough to warn.

Taya translated the lieutenant's question.

"I— yes, I am. Doctor André Morell." The physician held out his hand, faltered, and looked from one of them to the other. At last his eyes settled on Cristof's blank, mouthless mask, its ivory expanse broken only by glass-lensed eyes and a gold wave inlaid over one cheek. Morell dropped his hand. "Er, what can I do for you, my lord?"

"This is his excellency, the exalted Cristof Forlore, ambassador of Ondinium," Taya said. "I'm the exalted's representative, Taya Icarus, and these are Lieutenant Amcathra and Lictor Kiraly. We have some questions about a murder victim who was brought here several days ago."

"Ah, yes," Dr. Morell said at once, nodding. He gestured to his clerk, who hurried back to the file cabinet. "Was he a member of your delegation…?" His voice trailed off as he looked from the mute exalted to her.

"No, but the exalted would like to learn more about him," Taya said.

"We want to see the corpse," Amcathra added, in heavily accented Mareaux. Taya looked at him in surprise. Since when did he speak Mareaux? And why did he know the word "corpse"?

"I don't suppose there's any harm in it," the doctor said, taking the file his clerk handed him. He glanced at it and offered it to Cristof. "These are his records."

Amcathra stepped forward and took the folder from the doctor's hands, gave it a cursory glance, and handed it to Taya.

Cristof's sleeve-covered hand slid off her arm as she took the file, which was written in Mareaux. She read it through silently and then began to summarize out loud.

"His name was Hubert Guisnard, a book merchant from Grimaucourt. He registered at his hotel a day before his death. His body was found behind a tavern where he'd been drinking, in the alley. His trousers were unbuttoned, so it's assumed he was surprised while he was relieving himself." She turned the page. "His throat was cut and his body was left on the ground. The coroner's report says that he died from blood loss; he was dead when the body was found." She showed the coroner's sketch to Cristof, and then handed the folder to Amcathra.

"We store his body here," Dr. Morell said, speaking in hesitant, accented Ondinan. "We bury it after five days. Five… no, fifteen." He repeated the word in Mareaux, giving Taya an uncertain look.

"Fifteen," she confirmed.

"In Ondinium we store unidentified bodies for a month," Amcathra said with disdain.

"In Ondinium we have easier access to ice," Taya pointed out. She turned to the doctor, switching languages. "Is the body well-preserved?"

"Yes. We store our corpses on ice, too," he said, sounding put out. She translated that for Amcathra, who grunted and handed the doctor the folder.

"Good. Then let us view it," Amcathra said, still speaking in Ondinan. She wondered if he'd only memorized the one Mareaux phrase.

"I hope I'm not going to regret this," she said, switching to Demican. Now that she knew the doctor understood at least a little Ondinan, she preferred to be careful. "My stomach isn't as strong as it should be. And neither is *his*."

"Do not look," Amcathra advised.

She sighed.

"Doctor Morell, would you please lead us to the morgue to see the body?" she asked in Mareaux.

"Of course." The director nodded and walked out. They trailed behind him in the same order they'd come in, Taya slowing to lean her head close to Cristof's mask.

"Try not to puke," she whispered, in Ondinan. "If you want to close your eyes, I'll lead. I'm just going to look at the floor, myself."

He made a noise she couldn't quite interpret — a stifled laugh? — and tapped *no* on her arm.

"I don't care *how* many bodies you've seen," she hissed in his ear, "you've been ill!"

This time he tilted his head toward her, his fingers sliding over her arm in a caress.

"And don't look at me," she scolded. An exalted's public gestures were supposed to be slow, dignified, and minimal. *Like a man-sized doll*, Cristof had once said to her with disgust.

The morgue was in the basement. The temperature dropped as they descended, Cristof negotiating the stairs with some effort. Public stairs in Ondinium were wide and shallow to facilitate exalteds' measured movements. Mareaux's stairs were steep and narrow and difficult to descend in long, heavy robes and a mask.

When the doctor opened the door to the morgue, Taya's stomach lurched. The smell was an unpleasant combination of chemistry lab and butcher's shop.

I'm not going to get sick. I've puked enough over the last two days to last me a decade.

"Unclaimed bodies are sometimes passed along to university anatomists for specimen gathering," Doctor Morrell said, noticing her discomfort. "The room next door is used for tissue preservation. I'm afraid the ventilation isn't very good."

"Will— will this body be given to the university?" she asked, breathing through her mouth. It didn't help.

"Probably not. I assume he has family or friends who'll claim the body. We've sent a letter back to Grimaucourt to inquire."

Amcathra made an impatient gesture that needed no translation. The doctor opened the next door.

The room was small and almost entirely filled by a thick-walled box on a wheeled rack. Morrell pulled it out, and water sloshed over the edges of a pan at the bottom of the rack. He opened the box's lid, revealing a naked body packed in ice.

"The ice drips into the drainage pan as it melts. We drain the pan twice a day and take the water back to the ice house to be re-frozen," Morrell explained.

"Is that healthy?" Taya asked.

"I wouldn't use the ice in my lemonade, but we haven't received any complaints. So, do you know him?"

Cristof stepped forward, forcing her to move with him. She averted her eyes as his mask tilted over the corpse.

His hidden fingers tightened on her arm.

Oh, scrap. She swiftly glanced at the face but didn't recognize it.

"Should we claim the body?" she asked, barely breathing the question. A tapped *no*. "His things?" *Yes.*

"The exalted would like to know if we may examine his clothing and belongings," she said, raising her voice and addressing the doctor in his own language, then repeating herself in Ondinan for Amcathra and Rikard.

"You'll have to ask at the police office," Doctor Morrell replied. He gave Cristof a newly uneasy glance, as if reminded that the masked figure wasn't a wind-up mannequin. "He was murdered, so everything he owned was confiscated as evidence."

Amcathra didn't look pleased as Taya translated.

"Does the exalted recognize him?" he asked, in Demican.

Taya hesitated, then realized that the lictor's sharp eyes had caught her hesitation.

"Maybe," she hedged, also in Demican. The lictor nodded.

"We are done here."

"Thank you for your time," Taya said to the doctor, holding out a hand in Mareaux fashion. He shook it, looking curiously from her to the others.

"I'm sorry, but I can't help noticing that you look Mareaux...."

"I'm second-generation Ondinium," she explained. "Icarii don't wear castemarks."

"Ah, yes. The flyers." He glanced at her shoulders as though expecting wings to suddenly appear. "Well, I hope this was of some help to the ambassador."

"Yes, thank you. You were very kind to see us without any prior notice."

"I'm happy to be of assistance to, er, our esteemed neighbors." The doctor released her hand and made another awkward Mareaux bow to Cristof. "My lord. It's been an honor."

A crowd had gathered around the carriage in their absence, and a buzz arose as Cristof exited the building. Taya straightened her shoulders and kept a wary eye on the crowd and her husband, but within a few minutes he was safely stowed in the curtained carriage.

Amcathra again surprised Taya by ordering the driver to *police headquarters* in heavily accented Mareaux. Taya wondered if the lictors had been issued a special vocabulary list.

When the driver nodded, the lieutenant took his place inside while Rikard climbed to the driver's bench.

Taya untied Cristof's mask and pulled out a handkerchief to pat the sweat off his flushed face. He drew in a deep, relieved breath.

"Lady, those stairs nearly killed me." He rubbed the tip of his nose with his sleeve. "I can't wait to get back to Ondinium and throw that damn mask in a drawer where it belongs."

"You did very well," she said, wiping down the inside of the mask. Small leather pads lifted it off his skin, but his breath condensed on the ivory interior whenever he exerted himself.

"And this wig itches, too," her husband grumbled, adjusting it.

"Who was the dead man?" Amcathra demanded.

Cristof lifted a narrow shoulder.

"He sold me some books on criminal phrenology. They'd just come out of Alzana."

"I thought you hated Alzana," Taya remarked.

"They make good criminal anthropologists." Cristof raised an eyebrow. "Probably because they have so many criminals."

"When did he sell you those books?" Amcathra interrupted.

"Soon after we arrived. Two weeks ago, I think."

"You talked to him without me?" Taya asked. "You know you aren't supposed to do that!"

"I was careful. I stood behind a changing screen."

"It doesn't matter! Commoners aren't even supposed to hear your voice. And I'll bet you passed books back and forth, didn't you?"

"I hate to bother you with every little meeting...."

"It's my *job*, Cris."

Amcathra cleared his throat. "The bookseller returned to Echelles a day before his death. Did you give him reason to do so?"

"I don't know." Cristof sounded nettled. "Maybe he found some of the titles I'd asked about. Why don't we call the chief of police to the palace instead of visiting him? I can't ask any questions in this mask."

"It is no longer your job to ask questions." Amcathra said.

"Well, I'm not going to sit in my suite hiding from assassins."

"No. You will sit in your suite planning our withdrawal from Mareaux."

Cristof scowled.

"Taya's better at making polite excuses than I am."

"Then you want to keep it polite?" she asked.

"The exalted should withdraw in offended dignity," Amcathra instructed. "Mareaux has failed in its responsibility to guarantee his safety."

"The queen won't like that. You're just going to strengthen Ondinium's reputation for arrogance."

"Ondinium *is* arrogant."

"Lieutenant!" Taya glared at the lictor.

Cristof shook his head. "He's right; it is. But Taya's right, too, Janos. I don't want to make so much of a fuss over this that we risk our alliance."

"A show of offended dignity is hardly a declaration of war."

"You'd *both* better let me do the talking," Taya muttered. At least the Ondinium delegation was already close to its scheduled departure; leaving a few days early wouldn't cause much of a disturbance. She should be able to bring Queen Iancais around to some sort of mutually agreeable diplomatic pretense that would allow both sides to save face. Storms in the mountain passes, maybe. Weather was always a good excuse for adjusting travel plans.

The coach slowed as they reached the police station. Taya restored Cristof's mask and checked his robes to make certain they were still neatly arranged. By the time they left the carriage, a Mareaux man in a suit was speaking to Lieutenant Amcathra in Ondinan. The thin man paused when Cristof appeared and gave a precise Ondinium bow, his palm pressed against his forehead.

"Exalted Forlore," the man said in Ondinan, straightening. "I'm Martin Gifford, chief inspector of the Echelles Constabulary. Your presence honors us."

"We hope we haven't inconvenienced you," Taya replied, following his lead and speaking in Ondinan. "The exalted has some questions about a man who was recently murdered."

"Hubert Guisnard, yes; I reviewed his file after Lieutenant Amcathra wrote yesterday."

Taya gave the lieutenant a surprised glance. A police station wasn't a crime scene, then? Must be caste bias.

"Please, won't you step inside?"

Their walk through police headquarters didn't cause as much of a stir as in the hospital, although Taya saw the staff and officers shoot surreptitious glances their way as they pretended to be unimpressed. Chief Inspector Gifford led them into a cluttered office with large windows that overlooked a busy street. He pulled around a leather wing-backed chair and set a smaller chair next to it. "Please, Exalted." He gestured to the larger of the two.

Rikard stepped outside and closed the office door, leaving the four of them alone.

Taya brushed Cristof's layers of robes aside as he sat, then arranged them in portrait perfect drapery. She scooted the smaller chair closer and sat, draping his sleeve over their touching arms. She was impressed that Gifford understood Ondinium seating protocol.

"Guisnard sold Exalted Forlore some books approximately two weeks ago, shortly after our delegation arrived," Amcathra said, still standing. "Your report indicated that he had only checked into his hotel recently. Did he leave Echelles after seeing the exalted?"

"I hadn't realized Guisnard had been in town earlier, Exalted, and I had no idea that he'd spoken to you." Gifford also remained on his feet, ignoring the chair behind his desk. He spoke directly to Cristof. "However, he worked for a publisher in Grimaucourt, so it makes sense that he'd travel back and forth in the course of his work. Did you place an order? Perhaps he was planning to deliver a book to you?"

"The exalted didn't place an order," Taya replied, at Cristof's negative. "But it's possible that Mister Guisnard found something that might interest him."

"I'm sure Lieutenant Amcathra told you that Guisnard's hotel room had been torn apart," the inspector said. "The door wasn't forced, and no key was found on his body, so we assume his killer took his keys and searched his room."

"Was anything taken?" Amcathra asked.

"Difficult to say. He had a traveling desk that was forced open. There were no letters or files inside. Of course, we can't prove they were stolen, but it doesn't seem likely that a salesman would travel without any business records or receipt books. He had an entire crate of books in his hotel room. They were pulled out and left on the floor."

"Money?" the lictor asked.

"We didn't find any money on Guisnard's body, but he had cash and several bank notes in the hotel safe. We also found two books there."

"Were they rare volumes?" Taya inquired.

"I don't think so, but they may have been set aside for a particular buyer, as you suggested." Gifford pulled a ring of keys from his coat pocket, walking to a safe behind his desk. After a moment he turned, holding two slim volumes toward Cristof. "Would these have interested you, Exalted Forlore?"

Taya took the first with her free hand and held it up for Cristof. The title was in Alzanan. *Delinquency, Deviance, and Disorder: A Call for the Reformation of the Poor Law.*

His fingers dug into her arm.

She set it down on her lap and picked up the second, also in Alzanan. *Dangerous Women: Infamous Murderesses of History.*

Again.

She set it down, keeping her face blank.

Neither book looked like a work on criminal phrenology, to her. But Cristof wanted them both. The first made sense, but the second? *Infamous Murderesses of History*? Cristof didn't read sensational literature.

Which implied that he was up to something.

When she found out *what*, she might qualify for a page in the book's second edition.

"Yes, they would have interested him," she said with studied calm, handing the volumes back to Gifford. "Exalted Forlore studies criminal investigation and social reform. It's very likely Guisnard wanted to show him these books."

Cristof signaled again, his gloved fingers tapping a pattern on her arm: *obtain.*

"Are they rare?" Gifford asked.

"No," Taya said, after Cristof's negative. "At least, not here. The Oporphyr Council is very selective about what books are allowed into the country. The exalted has been able to expand his private library during this visit to Mareaux; I suppose Guisnard may have realized that and brought back books he thought might be difficult to find in Ondinium."

Gifford set the books on his desk, his dark blue eyes troubled.

"Did Guisnard sell books to anyone else in your delegation?"

"Not that we know of," Taya ventured, getting no signal from Cristof. She looked at Amcathra.

"I will inquire," he said, then inclined his head toward the inspector. "Or you, if you prefer."

"It might be useful for us to inquire together," Gifford said, politely. Lieutenant Amcathra nodded in what Taya considered a startling demonstration of diplomatic acquiescence. He really *must* think of Gifford as another lictor.

"Did Guisnard have anything else in the safe?" she asked.

"No."

"If the books were searched and the correspondence taken," Amcathra said, "the killer may have thought Guisnard was carrying a message."

"We've been operating on that assumption," Gifford agreed. "Unfortunately, if he had a list of clients, it was taken. I appreciate your coming forward to tell us that you'd done business with him, Exalted. I don't suppose you know any of his other customers?"

"The exalted regrets to say that he doesn't, Inspector," Taya replied.

"Or where he was staying on his previous visit?"

"No. I'm sorry."

"No need to apologize; I would have been surprised if you had." Gifford fell silent, the frown still in his eyes. Then he shook his head. "Let me pull out the rest of Guisnard's belongings, in case they mean anything to you."

Several minutes later, all four of them stood around the inspector's desk, gazing at the dead man's clothing and possessions. Taya picked up each item and turned it for Cristof. Lieutenant Amcathra inspected everything, as well, looking dissatisfied.

Nothing stood out. Guisnard owned exactly what one would expect of a traveling book seller: several changes of clothing, nondescript toiletries and luggage, a crate of books — all science and philosophy — a portable writing desk, and notes on a Mareaux bank that had branches in both Echelles and Grimaucourt. There was no sign of money, jewelry, or a watch. Gifford said they may have been taken by the murderer or any passer-by.

"I can draw no conclusions," Amcathra said at last, setting down the clothing. "Perhaps there is no link between this murder and the exalted."

"Perhaps not. You've given us more information, at least." The inspector replaced the valuables in his safe and called constables to carry the rest back to storage.

Cristof resumed his seat. Taya sat next to him.

"Well, Exalted," Gifford said, "if you don't mind, I would like to question the rest of your delegation to see if he sold any books to them."

Cristof signaled his consent to Taya, then repeated his order to obtain the books.

"The exalted says you're welcome to ask any questions you like," she replied to the inspector, and then made a show of hesitating.

"Is there anything else?" Gifford asked.

"When the case has been closed, Inspector, what will happen to Mister Guisnard's books?"

"They'll be held with the rest of his possessions, to be picked up by his family or his employer."

"Would you consider selling them to us?"

"That's not something I can arrange. Besides, I wouldn't know what price to ask."

"Perhaps another bookseller could price them for you— the exalted is willing to pay an appraisal fee."

Gifford narrowed his eyes, concentrating on Cristof as though he could see through the ivory mask and its glass lenses.

"Are you that much of a collector, Exalted Forlore?"

"Inspector, have you ever visited Ondinium?" Taya asked, grasping at straws.

"Yes. I took a year-long course on chemical analytics at the university."

"I thought you might have; you seem comfortable with our language and customs. Are you also familiar with our religious beliefs?"

"The Lady of the Forge?"

"Yes. The Lady forges our souls anew with each birth, although their substance remains the same, affected by the strengths and weaknesses accrued over past lifetimes. Many things can hinder a soul's successful rebirth— great sins, great debts, great anger, great love. It's our job, as the living, to facilitate each soul's path into the next life by resolving those obstacles. That's why Ondiniums place so much value in finding and punishing criminals, especially murderers. The lictor caste performs an important service for the living and the dead. As does Mareaux's police force."

"And…?" Gifford looked mystified. Taya took a breath and continued.

"Mister Guisnard's life has touched ours, so we'd like to assist his rebirth. We will do all we can to facilitate your investigation, and, if you'll permit us, we'll finish the job that bought him to Echelles by purchasing his unsold books."

Cristof's gloved fingers squeezed her arm with approval.

"I…" The inspector shifted in his seat and cleared his throat. "You know we don't have quite the same beliefs about the Lady here in Mareaux."

"We understand, and of course we'll respect your decision in the matter. But if you decide no harm will come of it, will you please consider Exalted Forlore's request? It would benefit Mister Guisnard and the exalted, both spiritually and materially."

The inspector gave her a long look.

"We would need to inspect the books very carefully before releasing them," he said, "just to make certain there's no evidence in them that we may have missed. And, of course, the decision is ultimately the publisher's."

"We understand." Taya felt Cristof shift. She rose to her feet, supporting him as he stood. "Lieutenant, I don't think there will be room for all five of us in the carriage."

"That's all right. I can't leave the office immediately," Gifford said, glancing at the clock on his bookshelf. "Lieutenant Amcathra, will you be free in an hour to help me question the rest of your delegation?"

"Yes. Shall we meet at the palace?"

"I'll be there." The inspector shook the lieutenant's hand, and then Taya's, and then made another deep, correct bow to Cristof. "Thank you for your assistance, Exalted Forlore."

They gathered Rikard at the office door and headed outside. The wind was picking up again, carrying a chill. Taya looked north. The snow would be falling along the mountain range that divided Mareaux and Ondinium, and the trip from the capital of Mareaux to the capital of Ondinium would be a long one.

Using the weather to excuse their early departure would be believable, she decided.

They climbed into the carriage. Amcathra swung the doors shut and pulled the curtains.

"Why do you want those books?" he snapped.

"Give him a moment," Taya objected, untying her husband's mask. "There."

Cristof rubbed his face, then leaned over and kissed Taya on the cheek.

"My wife explained it perfectly."

"The icarus would have provided a compelling explanation for their purchase if you were a religiously observant man, Exalted."

"They'll be good additions to my library."

"*Infamous Murderesses of History*?" Amcathra's tone was politely skeptical. Taya made another mental note. The lictor read Alzanan.

Then again, "infamous murderess" *would* be the kind of phrase he'd know in another language.

"I want to see if there are any Mazzolettis in it."

"Was Guisnard an agent for the Council?"

"Wouldn't you know better than me?"

"I am the Council's spy only inasmuch as I have been ordered to evaluate your competence as a diplomat and report back any erratic or suspicious behavior in which you or your wife may indulge. I am not privy to the Council's secrets. Is Guisnard an agent?"

"Could we discuss this later?"

"I cannot oversee security if I am kept unaware of issues that may affect your safety."

"Please. I'd like to hear what the mercates have to say to the inspector, first."

"You intend to be present?"

"I'll stand behind a door."

"And then you will tell me whether Guisnard reports to the Oporphyr Tower."

"Yes."

Amcathra leaned back in the seat, folding his arms over his chest, and gave Taya a stern look.

"Make him see sense, Icarus."

CHAPTER FIVE

TAYA WAITED WHILE Cristof shed his heavy robes and gave them to Jayce to be brushed off and folded. He'd changed into the same famulate trousers and shirt he'd worn when he'd been a watchmaker on Tertius, making him look much like he had when they'd first met.

Except for his hair.

"By next summer you won't need the wig," she observed as he impatiently twisted his long black locks together and reached for a ribbon.

"I look like an idiot," he grumbled. "The only reason I don't cut it is that I hate wearing that wig even more than I hate long hair."

"You don't look like an idiot. But if you *do* decide to cut it, go to a barber. No more do-it-yourself hairstyles, Ambassador."

He shot her a wry glance over the rims of his spectacles, then turned back to the mirror and frowned as he finished tying his hair back in a ponytail.

She smiled, curling up on the divan.

"So, what am I going to tell Janos?" he asked, pushing his glasses higher and turning.

"Then the books *are* important?"

"Almost certainly." He walked over to a stack of books on his desk, chose one, and sat beside her on the divan. "This was Alister's last message, two weeks ago."

She took it. *Criminal Character: The Thirty Fundamental Physical Characteristics of the Criminal Type*. She flipped through it, pausing to study the lithographs. Some of them looked like people she knew, but she didn't see any underlining or other signs of a message hidden in the text.

"I don't understand."

"It's coded." He took her hand and laid her fingers on the page. "By the gutter."

Taya ran her fingers down the paper and felt bumps. She lifted the book and tilted it toward the light.

"Are those... punches?"

"Same concept. Alister hid a key card in the first book he sent me. It's just simple substitution — nothing like a real program — and it's time-consuming to translate. But he can read and write it on his own, instead of having to ask someone...." Cristof's voice trailed off.

"But why does he bother? What's he sending you that's so important?"

Her husband took the book back, weighing it in one hand before setting it on a side table.

"This book contains information about a pact the Alzanans are trying to make with Tizierian leaders to guarantee an open trade route from the coast up to Samaras. Alister is worried about what will happen if the Alzanans make diplomatic inroads with the Samarians. That could be a dangerous alliance for Ondinium."

"But why does he care?"

"He says he still loves his country."

"He says a lot of things." Taya realized her voice had become sharp, so she shifted and laid a hand on Cristof's knee. "Look, I don't mind you sending him money, but don't *trust* him."

"This is the third tip he's sent me. The first two checked out when I passed them along to the Council."

"Do they know you're communicating with him?"

"Scrap, no! I told them I'm getting the information from other sources; tradesmen I worked with on Tertius." He paused. "That's probably why Amcathra asked me about Guisnard. The Council must have asked him to identify my sources."

"If he finds out you're in touch with Alister, he'll report you."

"I know. I hate lying to him, but... I don't have any choice, do I?"

Not unless he stopped corresponding with his brother, but Taya didn't think that would happen.

"The problem is, he already suspects I'm lying," Cristof added.

"You need to get rid of that book. What if Chief Inspector Gifford asks to see the other books Guisnard sold you and discovers the code?" Taya thought about the police officer's comments, back at the office. "He already suspects the books have some kind of message hidden in them. We shouldn't have asked for them so quickly."

Cristof sighed. "Wonderful. The chief inspector thinks I'm a spy and I'm about to pull our delegation out early. I'm the world's worst ambassador. I *told* the Council I would be."

"Nonsense. Besides, now that I'm working for the diplomatic corps, you *have* to be an ambassador." She patted his leg. "What would people think if I left my husband for months at a time?"

"That you'd finally come to your senses."

"Don't be an idiot."

"Didn't you just say—"

"I said you don't *look* like an idiot. But sometimes you think like one. Now, what are you going to do about that book?"

"I can't get rid of it. The publisher will have a record of its sale. If Gifford *does* ask for it, it will look suspicious if I can't find it."

"Maybe they'd believe whoever poisoned you stole it."

"Taya!" Cristof pinched the bridge of his nose. "Let's try to keep the poisonings and Guisnard's murder separate."

"What if they *aren't* separate? If Alister's sending you important information, maybe Guisnard was killed to keep it out of your hands. And maybe when the message wasn't found, someone tried to kill *you* to keep it out of the *Council's* hands."

"But that would mean Alister's spying has been discovered." Cristof shifted restlessly. "I need to find out what's in those books."

"What will you do if Gifford finds the code?"

"I don't know."

"Could he decipher it?"

"Someone could, I'm sure. It's not that complex."

They fell silent.

"What's Alister doing now?" Taya asked, at last.

"Something he shouldn't."

"That seems to run in the family. What, exactly?"

"Something that involves interpreting a very large amount of data."

"But he's blind."

"Yes."

Taya thought of the punch code in the book and groaned.

"He isn't working as a programmer, is he?"

"He hasn't given me any specifics, but... he's brilliant, you know. It wouldn't take him any time at all to figure out a way to decipher punch cards by touch."

Taya straightened, looking her husband in the eye. "Cris, the Council will *murder* him for that. They have a secret team of lictors that hunts down and executes runaway programmers. Alister was allowed to live because he was blinded and you cut a special deal, but if he's caught punching, they'll throw that deal off a cliff. And Alister, too."

"A secret team of lictors?" Cristof's lips twitched. "You've been listening to Pyke's conspiracy theories again, love."

"*This* conspiracy theory makes sense!" A new thought chilled her. "Is Alister working for the Mareaux government?"

"I don't know. If he *is*, he wouldn't be the first exile a foreign government has taken in to get at Ondinium's secrets."

"Oh, scrap."

"But I don't know anything for certain," he added, hastily. "He could be working for any private organization with a difference engine. Industry, finance...."

"If the Council finds out you know Alister's still punching cards, it'll call you a traitor." Taya bit her lip. What had Amcathra said about her husband being 'expendable'?

Cristof took her hand. She gripped it, ignoring the pain in her palms as she slid closer and leaned against his side.

"I'm sorry." He disengaged his hand and put his arm around her. "I shouldn't have told you."

"Yes, you should have. You should have told me right from the start. I'd be shouting at you right now for keeping secrets if I weren't so worried." She swallowed. "*Is* this treason?"

His muscles tensed. "You don't believe I'd betray our nation, do you?"

"Not *betray*, but there's so much in Ondinium that you don't like...."

"I want reform, Taya, not revolution. And this information is benign. I'm using Alister as an informer; Ondinium has lots of informers in other countries."

"What if he's sending you misinformation?"

"That's always a risk."

"An exalted shouldn't work as a spy."

"I'm not spying; he is. And he's outcaste. He has nothing left to lose."

"Except his life."

Cristof remained silent. She glanced at him and saw a familiar frown furrowing his brow.

She wasn't telling him anything he hadn't already considered.

"All right," she said, in her best decisive voice. She picked up the book and ran her hands over the pinholes again. "Then we need to keep him safe. Have you written this information down?"

"Yes." He straightened, drawn from his dark reverie by her tone.

"Then smooth down the holes as well as you can, so they'll be harder to notice." She handed the book to him. "How does Alister deliver the books when you're in Ondinium?"

"He sends them from the bookstore in Grimaucourt. The one Guisnard worked for."

"Have you ever ordered any books there on your own?"

"I don't need to. Alister just chooses a volume and has it delivered."

"Well, from now on, start sending regular orders to build a paper trail. Keep your requests vague, if your brother chooses the books. All you need is a record of mail going back and forth between you and the store. I'll find out which icarus has our delivery route and ask Cassi to let us know if your letters are ever pulled for inspection. Do you pay for the books?"

"No..." Cristof pushed up his spectacles, gazing at her with fascination. "There's never any bill enclosed. I presume Alister pays for the books and delivery beforehand."

"Then you need a record of payment, too, in case someone ever checks the bookstore's ledgers."

"Like the Council's secret army of lictor assassins?"

She glowered at him. "I know what records Dispatch keeps for ingoing and outgoing foreign deliveries, so do what I say. Cover your tracks. Don't leave any gaps that might be suspicious if the Council *does* decide to check your correspondence."

"All right." He stood and leaned over to kiss her, running his long fingers over her cheek. "Thank you, love. I don't know why you put up with me."

Taya relaxed. As long as Cristof listened to her, she could keep him safe.

"You're usually worth it."

"Usually?"

"Well, when you ask me to go to a morgue just to be your interpreter—"

She was interrupted by a knock on the door.

"Exalted?" Amcathra said, from outside. "The inspector is waiting. If you still wish to hide in an adjacent room, I have prepared one for you."

"Now?" Taya growled.

"I'll make it up to you tonight," Cristof promised, giving her one last, hurried kiss. She shook her head with exasperation as she followed him out.

Ondinium's staff consisted of two lictors besides Amcathra and Rikard; Jayce and his five-person team, who kept the delegation appropriately clothed and coiffed; two Ondinium University professors who'd already settled into temporary housing at Echelles University but returned to answer questions; their two research assistants; and the three mercates representing each of the Big Three mining consortia and their separate clerks.

Taya and Cristof listened as Amcathra and Inspector Gifford asked each person about Hubert Guisnard and came up with nothing except the confirmation from a lictor that yes, a bookseller had visited Exalted Forlore and yes, he thought the exalted had bought some books from the man. Yes, the exalted had bought a dozen or so books since coming to Mareaux, and several journals, too. His wife had, too. Yes, his wife was with the delegation. Hadn't they met? His wife was the icarus.

Taya made a face as the inspector began to stammer.

The icarus was the exalted's wife? Why hadn't she been introduced that way? Weren't cross-caste marriages illegal? Do we mean the same thing by the word "wife"?

Apparently the inspector thought the folk wisdom that "cross-caste marriages never work" was law. To be sure, the statement was implicitly sanctioned by hundreds of tragic cross-caste love stories. In fact, Cristof had assured Taya during their engagement that almost .025 percent of marriages in Ondinium over the last fifty years had crossed caste, and 90 percent of those marriages had been successful; a higher percentage than enjoyed by intra-caste marriages.

At last the chief inspector took his leave. Lieutenant Amcathra stepped through the room connecting the two chambers.

"The mercates have asked to speak to you. They are waiting, if you care to address them now."

"I suppose I'd better." Cristof reached out and squeezed Taya's hand. "Will you stay?"

"Of course." She followed him into the room, where the three mercates rose and bowed.

Within Ondinium, Cristof had given up wearing a mask and robes entirely. Outside Ondinium, he was required to cover in public, unmasking only before foreigners of the highest social rank. The compromise sounded good in theory, but in practice it had been impossible to maintain. Cristof had soon stopped wearing his mask and public robes when he was alone with the mercates and the rest of his ambassadorial staff. It had been awkward at first, but after a while the mercates had disciplined themselves to look at Cristof's naked face without flinching.

"Exalted," said Maximilian Trichas, straightening. He represented North Reach Consolidated Mining & Smelting Co. and was the youngest and most headstrong of the three. "We were hoping you'd tell us whether you're going to pull the delegation out of Mareaux as a result of these assassination attempts."

"How much would it inconvenience you?" Cristof asked, taking a seat. Taya perched on the edge of an overstuffed velvet chair on the other side of the room.

"We haven't finalized our negotiations yet, Exalted," said Patrice Corundel, the gray-haired woman who represented Allied Metals & Extraction. "I think we could reach a satisfactory agreement if we had another three days."

"Those are three days in which the exalted's life could be in danger," Trichas objected. "I think we should withdraw as soon as possible. The assassin has failed twice already. Who knows what will happen if he gets desperate? The exalted should take the next train to Terminal and wait there for the rest of the delegation."

"What do you think?" Cristof asked, turning to the oldest of the representatives, Auguste Macerain, of Ondinium First Standard Mining Co.

"Make sure you have a private carriage," Macerain advised. "It's twenty hours to Terminal. You can't ride all day in a mask, and how would you manage those robes when you needed to take a piss?"

"Good point," Cristof replied.

"How's the trade agreement going?" Taya asked, trying not to laugh. "Have you worked out that coal tariff?"

"Mareaux has dug in its heels at six percent," Trichas complained. "Our partners tell us Mareaux's Parliament will reduce it to five if the Council reduces the cotton tariff to five, but that's out of our hands."

"Unless you have any influence on these matters, Exalted?" Corundel inquired.

"I can take a recommendation to Council, but that's all. Still, the compromise doesn't sound unreasonable. Of course, ultimately it all comes down to the Great Engine's trade projections."

"We would appreciate anything you could do to help," Corundel said.

"Are the other negotiations going better?" Taya asked.

"As well as expected," Trichas said. "We've reaffirmed several agreements and discussed some mutually beneficial delivery and storage rate changes. Signed a few new contracts. Nothing to excite our investors."

"We could have done most of it by post," Macerain grumbled, standing and leaning on his cane. He turned to Cristof and touched his forehead with his palm. "If you will excuse me, Exalted, I'm leaving to attend a string quartet. The daughter of one of my old friends plays the cello. She's dreadful, but nobody in Mareaux has the good sense to tell her so. If she'd taken the Great Examination, she would have been culled out of music school right from the start, and dozens of family friends would have been saved these painful musical interludes."

"You aren't going to tell her, are you?" Taya asked, wincing.

"Don't advise me on manners, Icarus; I've been visiting Mareaux since before you were born." He headed out the door. "And nothing ever changes. Don't know why you insisted we come in person, Patrice. I could do this job in my sleep."

Corundel waited a beat for the old man's back to vanish down the hallway before adding, "and for the most part, he does."

"It's useful to have someone around who remembers all the precedents," Trichas said, diplomatically. He turned to Cristof. "Will we have a few more days to wrap up?"

"Janos, how long would it take to get a private car attached to the next train out to Terminal?" Cristof asked, looking at the lictor.

"Two days, if you want your staff and luggage to accompany you."

"I do, and I see no reason to rush. We'll give you the three days you requested, Mercate Corundel. Lieutenant Amcathra will figure out the timetable and keep you informed."

"Thank you, Exalted." "Thank you," the two mercates chorused, taking their leave.

"Will you let us know as soon as you've set a departure date?" Cristof asked Amcathra.

"Yes." The lictor folded his arms over his chest and fixed the exalted with his ice-blue gaze. "Was Guisnard a Council agent?"

Taya grinned as Cristof blew out an exasperated breath.

"He was an informant, but as far as I know, he wasn't working for the Council. He brought me some useful news the last time he visited, and I can only assume he returned with an update. I hope that wasn't why he was killed, though."

"How do you come to have informants outside of Ondinium?"

"When I ran my repair shop, I corresponded with clockmakers all around the continent. I also worked with a number of foreign tradesmen and met foreign customers shopping for an Ondinium timepiece." He shrugged. "Now that I'm a diplomat, some of my old contacts send me information."

"Then there is a message hidden in the two books."

"Probably."

Amcathra's blue eyes narrowed.

Taya held her breath, wondering if he was going to ask about Alister again.

"There is no way to forcibly retrieve the books that would not risk an international incident," he said at last.

She softly released her breath.

"No." Cristof sounded glum. "Which means we may never find out why Guisnard was killed."

CHAPTER SIX

"THERE," SAID JAYCE proudly. "What do you think?"

Taya gave a very unladylike whistle of admiration as she gazed at the four silk robes he'd spread out over the bed.

"Have you been holding these back?" she asked, running a hand over the outer robe. It was covered with an embroidered arabesque of flowering vines picked out in precious and semi-precious stones, and the inner lining was a mirror-match in gold thread. She lifted one heavy sleeve. "This must weigh a ton."

"It does. The exalted won't do much walking around tonight." Jayce sounded pleased by the thought. "Look, every flower is native to Mareaux. And the back? Mareaux's grapevines. Each grape is a single ruby. Do you think the queen will appreciate it? I knew the exalted would need something impressive for his last night at court."

"Did the Council pay for this?"

"We have a wardrobe budget." Jayce gave the garments a calculating glance. "I'll tear the robe apart when we get back and re-use as much of it as possible. So, please, no *adventures* tonight."

"We haven't scheduled any." Taya ran a hand over the other garments. The second robe was celadon and embroidered with a darker leafy pattern. The third robe was a solid deep burgundy, and the fourth a rich sienna. "Oh, he's going to *hate* all this."

"Your husband has even less fashion sense than you do."

"That's true. But for what it's worth, they're beautiful. Can we keep this one?" She pointed to the sienna robe. "Cris would look good in it around the house."

"Have you convinced him to start wearing robes again?"

"I'm working on it." Not with much success, but she hoped if she kept flattering him whenever he wore one, he might come around. She enjoyed seeing him dressed up in proper silk and jewels.

"Good luck." Jayce turned to the wig on the dresser. "And what about this?"

"He'll hate that, too," Taya said. "But you did an amazing job. I can't even tell it got soaked."

Jayce gave the wig an affectionate pat. "One of my assistants is an incredible stylist. You should use her. When will the exalted give up his wig?"

Taya ignored his jab about her hairstyle. "His hair is almost long enough to style now, even though he keeps threatening to cut it off."

"Don't let him do that!"

"I'm working on that, too." She looked around. "What am I going to wear tonight?"

"A traditional Mareaux gown, of course."

"Of course." She sighed as he lifted it off a chair for her. Long, tied-back skirts, a tight bodice, a high collar, and sleeves down to her wrist. "I wish you'd make me something *practical*."

"I give you practical in Ondinium, where you're an icarus. But I give you formal in Mareaux, where you're the ambassador's voice. This is the *height* of local fashion. Do you like the bodice?"

Taya saw that he'd cut the fabric in long, curving strips, creating a suggestion of wings wrapping around her midsection.

"That's a nice touch," she admitted, although she'd rather wear her real wings.

"I work for barbarians," Jayce grumbled.

"No, it *is* nice. You always remind people that I'm an icarus, and I appreciate it. I'm just tired of wearing dresses every day."

"You haven't worn dresses every day. I've seen you in that ugly flight suit."

"Only when I'm on my own."

"You need to wear a dress two more times. Tonight, for the concert and reception, and tomorrow, for the farewell ceremony. Once you're back in Terminal, you can wear your flight suit every day, if you like."

"I can hardly wait." She smiled. Despite the social awkwardness of the delegation's withdrawal, she was looking forward to getting back home, where she could act — and dress — like herself again.

Jayce waved at the garments. "Then this will do?"

"Of course. Thank you. Can you deliver everything to our suites within the hour?"

"Naturally."

"I don't know what we'd do without you." She squeezed his hand and left. She had to find Lord Pomeroy to make certain the palace would provide a translator for the morning's departure ceremonies. She wouldn't be accompanying Cristof, since she had to oversee the transport of her armature.

Taya turned the corner into the grand hall and froze when she saw Lord Gaio Mazzoletti leaning over Rikard. The young lictor's fair complexion was flushed and his jaw and fists clenched as the Alzanan courtier berated him. Their faces were only inches apart.

"Excuse me." Taya raised her voice as she strode across the inlaid marble floor. "Is there a problem?"

Lord Gaio straightened, his dark eyes flashing.

"This young hoodlum ran into me and refused to apologize. He has no respect for his betters!"

Taya looked at Rikard, whose black lictor's stripe stood out against his reddened face.

"I apologized," he said, his voice tense.

"He said 'Sorry,'" Lord Gaio mimicked, in a bad Ondinium accent. "Without even stopping. I do not consider 'sorry' an apology. In Alzana, I would challenge this boy to a duel for such an insult. Only my respect for the ambassador keeps me from doing so here."

Taya's lips tightened. She didn't like Lord Gaio browbeating a member of her delegation, but she had no trouble imagining Rikard rudely brushing by the Alzanan ambassador.

"Lictor Kiraly, would you please give Lord Mazzoletti a more suitable apology?"

Rikard shot her a dark look, and then straightened, dragging his eyes away from her to fix them on the Alzanan. He gave a Mareaux-style salute.

"I apologize for running into you, Lord Mazzoletti," he said, stiffly. "It will not happen again."

Lord Gaio grunted with disgust and then waved a hand. "See that it does not." The Alzanan turned to Taya. "The exalted should not travel with children who cannot be trusted to do their duty."

Rikard jerked around and strode away, his shoulders high.

"I'm sorry," Taya said to the Alzanan ambassador. "This has been a stressful time for our security personnel. I'll see that Lieutenant Amcathra has a word with him."

"He is still in charge? I'm surprised. If an Alzanan bodyguard had failed to prevent two assassination attempts, he would be dismissed. Or executed."

"The lieutenant is not exactly the exalted's bodyguard, and his fate is up to the Council," Taya said, hiding her annoyance.

"Exalted Forlore doesn't have the power to dismiss a member of his own staff?"

"Exalted Forlore is content to wait until a formal investigation determines whether any of our lictors were negligent in their duties."

"How can there be any doubt?" Lord Gaio reached out and touched her cheek. "*I* would take better care of my wife, if I were the exalted."

"The exalted's wife prefers to take care of herself." Taya stepped backward. "If you'll excuse me, Lord Mazzoletti?"

"Of course." His smile mocked her.

Taya caught up with Rikard on the other side of the hall and tugged him into an empty side hall.

"What was all that about?" she demanded, keeping her voice low.

The young lictor avoided her eyes.

"You shouldn't trust him."

"I *don't* trust him. But he's Alzana's equivalent to an exalted, and he deserves to be treated with the respect due his rank."

"In Demicus, people are respected for what they do, not how they're born."

Taya took a deep breath. If Rikard wasn't careful, he was going to fail the lictors' annual loyalty test.

"Demicus has several families who have headed their clans for multiple generations. Isn't that a form of birthright?"

"They lead because they're good leaders," he shot back. "If they were weak or corrupt, they'd be challenged and someone else would take over."

"Well, it isn't that different in Alzana. The Families also recognize right of combat. In fact, you were lucky Lord Mazzoletti didn't challenge you on the spot. Alzanans duel with sabres, not guns. How good are you with a sabre?"

The question was rhetorical. Ondinium didn't teach its lictors how to use such old-fashioned weapons.

Rikard scowled at the floor.

"Alzanans duel with poison and bombs," he countered, his voice flat.

"Are you suggesting that the Mazzolettis were behind the attacks?"

"Of course they were."

She sighed. She needed to have a stern talk with Amcathra and Cristof about airing their suspicions in front of impressionable young lictors.

"We have no proof of that. Look, the political situation is difficult enough for the ambassador without throwing an offended Alzanan into the mix." She laid a hand on his shoulder, feeling silent anger in his taut muscles. "I know Lord Mazzoletti is annoying, but he's a powerful nobleman and, if we're very unlucky, he could be the queen's next consort. So keep your temper, do your duty, and make your uncle proud."

At last Rikard glanced up.

"I will," he said, grimly.

She nodded and released him, heading back out into the hall.

The farewell concert was held in Echelles' Royal Opera House. Traditionally the Mareaux would hold a ball, but the queen was doing her best to adapt tradition to an ambassador who barely moved and refused to take off his mask in public.

A concert required only that he sit and listen.

Queen Iancais had invited them to her royal box, which had a dark, gauzy curtain drawn across the front.

"Nobody can see us, as long as we keep the lights low," the queen said, gesturing to a servant to light only one of the gas candelabrae on the walls. After he'd bowed and withdrawn, Lieutenant Amcathra locked the door.

"Thank you, your Majesty," Taya said, untying her husband's mask. "You're very thoughtful."

"I would like Ondinium's exalteds to feel welcome in my country."

"You've made me very welcome, your Majesty," Cristof said, bowing and lifting one sleeve-covered hand to his forehead in an Ondinium bow. Like the sight of his bare face, the bow was an honor no foreigner had the right to receive. "I appreciate your generosity."

"Please, sit. That robe looks as heavy as the one I wore during my coronation."

"Thank you." Cristof waited for Taya to help him into the chair, arranging the jewel-encrusted fabric around him. Keeping his feet and hands covered didn't matter in front of the queen, of course, but Taya thought the richness of his robes demanded extra attention. She laid the ivory mask on his lap and slid his glasses onto his face.

"Take the chair beside him, Icarus," the queen directed. "You can't stand for the entire concert."

"Thank you, your Majesty."

"I regret that you're leaving under such circumstances."

"I hope you understand that this isn't my preference," Cristof said. "My lictors are under orders to return me to Ondinium if my life is threatened."

"One might construe your departure as an insult."

"The security lapse was our own."

"Your lictors have been less than subtle about casting suspicion on the Alzanan contingent."

"...I apologize on their behalf. I'm afraid lictors aren't trained in diplomacy."

"Indeed. I find myself in an awkward position, Ambassador. The Mazzolettis are offended by your men's insinuations. They feel unjustly accused, as we did not, in fact, find any evidence to suggest that they were involved in either incident."

Cristof hesitated. Taya silently sent up a prayer to the Lady that he wouldn't air his own suspicions.

"I have the utmost confidence in Mareaux's investigation," he said. Taya breathed a silent 'thank you.' "And I will convey that to the ambassadors this evening, if we may be allowed a private room at the reception."

"Mareaux would be happy to facilitate a sense of goodwill between its two valued allies," the queen said, formally.

"And Ondinium wants nothing more than to strengthen its ties to Mareaux," Cristof replied, just as formally.

"Then I shall see that the Mazzolettis are told that you'd like to say a personal good-bye," the queen said. She turned toward the stage, a shadow-show through the translucent curtain. "Are you familiar with our national composer, Ambassador?"

By the time the two-hour concert was over, Taya was in love. In Ondinium, she'd heard musicians play in the theater and at parties, and of course at weddings and funerals and holy days, but she'd never been exposed to the power and passion of a full orchestra before.

"Did you enjoy the concert, Icarus?" the queen asked, smiling as Taya finished applauding.

"It was wonderful!" Taya turned to Cristof, her eyes shining. "Wasn't it wonderful?"

"Magnificent," he agreed, gazing affectionately at her. "Should we have some of the compositions sent to Ondinium, so we can hear them played again?"

"I shall see that you receive the best," the queen said. "It would please us to have Mareaux's music played for Ondinium's exalteds."

The farewell reception was held at the palace. The Ondinium professors clustered in one corner, talking shop and working their way through several bottles of wine. The Big Three mercates mingled more comfortably with the foreign courtiers and ambassadors, although Taya suspected that they were also talking shop. Mareaux's aristocracy had no caste prohibitions to prevent them from chatting with mercates. The Mazzolettis were conversing with the elderly mercate Auguste Macerain, who smiled and nodded pleasantly as he held a glass of wine. Trade with Alzana was strictly regulated by the Council, but she assumed Ondinium First Standard Mining Co. did *some* business with the country.

"The queen has set aside a private salon, Ambassador," Pomeroy said, joining them. "If you'll follow me?"

The salon stood just off the reception room, spacious and glimmering in the warm light of candles rather than the harsher glare of gas. One of the palace guards stood by the door. "He'll make certain nobody of lesser rank intrudes on you, Ambassador," Pomeroy explained as he shut the door behind them.

"That's perfect." Taya untied Cristof's ivory mask and set it on a small mahogany console table.

"Yes, thank you," Cristof agreed, starting to lift one heavily jeweled sleeve to his forehead before changing his mind. He gave Taya a look of appeal. She pulled out her handkerchief, drying his forehead. "I apologize for the inconvenience."

"Not at all," Pomeroy replied. "Please, make yourself comfortable. Can I pour you a glass of wine?"

"Not right now, thank you. But I'm sure I'll need a drink soon."
Pomeroy smiled slightly. "Icarus, is there anything I can provide you?"

"No, thank you." Taya moved a chair to ensure that Cristof's back was to the door.

"Then I'll make certain everyone knows where to find you," Pomeroy said as he left.

"Meaning the Mazzolettis," Taya murmured, straightening her husband's robes.

"Well, I promised," Cristof said. "Would you please stop that?"

"I want you to look your best in front of them." She made sure the jeweled outer robe was turned to reveal the gold embroidery on the inside. "Do you want your spectacles?"

"No. I hate wearing them while I'm decked out like a holy-day centerpiece."

"Oh, that reminds me. Rikard bumped into Lord Mazzoletti today and wasn't fast enough with an apology," Taya said, pulling up a chair so she could sit by his side. "Lord Mazzoletti was ranting, so I made Rikard apologize again."

"I suppose I'll have to apologize, as well."

"Just say whatever needs to be said to get us all out of here without any trouble." She leaned over and kissed his forehead. "Remember, you're a diplomat."

"The worst diplomat in the history of Ondinium," he muttered, as someone knocked on the door.

The other ambassadors and courtiers visited in small groups, seeming more comfortable around Cristof when his mask was off. He remained seated while they clustered around him, helping themselves to wine and gossip. Soon the small room grew crowded as those privileged to see the Ondinium ambassador's naked face moved from the reception area to the salon. Taya began to worry that somebody was going to knock over a candle and set them all ablaze.

The crowd's tone suddenly changed. She turned to see the Alzanan ambassadors entering.

As usual, the Mazzolettis looked as though they'd walked to the reception directly from their servants' care rather than from the same two-hour concert and bumpy carriage ride back that everyone else had endured. They glittered in militant blue and gold, Lady Fosca's hair pinned and swept up in a style almost as elaborate as Cristof's.

"Ambassadors." Taya stood and curtsied, taking solace in the fact that their finery was beggared by the shameless ostentation of Cristof's robes.

"So nice to see you again, Taya," Lady Fosca said, making a perfunctory curtsey before sweeping around to plant herself on the chaise lounge opposite Cristof's chair. The Tizierian ambassador already sitting on it politely shifted to one side. "Exalted! It's so lovely to see you without your mask. I wish you didn't wear that thing in public all the time."

"It's not my choice, Ambassador," Cristof said, more honestly than Taya thought was proper. "The Council insists I obey the traditions of my caste."

"Of course it does," Lord Gaio said, following his sister at a more sedate pace. Taya rested a hand on the back of her chair but stayed on her feet. "Ondinium is mired in tradition. Its lack of social progress is what doomed it the first time."

"Every country has traditions," Cristof said mildly. "They're what give us our national character."

"Is it tradition for an Ondinium ambassador to flee at the first sign of trouble?" Lord Gaio asked. Taya's hand tightened on the chair. Small gasps and murmurs traveled through the onlookers.

Lady Fosca tapped her brother's leg with a look of mild disapproval.

"Come, Gaio, don't be rude. The exalted isn't obliged to stay in a country that is inimical toward him."

"We don't believe Mareaux is behind the attacks," Taya said quickly, sensing the danger in Lady Fosca's phrasing. The last thing they needed was for the other ambassadors to think Ondinium was turning against its long-time ally.

"No, you believe Alzana is behind the attacks," Lord Gaio said, his expression barely escaping a sneer.

"If anything my staff or I have said or done has given you that impression," Cristof replied, "I apologize. My lictors and the queen's guard have investigated, and we have no idea who was behind the attempts. As for myself, I wouldn't expect Alzana to carry out such *inadequate* attempts on my life."

Taya cringed as she struggled to maintain a neutral, pleasant expression.

"No," Lord Gaio agreed with a small smile. "Those attempts *were* particularly inept."

"I'm sure you'll be safe once you're home," Lady Fosca said, brightly. "Everybody knows how securely Ondinium keeps itself locked away in its mountains."

"Do we seem isolationist?" Cristof asked, mildly. "If so, I hope to change that impression. The Council hopes to strengthen the alliances we already have, such as with Mareaux, and build new alliances elsewhere." He glanced at the Tizierian ambassador, who straightened up, his kohl-rimmed eyes widening.

Taya felt a surge of pride. For all his self-deprecating remarks, Cristof wasn't so bad at the diplomatic game. Tizier might hesitate to ally with Alzana if it thought Ondinium were open to negotiations.

"And yet you are still leaving so soon?" Lady Fosca pressed. "The queen of Mareaux must fear what news you'll report to your Council."

"I plan to take back nothing but the highest praise for Queen Iancais and the rest of my kind hosts and colleagues." Cristof inclined his head to indicate the ambassadors and nobility around them, who murmured with satisfaction. "I assure you, Ambassador Mazzoletti, Ondinium prides itself on being a staunch friend to its allies... and a perilous foe to its enemies."

"And what *has* Ondinium done for its allies lately?" Lord Gaio murmured, almost too softly to be heard.

Almost.

"I'm sure the queen will be relieved," Lady Fosca added. "It can be quite nerve-wracking whenever Ondinium deigns to notice any of us lesser nations."

"'Lesser' is an unusual word to use, when Ondinium is the smallest of the nations represented here," Cristof said, still doing his best to retain a pleasant tone. "I am the one who has been honored by the welcome I've received. I hope," he glanced again at the Tizieran ambassador, and then up at the others who stood around them, listening intently, "I may visit all of your countries someday."

Lady Fosca smiled and leaned forward, touching his arm.

"We would love to have you in Alzana, Exalted."

"Perhaps this spring," Lord Gaio agreed, surprising Taya.

"If the Council permits," Cristof demurred, even as the other ambassadors spoke up, inviting him to their countries.

CHAPTER SEVEN

CLOUDS OF ASH-IMBUED steam billowed from the loco-motive, coating the platform and everyone on it in light gray soot. Uniformed porters bellowed back and forth as they loaded the delegation's trunks into the ambassador's car. A brass band played, the train's engine rumbled, and passengers milled to and fro, stretching their legs, looking for seats, or craning their necks to gawk at the assembly at the rear of the platform. An early morning storm pounded on the glass-and-iron canopy that arched over the vast, sprawling length of Echelles Central Station.

The formal farewells were over, but the informal goodbyes seemed interminable. Taya had slipped away, leaving her husband with Lieutenant Amcathra. The palace translator could handle whatever was left to be done; her job was to watch as her wings and the chest containing her ondium counterweights were loaded into their private carriage and locked to the heavy rings bolted to the walls.

Rikard had been ordered to guard the delegation's luggage during the farewell ceremonies. Now he stood next to Taya, one hand resting on the air rifle that hung from his shoulder by a leather strap. The Mareaux porters gave the forbidding young lictor a wide berth as they worked.

"Are you going to fly after us?" Rikard asked.

"Not in this rain," Taya replied, securing the armature. The tips of its metal wingfeathers tapped against the carriage ceil-ing. Rikard looked out the window.

"Someone is shouting," he said, swiveling his rifle around. He frowned. "It's that Mareaux lictor. The *inspector.*"

Taya yanked on the armature's chain to make sure it was tight. "What does he want?"

"I don't know. He's shouting for *missus* Forlore. What does *missus* mean? Is it Mareaux for exalted?"

"Oh, Forgefire!" Exasperated, Taya turned and leaned out the passenger car door. Chief Inspector Gifford stood there, breathing hard, his oilcloth coat streaming water and creating great, murky puddles of ash on the platform by the stairs. He was carrying a leather suitcase.

Taya hiked her skirts over her ankles and stepped down to the platform, maneuvering well away from the muddy puddles.

"Chief Inspector," she said. "It's good to see you again."

"Um, Missus Forlore?"

"Just Taya, please. Icarii don't use last names."

"I'm sorry… I'm not accustomed to calling noblewomen by their first names."

"I'm not noble. I didn't become an exalted just because I married one, Inspector."

"Oh." He looked mystified. "Caste is complicated, isn't it?"

"Not really." Taya wondered why he'd think so. One was born into one's mother's caste and stayed in it unless one took the Great Examination and qualified for another. Of course, nobody could qualify for the exalted caste except through birth.

Simple.

Complicated was figuring out social rank in countries where it could change according to birth and death and marriage and royal decree. Other countries' systems of precedence struck Taya as completely irrational.

"How may I help you, Chief Inspector? If you're looking for Exa— no, you aren't, are you?"

"I was looking for you. I know the exalted is busy." Gifford glanced at the diplomatic party, then back at her. "This is a bit awkward, but I didn't know whom else to ask— Lieutenant Amcathra's busy, and I'm not well acquainted with the other members of your delegation…."

"Ask me whatever you want, Inspector. I'm the exalted's liaison with the public."

"Then maybe you can tell me… are Ondinium and Mareaux going to war?"

Taya started, surprised.

"No, of course not. Why? What have you heard?"

Gifford studied her intently. "People are saying someone tried to assassinate the exalted and that his sudden departure means Ondinium is angry with the queen."

Taya stepped closer, lowering her voice.

"There *have* been a few suspicious events that may have been assassination attempts. That's why we were interested in Guisnard's murder, in case it was connected. But the Council's not going to declare war on its strongest political and economic ally over a few failed attacks that we can't even prove were aimed at the exalted. Exalted Forlore is leaving because he must; Ondinium has strict security protocols that demand his return to the capital. But that has nothing to do with war. Please let others know that."

"They say you're taking our aerostats with you so you can improve them and turn them against us. They say the trade negotiations didn't go well, and that Ondinium plans to annex our land to increase its power."

"'They' have an active imagination, don't they?" Taya made a face. 'They' did in Ondinium, too. "Chief Inspector Gifford, Ondinium prides itself on rational governance. The Council would never go to war without first calculating all the pros and cons and modeling dozens of alternative strategies and outcomes, first. Even if Cris — if the exalted went back in a huff, offended by his treatment here, as long as the Great Engine calculated that a war wasn't in the country's best interest, the Council would ignore him. And the Engine won't advise war — it would be strategically stupid for Ondinium to attack Mareaux. You'd simply team up with Alzana and we'd end up fighting on two borders. That's the last thing Ondinium wants."

Gifford studied her face.

"You sound convincing."

"The truth *should* sound convincing." She looked at the suitcase sitting on the dirty platform next to him. "Although I hope I haven't put a crimp in your plan to defect."

"Defect?" He followed her gaze down at the case. "Is that what you thought I was doing?"

"Well, defect or ask me to run away with you." Taya grinned as the inspector's concern gave way to a startled laugh.

"I'm sorry, Mis— Icarus. But my wife wouldn't approve."

"My husband wouldn't, either. So where are you going?"

He met her eyes.

"No war?"

"No war."

"No plans to invade?"

"I swear by the Lady, I don't know about any plans to invade Mareaux, and my husband and I would be the first to protest if anyone suggested it."

"All right. I'm going to trust you, Icarus. Please don't let me down."

Taya raised her hand as though she were taking her annual loyalty oath.

"I won't."

He gestured to the suitcase. "Those are Guisnard's books. My men searched them and didn't find anything suspicious, and Guisnard's employer wrote that he was willing to give them to the exalted as a gift. I have to confess, I'm uneasy about handing them over. If they contain some kind of secret plan to overthrow my country, I'll never forgive myself. But if they don't... I hope the ambassador will consider them a gesture of goodwill under these strained circumstances."

Taya's heart leaped.

"Inspector, you've just made Cri— the ambassador's day."

And hers, too. Cristof had paced back and forth across his suite for an hour last night, frustrated about missing a message from his brother. She hadn't been looking forward to dealing with his bad mood during the twenty-hour ride back to the border.

"I hope I'm doing the right thing." Gifford looked at the train. "I'll carry the case to your car. It's heavy."

"That's all right; we can take care of it." Taya waved to Rikard, who was keeping an eye on them through the half-open window.

"Really, I don't mind—"

"No," Rikard said in Ondinan, blocking Gifford. He slung his rifle across his back. "I need to inspect it, first."

"It's— oh, of course." Gifford stepped back.

"I'm sorry, Inspector," Taya said as Rikard unsnapped the suitcase latches and opened the lid. "The exalted's lictors take his security very seriously, especially now."

At the head of the platform, the brass band fell silent and Taya heard applause. She glanced over and saw that the ambassadors were starting to drift away, no doubt eager to return to the palace for a proper breakfast.

Rikard finished flipping through the last book, ran his hands over the top, bottom, and sides of the suitcase, and then re-stacked the books and closed the lid.

"It looks safe. Where do you want it?"

"I think the exalted would like to read during the long ride," Taya said. She turned to Gifford as Rikard picked up the case. "Thank you very much, Chief Inspector. If you can wait here a few minutes, I'll bring the exalted over so you can tell him what you brought. He won't be able to thank you in person, but I know he'll be pleased."

"No, that's all right; don't disturb him. I'd rather keep this informal, just in case I *am* making a mistake." Gifford looked rueful. "Besides, I'd only end up talking to you again."

She held out her hand. "Well, we won't forget your assistance."

"Have a good trip, Taya Icarus," he said, shaking her hand.

"Thank you, Chief Inspector Gifford." She watched as the thin man turned and walked off, working his way through the crowds toward the front building.

A whistle blew, and porters began calling out to the passengers to move aboard. Cristof and Amcathra were walking toward her, Cristof's ivory mask dulled by the moist ash in the air. The two other lictors jogged down the platform, their rifles slung across their backs.

"Everything's secure, sir," one reported as Amcathra stopped and let Taya take Cristof's arm. "No sign of trouble."

"Good." Amcathra turned to Taya. "Who was that?"

"The chief inspector." Taya glanced at Cristof. "Let's talk inside."

The hems of her skirts and Cristof's outer robe were soaked and muddy by the time they got into the diplomatic car. Macerain, Trichas, and Corundel were already aboard and had taken seats around a small table covered with farewell gifts of flowers and fruit baskets. Jayce and the other staff members were rummaging through their bags, opening books and pulling out packs of cards.

Their Mareaux guest, Professor Cora Dautry, stood as Cristof entered.

"Exalted," she said politely, glancing from the featureless mask to Taya. "I wasn't sure if I should travel in here...."

"That's fine," Taya said as the doors were closed behind them. She shook the professor's hand. "I hope you won't be offended, but we have to dispense with some formalities when we traveling together so closely."

"Er, of course…." Dautry looked confused.

Rikard and the two other lictors stationed themselves at the front and back of the car while Amcathra drew heavy velvet curtains across the windows. Taya unfastened Cristof's mask and helped her husband out of his ornate wig and public robe. She handed both to Jayce, who looked with dismay at the soot that stained them.

"I'm glad that's over," Cristof sighed, rubbing his face and then leaning forward to kiss her. "Home at last."

"In about twenty hours." She handed him his spectacles. He put them on and looked around, tugging at his multiple layers of inner robes.

"Jayce has your regular clothes back there," she said, pointing to the curtained facilities at the end of the car.

"Then I'll be back in a few minutes." Cristof gave Dautry a distracted nod. "Excuse me, Professor, but I'll feel better once I'm out of these. By the way, Taya, Lord Pomeroy gave us two crates of wine. I can't even think about drinking it."

"I hope you didn't tell him that."

"Fortunately, the exalted was masked when he received the news," Amcathra said, looking down at the old suitcase by the door. "What is this?"

"I'll tell you when Cristof gets back. Rikard already checked it." Taya sat across from Dautry. The professor wore a business-like traveling dress, and wire-rimmed reading glasses hung from a chain around her neck. "It's good to see you again, Professor."

"And you, Icarus. I was wondering how traveling with an exalted was going to work. I'm glad to see that we won't sit in silence for the entire trip."

"Do you know much about Ondinium customs?"

"I've done a great deal of reading in preparation for this trip, and of course I was briefed by the university. But I thought exalteds hid their face from everyone except each other and their household staff."

"It's true, but that would make the ambassador's job a little difficult, as you might imagine."

The train whistle blew again. They were almost ready to set off.

"Exalted Forlore follows strict covering protocol whenever he can, but sometimes he has to dispense with his mask and robes for practicality's sake."

"How do his peers feel about that?"

Taya blinked. Nobody had ever asked that before. She leaned forward, compelling Dautry to do the same.

"Most of them understand the importance of his position," she murmured. "However, that doesn't mean they approve of his behavior. You need to understand that most Ondiniums are as uncomfortable seeing an exalted walking around with a naked face as your Mareaux would feel... oh, seeing your queen walk around with naked breasts."

"I see." Dautry leaned back in her chair, smoothing her dark gray skirt. "That's a... vivid analogy."

Cristof reappeared in his usual ensemble of white shirt and plain black suit. A whistle blew and the train jerked into motion. He stumbled and grabbed the back of the big leather chair Taya had reserved for him.

"Is there anything to eat?" he asked, sliding into his seat as the rocking became steadier.

"The kitchen will open in an hour," Amcathra replied, still standing by the door and the suitcase. He gave the case a pointed look, which Taya ignored.

"Cristof, you remember our dirigible pilot Professor Cora Dautry. Professor Dautry, this is Exalted Forlore," she said.

Reminded of their pretense, Cristof leaned forward and shook the professor's hand.

"How do you do? I'm sorry we couldn't speak the first time we met. I'm looking forward to learning more about your work."

"Thank you, Exalted," Dautry said, studying his face with curiosity. "I'll be happy to tell you anything I can."

"He'll want to know all about the aerostat's instrumentation," Taya warned. "And he's a gearhead, so when I say *all*, I mean all."

"I think I can accommodate you, Exalted," the professor replied, her green eyes brightening.

"The suitcase," Amcathra demanded, cutting through Cristof's reply. All three looked at him. The lictor pushed the case forward with one booted foot. "Icarus?"

Taya rose and picked the case up, made a face, and set it back down again with a grunt. Gifford had been right; it was heavy.

"Chief Inspector Gifford hoped this would make you feel a little kinder toward Mareaux." She dragged it across the muddy floor to Cristof's chair and set it flat. Amcathra kept pace with her, although, she noticed, he didn't offer to help.

"Is it the books?" Cristof's voice was eager as he crouched next to her, unsnapping the latches and pulling the lid open. "Taya! It's the books!"

"I know." She grinned as he started stacking them on the floor. She hadn't seen him so animated in ages. "I'll remind you to write a thank-you letter."

"Excellent, please do," he muttered absently, picking out *Delinquency, Deviance, and Disorder: A Call for the Reformation of the Poor Law* and paging through it.

"Do not forget this one," Amcathra said coolly, leaning over and picking up *Dangerous Women: Infamous Murderesses of History*. He flipped open the cover and glanced at a few pages. Taya caught a glimpse of lurid engravings featuring bared bosoms and wild hair before the lictor snapped it shut again. "I am sure you will find it intellectually stimulating."

Cristof held out a hand and Amcathra handed the volume over, his blue eyes narrow.

"Thank you, Janos. Feel free to pick something out for yourself." Cristof tucked the two volumes under his arm and rose. "Taya, Professor, if you'll excuse me, I'm going to relax for a while. Ceremonies wear me out."

"Of course, Exalted," Dautry said, looking curiously at them. "I brought a book of my own."

"Then I'll just put these away, shall I?" Taya asked, glowering at Cristof's back as he moved to a seat by the window.

Lieutenant Amcathra nodded and strode back to his chair by the door.

For a moment Taya was tempted to leave the books to slide around the dirty floor every time the train went around a bend or up a hill. Then she sighed and put them back into the suitcase, snapping it shut.

Somebody in the delegation had to be the responsible one.

A few hours later she looked up from the third book in Cassie's romance series, sighed, and moved over to sit next to Cristof. Her husband had hooked his spectacles in the collar of his shirt and held *Delinquency, Deviance, and Disorder* a few inches from his nose, his brow furrowed as he read.

"Did you find what you were looking for?" she asked, pitching her voice to avoid being overheard. She didn't have to try too hard; the poker game in the back of the car was getting rowdy.

He blinked and focused on her, lowering the book.

"Yes. Although the rest of the book is interesting, too."

"Any ideas we can use in Ondinium?"

He reached for his spectacles and slid them back on.

"The poor laws in Alzana are different from ours, but the author's arguments sound very much like arguments I heard in Ondinium from a certain mutual acquaintance."

Taya's eyes widened. She plucked the book from his hand, turning it over to look at the author's name. "That's not... anyone I know."

"No, of course not." He took it back, folding over a page to mark his place. "But the book was printed a few months ago."

"So...."

"So," he lowered his voice even more, "I don't think our mutual friend chose it randomly."

"But it was published in Alzana."

"Yes, it was."

"Scrap."

"It doesn't mean he's living there. He may publish with an Alzanan press, but he'd never work for the Alzanan government."

Taya wished she were certain of that. "What did he have to say?"

"I don't know yet. This book contains a very brief message, and the other one contains an even briefer one." Cristof shot a glance toward Amcathra, who was writing in a black, leather-bound journal— drafting his report to the Oporphyr Council, Taya guessed. "I'll decipher it later. If it needs a response, I'll send a letter from Terminal."

"Give it to me to post. You're being watched too closely." Taya picked up *Dangerous Women*. "How's this book?"

"Sordid. You should give it to Cassie. It's the sort of lowbrow literature she enjoys."

"Hey!" Taya swatted him with the book. "That's my best friend you're talking about."

"Yes, I'm aware of that," he said with regret.

Rain pounded against the windows as the train made a turn. Taya leaned over her husband to look outside, but between the streaming water and the gray day, she couldn't see much.

"No sign of the storm letting up," she observed, leaning back again. "If it keeps pouring like this, I won't be able to fly while we're in Terminal, either."

"I'm sorry."

"I hate it. What's the point of being an icarus if I'm grounded?"

"You know, Taya, the rain is going to turn into snow when we get to the high passes." Cristof tentatively laid his hand over hers. "I'd rather you didn't go aloft in bad weather."

"I won't if there's sleet or hail. But if it's just a little snow...."

"You know how swiftly conditions can change at high altitudes."

"Better than you," Taya said, a little tartly.

Cristof lifted his hand, gazing at her over the tops of his glasses.

"If you get lost in a snowstorm, the Council will dock the price of your wings from my salary," he pointed out in a dry voice.

"Plus, you'd have a hard time finding another icarus patient enough to put up with you."

"Precisely. So I have a vested interest in keeping you safe."

She handed *Dangerous Women* back to him.

"I'll take your concern under consideration, Exalted."

"Please do, Icarus."

They opened their books again, content to read side-by-side.

CHAPTER EIGHT

RAIN CONTINUED TO scour the train as they headed north, skirting the Corundiel inland sea and climbing up into the foothills.

Amcathra vanished around noon to monitor the preparation of their lunch. Cristof asked him to open a few bottles of Lord Pomeroy's wine. He and Taya refrained from drinking any, and the rest of the staff made morbid jokes as they toasted each other, but soon the bottles began to empty and the noise in the back of the car grew louder.

After lunch, Taya listened while Cristof and Professor Dautry discussed aerostats, but she lost interest when the conversation shifted to the difficulty of making accurate measurements in differing temperatures and on unstable platforms. She wandered back to play a few hands of poker. After a string of losses, she excused herself to step out on the rear platform for some fresh air.

Damp, freezing wind wrapped her skirts around her body as she held on to the oak railing. The train had passed through Grimaucourt shortly after noon, and now, just several hours later, the cloudy sky was already as dark as twilight. The pine forest seemed shadowed and ominous as the train clattered through, its trail of smoke streaming in its wake like a banner.

Taya stretched out a hand. The rain was turning into sleet.

Rikard stepped outside, maneuvering around her windwhipped skirts.

"Are you well, Icarus?"

"It was getting too stuffy and loud in there."

He nodded, his pale blue eyes checking the car roof and then skimming the tracks before returning to her face. "Eleven more hours."

"More, if the tracks get icy." She shivered, wishing for her leather flight suit. "Did you enjoy Mareaux?"

"I was working. And I don't speak the language."

"Well, what did you think about the scenery?"

"Mareaux is very flat."

She laughed. It was true. None of them were used to seeing wide fields and low, sprawling buildings. Ondinium was built on verticals.

"What about the people?"

"They were frightened of me."

"I suppose they don't see lictors very often."

"I wasn't there to make friends."

"Maybe on the next trip you can take some time off. You could do some sight-seeing without your uniform." Although even in civilian clothes, Rikard's castemark and military bearing would make him stand out. Still, he shouldn't spend all his time working on behalf of his little sister.

The train turned a corner and the wind blasted them with wet sleet. Taya yelped and Rikard grabbed her.

"Be careful," he said, his fingers tightening on her shoulder. "You might slip and fall."

"Don't worry; I'm getting out of this cold."

For a moment she thought he'd say something, but then he nodded, lifting his hand and opening the carriage door.

The train would arrive in M-O Terminal around dawn instead of 3 a.m., Amcathra informed them several hours later. The tracks were slick and the engineer was taking the slopes and curves with more care than usual, cognizant of the Ondinium ambassador's presence.

The group groaned with dismay, but more wine quieted everyone down. At dinnertime the mercates and staff retired to the dining car with Professor Dautry. Lieutenant Amcathra brought dinner in for Taya, Cristof, and the other lictors.

"So much for having time to crack the message in private," Cristof muttered, disgruntled. "If we get to Terminal at dawn, we'll have to jump right on the next train."

"Decipher the message tonight and tell *him* that it's private business," she advised. "You're an exalted, after all."

He shot her a skeptical look.

"I worked for Janos for too many years to start giving him orders."

"Cris, you were *born* to give him orders. I don't think the Lady would approve of an exalted who allows himself to be pushed around by a lictor."

"But it's all right to be pushed around by an icarus?"

"Icarii are caste exceptions. And so are wives, in case you were wondering."

"The Lady help any poor soul who takes an icarus wife, then."

"She'd *better*, especially if those poor souls don't mind their tongues."

His lips twitched. "What are the odds I'd knock all the silverware off the table if I leaned over to kiss you?"

"You'll never know until you try."

He accepted the challenge, managing to catch and stabilize his water glass just as the chain on his pocket watch threatened to knock it over.

"You're getting better at romantic gestures," Taya said, grinning as she dropped back into her chair. "Now you just have to develop some spontaneity."

"Spontaneity isn't in my nature." Still, Cristof looked pleased with himself as he sat back down.

"Let me know if we should leave," Amcathra grumbled from the other side of the car, where he was eating dinner with his nephew.

"Would you?" Cristof inquired.

"No." The lieutenant paused a moment, reconsidering. "Yes, under certain circumstances. But I am certain that the product of a thousand fortuitous rebirths would not be so shameless as to drive me away in such a manner."

"I *do* have some important work to do," Cristof said. "Nothing shameless; just official. Maybe you could guard outside for a few hours."

"Could I?" The lictor eyed him. "And what about the rest of the delegation?"

"Oddly enough, the rest of the delegation gives me the privacy my rank is due."

"After dinner, I intend to confer with the conductor about late-arrival procedures. Rikard will guard your door."

"Thank you."

Amcathra turned his attention back to his plate. "Do not make me regret leaving you to your own devices, Exalted."

Taya smiled, then kicked her husband under the table. "What was that for?" he objected. "I did exactly what you wanted me to do."

"I thought you were going to ask him to leave so we could spend some time together."

"Why?" He grimaced as she kicked him again. "Oh. Right. But I *do* have to work."

She gave up. Cristof *was* getting better at romantic gestures... but then again, he'd started from scratch.

"You'd better be thinking about how you're going to make up for all that lost time in Mareaux. Separate suites, my grounded tailset...."

"I'll make amends," he promised.

Taya allowed herself to be mollified. One advantage to marrying a gearhead was that whenever she gave him a problem to solve, he addressed it in the most earnest, meticulous manner possible. It had made certain aspects of their marital life more interesting than she'd anticipated.

After dinner, the rest of the delegation returned. Another hour or so of idle chatter passed, and then they began to settle down for the night, making themselves as comfortable as they could in chairs and padded benches and pulling railway-provided blankets over their shoulders as the temperature dropped.

Amcathra left the car, putting Rikard in charge.

Cristof moved to the table where the mercates had been working and began deciphering his books while everyone else drowsed, lulled by the slow rocking of the train. Taya watched him frown over his note-taking for a while, and then fell asleep.

The train's whistle and squealing brakes woke her up. Taya groaned as she straightened, feeling her stiff muscles protest. Gray sunlight filtered through the curtains and soot-smudged train window.

"Cris?" She looked around and saw the others in various states of wakefulness.

"He's getting your papers together," Professor Dautry said, combing out her unpinned hair. "He didn't want to wake you."

"Good idea; make sure all *your* papers are in order, too, and someplace where they're easy to pull out."

"I did that last night. I've read about Ondinium's security checks."

"Yes; it's important to carry your papers wherever you go. You'll need them to move from sector to sector, and you could be ordered to show them at any time."

"Do citizens have to carry papers, too?"

"If they want to move across city sectors, yes. Otherwise, our castemarks act as identification within our own sector of residence."

"But icarii don't have castemarks."

"As long as we're wearing our wings, we aren't questioned. When I'm out of my armature, I wear an identifying pin and keep my papers with me."

"I don't think Ondinium's custom of requiring identification papers ... or tattoos ... could ever be adopted in Mareaux. Our citizenry would be up in arms at the mistrust it implies between government and populace."

"We see identification papers and castemarks as a protection from crime, not a sign of mistrust." *Well, most of us see it that way,* she amended silently. She had a few friends who thought otherwise. "It's a small inconvenience for the sake of national security."

"Yet Ondinium suffers more terrorist attacks within its borders than any other nation," Dautry observed.

"That's because we're richer and more powerful than any other nation," Taya countered. "A powerful country attracts powerful enemies. That's why we take our security so seriously."

"Caste stratification, identification papers, spot checks, censorship...."

"Every one of those policies helps keep Ondinium safe. We've had a stable government since the Last War, nearly two thousand years ago. What other nation can say that? Certainly not Mareaux."

"But you've had internal upheavals."

"We've experienced occasional shifts in national policy and divisions within the Council, but we've never had a civil war or revolution."

"What about your political dissidents? Wasn't there some problem with the Torn Cards last year? They're citizens, aren't they?"

"We had some bombings that were blamed on the Torn Cards, but we found out they were really the work of Alzanan spies." *Except for the bombings that were the work of a decatur,* but nothing short of torture was going to compel her to admit that to a foreigner.

"Aren't the Torn Cards radical discontents?"

"Radical. Not revolutionary." Taya stood. She didn't like talking about things like this. "Anyway, I suggest you don't talk about terrorist attacks at the checkpoint. Lictors have no qualms about denying a suspicious visitor entrance, and it would take a lot of work to get you a new pass if you don't get through the security check today."

"I didn't mean any offense," Dautry said, quickly. "I was just questioning the efficacy of Ondinium's social choices."

"Don't. Not until you're in the capital, and even then, I wouldn't make those kinds of comments outside the University."

"You can't express yourself freely in Ondinium?"

"*I* can. But I'm a citizen. Ondiniums don't appreciate foreigners who criticize our way of life. You'll get away with it at the University because it's a dedicate's job to analyze, criticize, and evaluate, but you'd better be ready to defend your point of view. Dedicates love debates."

Dautry raised her eyebrows. "I see that Ondinium will take some getting used to."

"It's a good place to live." Taya excused herself to find her traveling case.

Some time later, Cristof sat next to her, encased in his robes. His glasses were off and he held his ivory mask in one hand.

Taya grinned and patted his cheek, enjoying his put-upon expression.

"At least all those layers will keep you nice and warm."

"I'd rather wear a flight suit. Is it too late to become an icarus?"

"You don't like heights."

"A lictor, then. I should have taken the Great Exam and tried for lictor caste," he muttered.

"Hush. Exalteds never change caste."

Cristof gave a disgusted snort, but his retort was cut off as Jayce joined them.

"I've put fresh clothes and your outerwear in your trunk, Exalted. If you'll put your robes and mask inside when you change, I'll clean them when we're back in the capital."

"Thank you." The whistle blew again, announcing their arrival.

Taya sorted through the papers in her attaché case, making sure she knew where their identifications and letters from the Council were located. She pulled out her feather-shaped badge and pinned it to the lapel of her coat.

"Ready to get back into your wings again?" he asked.

"I plan to wear them to bed."

"That will make it more difficult for me to apologize for my neglect during this trip."

Taya gave him an arch look.

"I *might* be persuaded to forgo them for a night."

He started to reply, but brakes screeched as the train jolted several times. It came to a shuddering stop to the sound of more whistling.

"All set," she said, putting everything back into the case and throwing the latches. She leaned over and picked up his mask. "Last time, Cris."

"At last." He sat still while she tied it on. With a quick squeeze to his shoulder, she grabbed her coat and case and stood. "Lieutenant Amcathra will get you when everything's ready."

She edged around the bustle of packing and pulled on her coat. Amcathra handed her a key and she felt a leap of joy as she unlocked her armature. She wanted to put her wings on at once, but the armature would never fit over her heavy winter coat, not to mention that she was wearing a dress underneath.

"All out!" the conductor shouted.

Lieutenant Amcathra checked over his shoulder to make certain Cristof was masked, then grabbed the counterweight chest, opened the door, and stepped out. Great arching roofs protected the station from the snow, but the air was freezing and a sharp, chilly wind gusted down the length of the platform. Smoke dribbled out of the locomotive's stack as the fire in its engine cooled. Condensed snow hissed off its hot metal body.

Two lictors wearing Mareaux-Ondinium Terminal Station badges pinned to their coats waved them over.

"I am Lieutenant Janos Amcathra. This is Taya Icarus, Exalted Forlore's representative," Amcathra said, half-turning to her as she maneuvered her wings out of the door, one arm looped through the metal armature.

"Icarus." The lictors nodded to her. "How many are in the exalted's private party?"

"Just the two of us," she replied, "and four lictors."

"Very good." The station lictor pointed down the platform. "Lieutenant, you can escort the exalted along the edge of the terminal to the red door. Please have all your papers and documentation ready. Will you be waiting for anyone else or passing straight through?"

"The rest of the delegation will go through regular border check procedures," Amcathra stated.

"Then once you've passed check-in, Security will show you to a private waiting room. We'll have it prepared with hot food and drink before the exalted arrives."

"Acceptable." Amcathra strode back into the car, ordering away the members of the delegation who were trickling out, pulling on their coats and calling for porters.

A minute later Cristof appeared, robed and masked. Taya hurried to help him down, moving her armature to the arm carrying the attaché case. Her wings bobbed and swayed as they were tugged by the gusting wind.

Lieutenant Amcathra gathered his lictors and the small procession solemnly traversed the platform to the terminal. Exalteds seldom left the heavily secured Primus sector of the capital, so the figure in the ivory mask and jewel-covered robes was an exotic sight to everyone in Terminus. Ondiniums bowed as he passed in a ripple of bobbing heads.

Two lictors, a man wearing an icarus pin like hers, and a man in the uniform of the Mareaux army, stood up as they entered the private security chamber. The Ondiniums bowed, palms against their foreheads, and the Mareaux soldier saluted.

Amcathra waved their own lictors aside.

"This is his excellency, the exalted Cristof Forlore, ambassador of Ondinium," Taya said, leading her masked husband up to the check-in desk.

"Please, allow me." The icarus stepped forward and took her wings.

"Thank you." She swung her attaché case around and set it on the desk, snapping it open one-handed. "I'm Taya Icarus, the ambassador's spokesperson."

"We've been expecting you," one of the station lictors said. "We'll need to see your papers, Exalted Forlore, and we'll need to ask you to step into the side room to unmask in front of our icarus for identification verification. Your icarus may remain with you."

"That's fine," Taya said, pulling out the leather wallets that held their identification papers. The lictors and the Mareaux soldier inspected the documents carefully while she, the other icarus, and Cristof entered a small, wood-paneled room set off to one side.

Taya untied Cristof's mask and the station icarus studied his face.

"Exalted, may I touch you?"

"Yes, let's get this over with," Cristof grumbled. "Do you have any tea in the station?"

"We put a pot on as soon as the train pulled in. It should reach the waiting room before you do." The icarus dipped his thumb into an alcohol-scented solution, reached out, and rubbed the wave-shaped castemarks on Cristof's cheekbones. Seeing that they didn't smudge, he nodded and dropped his hand. "Welcome back to Ondinium, Exalted Forlore."

"It's good to be back," Cristof responded. Taya tied his mask back on and they left the room.

"Everything's in order," the icarus reported, returning to the table and signing a document. Lieutenant Amcathra, Rikard, and the other two lictors handed over their own identification papers while a clerk slid a card into a holder and methodically punched it.

Taya spent several more minutes signing papers for herself and Cristof that declared that they weren't carrying any contraband (*censored romances don't count*, she thought with a twinge of guilt), that they hadn't engaged in any illegal activities abroad, that they hadn't foresworn their citizenship, and a variety of similar but, she thought, ultimately pointless statements. Was anyone ever stupid enough to admit to such things?

At last their papers and her wings were returned. They were led across the crowded terminal, past long lines of incoming and outgoing passengers waiting at security points, and into a private waiting room.

Taya looked around the comfortably appointed room as Amcathra closed the curtains. A table held a full tea service and a silver tray full of tiny frosted cakes, as well as more mundane rolls, butter, and imported strawberry jam. She let her armature float to the ceiling and helped her husband out of all but his two inner robes.

"Thank you," he said, sinking into a leather chair with a sigh. "Lady, I'm exhausted. I barely got any sleep last night. Do we *have* to leave again today?"

"Yes," Amcathra replied.

"Exalted." Rikard handed him a cup of tea, then carried one to Taya. "Icarus."

"Thank you." Taya sat on a sofa across from her husband and sighed with contentment as she sipped the black brew, an import from the Cabisi isles. Sweet, milky, and strong— another three or four cups and she might feel ready to face the next leg of their journey.

"You can post your letter on the next outgoing train," she told her husband after the cup was half-empty. She set it on the side table and stood to explore the selection of pastries. "There's a writing desk in the corner."

"What letter?"

"A thank-you to Chief Inspector Gifford for the books."

Cristof sighed, shoving himself back to his feet. "Yes, very well. Would you bring me some more tea? And maybe a pastry?"

She brought him his breakfast, stealing a sweet, tea-flavored kiss as a reward, and then refilled her cup and nudged the window curtain aside.

Their train was surrounded by porters moving luggage back and forth and cleaning crews heading in with buckets, mops, and polishing rags. Up front, on the track side, the locomotive's stores of coal and water were being replenished.

M-O Terminal was the second-largest city in Ondinium, after the nation's eponymous capital. Most of the traffic in and out of the country ran through M-O, although a heavily guarded border station stood on the Alzanan border, two stations sat on the Samarian border, and several small stations dotted the border with Demicus. The Demican border, Ondinium's longest, was also its most lightly guarded. The Oporphyr Council wasn't worried about a horde of northern clansmen wielding spears and secondhand rifles.

Someone knocked. "Luggage! I'll leave it by the door."

"Thank you," Taya called back. "Our clothes are here, Cris."

"You go first," he said, still bent over his letter. "I'll change as soon as I finish."

"Then, if you'll excuse me, gentlemen." Taya stepped out and grabbed her case. Staff directed her to the nearest washroom, where she sent several buttons skittering across the floor before she managed to squirm her way free of her dress.

Its tight bodice had left creases in her skin, and she felt bruised where its buttons had dug into her back all night. She dropped the dress on the floor and swiftly pulled on her winter flight uniform and boots, reveling in the comfort of fresh underwear, thick socks, and the soft wool padding of her leather suit.

The only thing that would have made it better would have been a long, hot bath and several hours snuggled in a soft bed with her husband beforehand.

Taya retrieved the lost buttons, folded the dress back into her case with a touch of guilt, and returned to the waiting room.

About twenty minutes later Cristof finished his letters and gave them to her to post while he changed his own clothes. She glanced at the addresses— Inspector Gifford, Lord Pomeroy, and A. Gryngoth, the last c/o a bookstore in Grimaucourt. She took them outside and dropped them into a mailbag. On her way back, she checked on their delegation's progress.

"We're all through the identification checkpoint," said Auguste Macerain, who sat on one of his trunks holding a peach from one of the fruit baskets. "Now we're going through luggage search. Professor Dautry is being given the third degree."

"Her paperwork should be in order."

"Oh, I'm sure it is." He gestured vaguely. "They'll let her through once they're sure she's impressed by Ondinium's security procedures."

"You're a cynic, Mercate."

"I've been doing this for forty years, Icarus."

Taya remembered him laughing with the Mazzolettis at the farewell reception and studied him afresh. "How well do you know the Alzanan ambassadors?"

"The new one?"

"Are they new?"

"Since about three years ago." Macerain took another bite of the peach and chewed a moment, then swallowed and shrugged. "Lady Fosca's the ambassador; her brother's a military officer sent to Mareaux to suck up to the queen. Fosca's powerful in her Family, but she's new to the diplomatic game. Mareaux's a good place for her to learn the ropes."

"Do you get along with them?"

"I represent First Standard. It's my job to get along with everybody."

"Have you done business with the Mazzolettis?"

"With the Family, yes. Transportation and construction; all licensed by the Council." He gave her an amused look. "Which didn't stop Lady Fosca from plying me with food and wine in the hope that I'd slip up and tell her something important. She thinks I'm an idiot because I'm old, and it serves First Standard's interests for me to play along. So I eat her food and drink her wine and tell her a little truth mixed in with a lot of lies. If I'm lucky, I'll retire before she figures out how useless I've been."

Taya nodded, trying not to let her reservations show. It seemed like an unpleasant way to live, putting on a false persona just to secure more business. She preferred things to be exactly the way they looked. Secrets and lies upset her.

"Do you think they were questioning the rest of the delegation, too?" she asked.

"Undoubtedly. I'm sure they invited all of us," he nodded toward the two other mercates, who stood over their luggage as it was inspected, "to dinner at least once, and they probably had the professors over, too. It's all part of the game, isn't it?"

"I guess so." She hoped the rest of the delegation had been as wise to the Mazzolettis' tricks as Macerain.

One of the lictors shouted the mercate's name. Macerain grabbed his cane and stood.

"Well, if you'll excuse me, Icarus, it's time to let security paw through my underwear."

She waved goodbye and headed back.

"Looks like it may be another hour or so," she announced when she returned, "although I think our people were moved to the front of the line."

Cristof grunted. He'd stretched out in her spot on the sofa, his long legs dangling off one end. She perched next to him and pulled off his glasses.

"So, who's a fan of Lictor Gryngoth?" she asked, her voice low. Amcathra, Rikard, and the rest were half-dozing in chairs of their own. Taya didn't begrudge them a nap. They'd kept watch throughout the long train ride, and there could be few places safer than the middle of Terminal station.

Cristof opened his grey eyes and gave her one of his crooked smiles.

"When we were boys playing Last War, he *always* wanted to be Gryngoth," he replied, just as softly. "And of course he always got his way."

"Who did *you* play?"

"Imperate Viridinion, usually. That way I got to boss him around."

"But the imperate dies in the end."

"Our games weren't exactly historical re-enactments. They were more like two gangs of neighborhood children trying to wrestle each other into the gutter."

"So the imperate survived? I don't think that would have been good for Ondinium."

He took her hand and kissed it. "I promise I would have seen the error of my ways and become a strong and benevolent leader instead of a weak-willed hedonist."

"Exalted!" Somebody pounded on the door, startling them. Amcathra grabbed his rifle and sprung to his feet as the other lictors fumbled for their weapons.

"What is it?" he asked, opening it. The lictor outside froze as she stared into the barrel of Amcathra's weapon.

"There's been an incident," she said, voice tense. "One of your delegation died in security."

"Was it the wine?" Cristof demanded. The lictor's eyes flickered toward him and then hastily away. Her cheeks colored.

"We don't know what happened, Exalted," she said, keeping her eyes fixed on Amcathra's rifle. "It seems to have been his heart."

"Macerain?" Taya gasped. "Not Auguste Macerain— an old man? From First Standard?"

"I'm sorry, yes."

"Oh, no." A lump rose in her throat. "I was just talking to him."

Cristof took her hand and squeezed it. She swallowed and stood, letting his fingers slip from hers.

"I'll— I'll go find out what happened," she said, trying to collect her thoughts. "You stay here."

"Don't be ridiculous!" Her husband rose, frowning. "This is Ondinium."

"Technically, the station is owned by both Mareaux and Ondinium," Amcathra pointed out.

"Good enough."

"As you wish." The lictor lowered his rifle. "Rikard, come. The rest of you, guard the exalted's luggage and the armature. Do not leave the room without securing them."

"Sir." Their lictors saluted as Amcathra slung his rifle over his shoulder and gestured for the station lictor to proceed.

Mareaux soldiers and Ondinium lictors had cordoned off the area around their delegation. Patrice Corundel and Maximilian Trichas hovered next to Macerain's corpse, looking anxious, while the rest of the staff huddled together, whispering. Professor Dautry stood noticeably alone, her knuckles white as she clutched her identification papers.

A man with a dedicate's castemark knelt next to Macerain, jotting notes. Macerain's face was twisted with pain, and his hands were bent like claws as they clutched his heart. Taya looked away.

"What happened?" Cristof asked, at the same time as Amcathra. The lictor glanced at him and nodded, taking a step back.

"I think—" the dedicate looked up and faltered as he saw the wave-shaped castemarks on Cristof's cheeks. He leaped to his feet and bowed. "E-exalted— Forlore?"

"Of course," Cristof growled. "Now, tell us what happened!"

"Er, yes, Exalted." The man couldn't bring himself to look at Cristof's bare face. "I'm a physician, sir. I was called to security as soon as this man began showing signs of distress. When I arrived, he was having difficulty breathing and was holding his chest. His heartbeat was rapid and he was sweating. I tried to give him an emetic, but— his death was very sudden."

"A heart attack?"

"It might have been," the physician said, hesitantly, "but his companions seem to think he was poisoned."

"He was eating from one of those fruit baskets right before he died," Trichas said, urgently. "He never had a heart problem in his life, but then he ate a peach and died— it had to have been poison, Exalted!"

"But the rest of us have been nibbling from the baskets, too, and we aren't ill," Corundel objected.

"Maybe it was just the one."

"Or maybe it was just his time to pass."

"He seemed fine when I was talking to him about twenty minutes ago," Taya said, her eyes drifting back against her will to Macerain's twisted face. "He was joking and alert."

"Cardiac arrest can come on unexpectedly, but if you like, we can take him and the fruit back to the hospital and run some tests, Exalted."

"Yes, I think you'd better." Cristof glanced at Amcathra, who nodded.

"Take the rest of the fruit baskets with you, too," Taya said, shuddering. "All of them. Just in case."

"I will make arrangements." Amcathra gestured to Rikard and pulled the physician aside. Trichas shrugged out of his expensive coat and laid it over Macerain's body, covering his face.

"We weren't close friends, but I respected him," the young mercate murmured to Taya. "Auguste was a good negotiator, and he never let the competition between our companies blind him to the bigger picture. It was always Ondinium's interest first, and then First Standard's."

"Do you think anyone would want to kill him?" Taya asked. Trichas shook his head.

"Any one of us could have eaten that peach," Corundel said, looking angry. "What a stupid, haphazard way to kill someone!"

Taya nodded, not willing to voice her fears.

Cristof was fond of peaches; he'd eaten a number of them in Mareaux. And the fruit had been a gift to him. Had this been a last-ditch attempt to kill Cristof before they reached the safety of Ondinium's borders? Maybe the would-be murderer hadn't expected him to share his farewell gifts with the rest of his delegation.

Or could it have just been an old man's heart giving out at last?

She turned. Cristof was speaking solemnly to Professor Dautry. Taya walked over and laid a hand on his arm.

"—do with you," he was saying. Dautry nodded, still looking alarmed.

"Will this delay us any longer?" the professor asked. "Are we going to be interrogated again?"

"I'm afraid there will be delays." Cristof turned to Taya. "Would you ask the remaining mercates to stay in Terminal until Macerain's body is released? We'll leave one of our lictors, too." He laid a hand over hers, squeezing it. "The rest of the diplomatic delegation will travel back alone."

Taya nodded, wondering what was on his mind. She walked back and delivered the request to Lieutenant Amcathra and the mercates.

"But we need to get back to our offices!" Patrice Corundel protested. "We have contracts to deliver!"

"I'll carry them for you." Taya tapped her feather pin. "Just put all your correspondence in a bundle."

"Some of it—" the mercate stopped and pursed her lips with frustration.

"Of course we will, Icarus," Trichas said. "I'm sure the examination won't take more than a day or two. First Standard will appreciate the gesture, Patrice."

"First Standard has representatives here who can take Macerain's body back to Ondinium!"

"The exalted has made a request," Taya said, making her voice hard and flat. "Mind your caste, Mercate Corundel."

Corundel stiffened and bowed, her expression grim.

"Very well, Icarus," she grated. "I hope you'll give us time to write cover letters?"

"We can spare half an hour," Lieutenant Amcathra said. He pointed to the benches by the wall. "Sit and write."

Corundel's growl was audible as she snatched up her leather dispatch case and called to her clerk.

"I don't know why she's so upset," Trichas apologized. "I think Auguste's death has shaken her."

"I understand," Taya said. "And speaking of Mercate Macerain, would it be possible for you to go through his documents and give me the contracts he signed in Mareaux, as well?"

"My employers would probably fire me if they knew I let an opportunity like this slide through my fingers, but I think you should ask his clerk to do it."

"Oh, of course. Thank you."

About forty minutes later, Taya had each mercate's mail in her courier's case and was snapping herself back into her armature. Despite the tragedy, her heart lifted at the familiar tug on her shoulders. It felt good to be a proper icarus again, even though the weather was too poor to go aloft.

As they left Terminal Station, Cristof's naked face caused a flurry of averted eyes, hasty bows, and scandalized whispers. He grit his teeth and stared at the sleety snow that whipped and gusted across the busy road.

"Here." Taya tugged up his woolen coat collar and untied the ribbon that held back his long hair. "That will help."

"I hate being stared at."

"You could wear your mask."

"I hate the mask more."

The wide thoroughfare outside Terminal Station was crowded and noisy, its surface churned up into black, muddy slush from the falling snow. Porters hurried back and forth, packing luggage onto wagons and coaches and trying not to slip on the icy puddles. The city beyond the main road looked comfortably crowded, even though its skies weren't criss-crossed by wireferry cables or darkened by smoke-belching factories. Taya drew in a deep breath and slowly let it out, relaxing muscles she hadn't known she'd been holding tight.

They were home again.

She hadn't realized how good it would feel to be back in Ondinium. She reached out and twined her fingers through Cristof's.

"Our coaches are coming," Lieutenant Amcathra reported. "You two will take the lead coach to the junction lift and the rest will follow. Strap your armature to the roof, Icarus."

"Thank you." Taya glanced up at the steep, dark cliff in the distance, where the junction lift was located. MB-1 Junction was the beginning of the short-haul, narrow-gauge railroad that led from Ondinium's side of M-O Terminal through the mountains to Safira. Safira, officially known as O-Base-0, was the end of the track and the beginning of the well-guarded periphery encircling the capital.

"So, what did Alister's message say?" Taya asked, once they were alone in the coach.

"I'll need help deciphering it." Cristof removed his gloves and pulled out his leather wallet. From beneath his identification papers he drew a small, flat bundle of paper punch cards. "These were pasted under the endpapers of *Dangerous Women*."

"Oh, Lady." Each individual punch looked neat, but the cards had been numbered in ink, and the numbers were off-centered and scrawling. "He *is* programming, isn't he?"

"Maybe. Or maybe it's easier for him to send a lot of data this way, instead of punching it out in the substitution code he's been using."

"Do you have any idea what they say?"

"They're a record of payments from an Alzanan bank to a fake corporation in Mareaux that he thinks is a front for one of the Big Three. He says we can use the information to track down the shell corporation's backers. He thinks one of our three mercates was doing some back-room dealing with the Alzanans during our visit."

"Macerain?"

"Maybe. At any rate, I'll ask Mr. Deuse to run the cards when we get back."

"Good idea. So that explains why you wanted Trichas and Corundel to stay behind."

"I thought it would be wise, under the circumstances. If they're innocent, no harm has been done, and if they're not, it keeps us a little safer."

Taya looked out the dirty, sleet-crusted window, trying to put all the pieces in their mystery together. She sighed with frustration as the coach slowed. Voices demanded identification, and then iron hinges creaked as security gates were opened.

They'd arrived.

The junction lift was a steeply inclined cable rail on which a pair of trams ran on short tracks back and forth, each counterbalancing the other. Billows of steam rose from the chugging engine that drew the cables. Taya eased her wings out of the coach and into the lift car. Lictors stacked their luggage behind the wings. The lift operators leaned out to gaze curiously at Cristof after the wind whipped his hair off his face and revealed his castemarks.

Amcathra slid in beside the two of them at the last minute.

"We will ascend first," he announced. "The others will follow."

A bell rang and the car started to slide up the angled tracks. Sleet hammered the large front windows, turning them opaque.

"Janos, I'm told one of the Big Three may be selling illegal goods to the Alzanans," Cristof said. "I don't know who yet, but I was given enough information to start an investigation once we get back to the capital."

Amcathra's cool gaze rested on Cristof's face a moment and then shifted to the back window.

"That is why you left the mercates behind."

"Yes."

"Tell me what you know."

Cristof quickly summarized the matter, avoiding any mention of Alister and punch cards. The lictor listened in silence as the lift reached the top of the cliff.

"Very well," he said as they disembarked. Porters from the junction station began lifting out their luggage. Taya grabbed her wings before anyone else could touch them. "I will keep you isolated for the rest of the trip."

"We should be safe now that we're back in Ondinium," Cristof objected.

"Isolating you is a simple precaution. And it will give you a day of privacy with your wife."

Taya grinned at the lictor as she pulled on her wings.

"Oh. Well." Cristof blinked. "In that case, I appreciate the precaution."

"Indeed." Amcathra turned to give orders.

They waited for the rest of the staff on the observation platform at the top of the junction lift. On a nice day, the platform would provide a panoramic view of Terminal and the forested mountains beyond. Today all they could see was whirling ice and snow. Cristof raked his hand through his hair, which kept whipping into his face.

Taya smiled, leaning on the railing and looking up at him. Her husband's heavy black coat flapped around his legs and his silver-rimmed spectacles gleamed on his sharp-featured face. His long black hair made him look more exalted than he had when she'd first met him, but he still had an unkempt air.

"What?" he demanded, noticing her gaze. She straightened and grabbed his coat lapels, rising on her toes to give him a swift kiss.

"I'm happy to see my crow out of captivity."

He leaned over to rest his forehead against hers, his hair blowing around their faces like a curtain.

"And it's good to see you in your wings again. I'm sorry the weather's so miserable."

"Not your fault."

"But I'm still not going to let you wear them to bed."

"Maybe you should consider the possibilities."

He pulled his head back, cocking it as he studied her face. Taya tried to keep her expression as earnest as possible, but at last she broke into a laugh. He looked relieved.

"I could see the gears turning," she teased.

"I was thinking that an armature's straps would chafe without a flight suit."

"You could fix that."

"And your wings would get tangled in the four-poster."

"True. We'd have to go someplace else."

"I'm not going flying again."

"Not without a flight suit, anyway. Not unless you fixed that chafing problem."

Cristof rubbed his forehead. "As if baring my *face* in public weren't scandalous enough."

She laughed and he gave her a crooked smile.

From the lift it was a short, muddy walk to MB-1 Junction. The train waiting there consisted almost entirely of freight cars. Amcathra pointed to the only two passenger cars, at the back of the train.

"The exalted and the icarus will ride in the last car," he said. "The rest of us will ride in the dining car. I will post a lictor at your door for the duration of the journey, Exalted, to ensure that you are not disturbed."

"You're a good man, Janos," Cristof said. Amcathra raised a pale eyebrow and turned, directing the porters to carry the trunks inside.

CHAPTER NINE

IRON CHAINS RATTLED on her armature and the crystal glasses chimed in their racks. The train was straining up another steep, curving incline. Oil lamps rocked, suspended by gimbals on the ceiling, and provided a warm glow over the wood, leather, and brass interior of the car.

Taya pulled the railway blankets closer around her bare shoulders.

She couldn't see anything through the windows except a swirling grayness, although she heard something tap against the glass. Either the sleet was getting worse or it had turned into ice rain.

She looked around for her flight suit. Cristof's vest was closer, so she reached over his shoulder and grabbed it, fishing his gold watch out of its pocket.

A little after four.

Cristof yawned and slid his hand over her leg.

"What is it?" he asked, sleepily.

"Nothing." She burrowed back under the covers and rested her head on his shoulder. "Just checking the time. Four fifteen."

He groaned.

"We're supposed to reach the cable-haul by five." His arm tightened around her, hugging her close. They shared a long kiss.

"There's no rush," she murmured, loathe to give up her quiet, warm haven. "I'm sure we're behind schedule. This ice can't be any good for the tracks."

"What ice?" He rolled to one elbow and squinted toward the windows, then groped around the expensive Cabisi rug for his spectacles. She found them first, tucked under one of the chairs. He slid them on and looked up again. "I can't see a thing out there."

Taya sighed, sensing the end of their comfortable idyll. Just as well, she supposed. No doubt Amcathra would knock on the door soon to make sure they were ready for the haul.

"If the ice gets bad enough, will the train get stuck?" she asked.

"The engineers have bags of salt and sand for the tracks," Cristof assured her, gathering his clothes and starting to dress under the blankets. "Although if the weather's bad enough, we might get stuck waiting at the cable station for the storm to blow over."

He sounded enthusiastic; Taya imagined he was looking forward to poking at the station's inner workings. She pulled on her clothes and hoped they wouldn't be delayed. She was ready to sleep in their own bed, on their own sheets and pillows, and enjoy their own fireplace and kitchen and water closet and wardrobe. She expected it would be several months before she felt the itch to travel again.

By a quarter to five, they had straightened themselves and the car back up and secured the trunks and cabinets.

"I'll see if we're still on schedule," Cristof volunteered while Taya secured her case of ondium counterweights. "Do you want anything from the dining room?"

"Something hot. Tea, maybe?"

"I'll bring back a pot." He opened the door, letting in a blast of even colder air and a swirl of snow. The lictor greeted him as he stepped through.

Taya rattled the chains holding her armature in place and made sure the key was in her flight suit pocket. Then she walked over to the nearest window and pushed the pane down. Cold air swept through the car, and she still couldn't see a thing. She thrust her hand outside. Ice stung her fingers.

Ugly weather. She closed the window and wiped her fingers on the leg of her flight suit. They were in the high passes now. They would drop a little before reaching Safira, but O-Base-0 was still higher than Terminal by several thousand feet. She suspected the weather was going to be bad there, too.

Spending the night at a cable-haul station wouldn't be much fun, but Safira boasted a number of comfortable hotels for the mercates who traveled back and forth....

The train jerked and she stumbled, grabbing the nearest chair. A deep, low whistle sounded as the train jolted again, making an unnatural shuddering movement. Taya's heart sped.

Something pounded against the roof of the car, like running footsteps. The air filled with the screech of tortured metal and a sharp but muffled retort.

"Cris? Cris!"

The train shuddered again and people in the next car began shouting. Taya pulled herself toward the door, fighting to keep her balance as the train jolted and rocked. The door burst open before she could reach it and Rikard threw himself inside. Snow covered his hair and overcoat, and he held his air-rifle in one gloved hand.

"Where's the exalted?" he demanded, looking around.

"What—" Taya gasped as the young lictor grabbed her and pushed her against the paneled wall of the car.

"Where is he?"

The train's whistle gave three more urgent blasts as the cars shuddered. Taya grabbed Rikard's arms just as she heard a crashing sound.

The lictor yanked her down into a crouch as the train began moving *backward*, sliding the wrong direction on the tracks with a sickening shimmy. Someone was screaming, the whistle was blowing, and the car's heavy, leather-covered chairs and tables began to slide across the Cabisi rug.

Then everything gave a sharp lurch. Rikard wrapped an arm around her as the metal of the train shrieked. His rifle hit her in the shoulder. Taya stopped trying to resist him and clung to his coat lapels instead. She cried out as the car rolled, bouncing them like rocks in a box. Tables and chairs tumbled around them and the oil lamps went out. Something hit her head. She heard shattering and crunching and more screams. Her cheek was pressed against glass and she realized the car was on its side and a window's glass was cracking beneath her. The train jolted and ground against rock and dirt, shrubbery and trees.

Then the car gave another jerk. She and Rikard began to slide backward. She looked over her shoulder but couldn't see anything in the darkness. Blood ran down her face— she tasted it as it trickled between her lips. She clawed for something to hold on to, feeling Rikard doing the same, one hand still locked around her flight suit collar. Then the car hit something big — a boulder, a tree, another car, maybe — and they were torn apart. Metal screeched and tore. Taya screamed, panicking as the train self-destructed around her. Glass slashed her palms, her shoulder hit something hard, and a heavy object slammed into the side of her head with sickening finality.

Taya awoke to the sound of a gunshot and shouting. She couldn't move. She hurt all over. A scream, a Demican curse, a quieter pop. She smelled gunpowder and blood and burning wood. She tried to open her eyes, but they were glued shut.

"Icarus!" The hands on her were cold, and so was the ground beneath her head and back. She groaned. Rough hands ran down her arms and legs, then prodded her ribs. She twisted and gasped at the pain in her neck and back. Her head pounded as if it were going to split open.

Then the intrusive fingers pushed her eyelids open. Sticky, crusting blood crumbled into her eyes. She blinked back involuntary tears.

"Icarus." Flames danced off a bloody mask. The voice was rough and gravelly but familiar. Taya blinked again, feeling cold tracks running down her face as her tears overflowed; or maybe it was the ice rain. She tried to focus. Pinpoints of light flared around the edge of her vision.

"Lieu—"

"Can you fly?"

She stared, struggling to understand. His face and pale blond hair were black with blood and soot and there was something in his expression that she had never seen before. His hands tightened on her shoulders as he pulled her into a sitting position. She cried out as her strained muscles protested.

"Can you fly, Icarus? We need help."

This time the words registered, and so did his expression. She crooked her head to one side, wincing at the effort.

Amcathra had jammed a makeshift torch between two sheared-off edges of metal jutting from an overturned train car. Broken glass glittered around them. Or maybe it was ice, because the ice rain still pounded, clanging off torn metal and skittering down the lieutenant's tattered and bloody uniform. He held his rifle in the crook of his arm.

At the edge of the torchlight she saw another person, prone. Rikard's blue eyes stared blankly at her as snowflakes fell on his face. Steam rose from the blood that covered the front of his uniform jacket and the snow around him, shockingly red in the unsteady torchlight.

Dead? Rikard was dead? How many— who else—

"Cris!" She lurched forward, grabbing Amcathra as she struggled to stand. He hissed in pain and collapsed, and she realized he'd been crouched with one leg stretched out, off-balance. She ignored him, ignored the pulling sensation in her muscles as she got to her feet, ignored the way her vision blurred and darkened. Tears ran down her face. She spun. There, on the edge of the firelight, another corpse sprawled in a pool of blood with a percussion-style pistol in one hand. She drew in a ragged breath, feeling as though somebody had hit her in the stomach. "Cris!"

"He is alive," Amcathra said, his voice tight. "Fly to the cable station. He needs help."

"Oh, Lady!" She started toward the body with the pistol. Amcathra reached up and grabbed the armature buckles around the waist of her flight suit. She staggered, ready to strike out— but that look in his face stopped her.

"That is not your husband. Listen. The exalted was bleeding. I stopped it. But he needs help. *Now.*"

Taya felt a roaring in her ears. Cristof was bleeding? Cristof was in danger? But now she saw that the second corpse was also a lictor, also shot to death.

"Where is he?"

The lieutenant fought back to his knees and clutched his injured leg. Sweat or melted ice ran down his face. He lifted his arm, pointing.

She turned. Cristof wasn't there, but her wings were visible, half-caught in an open window, still locked to the floor of the passenger car.

"No, no... where's Cris?"

"*Now*, Icarus!" he roared. "Before anybody else dies!"

The threat snapped her back to her senses.

"Oh, Lady," she whispered again, staggering toward her wings and fumbling for the key with blood-covered fingers. "Oh, Lady, no. Not yet. Not now."

She tried to climb up the bent side of the car, slid back down, screamed with frustration, and tried again. Ice and blood made her hands slip on the cold metal. She threw herself against it and dug her nails into the splintered oak paneling that bore the train's name and the car's number. Her grip held and she dragged herself forward until she was flat on the tilted side-turned-roof. She reached down and groped for the armature's locks.

The key fell from her numb fingers into the darkness below.

Taya howled oaths and pounded her fist on the side of the car, then looked at Amcathra. The lictor had pulled himself back to his feet and held up the torch to give her more light. His face was drawn and horrible, and his back was turned to his dead nephew.

With a surge of shame, Taya forced herself to sit up and swing her legs into the shattered window. She let herself drop.

Her legs collapsed beneath her and she fell to her knees, groaning. Her head pounded. The torchlight didn't reach inside the car; everything was pitch black.

He needs help. Now.

"Please, Lady, please," she moaned, her voice cracking as she ran her hands over shattered glass and threw broken furniture out of the way. Then, as if in answer to her prayer, her fingers touched the key. With fervent thanks, she yanked her wings toward her, ran one arm through the keel struts to hold it in place, and turned the key in the lock.

It opened. She pulled it from the chains, letting them fall.

Now. She had to get back out again.

Taya groped around for something to stand on— one of the pieces of furniture she'd thrown aside. Her fingers touched a smooth edge and she pulled it forward, startled by its lightness.

The case of counterweights.

Her free hand shook as she unsnapped the latches and felt the long, flat counterweights buckled against the sides of the case. She pulled out the ondium oblongs and slid them into the counterweight pockets on her flight suit belt, then shoved the rest into the tool pockets that ran along her suit's arms and legs.

Nearly floating, she latched the case and set it on its end. She pulled the armature toward her, low enough to run her uniform straps through it. Wing feathers rattled against the metal edges of the window.

Still trembling, Taya climbed up on the edge of the narrow case and reached as high as she could. Her shoulders ached. The case tilted beneath her and she stopped, catching her balance. Moving more slowly, she reached up again. Her fingertips brushed the edge of the window.

If she had time, she'd check the feathers for damage and examine the rest of the armature for bends, cracks, and foreign matter. But she'd wasted enough time already.

He needs help. Now.

Taya jumped, her hands closing on the edges of the window sill. She twisted as the case tipped and fell beneath her and pulled herself through.

Ice rain pelted her head and face as she knelt on the side of the overturned car. The gusting wind caught her feathers and shoved her to one side. She'd counterweighted herself too much for a storm, but she was afraid she wouldn't be able to get aloft without its help.

Amcathra picked up his torch and turned to leave.

Taya ran her suit's straps and buckles through the struts and snapped the keel around her chest, watching as the lictor paused next to Rikard's bloodstained body. He started to reach down, then jerked his hand away and limped into the wasteland of broken trees and twisted metal.

Her vision blurred, turning the lictor's torch into a fuzzy ball of fire.

She wanted to stop what she was doing. She wanted to run after him, screaming for Cristof. She wanted to find out what he meant when he said her husband had been *bleeding*.

Nightmare images swam before her mind's eye.

She shoved them away, although she couldn't stop the tears that ran down her face. Then, stifling another groan, she lifted her arms and slid them into her wings, shrugging out of the locked-high position.

Lady save her, there was no way to get a running start in this field of natural and man-made wreckage. She swallowed, looking at the tilted, ice-slicked surface of the car, then stamped her feet, wincing as the jolts made the pain in her head even worse. Light flared in her vision again and she blinked it away.

Now.

Why was she wasting more time?

Taya backed up as far as she could, put her back to the wind, and sprinted down the truncated length of the wrecked car.

The wind caught her as she jumped and spread her wings. She narrowly missed one of the broken trees and beat furiously, trying to gain enough altitude to get over the dangerous treetops. Too light— she was too light, even though her strained shoulders and back were already protesting at the effort of balancing her weight. She kicked down her tailset, sliding her legs up to take some of the pressure off her back, and squinted against the pelting ice. The mechanisms in her armature were pulling and she felt a drag that suggested her feathers weren't in alignment, but nothing could be done about it, and she *had to fly*.

No moon or stars were visible to guide her, but she saw glimmers of light below. Amcathra wasn't the only one moving in the woods. Other survivors at the front of the train were carrying torches and lanterns, as well. They were all but impossible to see through the blowing snow.

The wind shifted and she struggled against it, searching the dark, featureless horizon. They'd been close to the cable lift station, but she had no idea where she was. Up— the train had been climbing up, so the station must be up, but in the middle of the storm and darkness, she was completely disoriented.

Cold air tore into her chest and she coughed.

This was madness, and somewhere below her, Cristof was hurt.

There— she saw a light glimmering well away from the crash. She fought toward it, unable to predict the tumultuous winds, hampered by the pull and drag of her battered armature. Tears blinded her and ice stung her face. Her bare hands were numb as she clutched the cold metal handles of her wings. No, the light! — where did it go? Gone? — no, there it was, flickering through something, trees maybe, but was it the wreck or the station? For all Taya knew, she was flying in circles.

The light blinked in and out.

She had to get higher, but there were no warm air currents to ride. Instead, she battled for every inch of progress, straining to ascend against a storm that wanted to dash her into the treetops. A cut on her face cracked open and she tasted blood.

The exalted was bleeding.

If Cristof died — if he was dead — the thought was like staring into an empty, bottomless chasm, and she mentally recoiled, focusing on the horizon.

The dark treetops dropped away and at last she saw the light she'd been tracking— an incandescent flare reflected by a giant parabolic mirror. She could just barely hear the chugging of the generator that powered it.

The cable-haul station was equipped with a military signaling station, and it was being used.

Her breath catching in a grateful sob, Taya veered and tacked against the tossing winds. As she drew nearer she saw train tracks, a cleared cliff incline where the cars were to be hauled up to the second set of rails, and men waving torches, signaling her. They were already on the lower tracks, next to some kind of warehouse — was it a search party? Had they heard — of course they'd heard the wreck.

She dived, buffeted by the winds and blinded by the ice and snow. A graceful landing was out of the question. Now, at last, the extra counterweights might do her some good. Men and women scattered as she twisted and backbeat, preparing for a sliding landing that was going to hurt like hell because she wasn't wearing any knee pads. She aimed for what she hoped was a muddy patch to the side of the train tracks and arched her aching, protesting back.

Mud and sleet, yes, but rocks, too— the leather of her flight suit tore across her knees, and then she was surrounded by famulates and lictors picking her up and asking where the train had derailed. She slid her arms out of the wings, carelessly letting them float around her.

"Fifteen, twenty minutes away," she gasped, pointing the way she had come, or at least what she thought was the way she'd come. "A steep switchback. Hurry!"

Shouts, directions. A man in a parka with a famulate's circular castemark on his forehead was steadying her.

"The exalted? Is he all right?"

She gave him a terrified look. Lieutenant Amcathra's warning echoed through her head.

"He's hurt. Bleeding. You have to do something."

"The exalted's injured!" he bellowed, turning. "Get Marchand down there, fast!"

The workers had dragged a cart onto the rails, a miniature engine pulling a platform loaded with boxes. At the man's shout, the searchers riding it released the brakes and it shot forward faster than a man could run.

"What about the others?" the famulate asked, steadying her.

"I don't know." She shuddered, clutching his lapel. "Rikard's dead. There's a gunman— someone was shooting. Amcathra's hurt— I think he broke his leg. Cristof's bleeding. You have to help him."

"We will," he said, pulling his coat out of her grip. She let the heavy, fulled wool slide through her numb fingers and leaned over, nauseous. Gusts of wind yanked her loose wings back and forth, jarring her.

"Stefan," she heard the man say, "get the icarus inside."

"No…" she straightened up, her head pounding. "I need Cris." She had to get back. She had to make sure her husband was alive.

"Wings up, Icarus," someone else said, not unkindly. She blinked her dizziness away. A young man, as young as Rikard, his face filled with sympathy.

Oh, Lady, Rikard!

She turned, dazed, remembering Rikard's blank blue eyes. The workers were hauling a second rail-cart out of the warehouse, rattling it onto the tracks from a short spur and stoking the fire inside its miniature metal engine. Sleet hissed and melted against the steel.

"Icarus." A hand on her arm. Stefan. "Your wings. They'll get damaged in this wind."

She groped for the arm struts and slid her arms inside until she could lift and lock the wings tight against her body. The armature and counterweights in her suit tugged upward, trying to pull her back into the wind.

"I'll show you where they are," she volunteered.

The leader looked up and shook his head.

"Stefan, talk some sense into her."

The youth laid the back of his hand against her cheek. She could barely feel it.

"You're in shock, Icarus. You look like hell, and you're shaking so hard I'm surprised you can stand. Come inside and get warm."

"No!" She turned as the cart's searchlight switched on and staggered to the shallow wagon behind the engine. "Take me with you."

The workers glanced at her, then away, searching for guidance. Their boss shrugged.

"We don't have time to argue. Stefan, watch her. Let's get this thing rolling."

Taya huddled with the workers, her cut and bruised hands numb as she gripped the sides of the wagon. Her appointed guardian crouched beside her, his parka hood pulled close around his face.

The brakeman released his lever and they began to chug forward, slowly at first, then gaining speed. Taya closed her eyes, every muscle straining against the cold and her own impatience, and prayed.

It didn't seem long before she heard the brakes squeal again. Someone laid a hand on her shoulder. She only realized it when he shook her.

"We're getting off," Stefan said in her ear. "We'll walk while the engineer eases the cart down."

She opened her eyes and climbed out.

The railcart's bright lamp picked out the steep hill below and the terrible scar where one of the rails had broken. The train's wreckage sprawled beyond it, a twisted and horrific shape that glittered in the darkness against the whirling snow and dark pines.

The first rescue cart had stopped above the broken rail, its light shining on the last of the derailed cars— their car, the ambassadorial car, with its splintered wood paneling and once-cheerful paint. Figures sat or laid next to it, wrapped in blankets.

"Cris...." Taya scrambled down the slope, her boots slipping on ice-covered gravel and soil. The rest of the rescuers were with her, though, moving just as quickly, carrying lanterns and backpacks.

She found Amcathra sitting on a leather trunk while one of the rescue workers splinted his ankle. Taya staggered to a halt, her breath a lung-shredding plume of white.

"Where—"

"She's looking for someone named Cris," a voice explained, panting almost as hard as she was. She spared a second's glance to see Stefan stopping next to her and leaning over, puffing. "Wouldn't stay at the station."

"He is alive." Amcathra turned, making the man wrapping his splint protest, and grabbed her wrist. Taya was too tired to be shocked by the ferocity of his grip. "Stay here. A doctor is examining him."

"I need—" She tried to tug her arm away, but even if she hadn't been counterweighted, the Demican lictor was larger and stronger than she was. "I need to see him."

"You will only be in the way, Icarus." His grasp was as relentless as his voice.

She stopped struggling, searching his black-striped face for some indication that he was holding back bad news, trying to shield her from the worst. But Amcathra was nothing if not honest. If Cris were dead, Amcathra would tell her.

She sank into a crouch next to him, drained.

"Lictor," Stefan said, "I was told to keep an eye on her, but if you could..."

"Yes. Go."

They sat motionless. The freezing wind insinuated itself into the rips in Taya's flight suit. The rescue worker finished with Amcathra's ankle and stood.

"Good enough for now, Lieutenant," he said. "We'll do a better job up top. I think it's just sprained."

"Thank you."

"You need any help, Icarus?"

She looked up at the stranger.

"How's Cris?"

"Who?"

"Exalted Forlore," Amcathra clarified.

"I don't know. Doctor Marchand's taking care of him."

She started to move, and Amcathra's grip tightened.

"Do you need any help?" the rescuer repeated, holding his bundle of bandages.

"No."

He nodded and moved away, looking for anyone else who needed his attention. Amcathra made no attempt to stand, his gloved hand locked around Taya's wrist. Lanternlight cast the hard planes of his face in unforgiving chiaroscuro. Taut, pained lines were carved around his mouth.

"I'm sorry," she said, shaken out of her self-absorption. "I'm sorry about Rikard."

"He killed Petre."

"Who—"

"Petre. One of my lictors." Amcathra's voice was as cold as the weather around them.

"Oh, Lady." Tears stung her eyes. "I'm sorry. Rikard— he was looking for Cris. When the train started to roll, he tried to hold me, but we were torn apart and I blacked out."

Amcathra released her wrist to pull his torn coat closer around him. She was dismayed by the expression on his face.

"His mother is my sister."

She swallowed.

"I know. He told me. And he told me about his sister...."

Amcathra didn't say anything else. Taya tried to stand, staggered as her cold-stiffened muscles failed to respond, and grabbed the edge of the box to push herself to her feet.

"What happened to Cris?" she asked, bracing for the answer.

"He was standing next to a dining car window when the train derailed. A branch drove through the glass. The broken glass struck him."

She drew a sharp breath. Amcathra touched her sleeve, a mute warning that he would stop her again if he needed to.

"Your presence will change nothing."

"But—" She couldn't say it. *But if he dies....*

Her presence would still change nothing. Except she'd be with him at the end.

She'd seen Cristof thrown into an abyss and shot at by terrorists, but she'd never felt as helpless to save him as she did now.

"H-how bad is it?"

"He was bleeding and unconscious when the train stopped moving. One of the seamstresses helped me bind the worst of his lacerations. A sharp piece of glass was driven through his left hand— we left it in place. One of his lenses had broken over his left eye. We did not dare to remove the glass."

Taya's knees weakened again. She sat in the snow next to the lictor, clutching the hand he'd laid on her sleeve. That horrible black chasm loomed before her again— the thought of life without her husband.

"He is alive," Amcathra reminded her. "He is in a doctor's care."

"I know." She leaned her head against the lieutenant's arm, fighting back her tears. If Amcathra could remain stoic in the face of his nephew's death, how dare she cry just because her husband was injured? "I know. I'm sorry. I can't help it. I love him. I thought we'd be safe in Ondinium. I thought we were all safe."

Amcathra shifted, but he didn't pull his arm away. Taya wanted him to say something to reassure her, but he remained silent.

Of course. Because no matter what she'd thought, they were clearly not safe.

"What about the others?" she asked after a moment.

"I think one of the tailors will not survive."

"Jayce?" She dug her fingers into his arm.

"He was unconscious when I left. He may have broken his arm."

She relaxed, minutely.

"Get 'er ready to move; we got the exalted!" someone bellowed. Taya's head snapped up. Four rescuers carrying a stretcher appeared out from the trees. She leaped to her feet, nearly fell, then stumbled forward.

"Give us room, Icarus," one of the stretcher-bearers snapped, holding out an arm to block her way. She stared at Cristof's pallored face, half-hidden by bandages and sticking plaster. One heavily bandaged arm had been tied down across his chest, but a blanket covered the rest of his body. Someone had cut his shirt sleeve open.

"I'm riding with him," she declared, struggling to keep pace as they marched up the incline beside the tracks.

"And I," Amcathra said, behind her.

Taya turned.

"Your ankle—"

"He said it was only a sprain."

"He said he *thought* it was a sprain!" Taya grabbed his arm, steadying him. The lictor couldn't lean on her while she was wearing her armature, but she did her best to support him as he stubbornly worked his way up the hill beside her. "No, wait, stop a minute."

"Why?"

"You'll walk better if you're lighter." She unbuckled her flight belt with numb fingers and tugged it out through its loops and brackets. Clutching the belt with one hand, she worked at it with her other hand and teeth, pulling on the straps and buckles to lengthen it. "Here."

Amcathra buckled the belt around his waist and continued forward. They reached the rail-cart just as the rescuers were running ropes across the stretcher to keep Cristof's prone body in place on the railcart bed.

"Hold his stretcher," one of the men ordered. "And keep his arm still."

She climbed on. Amcathra pulled himself up to the other side of the stretcher and let out a hiss of pain as he sat.

Taya touched Cristof's blanket-covered chest, reassuring herself that he was breathing. Then she ran a hand over his hair and bit her lip as her fingers encountered sticky blood and splinters of glass.

Four other injured men were put into the cart. Jayce, whose right arm was in a sling, sat next to the unconscious tailor. He stretched out his left hand and Taya grasped it.

"Don't worry, Taya," Jayce said. "He'll be all right."

Suddenly, she wasn't able to hold back her tears anymore.

CHAPTER TEN

THE SOUTH ALPHA Incline cable-haul station housed fifteen railway workers, four lictors, and one physician in the barracks-like simplicity of its solid stone construction. The government could have blasted a long series of switchbacks out of the cliff, but it preferred to take the time and effort to haul train cars up the steep hill by cable-pull and transfer them to a new set of tracks. Ensuring that no train could travel straight from the borders to the capital was one of the nation's many safeguards against enemy invasion.

With a commanding view of the surrounding mountains, the cable-haul station also served as one of the hundreds of signal stations built across Ondinium, its bright, incandescent lamp and parabolic reflector ready to convey messages across the mountainous nation. Right now it was alerting M-O Terminal to keep other trains off the track until the broken rail was repaired and informing stations farther up the line that the train had crashed and the exalted was injured.

Taya sat by the stationmaster's bed, which had been made available for her husband, listening to the distant rumble of the station's engine and the low, urgent conversations outside the room. Cristof had gained consciousness twice, but only for a few seconds each time. It was enough to give her hope, but not enough to alleviate her dreadful sense of loneliness.

All the things that exasperated her about her husband — his social awkwardness, his tumultuous moods, his gearhead enthusiasm for machines — and all the things she admired about him — his intelligence, his wry humor, his dedication, and his bravery — had suddenly become impossibly dear to her. Taya studied his bloody, bandaged face, dreadfully cognizant of how central he'd become in her life and how empty she would feel without him.

It wasn't that she hadn't known she'd loved him. Of course she'd loved him; she couldn't have put up with him if she hadn't loved him. But theirs wasn't the kind of grand, destined love affair described in the thick romance novels Cassie bought. They had to work at their marriage with humor and patience. Sometimes, the marriage took a *lot* of effort.

Taya ran her fingers over Cristof's unbandaged right hand, feeling a lump in her throat.

Some things were worth the effort, though.

Two hours had passed since the crash. Five men had died: Rikard, Petre, Tailor, the engineer, and the conductor. Many more were badly injured.

Taya had changed into a station worker's spare uniform. The physician's assistant had checked her over, bandaging and plastering her cuts. He'd warned her that she'd strained her muscles and wouldn't feel much like moving once her stress levels decreased. She already ached, and she was afraid that if she laid down, she might not be able to get back up again. Nobody would let her lie down, though, because the assistant had also diagnosed her as mildly concussed.

She preferred to stay awake and watch over her husband, anyway.

"Taya?"

She looked up. Jayce walked in, holding a flask, and handed it to her. His broken arm had been splinted and bound, and a fresh sling secured it close to his chest.

"Whiskey. Belongs to one of the men here. The doctor said you could have some."

"Thank you." She didn't like whiskey, but she took a sip anyway, flinching as the alcohol stung her cut and chapped lips.

"How are you doing?"

"I want him to wake up. *Really* wake up."

"I know. He will. How are *you* doing?"

She looked up and saw concern in his dark eyes. She mustered a weak smile that quickly collapsed.

"Rikard… Rikard died protecting me."

"I'm sorry." Jayce lowered his voice to a whisper. "They put the bodies in the warehouse, but the lieutenant hasn't gone down yet. He won't talk to anybody, either. He just sits outside like a statue."

She nodded. She couldn't imagine that Lieutenant Amcathra would willingly reveal his grief to strangers.

Her heart ached to think about what Rikard's mother would say when she heard the news. And what about his little sister? The one Rikard had been saving up his money to help?

They would do something for her, she decided, touching Cristof's bandaged arm. As soon as they were back in the capital.

"What do you know about Petre?" she asked, at last.

"I didn't know him before this trip, but we got along fine. He seemed normal." Jayce looked unhappy. "It's hard to believe he was behind all this."

"I know," Taya whispered. "You'd think the lieutenant would have noticed something, if one of his men was a turncoat."

"Maybe that's why he's so upset."

"Excuse me? Icarus?"

They looked up. Doctor Marchand, the station physician, stood in the doorway. Jayce excused himself and the doctor took his place.

"I'm told you're the exalted's wife?"

"Yes."

"I'm sorry. I hadn't realized that. You are also the head of the delegation in his absence?"

"Yes, I suppose so." She glanced at the small table by the bed. Cristof's pocket watch was there, next to her own. Their twin ticking reassured her. She realized it was a groundless superstition, but somehow she couldn't believe that Cristof would die as long as his watch was working.

"Very good. We plan to retrieve everyone's goods from the wreckage tomorrow." The physician rubbed the spiral caste-mark on his right cheekbone. "There's nothing that needs to be retrieved sooner than that, is there?"

"Not that I know of." She'd found Alister's punch cards tucked behind Cristof's identification papers in the coat they'd cut off his body, and she had her armature. "I'll need my box of counter-weights tomorrow, and my dispatch case contains confidential material."

"We'll prioritize them, then."

Her husband groaned and she looked back down at him.

"Will he be all right?"

"He lost a lot of blood, but none of his lacerations were life-threatening...."

"But...?" Taya bit her lip. Marchand shook his head.

"The fact that he's regained consciousness a few times is a good sign."

"When can we leave, then?"

"That depends on what the signalers have to say." He gestured toward the door. "Do you want to come with me? We can ask if they've received orders from Ondinium yet."

Taya hesitated.

"Walk with me," the doctor urged. "It will do you good."

She reluctantly stood, leaning over to kiss Cristof's forehead before following the physician out. Walking hurt. She rotated her aching arms and neck, and rubbed her trembling legs. Her skinned and bruised knees were on fire.

"We're going up to the station," the doctor announced to the room in general. Nods and grunts arose from those who were still awake. Taya pulled on the heavy coat and gloves Marchand handed her and followed him out the door and up a steep flight of stairs cut out of the cold mountain stone. The snow wasn't as bad now, though the wind was still bitterly cold.

Taya had never been this close to a signaling station before. Several were near the capital, but they weren't on her courier route. The steam engine chugged and giant mirrors clattered around metal tracks while a metal hood snapped back and forth in front of the bright signal light.

A small door at the base of the mechanism led to a spartan operator's room. Long windows ran across the room's walls, revealing distant flashes through the swirling snowflakes. On the far side of the room was a metal panel in which were set levers and cranks.

The famulate at the desk raised her hand in a stalling gesture as she scribbled on a sheet of paper. A stack of blank punch cards and a punch machine sat on the desk by her right hand.

"Are the signals run by difference engines?" Taya asked Marchand in a low voice.

"No— it's a much simpler system," he replied. "More like a mechanical loom, or a wireferry."

The signaler finished writing and walked over to the control panel, making adjustments. She removed a card and replaced it with another, hanging the used card on a labeled board. When she was done, she turned.

"Doctor?" Her face darkened. "Is it the exalted?"

"No, no, he's well. This is Taya Icarus, Exalted Forlore's wife."

"Er, how do you do, Icarus?" the famulate said, taken aback. "I'm sorry about the accident."

"Thank you." Taya glanced at Marchand, wondering why they'd come. She'd rather be sitting by Cristof's side.

"Has there been any word from Ondinium?" Marchand asked. The signaler nodded, picking up the papers from the table.

"I'm acknowledging it right now, right?" she replied. "We're to divert all rail traffic until repairs are made and get the exalted to safety as soon as possible." She hesitated, looking down at the papers, then folded them and handed them to Marchand. "These coded orders are for the stationmaster, aren't they? Will you deliver them, as long as you're here?"

"Of course."

"Does that mean we can travel?" Taya asked as they headed back down the icy stairs to the main station.

"If this is the authorization we've been expecting, then yes." The doctor stopped before they reached the station door. "Icarus, I'd like to show you something down below. Something about one of your dead."

She recoiled. "Is it important?"

"I think it may be, yes. Will you come?"

She glanced at the station door. She wanted to go back to Cristof, but it wouldn't be fair to ask Lieutenant Amcathra to do it. He had a twisted knee and a sprained ankle, and he clearly wasn't ready to confront his nephew's corpse yet.

"All right," she acquiesced without enthusiasm.

Marchand led her down more stairs to the detached storage shed where the bodies had been taken. Taya stopped when she saw him reach for the oilcloth covering the face.

"That's Rikard."

"I don't know his name. But I'm concerned about how he died."

"One of our lictors, Petre, shot him." She didn't want to see Rikard's dead face. She didn't want to see his wounds. All she wanted to do was go back inside to check on Cristof.

"I don't think so."

Taya forced herself to set one foot in front of the other until she stood by his side.

"Why not?"

He pulled down the oilcloth. She made a small, strangled noise at the sight of Rikard's waxen face. Someone had closed his eyes and set steel washers over them to keep them shut. But the doctor was gesturing to the dead lictor's chest, where his tattered uniform jacket and shirt had been cut open.

Rikard's chest had been blown apart. Frozen blood glittered in the light of the lantern that hung from the shed's rafters. The bear's head tattoo on his upper arm, heartwrenchingly identical to his uncle's, was livid against his colorless skin.

"This wound is the result of a very high-caliber weapon."

"So?" Taya swallowed back a surge of nausea, looking away. Marchand pulled up the oilcloth.

"The other lictor, Petre, was holding a handgun, not a rifle. The only man we rescued who was carrying a high-caliber weapon is your lieutenant."

"Lieutenant Amcathra didn't shoot his own nephew!"

"Perhaps not intentionally, but if it was dark, and the two men were shooting at each other... he might have made a mistake."

"No. That's impossible." Taya felt sick just thinking about it. "Amcathra wouldn't make that kind of mistake."

"At night? In the middle of a storm? After crawling out of a train wreck? *Anybody* could have made that kind of mistake." Marchand gave her a grave look. "Unless, of course, it wasn't a mistake. Are you certain the man with the handgun was the saboteur?"

"I'm not talking about this any more." Taya jerked around, hugging herself.

"You trust your lieutenant?"

"Implicitly!" she snapped. Of course she trusted him. That wasn't the issue. The issue was... if he'd killed his sister's son by accident....

Her stomach churned as she remembered the despair on his face when she'd first opened her eyes.

How was he ever going to live with himself?

When they returned to the station, Taya peeled off her parka as Marchand handed the signal message to the stationmaster. He called over a lictor, and the three conferred in low voices. The stationmaster gestured to her as she was about to check on Cristof.

"Icarus, we've been given permission to transport Exalted Forlore to Overlook by restricted rail," he murmured, standing close to her. "The trip takes about two hours. Your lieutenant has been ordered to escort him. Do you want to accompany him, too, or would you rather stay here to oversee the salvage operation?"

"I'll go with him," Taya said at once. The stationmaster nodded and headed to Lieutenant Amcathra, who was sitting by the door with his arms folded over his chest and his eyes all but closed. He looked up as the stationmaster spoke to him.

Taya slipped past them to re-enter Cristof's room, unable to look the lictor in the face. Her heart leaped when she saw her husband's unbandaged eye open.

"Cris?" He was still prone, and Dr. Marchand was pulling a needle attached to a syringe out of her husband's arm. "Cris, are you all right?"

"Taya." His voice was weak and strained, but she recognized the relief in his bruised face. It was a reflection of her own. She grabbed his bandaged hand, then tore off her gloves and took it again.

"Shhh." She rubbed his bare fingertips, afraid to squeeze too hard. "I'm all right."

He nodded, just the slightest twitch.

"I've administered a subcutaneous dose of morphine to help him with the pain," Marchand said, cleaning the needle with a cloth and setting it aside. "I'll show you and the lictor how to do it, in case he needs another dose during the journey."

Cristof tried to say something, but it came out as a whisper. She leaned closer.

"...safe?"

She drew in a deep breath.

"We lost Rikard," she said, squeezing his hand. "Petre... Petre shot him," she said, with a touch of defiance. The doctor was wrong. He *had* to be wrong. "Petre's dead, too, and one of Jayce's tailors, and an engineer. Everyone else is alive."

He slid his other arm across the blanket and grasped her hand.

"Please, Exalted, don't move." Marchand looked at Taya. "The morphine will put him to sleep for the journey."

Taya leaned over and kissed her husband.

"I love you, Cris. Don't worry about anything. Amcathra and I will take care of you."

He murmured something she couldn't make out before his eyes closed and his hands relaxed.

She waited until his breathing was deep and steady, then straightened his arms and looked at Marchand. The physician took the exalted's pulse, listened to his breathing, and nodded with satisfaction.

"He should sleep through the trip, but I'll give you more morphine in case he awakens."

Marchand asked Lieutenant Amcathra to join them and demonstrated how to give Cristof a second injection. Taya put the glass-and-steel syringe and small bottle of morphine into her coat pocket for safekeeping.

"How are you?" she asked Amcathra after Marchand left.

"Mobile," he said, tersely. "Did the stationmaster say how long it will take to reach Overlook?"

"Two hours."

Amcathra scowled and limped out of the room on a makeshift cane someone had made for him from a tree branch. Taya checked on her sleeping husband one more time and followed the lictor out. She found him studying a large schematic map of the rails that hung on one wall.

"Where are we?" she asked.

Amcathra pointed to a dot.

"And Overlook?"

He pointed to another. Taya frowned. The schematic didn't tell her much about the terrain, but her rough mental map of Ondinium told her that Overlook was on the other side of the mountain, much more than two hours away.

"Maybe they have a wireferry?" she suggested. Going straight over the peak instead of around it would reduce the travel time.

"No."

"I might be able to fly to Overlook in two hours," she tried again, puzzled. "But I don't think they're going to give you a pair of wings and hang Cris from a sling between us."

"That might be preferable." Amcathra turned, his attention caught by the stationmaster's return from outside.

"Icarus. Lieutenant. If you're ready to depart, we'll be traveling to the restricted line by rail-cart."

They bade the rest of their small group good-bye as the lictors fastened Cristof's stretcher to the rail-cart. Taya, back in her torn flight suit and armature, hugged them all while the stationmaster warmed up the rail-cart's engine.

Nobody in the cart tried to speak as they sped along zig-zagging side-rails through the dark, snowy forest. Several times the tracks ran under camouflaged tunnels. Taya held Cristof's motionless hand, her heart aching. Her husband looked too small under his blanket and bandages. Beside her, Amcathra remained silent. He'd changed into a clean uniform one of the station's lictors had found for him and held his makeshift cane as he observed their route. She kept expecting to see some sign of grief or guilt in his face, but if he was feeling either emotion, he hid it well.

At last the stationmaster braked as they approached a locked mine entrance; the tracks ran under the doors. The two station lictors jumped off to unlock the two heavy, iron-banded doors and swing them open. The rail-cart chugged inside a stone tunnel, then braked again. Its front-mounted searchlight snapped on. The stationmaster lit several lamps, hanging them on hooks on the back of the engine, while the lictors closed and locked the doors from the inside.

"Mines…" Taya breathed, looking at Amcathra. "We're not going *over* the mountain; we're going *through* it."

The lictors climbed back aboard, shooting them smug glances.

The rail-cart carried them into a dark shaft. They descended steadily, passing two more sets of gates that had already been drawn back. Taya squirmed. She'd never been inside a mine before. The close, dark tunnels made her uneasy, and the sound of the engine and wheels clattering on the rails seemed ten times as loud as before.

She didn't know how long it was before they slowed and turned. She laid a hand on Cristof's chest, reassuring herself with his heartbeat. Steam hissed as the cart stopped and the engineer set the brakes. The lictors slid off and grabbed their lanterns.

The chamber was strangely muggy and warm, trickles of water running down its stone walls. Once the rail-cart's engine was off, Taya could make out the thundering rumble of a much, much larger steam engine nearby.

"Where are we?" she asked, looking around. She had to raise her voice to be heard over the noise. "What *is* this?"

The chamber was taller and wider than the small tunnel they'd taken down, its walls and square support pillars decorated with great, ornately carved stone slabs. The carvings reminded her of ancient designs she'd seen preserved in the state museum years ago: flowers and animals and mask-wearing figures out of legend.

The rail-cart tracks circled next to a broad wooden platform, but the vehicle next to the platform was no train Taya had ever seen before. It was slender, cylindrical, and windowless, its sides smooth and lacking any of the decorative panels or paint she was used to seeing on passenger cars. The vehicle's front end was pointed like an air-rifle cartridge.

The tunnel it was aimed at was hardly wider than the vehicle itself. The entrance was faced with huge blocks of stone incised with ancient Ondinium script.

"This," the stationmaster announced with pride, "is Ondinium's subterranean atmospheric railway."

"It runs through the mountain?"

"Yes. These tunnels date back to the Imperial days. They've been reinforced, of course."

"What do the words over the tunnel say?"

"No idea."

Taya dropped her eyes to the vehicle again, confused.

"Where's its engine?"

"It doesn't have one." The stationmaster pointed to a building on the platform where one of the lictors was working. "That's an air compressing station. We have a giant, steam-powered pump in there and pumps at regular stations down the line. Together they'll push the railcar through the mountain on a cushion of compressed air. It's clean, quiet, and much, much faster than a normal locomotive."

"This is not quiet," Amcathra objected, studying the pumping station with perceptible mistrust.

"Well, the pump makes noise, and it generates some smoke, as well, but once you're inside the tunnel, you'll hardly hear a thing except the wheels on the track."

"Is it safe?" Taya asked.

"Absolutely. The atmospheric railway was designed for exactly this sort of thing— moving exalteds through Ondinium swiftly and secretly. I don't need to tell you that this is all top secret, of course. On penalty of death."

Taya nodded. For Ondinium to have kept such a major railway system secret for so many years, the punishment *had* to be death. The stationmaster and lictors must have passed a battery of loyalty tests before earning their clearance to work on it.

Her eyes rose again to the carved walls of the chamber. She had never heard that the Ondinium Empire had dug train tunnels through the mountains.

"Of course," the stationmaster continued, heading back to the rail-cart to unbuckle her husband's stretcher, "the three of you were given a need-to-know clearance, but you won't be permitted to discuss this with anyone else, either."

"Do these... these air trains run underneath the whole range?" Taya asked, moving over to help him. She wished Cristof were awake to hear all this. He'd be fascinated. Did any of these tunnels run beneath the capital proper? Maybe that explained how the vast, floating Great Engine had been constructed inside a hollow mountain.

"It's an atmospheric railway," the stationmaster corrected her. "And I don't know how far the system extends. That's confidential, too."

He and one of the lictors carried Cristof into the strange-looking carriage. Taya had to take off her armature to fit into the short, narrow doorway. She set it to one side, letting the wings float as she looked around.

The carriage was narrower than a regular train car, both walls lined with long, leather-padded, high-backed seats with projecting wings that curved around either side of each passenger's head. Cabinets beneath the seats provided storage for luggage they didn't have. Metal doors were set in both ends of the carriage, and the front door bore a framed sign. Amcathra hobbled past the two men and the stretcher to read it.

"What is it?" Taya asked.

"Emergency instructions for exiting the vehicle."

"I thought you said it was safe!" she exclaimed.

"It is, it is," the stationmaster assured her. "But there's always a small chance that we'll lose vacuum or air pressure along the line. Shouldn't happen — we test the lines twice a year — but an earthquake or even normal subsidence could crack the pneumatic tubes, or the timing on the relay pumping stations could be thrown off."

"An earthquake...?" A vision of the dark, cramped tunnel collapsing on them made Taya's mouth grow dry.

"Unlikely in the extreme, I assure you." The stationmaster cocked his head. "I guess it's true, what they say about icarii being afraid of enclosed spaces."

"I'm not afraid. I just don't like the idea of an earthquake trapping me in the middle of a mountain."

"On my honor, Icarus, this is safer than a regular railway. This train can't derail and it can't hit another train. It's going to pass straight through the mountain and shoot you out the other side, right into Overlook. You'll be there before you know it."

"I hope you're right," she muttered, already feeling the weight of the mountain pushing down on her.

The lictors secured Cristof's stretcher to the floor with a complicated array of straps and bade Amcathra and Taya goodbye.

"Strap in; the initial take-off is quite a jolt," the stationmaster said, gesturing to the straps that hung from the tops of the chairs. "I recommend you keep your belt on for the entire ride. The route is steep, and you might get hurt if you aren't secured."

Taya scowled as he waved and left, and then moved over to snap her wings' keel around one of the extra sets of straps. The last thing she needed was for her armature to bounce around the car, suffering more damage.

A warning whistle sounded. Amcathra took a seat on one side of the car, at Cristof's feet, and Taya sat on the other side, at Cristof's head. Both of them puzzled over the network of straps and buckles. The train rolled forward and stopped again. Taya swallowed hard and swiftly fastened herself in.

"Do you know anything about atmospheric railways?" she asked the lictor. Amcathra grunted, buckling the straps that ran across his lap and shoulders and taking a firm grip on his crude cane. His face was impassive, but Taya couldn't help but notice that his knuckles were white.

That was *not* reassuring.

The train jerked forward, throwing them both against their harnesses, and abruptly plunged downward.

Taya closed her eyes and bit back a scream.

Chapter Eleven

TERROR CAN ONLY be sustained for a short period of time. Despite the car's disconcerting habit of making abrupt shifts and stomach-dislodging drops, Taya's heart gradually began to beat more regularly. She warily loosened the buckles and clips holding her in place and leaned over to check on Cristof. He'd been securely wrapped in blankets and strapped between the chairs, and his breathing remained deep and steady. Deeper and steadier than hers, that was for certain.

"I think I prefer normal trains," she declared, sitting back up and re-tightening her straps. Her palms were damp with nervous sweat.

"I agree," Amcathra said. Taya couldn't tell for certain in the unsteady light of the gimbal-mounted lanterns, but she thought the lieutenant looked paler than usual.

Maybe Demicans, like icarii, were also more comfortable in open spaces.

The pneumatic train *was* quieter than a regular train, though. Sometimes she heard a distant rumble that she supposed was another pumping station, but for the most part the only sound was the metallic rattle of the wheels on the tracks and the creaking of the leather straps fastened across their waist and shoulders. When they arrived in Overlook — she fished out Cristof's heavy gold pocket watch and snapped it open — when they arrived in Overlook in another hour and a half, she'd have to look more closely at the train. She wanted to be able to describe it to Cristof when he woke up. A subterranean method of crossing mountains would appeal to him.

She put the pocket watch back and wondered if she should have brought a book.

The train lurched again, making her stomach tighten.

Maybe not.

"Lieutenant…." She considered asking about Rikard, but then she cringed from the thought. How did you ask a man if he might have shot his own nephew in the dark? "Tell me a little about yourself."

His reluctance was visible.

"How did you and Cristof meet?" she pressed, fearing that otherwise they'd sit in an awkward silence for the rest of the ride. "How long have you known each other?"

"We met six years ago," Amcathra said, looking down with a hooded gaze. "I was working for Captain Scarios when the exalted decided to involve himself in one of our investigations. The captain instructed me to keep him away. It was more difficult than I had anticipated."

"Didn't he have a license to work with the lictors?"

"He turned out to be persistent and occasionally useful. Even a misfit exalted can do things and go places a lictor cannot. Captain Scarios began to call on him for regular assistance. It finally became necessary to secure him a special license to avoid a lawsuit."

"Why? What kind of lawsuit?"

"The exalted was caught breaking and entering."

"Where? What happened?"

"I do not think he would appreciate my revealing his more embarrassing moments to his wife."

"Well, what are friends for?"

Amcathra hesitated. The train took another short, steep dip and Taya flinched.

"I'm sorry," she said, as it straightened out again. "If you don't want to tell me, I understand. I'm just talking because I'm nervous."

"I am aware of that." Amcathra paused again. "My parents came from Demicus to find work."

Taya nodded, puzzled. Rikard had told her as much.

"My family still practices many of the old traditions," he added.

Taya waited a moment, then ventured, in Demican, "I don't understand."

"While a man is alive, he should tell his own stories. It is only after a man is dead and his spirit has moved on that my people will freely tell stories about him."

"Oh." Taya drew in a deep breath. She touched the lump Cristof's watch made in one of her flight suit pockets, feeling it vibrate with each tick. It was oddly comforting to know that the lieutenant held some superstitions, too. "Do you… do you want to talk about Rikard?"

"His spirit cannot move on until his body has been destroyed."

Taya swallowed.

"Maybe we should have brought a pack of cards," she said, finally, into the silence.

He nodded.

Taya sighed, squirmed, tugged on the straps around her waist and chest, checked her husband, and then folded her arms around herself and leaned back against the seat.

I wish I could be more like a Demican, she thought. Amcathra seemed perfectly content to sit motionless with his own thoughts. Was he thinking about Rikard? His sister? His niece? Cristof?

She didn't want to think about any of those things. If she thought about Rikard, she'd remember those blank blue eyes staring at her in the snow. If she thought about Rikard's family, she'd imagine them mourning. And if she thought about Cristof, she'd only worry that he wouldn't recover, that he might be suffering from internal bleeding or some other terrible complication.

"Stop it," she muttered aloud, shaking her head to banish the visions. Amcathra glanced at her, then dropped his eyes again, gazing at his scab-covered hands and the top of his crude cane.

She ground her teeth together and almost welcomed the next lurching turn and drop. At least terror took her mind off despair.

"I didn't know Ondinium had tunnels like this," she said at last, giving up on being Demican. "Did you?"

"Yes. They are secret and restricted to military use."

"They're imperial?"

"Yes." Amcathra hesitated, then seemed to force himself to keep speaking. "Of course the imperial Ondiniums did not use railways."

"What did they use them for?"

He studied her. Taya was afraid he'd fall silent again, but he took a deep breath and replied.

"The tunnels are said to extend to the ends of the empire. They were probably used to move supplies and troops."

"The ends of the empire…."

"Well beyond Ondinium's current political borders. They were dug by colonial slaves."

"Ondinium kept slaves?"

"It was one of the reasons for the Last War."

Taya fell silent. She'd never read about the empire's slaves in school. It was, she thought gloomily, yet another of Ondinium's dark secrets. She wondered if she'd ever learn them all.

Taya jerked awake from a frightening dream, disoriented and panicked when she realized she couldn't move. She yanked her hands free from the straps and looked around, her eyes wide and her muscles trembling against the train's harness.

"The vehicle is slowing," Amcathra reported.

"Good." Her heart still pounding, she leaned over and checked Cristof. Still asleep. She watched until she was certain his chest was moving, then rubbed her face and opened her husband's watch.

A little after noon.

Now she could feel it, too, a subtle difference in the way the straps pressed on her that suggested they were easing to a halt, even though she couldn't hear the usual scream of brakes being applied to the rails. Then, at last, with an abrupt jerk, the train stopped.

She looked at Amcathra.

"I guess we'd better get up?" she asked.

"Somebody will come."

"Are you sure?" She reached for the buckles on her harness just as someone pounded on the side of the car, startling them both. Metal bars moved and the side door was rolled open, ushering in a blast of cool but fresh air.

"Please stay seated," the lictor said, climbing into the car and ducking around Taya's wings. She was middle-aged and sturdy, carrying an air rifle slung over her back. "Everyone all right?"

"Yes." Taya craned her neck to see outside, but the angle was wrong.

"Good. We have to do a little maneuvering to tow this thing to the platform. The braking mechanism isn't exact, so we like to stop the car well before the end of the tunnel. If you'll be patient, we'll have you out of this box in about ten minutes."

"Are we in Overlook?"

"Yes, Icarus. I have a team standing by to take Exalted Forlore and the two of you to the hospital. The Council wants a second opinion on the ambassador's condition." The woman leaned out the open door and signaled. A steam engine rumbled as the train shuddered and started to move again.

Taya felt a rush of relief when she finally stepped out. Every muscle in her body was stiff, and the train harness had dug into the bruises on her shoulders and hips. She stretched, groaning, and looked around.

The Overlook platform, too, was inside a low-ceilinged tunnel covered with ancient stone carvings. Two lictors carried Cristof's stretcher down the steps to a waiting railcart.

As before, they rode a railcart out of the tunnels, which opened up into a vast wooden warehouse. A horse-drawn carriage waited in its dimly lit interior, and the lictors transferred the still-sleeping Cristof into it. Taya glanced inside with dismay. There wasn't enough room for her wings.

"Stay outside," Lieutenant Amcathra directed. "I will ride with the exalted."

She nodded, unhappy about it, and strapped on her armature. Her muscles were stiff again.

"We're about twenty minutes away," the older woman said, climbing up into the driver's seat. "Do you want to meet us there, Icarus? The hospital roof is clearly marked."

"No... no, I'll stay." Taya climbed up next to her, fastening her collar. She wasn't sure she could get aloft, anyway, aching as she was.

"Do you want to cover the exalted's face? We don't have masks, but I brought an extra scarf." The lictor pulled a rolled bundle from her coat pocket.

"No. That's all right. Thank you."

"You'd better take it, then. It's cold out." The lictor thrust it at her, so Taya accepted it, wrapping the black length of wool over her head and around her ears. Her own scarf and hat had been lost in the wreck.

Outside, the sky was gray and snowflakes drifted down from the heavy clouds. A fresh coat of snow already covered the ground, making everything around them look fresh and white. The lictors locked the warehouse doors as the carriage started down the road.

Overlook was a high town, as its name suggested, built along a ridge that commanded a striking view of the surrounding valleys. It wasn't very large, but it sprawled over a wide area marked by clearings and buildings that dotted the hills and valleys. The surrounding forest was broken up into rectangles of varying colors— different years of growth that spoke to Ondinium's careful husbanding of its timber. As the carriage jolted along the rough trail, Taya spotted the train track winding its way through a series of switchbacks, its rails glinting silver whenever the clouds broke. The wind kept the air clear, despite the sawmills around town. An icarus would be able to see for miles out here.

When they reached the hospital, Cristof's stretcher was rushed to a private room on the second floor. Taya lurked as close as she could while orderlies unbuckled her husband from the stretcher, pulling the blankets off his chest and lifting his bandaged arm out of the way so that he could be transferred to a bed. Taya ached to see the dark bruises and scratches that stretched over the few parts of his body that weren't wrapped in bandages.

"He's been drugged?" one of the doctors asked, lifting Cristof's eyelid and checking his pupils.

"Dr. Marchand gave him morphine."

"How long ago?"

"Right before we left. About three hours ago."

"Thank you." The two doctors continued their examination.

The lictor who had driven them spoke quietly to Lieutenant Amcathra. Taya dragged herself away long enough to shake the driver's hand and thank her before she left. Then she stood close to the bed again, struggling against the urge to hold her husband's hand while they worked.

"We're going to take off his bandages and clean him up," the female physician said at last, straightening. "We'll replace some of these sutures and sew up one or two of the cuts that Marchand only plastered. Why don't you let my assistant examine you and get you something to eat?"

"I'd rather stay."

The doctor paused, looking at her, and then held out a hand.

"I'm Doctor Placius."

"Taya Icarus." She shook.

"Icarus, Dr. Talevi and I need space and light while we work, and we don't want to be distracted by observers. I'd like you and the lictor to go outside and get yourselves inspected by our assistants. After they've cleared you, you can wait on the other side of the room, quietly, while we work. Is that acceptable?"

Taya forced a nod. It wasn't what she wanted, but it was acceptable.

After her examination, she washed and changed into a clean flight suit sent over from the small eyrie that served the mining community. She'd suffered nothing more than bruises, cuts, and strained muscles. As soon as she was dressed, she hurried back into Cristof's room, taking a seat by the window. Not long afterward, Lieutenant Amcathra joined her, washed, shaved, re-bandaged, and leaning on a proper cane.

"How are you?" Taya asked in a hushed voice as the lictor lowered himself into the chair next to hers.

"A sprain."

"Will that need stitches?" She gestured to the bandage on his forehead.

"It will heal on its own."

Taya remembered the blood that had poured down his face after the wreck. "But won't it scar?"

"Scars do not concern me."

"What about your—" Taya had no idea if Lieutenant Amcathra was married or seeing anyone. "—your family? Won't they care?"

"No."

Frustrated, Taya let the subject drop and turned her worried gaze back to the doctors working on Cristof.

"No permanent damage," Dr. Placius confirmed once they had finished. "The exalted simply needs time to rest and heal."

"When can he travel?"

"It would be best if he stayed here for a week or two, under our supervision."

"Impossible." Amcathra's voice was flat. "The Council awaits him, and you said he was not seriously injured."

"He *was* seriously injured; I simply said that he hasn't suffered any permanent damage." The doctor looked stern. "We'll keep him under observation for a day or two to make certain there's nothing we missed."

"Thank you." Taya crossed the room and looked down at her husband, who was sleeping again. She brushed the hair off his face. "He'll stay here as long as you say he should."

After the doctors left, nurses moved two military-style cots into the room, one for Taya and one for Lieutenant Amcathra. Taya set hers close to Cristof's bed. The lictor put his near the door.

"The storm is clearing," he said, walking to the window and gazing out.

She stood next to him and saw streaks of blue on the horizon over the mountains.

"That's good."

"Why would someone derail a train to kill Exalted Forlore?"

Taya let out a slow breath. Nobody had said it aloud at the station, but she was certain that everybody had wondered, deep inside, if the derailment had been sabotage.

"Are you sure it was another assassination attempt?"

"Yes. What has the exalted done?"

"Nothing! Nothing except what we told you. He was given some information about illegal trade between one of the Big Three and the Alzanans. We assumed the assassin was one of the mercates. I never imagined it would be a lictor."

Amcathra's face hardened as he stared out the window.

"Perhaps he was paid by a mercate. Or an Alzanan."

"That would mean that Cristof's information is pretty important."

"You must return to the capital and begin the investigation."

She was shaking her head before she even realized what she was doing.

"No. I can't. Not yet."

"Then tell me what you know, and I will go."

"…I can't do that, either." She bit her lip, feeling awful, but she couldn't give Amcathra the punch cards. The lictor was no fool. He'd guess at once that the cards came from Alister, and then he'd be duty-bound to report Alister to the Council. Cristof wouldn't want that. "Let me— let me wait. As soon as I'm sure Cris is all right, I'll go. I promise."

Amcathra leaned on his cane, studying her. Some indefinable emotion shadowed his normally clear, pale blue gaze, and the light from the window emphasized the cuts and bruises on his face.

"Do you think *I* am a traitor, too?"

Taya drew in a sharp breath, appalled.

"No! It's nothing like that. It's…." she faltered as she searched for words that wouldn't hurt the feelings she knew he must keep hidden under his stoic mask. "It's that you have too much integrity. If you were any less honest, I would give you the information at once. But… Cris doesn't want you investigating his sources. We know the Council's interested in them."

"That does not mean I would compromise the ambassador's contacts without good reason."

Taya bit her lip. This would be so much easier if she knew him as well as Cristof did. "What if we were pretty sure you'd decide you had a good reason?"

He was silent for a long time, long enough for Taya to be aware of her heart pounding. Then he turned and looked out the window.

"Does your reluctance have anything to do with... my nephew?"

"I—" Taya stared at his back, wondering if he was finally going to talk about the shooting. "No." She braced herself. "Why?"

Lieutenant Amcathra didn't turn.

"According to Council guidelines, if the ambassador is absent or incapacitated, *I* am in charge of the delegation, not you. However...." His voice trailed off a moment. "I will understand if you consider me unfit. I admit that my judgment may be compromised."

Scrap! She knew it— he was upset about the shooting.

"I know about Rikard," she said, hoping that if she said it first, somehow it would make his admission easier.

His head lifted.

"I thought you were unconscious."

"I saw the wound, later. Doctor Marchand said he'd been shot with a rifle, not a pistol." She clenched her fists, hating this conversation but knowing that it had to be finished. "It wasn't your fault. It was dark and snowy, and you were hurt. Anyone could have missed."

"I did not miss. I know it would have been more useful to incapacitate him, but... as you said, the conditions were poor, and I was injured. I had to aim for his chest to be sure I'd stop him in time."

"You— you *aimed* for his chest?"

"It was the safest choice, under the circumstances."

"*Rikard's* chest?"

"He shot Petre. I heard it as I stepped into the clearing. Then he turned and pointed his rifle at you."

Taya couldn't speak, aghast.

"I had to make a split-second decision. I shot to kill. I apologize. We would have learned more if we could have questioned him."

"Oh, Lady...."

"I assume Petre confronted my nephew about his actions in the clearing."

"But...."

"In the last few hours I have examined my memory of the accident very carefully." Amcathra's voice was heavy. "My nephew

left the dining room car before the exalted joined us. I did not
see him again until I saw him pointing his rifle at you. He was
wearing gloves, a hat, a scarf— garments he would not have been
wearing had he been inside a passenger car during the crash.
But they would have been necessary had he been on top of the
car, manipulating the emergency brake to cause the derailment."

Taya remembered the sound of footsteps pounding on the
roof of the car, and snowflakes on Rikard's coat.

"W... when he came in, he was shouting, 'where is the exalted?'" she said, dully. "He grabbed me and pushed me against
the side of the car. I thought— I don't know what he was doing.
He might have been threatening me. Or he might have been
trying to protect me."

"I searched him while you were flying to the station." Amcathra
reached into his coat pocket and pulled out a battered, leather-
bound notebook with his free hand. "Among other things, this
contains notes on the aerostat's security rotation and an address
for the bookseller's hotel."

"Then he...."

"I still do not understand why he sought to kill the exalted,
or why he failed to do so. Perhaps he was hoping to be stopped.
This last-ditch effort strikes me as a final act of desperation."

Taya sank into the nearest chair, her hands pressed against
her stomach. Amcathra offered her the notebook. She ignored it.

"I'm sorry," she said at last, as he lowered his hand. "This
must be terrible for you."

"The apology is mine, Icarus. You and the exalted have the
right to hold my family in blood-guilt for my nephew's attacks."
He spoke as calmly as though he were discussing the weather.
"By Demican tradition, the matter would be settled during the
cremation. However, we do not know when that will occur, so
you may wish to demand recompense now."

"Blood-guilt?" Taya fought to keep her own voice under control;
to emulate Lieutenant Amcathra's impassive manner. "There's
no blood-guilt. You *killed* him. You killed your own nephew to
protect me. How in the Lady's name could I consider you guilty
of anything?"

"You are not viewing the situation like a Demican."

"That's because I'm not Demican! And neither are you. Or
Rikard. Why should *any* of us care about Demican customs?"

"Not everyone who accepts Ondinium's mark upon his face has accepted Ondinium's mark upon his spirit. Otherwise, my nephew would never have dared turn his hand against an exalted."

"*You're* loyal to Ondinium, aren't you?"

Amcathra stiffened. "Of course."

Of course. She rubbed her face, thinking about Rikard. Their only real conversation had been the one over tea, where he'd both expressed his dislike for Ondinium and his admiration for his uncle.

"Did you know he got himself tattooed like you?"

"He was a lictor."

"No, I don't mean the castemark. The bear. He didn't want me to tell you about it. I think he did it to be like you."

Amcathra was silent, his face blank.

"It was a compliment," she added, hoping she hadn't upset him.

"He was working for the Alzanans," Amcathra said at last. "If he belonged to the *sheytatangri*, he must have been working for the Alzanans. I would have been told if he had been working for the Council."

Taya knew that *tangri* referred to a Demican religious or philosophical organization, but...

"*Sheyta*'s not the Demican word for bear," she said, confused. "What does it mean?"

"Self-governance." He considered. "Autonomy."

"I don't— doesn't Demicus already practice self-governance?"

"The *sheytatangri* consider their country under occupation by Alzanan and Ondinium colonists. They seek to drive out foreigners and return Demicus to a state of cultural purity."

"That sounds like something Rikard might have supported, but why would he work for the Alzanans?"

"The Alzanans have been known to provide weapons and financial support to extremist groups who oppose Ondinium." Amcathra's blue eyes were impassive. "Just as they support terrorist groups within Ondinium itself."

"Is that tattoo some kind of sign, then?"

"Yes."

She stared. He gave a slight nod, acknowledging the silent question.

"I joined the *sheytatangri* on a special assignment for the Council. My actions were such that the *tangri* now considers me a sympathizer within the lictor caste. I do what I can to keep the Council apprised of its actions."

"*Are* you a sympathizer? I'm not questioning your loyalty," she hastened to add, "just your personal beliefs."

"I believe it would be in Demicus' best interest to protect its people and resources against foreign exploitation. However, I do not believe that will be possible unless the clans unite into a cohesive political unit."

"That would require an enormous cultural shift, wouldn't it?"

"Yes. 'Demicus' as a nation is a foreign construct, not a native concept."

"You know a lot about it."

"I had to learn much Demican history to infiltrate the *sheytatangri*." He hesitated. "I did not know my nephew was a member. Nobody in the tangri told me."

Taya bit her lip, remembering Rikard's assertion that he would make his uncle proud of him. Had he thought his uncle was a secret nationalist?

"If he was working for the Alzanans, he was probably taking orders from the Mazzolettis." She remembered the argument between Gaio Mazzoletti and Rikard. Had they really been arguing about an accidental bump in the hall, or had their argument been about something far more serious? Rikard had warned her about Gaio. Had his warning carried a deeper meaning than she'd realized at the time?

She felt a weight around her heart, wondering if things might have gone differently if only she'd pushed the young man harder, demanded more answers.

"Are you going to be all right?" she asked at last, looking up at the lieutenant. Speaking of people who needed to be pushed.... "I mean, really?"

"I did what had to be done."

And *that* was why she couldn't give him Alister's punch cards. Because Amcathra would always do what had to be done, regardless of the consequences.

"We'll talk about my returning to Ondinium tomorrow," she said, standing. As she passed him, she laid a hand on his forearm. "Let's both get some rest."

He didn't move from the window as she walked over to her cot and laid down.

Chapter Twelve

TAYA PACED BACK and forth down the narrow aisle of empty seats. The train rocked as it hurtled down the tracks at top speed, making her stumble and catch herself on the back of a seat, but she was possessed by a restlessness that wouldn't let her sit.

She fished out her husband's heavy, well-worn gold watch and opened it. 7:33 p.m. The hands on its pearlescent gray face had barely moved since the last time she'd checked. She held it to her ear to reassure herself that it was still ticking. The steady sound was barely audible over the rattle and creak of the car around her.

Her own watch, with a wing engraved on its cover and a ruby heart on its face, was sitting next to Cristof's bed back in Overlook. Lieutenant Amcathra had promised to keep it wound until her husband could wind it himself.

A bright light flashed in the dark window. Taya peered out. A long string of generator-powered lamps lit the tracks as they entered a zone of illumination that stretched to the horizon, then rose into the sky as far as she could see. The first set of lights demarcated the city of Safira, which housed O-Base-0, the railway terminus. The towering mountain of lights beyond Safira was Ondinium, the capital, glowing with life and industry even at this time of night.

At last! She checked the watch again. One minute closer. They were on time, scheduled to arrive at eight. She continued pacing, stopping every few seconds to look out the window again.

She'd been on the train almost fifty hours. The express consisted of one engine, two fuel tenders, and her car, and it had rumbled through the mountains as fast as it could, its path cleared by signals flashing ahead of it. Every water stop had grated on her nerves, and she'd had to restrain herself from strapping on her armature and leaping out to fly ahead— a ridiculous proposition, because the train traveled much faster than she could.

Still, the sooner she wrapped up her business in Ondinium, the sooner she could rejoin Cristof.

The train had no sooner stopped in a burst of released steam than Taya wrestled open the doors and jumped out. She dropped her case of counterweights on the platform and began strapping on her armature as engineers and train crew hurried past her, securing the vehicle. Clouds of steam and ash drifted around her, giving the chilly night scene a ghostly air.

"Taya Icarus?"

A lictor was jogging toward her. She waved and finished pulling on her wings, locking them high.

"Your identification, please." The lictor halted in front of her as she slid counterweights into her flight suit pockets. She pulled out her wallet. He checked her papers, studied her, then nodded and handed the wallet back. "I have documents clearing you for a night flight into Ondinium. You're to report to Decatur Constante's estate immediately. Do you need directions?"

"No." Taya had spent most of her life working as a courier; she'd visited all Ondinium's exalted houses at one time or another. She took the flight clearance form and tucked it next to her identification papers.

"I know you're in a hurry, but we have hot tea and sandwiches in the station office if you need to eat before you leave."

"I'd rather go now, thanks." She snapped the counterweight case shut. "Will you hold this for me? I'll send for it later or pick it up on my way back."

"Not a problem. There's a flight tower on the east side of the station. Have you flown from O-Base-0 before?"

"Not at night."

"We keep a clear airspace corridor from the flight tower to the Great Gates. After you reach the Gates, it's business as usual. That form clears you straight up to Primus; we'll signal the stations and sector gates to expect your flyover. Average flight time to the city is about twenty to thirty minutes. The weather's cold but clear; snow on the ground but nothing in the air."

"Thank you." Taya bowed, then turned and thanked the engineers and crew for the speedy trip, forcing herself to smile and let them touch her wings for luck even though she was itching to go.

At last she hurried through the station to climb up the flight tower. She took a moment on the launch dock to stretch her legs and arms, feeling pathetically out of shape. Then she buckled on her leather flight cap, adjusted her goggles, waved to the guard, and hurled herself into the cold night air.

For a moment she dropped through the winter night, and then she tucked her ankles into the armature's tailset and snapped out her metal wings. The lighter-than-air feathers caught the air on a downstroke and lifted her over the train station's bright lights. Warm currents rose from the station's steam generators and busy junction. She eased herself higher.

The armature had been repaired and oiled by the Overlook eyrie, and even though it pressed against bruises and stiff muscles, Taya relaxed for what felt like the first time in days. Cold air numbed her nose as she flew over Safira's busy streets, crowded with citizens and foreigners. Uncurtained windows and streetlights provided her with plenty of illumination, and Safira didn't have the high-standing towers and suspended cables that posed such a threat in the capital.

Within minutes she shot past the town's outskirts. From Safira, a well-maintained road led through the next twenty-five miles of steep foothills to Ondinium's Great Gates.

Unfamiliar air currents and breezes forced Taya to concentrate. She wasn't accustomed to nightflights, and even with the lictor's assurance that no manufactory towers or stray cables crossed the approved flight corridor, her eyes automatically scanned the horizon, checking for obstacles as she sped over the winding road. Lights glowed from the windows of the guard stations that were set up every five miles. Once she saw a lictor standing outside his station who looked up and waved. She rocked her wings back and forth and kept going. After a moment, she realized she was smiling, and with that realization, the smile faded.

Yes, it felt good to be back in the air again. And to be home again, for that matter. But Cristof was two days away in the Overlook hospital, and until he was well, she couldn't remain happy.

Several miles later, she entered the sprawl of manufactories that covered Tertius with a haze of foul-smelling smoke and ash. Even in this cold weather, the familiar, choking scent of coal smoke lingered in the air. Had it gotten worse, or was she just unaccustomed to it after spending so much time in Mareaux? The air there had been fresh and clear.

The Great Gates of Ondinium weren't real gates anymore, since the city's industries had long since sprawled past Ondinium's ancient protective walls to create a labyrinth of high-walled manufactories and storage yards. However, the Gates marked the formal entry point into the capital, where travelers queued up to show identification before being allowed inside. Regular lictor patrols did their best to keep undocumented visitors out of the city's lowest sector, Tertius, with a limited degree of success. Entrance into the city's two higher sectors, Secundus and Primus, was more difficult— there, the city walls and gates remained intact and were consistently monitored and reinforced.

Taya dropped lower as the Gates' vast stone and iron frontage came into view, prepared to land if challenged. But the relay signal must have come through; she was given a "clear to pass" flag by the lictor on top of the wall. She wing-saluted and entered the city.

Close attention became necessary as she worked her way up the steep and endless urban sprawl that covered the mountain, its airspace broken by clocktowers and smokestacks and wireferry cabling. City-maintained streetlights lit the main thoroughfares, and hand-held lanterns bobbed through lesser streets. The lights helped her keep her mental map of the city aligned with the dark reality below her.

She flew past Tertius into the better-ordered Secundus, where the University towers beckoned. Kyle Deuse and his programming team worked there. She was tempted to stop to see if they were working late and give them Alister's cards, but the decatur had demanded her immediate presence, and she didn't dare disobey.

Cristof kept assuring her that the Council wouldn't ground an exalted's wife, but Taya wasn't so certain. Her husband might be exalted, but he was also a caste renegade and a traitor's brother; Taya was afraid that if either of them caused trouble, the Council's reaction would be swift and ruthless.

So she bypassed the University and continued to Primus, where exalteds' estates perched like eagles' nests on the top of a cliff. House Forlore's estate was there, and so was House Constante's, about a half-mile away.

Taya slowed, circled, and backbeat to an awkward, slippery stop in the icy street. The lictor at the Constante gate straightened but didn't reach for his weapon.

"Name?"

"Taya Icarus," she said, locking her wings high and sliding her arms free. She was exhausted. It had been too long since she'd flown regularly.

"The decatur's expecting you."

"Thanks." She pulled her goggles down around her neck and peeled off her leather helmet. Icy air chilled the sweat on her face as she ran her fingers through her hair. Pointless, she decided. After a fifty-hour train ride and a half-hour flight, she had no prayer of looking presentable.

The lictor unlocked the gate and swung it open.

"Straight through, knock on the front door."

"Thank you."

Ten minutes later she stood in Decatur Evadare Constante's warm, firelit study, her armature left in the hallway and her cold face thawing. A servant brought in a pitcher of water and a glass, and Taya drank as the decatur opened a leather portfolio and uncapped a bottle of ink.

"Thank you, Exalted." Taya set the glass down.

"Sit down, Icarus— you must be exhausted." Constante gestured to a chair and Taya gratefully sat. The muscles in her arms, shoulders, and legs had started to twitch and ping from the unaccustomed exercise. "How is Exalted Forlore?"

Not 'Cristof,' Taya noted, and not 'your husband.'

"He was hit by a pane of glass when the train derailed. The doctors at Outlook stitched his wounds, but they say he lost a lot of blood. When I left, he was still spending most of the time asleep." Taya reached into a leg pocket and pulled out the folded report Dr. Placius had sent with her. The ondium counterweights she hadn't removed from her suit tugged against the fabric. "This is the doctor's statement." She handed it over.

Constante opened it and read, squinting and holding the paper close to her face.

Taya didn't know Decatur Constante very well. In her seventies, she was one of the older members of the Council. Her face was creased with wrinkles and her hair was even shorter than Taya's, mostly white with a few lingering streaks of gray. She would wear a wig in public; most exalteds did, once they started going gray. It would be unthinkable for an exalted to show signs of aging to the lower castes.

Constante was conservative, leaning toward the System Analyst credo— a stance of respectful caution toward the technological advances that drove so much of Ondinium's progress. She likely disapproved of such things as cross-caste marriages.

Taya decided to be circumspect.

The decatur set down the report and looked up. "You must be rather concerned about him."

Or maybe she had Constante all wrong.

"I am, Exalted."

"Yet you returned to Ondinium, regardless?"

"Lieutenant Amcathra and I believe the derailment was another attempt on Cris— the ambassador's life. I have the lieutenant's and stationmaster's reports." She pulled those folded sheaves of paper out of her other flight suit pockets and handed them to the decatur.

"Very good." Constante reached over and pulled a cord. A few moments later, a dedicate appeared in the doorway of her study.

"Please take the icarus to the kitchen and see she has something to eat and drink," the decatur directed. "I shall ring for her soon."

"Yes, Exalted."

Taya rose, aware that she was being dismissed but not certain whether it was an insult or the decatur's normal manner. She gave a stiff bow, aching all over, and followed the dedicate out.

Most of House Constante's staff had retired for the evening, so Taya sat in the kitchen with the dedicate who'd led her there and the sub-chef on night duty. They shared a small meal and a pot of tea. After a few false starts, the conversation landed on the tepid but safe subject of Mareaux. Taya did her best to distract them with observations about a country whose culture revolved around agriculture rather than manufacturing while they did their best to appear interested. Constante's summons came as a relief to all three.

"Thank you for delivering these reports, Icarus," the decatur said briskly, standing by her desk as Taya entered and bowed. "Council will discuss them tomorrow. I assure you that Ondinium takes threats to its ambassadors very seriously. You will remain in the city awaiting our summons. You plan to stay at House Forlore?"

Where else? Taya wondered with a flash of irritation.

"Yes, although I have some errands to run tomorrow."

"Be certain your staff knows where to find you. The Council has been doing its utmost to contain the information about this crash and the incidents in Mareaux. I would appreciate your discretion, as well. I understand that you may feel obliged to discuss the details with Forlore's cousin, Viera Octavus. That is acceptable, but please impress upon her the Council's desire to keep the news out of the press."

"Viera understands Council business."

"Yes, she does. Good evening, Icarus."

"Good evening, Exalted." Taya bowed again and left, pulling on her armature on the way out of the house. Another brusque dismissal. Was the Council upset with her for some reason? Had she and Cris made a mistake somewhere along the line— in leaving Mareaux early, perhaps, or in sending the mercates home separately? In trusting Rikard?

Lost in thought, she walked through the broad streets back to House Forlore, her wings rattling in the cold breeze.

"Taya!" Their housekeeper, Mitta, met her at the door and swept her up into a hug. "Taya, how is he?"

"He's all right; he's going to be all right," Taya said, hugging the tall, angular woman back. Mitta helped her out of her armature with practiced ease. "How did you—" She spotted the other two armatures floating in a corner a moment before she finished the question.

"She has friends in high places," a familiar voice replied. Taya was engulfed in another hug, this time with her two best friends.

"Cassi! Pyke! How did *you* know I was back? What are you doing here?"

"Waiting for you." Cassi stepped back and cupped Taya's face, looking serious. "We heard you were in an accident. You look terrible."

"Lady!" Pyke scowled, one hand resting on the metal bars over her shoulder as he studied her. "You're bruised black and blue."

"Is it that bad?" Taya touched her face. She hadn't looked into a mirror since she'd arrived at the hospital.

"You look like you were in a bar fight," Cassi said.

"And lost," Pyke added. "Is that all from the crash?"

"It's supposed to be a secret." Taya looked from one expectant face to the other. "The decaturs are trying to keep it contained."

"It hasn't been in the papers, but I've got friends who monitor luxographs," Pyke said. "We were worried about you."

"As soon as Pyke heard your train was coming in, we hurried over," Cassi said, squeezing her hand.

"You can't tell anyone about this."

"We won't," Pyke promised. Taya shot him a look. "Really!"

"Why don't you talk in the parlor?" Mitta suggested, catching Taya's floating armature and slipping it over its stand by the door.

"You'd better join us, too, Mitta," Taya said. "You can decide how much to tell the rest of the staff."

"Give me a few minutes, then?" Mitta asked.

Pyke and Cassi already had drinks, but Mitta returned with the hot, spiced wine that Taya always enjoyed after a cold night out. Taya wrapped her fingers around her favorite mug and sank into her favorite chair, her eyes alighting on Cristof's collection of clocks lining the mantelpiece.

Home at last.

She took a deep breath and burst into tears.

It took her a few minutes to get control of herself again, held tight in Cassi's arms. Eight minutes, according to the clocks, which would be flawlessly accurate because Cristof had made them.

But at last she rubbed her eyes, blew her nose, and told the whole story, from the fire on the dirigible to the poisoned wine and fruit to the train wreck. She left out the shootings at the end. She wasn't ready to talk about Rikard and Lieutenant Amcathra yet.

"But the exalted will be all right?" Mitta asked, looking anxious.

Taya gazed at the dregs of her spiced wine.

"He'll have a few scars, the doctor said. But they're taking good care of him."

"Well, that's okay." Cassi reached over and patted her arm. "Some scars will make that gawky old gearhead look distinguished."

Taya gave her friend a half-hearted smile. She didn't care about the scars. She just wanted to be back in Overlook, watching over her husband while he slept.

"He needs to come home as soon as he can," Mitta said. "We'll take care of him here. An exalted belongs in his House, not out in the wild with a bunch of strangers, isn't that right?"

"Lieutenant Amcathra said he'd bring Cris back as soon as he can," Taya said, reassuring herself as much as Mitta.

The clocks chimed eleven, filling the first floor with noise. Pyke stood.

"We'll, you look beat. We should let you get some sleep."

"Wait— who told you I was on that train?" Taya asked.

"A mutual friend from Inquiry and Liberation," Pyke said, winking. "He's been keeping us updated on all the 'graphs about the exalted."

"You two are going to get yourself arrested." Taya pulled herself to her feet and groaned. Every part of her body hurt. "I'm glad you came. Do you want to stay over?"

"Nope; got work tomorrow." Cassi hopped to her feet and gave Taya another hug. "Now, get some rest and don't worry about anything. Cabisi for dinner tomorrow? That place by the university?"

"Sounds great. I might bring Kyle and the rest by, too."

"Perfect."

They said their farewells and Taya dragged herself upstairs, pulling off her flight suit and collapsing into bed in her underwear. She slid a hand over the empty side of the mattress where Cristof usually laid. Feeling a painful tightness in her chest, she sat up and fished her suit off the floor.

Cristof's watch was still ticking in its pocket. She pulled it out, wound it up, and curled under the covers, holding it in one hand.

It took a while, but the steady ticking eventually lulled her to sleep.

Chapter Thirteen

ALISTER FORLORE'S FORMER programming team still worked in one of the sub-basements of Ondinium University's Science & Technology building, surrounded by walls of clicking and hissing steam-powered analytical engines. Taya descended the stairs expecting to hear the usual voices, but all she heard was machinery. Wondering if she'd beaten the team to the office, she peered inside.

All four team members were sitting quietly around a cluttered wooden table. Kyle and Lars were punching cards while Victor and Isobel studied a map.

"Hello?" Taya ventured.

"Taya!" Isobel straightened and turned. While everyone else was pushing his chair back, she strode up and grasped Taya's arm. "It's so good to see you!"

Before she could answer, Lars shouldered Isobel aside. He grabbed Taya and lifted her, wings and all, into a giant bear hug.

"Welcome back," the big man exclaimed, swinging her around and setting her down by the table. His normally cheerful face darkened. "Now, what's all this about train wrecks and assassination attempts?"

"Give her a chance to catch her breath," Kyle chided, reaching past Lars to clasp her hand. "Come sit down, Taya. Cassi and Pyke dropped by last night and told us what happened."

"Oh, scrap." Taya shrugged out of her armature and joined them at the table. "They promised they wouldn't tell anyone."

"We already had the basics," Victor said, leaning forward and clasping his pale, thin hands on the crumpled map. "We knew there was a train accident and the exalted was injured.

We also knew that he was in Overlook hospital and that you were returning to Ondinium by express. Cassi and Pyke simply filled in the details."

"That's all supposed to be confidential."

"It still is."

Taya made a mental note to tell Lieutenant Amcathra that the lictors had a security problem. "Are you sure? A leak could put Cris into danger again."

"If there's a leak, Taya, it won't come from us."

"Cassi and Pyke said you might be dropping by," Kyle interrupted. "Is there something we can do for you?"

"As programmers or otherwise," Victor added, stressing the last word.

Taya glanced at the doorway to make sure nobody was walking by. Isobel, noticing, stood to shut and lock the door.

"Better?"

"Thank you." Taya reached into her flight suit to pull out her identification wallet. "Cris *does* need your help."

The programmers leaned closer to hear over the clattering difference engines.

"This needs to be kept secret," she said, looking at Victor. "No Council, no lictors, no Cassi and Pyke, and none of your shady I&L friends. Do you understand?"

Victor's dark eyes gleamed with interest as he nodded.

"Is it illegal?" Lars asked, dubiously.

"No, but it could be politically sensitive."

Kyle gave her an easy smile. "Don't worry. We've been cleared for top-secret work ever since your husband got us that job on the bank's security program. We're much better at keeping secrets than Cassie and Pyke."

"Then again, who isn't?" Lars added.

"I hope so." Taya slid out the punch cards, handing them across the table to Kyle. "Can you run these and tell me what's on them?"

All four programmers leaned forward.

"Standard size." Kyle rubbed his fingers over the paper. "But it isn't Ondinium card stock."

Isobel held up one of the cards against the card Lars had been punching. "Hand-cut, not die-cut. Somebody was working under rough conditions. We'd better trim them before we run them."

"Are they from Mareaux?" Lars asked, as the group checked the edges of the new cards against Ondinium masters and shaved off the rough spots.

"I'd rather not say."

The big man shrugged. "Seems obvious, under the circumstances."

"Diplomacy and espionage," Victor said with satisfaction. "Are these cards why you're so worried about Exalted Forlore's safety?"

"Maybe."

That silenced the group. One by one they handed their cards back to Kyle, who put them into order and stood.

"All right. Let's see what's on them. If it's a program instead of data, this could take a while. And let's hope your source verified his punches before he passed them to you, or they might not run at all."

Taya pulled up her feet to the seat of her chair and rested her chin on her knees. So Victor's friends were able to intercept and decode luxograph signals. Who else was reading them? She used to think that Ondinium was an impenetrable fortress protected by the Great Engine, but over the last year she'd learned more and more about its secrets and flaws.

Her friends loaded the cards into the feeder mechanism and moved around the machine, talking about output and chirography and typebars. Taya pulled over Victor's map. She liked maps; she liked the impression they gave of looking down at the world the way she did when she was flying. It took her a minute or two of study to realize what she was looking at.

His map showed the area where the train had derailed, marked with a graphite circle. That wasn't so bad, but the symbols around it looked like the locations of Ondinium's signaling stations.

"Victor... where did you get this?"

The bearded programmer glanced over his shoulder, then turned back to the machine. The last of the cards vanished into the input tray.

"Data collection is my specialty. The information is out there, if you know how and where to look."

"But this is a security breach!"

"Not my fault if Ondinium can't protect its secrets."

"Please tell me you're reporting any security weaknesses you find."

"I report them."

"To the *government*?"

"I'm sure some of my colleagues are Council spies."

Taya shook her head, folding the map and hiding it under a stack of punch card boxes.

"I can't believe you guys let him bring this in here."

"We wanted to see the accident site," Isobel explained. "But usually we make him keep his political stuff in his own rooms."

"It's not a crime to know where Ondinium's signal stations are located," Victor objected. "It's only a crime if you tell someone else."

"Like you told us?" Lars growled. Victor spread his hands and shrugged.

"I didn't *tell* you anything. I can't help it if you know how to read a map."

With a series of clicks, a new set of cards began dropping down into a tray. Lars pulled them out and numbered them with an ink pen, then turned and fed them into another machine.

"What's that?" Taya asked.

"Readable output."

A slower tapping sound joined the cacophony. Taya turned toward a tall metal-and-wood machine on an oak table by the end of the room. A long, thin roll of paper moved through it.

"That's new, isn't it?"

"It's an automated typography machine," Kyle said, checking the paper feed. "Got the idea from the bank. The output's printed backward, but it's not hard to read, once you get used to it."

"Someday I'll fix it to print out the right way," Lars said. "I just haven't gotten around to it yet."

"If you don't hurry, somebody else will do it first," Isobel warned.

"Then it'll save me the effort."

"You need to work on your ambition."

"I don't have any ambition."

"We've noticed."

"So what does it say?" Taya asked, sliding out of the chair.

Kyle leaned over to look at the ink characters that were slowly being impressed on the paper. His eyes widened and he straightened, giving her a startled look. "It's Nutcracker Six!"

"You're slagging kidding me!" Lars burst out, his eyes going as wide as Kyle's. "He's punching *blind*?"

"Either that or he taught someone else the code."

Isobel cheered and jumped forward, hugging Lars, who was laughing with delight.

Taya had a sinking feeling that their source wasn't anonymous anymore.

"Nutcracker Six," Victor announced, pulling a battered paper-bound volume from a shelf on the other side of the room. He came back and dropped it on the typography machine's table. It was a ten-year-old, dog-eared copy of *The Indices of Physical Output for Mining, Manufacture, and Agriculture, Southeastern Region*. Somebody had scrawled a big black 6 across the front cover and on the spine.

Taya turned and saw that the shelf contained a line of beaten-up volumes, their spines marked 1 to 10.

"All right," she asked, grimly. "What's Nutcracker Six?"

"A book cipher we worked up several years ago," Victor said with satisfaction. "'Nutcracker' as in 'this code is a tough nut to crack,' and numbered to correspond with whatever volume we used as a codebook. To keep it secure, we selected ephemera— incredibly dull reports with small print runs and specialized audiences, likely to be thrown away after a year or two."

"Alister enjoyed cryptography," Isobel added. "We created the ciphers more for the fun of it than anything else."

"So how is he?" Lars asked, eagerly. "Is he living in Mareaux? Is he doing all right?"

Taya rubbed her forehead. Of course they'd guessed. They'd worked with Alister for years before he'd self-destructed and become a murdering Eugenicist.

Sometimes she wondered if she was the only one who remembered the "murdering Eugenicist" part.

"Could we please avoid using his name?" she asked plain-tively. "If the Council finds out he's punching cards, they'll kill him, and that would make Cris very unhappy."

The four programmers glanced at each other, sobering.

"Anyway, we never saw him," she said. Her mind flew back to the rainy day with Rikard when she'd seen a blind man being led down the street.

Rikard had searched for the blind man a long time before returning to her. Why? Had the Alzanans asked him to be on the lookout for a blind exalted?

She thrust the memory aside.

"He sent us the cards by messenger," she said. "We don't *really* know who they're from. There's no name on them, is there?"

"No...." Lars murmured, glancing at *The Indices*.

"All right, then. It's still an anonymous source."

"Once we're sure the data's been transcribed, you can burn the cards," Kyle said. "If you want to be safe."

"Wait," Victor objected. "Don't burn them; leave them with us or hide them someplace safe. Just in case."

"In case of what?" Isobel demanded.

"In case the anonymous source who punched them ever needs to prove he's still serving the state." Victor looked around the table. "In case the Oporphyr Council ever suspected him of breaking the conditions of his exile, for example."

Taya understood. One thing she had to admire about Victor; he always planned for the worst.

"Let's see what he has to say."

The printout took time to run, and the team took more time to decode it. Taya left to go to the icarus central post office and deliver a letter from Lieutenant Amcathra to his sister. When she returned, the team had translated the mechanically printed numbers on the long strip of paper into a set of neatly handwritten pages. Lars was blotting the last page as she pulled off her armature.

"Interesting stuff," Kyle said as she joined them at the table. "Al— your *source* says military supplies are being shipped from a major corporation in Ondinium to another major corporation in Alzana through front companies: old shelf corporations legitimately established in Mareaux but sold to unnamed investors. It's a way of hiding the transaction from auditors. However, he managed to track the account numbers back to the Bank of Ondinium."

"Whatever's being sold must violate Ondinium's trade restrictions," Victor clarified. "You wouldn't build that much deniability around a legal interaction."

"Firearms?" Taya guessed. Laws strictly controlled the export of munitions and technology.

"The shipments are listed as raw material — sheet metal, cabling, things like that — but you can never tell what's really behind a bill of lading."

Taya skimmed over the notes, penned in a neat, miniscule handwriting that didn't suit Lars' size. Most of it was a list of account numbers, sums, and deposit/withdrawal records.

"But we still don't know who's behind it?"

"You'd need to get access to the bank's financial records if you want that information," Kyle said.

"If I gave this to the Council, they could get the records."

"Assuming none of the decaturs are affiliated with the corporation involved in the scheme," Victor pointed out. "And assuming you don't mind answering questions about how you obtained the information."

"Actually, we're a little curious about that ourselves," Isobel admitted. "It's hard to imagine any bank hiring— well, an exile."

"Plus, there's the question of how he could use the *Indices* as his codebook if he's blind," Lars grumbled. "He must have someone else working with him."

"Look, Taya, we can get you this information," Kyle said. "But we'll need a few days to get into the bank's system."

"How?"

"We can say we found a problem in one of the lines of code we wrote last summer and need to correct it. Standard maintenance, but we'll want to check all the records for the last few months to see whether any of transactions were affected. That'll allow us to cross-reference these account numbers for you."

"You'd be violating security."

"We'd be giving you a single name to help you track down a major corporation that's engaging in illegal trade with Alzana. We talked it over while you were gone, and none of us have any ethical problem with that."

"*But* you have to promise to report it to the authorities if it checks out," Lars added. He raised a hand as Taya started to speak. "I know you will, but I want to be sure, okay? I don't like shady stuff. It's bad enough to find out that Alister's punching again. I'm only letting it slide because it sounds like he's doing it for a good cause."

"I told you, if you want to take your holiday while we do this, nobody will blame you," Kyle said, earnestly. "I'm not going ask you to do anything that makes you uncomfortable."

"Since when?" Lars shot his friend a dry look. Kyle coughed, looking away.

"Ask you *professionally*," Isobel clarified, deadpan.

"I agree to your terms, Lars," Taya said, quickly.

"Then give us some time to get this worked out," Kyle said. "We'll send a memo expressing a slight concern with some of the code we wrote, and then another memo the next day that's worded a little more strongly, and then we'll recommend they let us come in to run the repaired program."

"Is this going to be bad for your reputation?"

"We'll make it something minor; a tiny glitch that doesn't make any difference in the short run but could add up to a serious imbalance over a year or two."

"A problem calculating interest," Isobel suggested. "Something that would ultimately cost the bank money; they'll be in more of a hurry to let us fix it, then."

"Will you be safe?"

"There's no risk involved at all," Kyle assured her.

"I mean— we think someone tried to kill Cris to get this information. Having it could put you in danger."

"Nobody will ever know," Kyle assured her.

"I've heard that before," Lars muttered.

"They'll know I visited you," Taya objected.

"If anyone asks, we'll say your housekeeper showed you some problems in the Forlore accounts," Isobel suggested. "You asked us to double-check the numbers, since we're friends, and that's how we figured out there's an accounting glitch in the bank program."

"Nice." Victor nodded with approval.

"We were worried because our accounts were earning too much interest?" Taya asked, skeptically.

"Just another example of our exalteds' scrupulous honesty." Victor smirked.

"All right. I'll make sure Mitta is in on the plan. But if the bank docks any of Cris's savings as an adjustment...."

Kyle laughed. "We won't let that happen."

"Please don't. It's not my money." Taya handed the papers back. "I have to make some visits today — Viera, my father, my sister — but maybe we can get together for dinner tonight? Cassi and Pyke wanted Cabisi."

"Sounds good," Kyle said with a smile. "We'll draft up the first memo and send it to the bank this afternoon."

CHAPTER FOURTEEN

TWO DAYS LATER, Taya stood on the Safira train platform again, shivering in the icy morning air. She held the Council's orders in one gloved hand, waiting for somebody to question her presence, but nobody gave her more than a passing glance.

The Council had contacted her the same day she'd given the punch cards to Kyle and his team: *The ambassador will be on the next train from Overlook.*

Exalted Constante had told her more when Taya had arrived on her doorstep biting back frustration and fretting about her husband's health.

"The Council wishes to talk to the ambassador and Lieutenant Amcathra," Constante had said, standing in the foyer of her mansion as her servants adjusted her robes and waited with her ivory mask. "We saw no point in leaving them in a relatively unprotected hospital when we can bring them here to the safety of the capital."

"Is he well enough to travel?"

"He is receiving the best care possible, under the circumstances. Now, if you will excuse me, I have a full day of meetings scheduled with every Lady-blessed man or woman who has anything halfway intelligent to say about the political and diplomatic situation developing in Mareaux."

"But we don't think the assassination attempts had anything to do with Mareaux."

"Some decaturs think otherwise." Constante gestured to the dedicate holding her mask.

"Rikard was from Ondinium!" Taya protested, before freezing. Had Amcathra's report mentioned Rikard?

"But who convinced him to become an assassin while the delegation was in Mareaux?" the decatur asked, before the mask was placed over her face and her servants fastened it into place.

Of *course* Amcathra's report had mentioned Rikard. Biting back the rest of her protests, Taya bowed, her palm against her forehead, and left.

An hour later she was summoned to the Tower to fill out reports and be debriefed by her superiors in the diplomatic corps.

Jayce, Professor Dautry, and the rest of the delegation had arrived in Ondinium the next day with Macerain's corpse. They'd heard rumors about the accident, and Taya's appearance did nothing to reassure them. She dutifully refrained from answering their alarmed queries, though she expected they'd learn the truth soon enough.

A whistle announced the incoming train. Taya's heart leaped as the engine rumbled past, followed by a long line of passenger and baggage cars. She hurried to the back of the platform as the train's brakes screeched and displaced air rattled her metal wings. Red-coated porters paced the cars as the train ground to a halt. More whistles blew, and they threw open the doors and pulled down the folding steps with a loud clatter.

Taya stopped at the last car, waiting as people surged off the rest of the train, shouting and waving and manhandling their luggage.

Nobody opened the door.

Taya was about to go in when a window slid down and Lieutenant Amcathra leaned out.

"We will wait until the platform is emptier," he said, his pale blue eyes sweeping past her to inspect the platform. "Does anybody know he is here?"

"Just the Council. I have the paperwork to get you through security." Taya handed the folded sheet of paper through the window. He perused it.

"No names. Good. I have disguised him. Nobody will know he has returned until he is safely in Primus."

"Is he all right?" All Taya could see in the window was the station's reflection in the glass.

"Yes. Do not greet him until we are alone."

"Lieutenant!" she protested, but Amcathra slid up the window, cutting her off. She muttered a rude word and strode away from the train, turning and folding her arms over her chest.

Twenty minutes later, most of the crowd had dissipated. Amcathra stepped out with his rifle nestled in the crook of one arm. He wasn't carrying a cane, she noted, and the cuts and bruises on his face, like the ones on hers, were healing. The gash on his forehead was going to leave a scar.

He looked around, nodded to her, and turned. Cristof slowly, carefully descended the steps, his long hair disheveled as it hung around his face. He was dressed in a laborer's rough clothing and wore manacles on his wrists.

Taya muffled a distressed sound as her husband lifted his head and squinted. His wave-shaped castemarks had been cosmetically hidden, replaced with an operate's hook and circle. Still-healing scrapes and wounds covered his bruised face, the stitches raw and visible to the world. He wasn't wearing his glasses, and his pale grey eyes passed over her without any sign of recognition.

"Come," Amcathra said, keeping his free hand locked high on Cristof's upper arm. They walked forward at a measured pace. Taya realized the lictor was supporting her husband in the guise of holding him captive. "Icarus, our bags are by our seats."

Cristof stopped and turned, squinting in her direction.

"Keep moving," Amcathra growled, jerking the disguised exalted forward. Cristof stumbled and closed his mouth on whatever he'd been about to say.

"I'll be with you in a minute," Taya promised, locking her wings in tight. She squirmed through the narrow car door, grabbed the two leather cases and the cane that sat there, and hurried back out. Amcathra's ramrod-straight, black-uniformed back was easy to follow. He paused to sling his rifle over his shoulder and present the Council's pass to the lictors at the end of the platform. When he gestured, Taya hurried forward to join them.

"A carriage is waiting for the— for the lieutenant," she said. The lictors waved them through, and a few minutes later they stood outside the station in a gentle snowfall. Taya scrambled on top of the coach and pulled off her armature, securing it to the roof with Amcathra's and Cristof's luggage. The driver, an old friend of hers, tugged the leather straps and nodded with approval.

She slid into the coach and slammed the door as Amcathra dropped the curtains over the windows.

"Cris! Are you all right?"

"Taya." Her husband smiled and Taya threw her arms around him. "Oof. Ouch. Wait. Let me get out of these cuffs so I can hug you back."

"Sorry— can't wait." She squeezed him again, more gently this time, and leaned back to study his bruised face. Stitches closed a deep cut over his left eye, and a raw but healing scar broke the concealed castemark on his left cheek. "You look terrible. How are you feeling?"

"Terrible. Janos is very sparing with the morphine."

"It is healthier for you to feel pain and keep a clear head." Lieutenant Amcathra slid Cristof's glasses from his coat pocket and handed them to Taya, who eased them onto her husband's nose as the lictor unlocked the manacles. They fell away with a clatter.

"There." Cristof reached up and brushed snow-dampened hair away from Taya's face, still smiling. "It's good to see you again." His fingertips caressed her face, tracing the areas where her own bruises were the same blotchy shade of yellow and green as his. The edges of a bandage were visible under his shirt cuff. She started to ask, but he leaned forward and kissed her, and she decided her questions could wait.

On the other seat, Amcathra slid the manacles into his overcoat pocket as the coach shuddered and began to move. He set his rifle on the floor between their feet and cleared his throat.

Taya ended the kiss with reluctance. Cristof's smile faded as he adjusted his fogged glasses.

"How soon does the Council want to see me?" he asked, leaning gingerly back in the seat.

"Now." Taya studied him, noting all the signs of exhaustion and pain he was trying to hide. "But I think they'll let you get washed and changed, first."

"What have you discovered about the secret sales to the Alzanans?" Amcathra asked, bluntly.

"We're— I'm still tracking down the accounts," she said, evasively. "I need a little more time."

"What is being traded?"

"Metal and machine parts, according to the bills of lading. No weapons, analytical engines, or other proscribed technologies. At least, not officially. So there's nothing to tell the Council yet."

Amcathra gave her an oblique look. "Then I will say nothing about it today."

"Thank you."

Cristof usually abhorred the wireferry, and today Taya was none too happy about riding it, either. The suspended car rocked back and forth in the gusty winter winds as it creaked and groaned up to Oporphyr Tower, which sat on the rocky, wind-scoured top of Ondinium Mountain. The wireferry's cables were new, replaced last year after they'd been sabotaged, but Taya couldn't help but remember the accident that had killed Viera's husband.

On the other hand, Cristof, for the first time ever, seemed oblivious to the ride. Washed and changed, his castemarks visible once more, he sat in the middle of the car with his eyes closed and his head thrown back against the seat-rest.

It wasn't a good sign, Taya thought, when her husband's exhaustion overcame his fear of heights.

The wireferry stopped inside a sheltered part of the tower, and lictors escorted them to the Council chamber.

Taya had only been in the vast circular room once before, when she and Cristof had broken in last year. Her eyes strayed to the oak panel that hid the tunnel to the center of the mountain. If she hadn't known it was there, she'd never suspect.

Then she squared her shoulders and moved closer to her husband, who walked to the head of the table and stopped.

The lictors closed the chamber doors. The ten motionless decaturs seated around the table stirred at last, removing their ivory masks and placing them face-down in front of them. A few shrugged out of their heavy public robes while others only opened them and folded back their overlong sleeves. Murmurs arose as they took a closer look at Cristof's battered face.

"A chair for the ambassador," one of the decaturs said, just as Taya was opening her mouth to make the same suggestion.

The Council clerk, a highly ranked dedicate licensed to gaze upon the unmasked Council, brought a chair from the side of the room. Cristof sat with obvious relief. Nobody offered Taya a place to sit.

Irritated, she stepped next to Cristof and rested a hand on the top of his chair to remind them of who she was.

Although she didn't really think they'd forgotten. That was the problem.

"How are you feeling, Cristof?" asked one of the older decaturs, a man Taya had been introduced to a year ago at a ball.

"Like I was in a train wreck and then dragged halfway across the country," Cristof said. "You could have permitted me a few more days to recover, Attelus."

The decatur sighed and tugged on the collar of one of his inner robes.

"We could have, but we needed to talk to you before word of your arrival spread. You left Mareaux in something of a mess. Their ambassador has written us several messages inquiring about your health and requesting a meeting to discuss the diplomatic relations between our countries." Attelus sighed. "Apparently he's heard rumors that Ondinium plans to declare war on Mareaux. And he doesn't even know about the derailment yet."

"We *assume* he doesn't know," another decatur murmured.

"Nobody threatened war," Taya said, defensively. "In fact, we made it clear that we were leaving for security reasons, not out of fear or anger."

"What you said and what the Mareaux believe are not necessarily the same thing, Icarus," Constante pointed out. "The ambassador's precipitous departure—"

"Was Lieutenant Amcathra's idea!" Taya protested. "And as I understand it, he takes his orders from you."

"Taya...." Cristof half-turned and gave her a pointed look over the top of his wire-rimmed spectacles. "Let me annoy the Council. They're used to it, and there isn't much they can do about it anymore."

She resisted a moment before giving in with a brusque, unhappy nod. He was right. The Council could confiscate her wings. It couldn't confiscate Cristof's birthright. At least, not without a great deal of unpleasant publicity in a city that had recently hailed the eccentric exalted as a hero.

"We've already received Lieutenant Amcathra's preliminary report," Constante said. Amcathra must have headed straight to the tower after they'd parted, Taya thought. "Now we'd like to hear your version of events, Cristof."

Her husband described what had happened, from the dirigible incident to the poisoning to what he remembered of the derailment. He sidestepped the issue of who was in the dirigible's gondola. Taya wondered if Amcathra had confessed to wearing an exalted's robes during the disastrous flight. None of the decaturs questioned Cristof's version, so she supposed not.

Perhaps the lieutenant didn't feel obliged to reveal secrets that carried the death penalty.

Or, she thought with a touch of penitence, perhaps he just didn't feel obliged to reveal secrets that weren't threats to Ondinium's security.

The decaturs grilled Cristof about his responses to the dirigible crash and the poisoning, what he said to the queen when he pulled the diplomatic party out of Mareaux, his relationship with Rikard, and a multitude of other issues. The questioning seemed endless, and Taya watched her husband with concern, knowing how much he was holding back and seeing the effort it took him. As an hour passed, his answers became more strained, and his copper complexion grew gray and damp with perspiration.

"Excuse me," she interrupted at last. She leaned over the chair, blocking the decaturs' sight, and lowered her voice to a murmur. "I brought the lancet and bottle. Do you need it?"

A muscle in his cheek twitched as he met her eyes. He nodded. "Please, yes."

She spun and glowered at the assembly.

"My husband's injuries are hurting him. If you'll excuse us, I'm going to give him an injection for the pain and take him out of here."

The decaturs began to speak all at once. Constante rapped on the table with her knuckles.

"We shall take a short break," she said, "so that you may administer the exalted's medication. However, we're not through questioning him yet."

"I think we are," Taya shot back. Cristof reached out and touched her arm, and she shook him off. "If you have more questions, send someone to talk to him tomorrow, while he's at home resting."

"The icarus is right," one of the decaturs said, giving her a kind nod. "Let Forlore rest. We have sufficient information to discuss the matter amongst ourselves."

"But we need to resolve this political tension with Mareaux as soon as possible," another objected. "Before the Alzanans step in and take advantage of it!"

"We don't need Forlore here for that," another argued. "He's not important anymore."

"Well, *somebody* thinks he's important, or they wouldn't have gone through so much effort to kill him…."

"He's here now."

"For the Lady's sake, the assassin was one of our own lictors! We have no idea how far this corruption extends."

"The report said he was a Demican nationalist."

"Enough! Enough!" Constante's voice rose over the disagreement. "Council, that will be enough!"

Taya stood in front of her husband, her fists clenched, waiting for the decaturs to quiet down. Exalted Constante glanced at her, then looked around the table.

"It is obvious that we still have a great deal to discuss," she said, her voice cold. "Perhaps a closed session would be best, after all. Exalted Forlore, Icarus, thank you for your time. We will be in touch."

"Thank you, Decaturs," Cristof said, standing and putting a hand on Taya's shoulder. She started to step aside, then stopped as she felt his fingers dig into her shoulder for support. "You know where to find us."

As soon as they returned to the wireferry, Taya administered the injection.

"So," Cristof said, closing his eyes. "Do you think they've finally realized that I'm a terrible choice as an ambassador?"

Taya brushed a strand of black hair away from the stitches in his bruised forehead. He was sweating, and his color was ghastly.

"As long as I'm in the diplomatic corps, you're stuck with the job."

He opened his eyes, looking strained. "Does that make you the important one, then?"

"You know, they seemed so *polite* when I met them at Viera's party last year."

"That was before you married the caste's most excruciating embarrassment."

"Shh; stop that," Taya scolded.

Lieutenant Amcathra joined them as the ferry car arrived.

"Exalted. Icarus." His pale blue eyes flickered over Cristof, and he took her husband's arm. "You have given him another shot?"

"He needed it. Have you been here long?"

"I reported to the Council before you arrived." He guided Cristof to a seat in the center of the wireferry car.

"Are you in as much trouble as we are?"

"The decaturs are not pleased that my nephew was a political rebel and would-be assassin."

"What are they going to do to you?"

"I have been chastised."

"Good thing I didn't mention that you impersonated me on the dirigible," Cristof said, leaning back. "They might have slapped your hand. How did you manage to make yourself the Council's pet, Janos?"

"I serve to the best of my ability."

"Even if it means omitting information from your reports? We're corrupting him, Taya."

Amcathra gave the exalted a disapproving look. "I am giving you an opportunity to gather enough evidence to support your speculation. Your fieldwork was always slow, Exalted Forlore."

CHAPTER FIFTEEN

TAYA WAS BUTTERING her second scone by the time Cristof dragged himself into the breakfast room, dressed but looking groggy.

"Good morning," she said, setting her book aside and reaching for the teapot. She poured him a cup. "How are you feeling?"

"Tired." He tilted up his glasses to rub his eyes, careful not to touch the stitches and bruised areas. "But I'm going to try to make it without any painkillers today." He eased into a chair and reached for the cup and saucer. "Thank—" he froze, his eyes glued to the book in front of her. "What's that?"

Taya fought back a smile.

"*Mrs. Melham's Advice for the Care of Infants*. Ann recommended it when she came by to repair your wig."

The color drained from his face. He set down his cup and saucer.

"Why are you reading it?"

She considered her options and decided to be merciful. He wasn't well, after all.

"My sister's pregnant. The baby's due in another five months. I'll fly the book down to her later today, if I have time."

Her husband exhaled with relief. "Thank the Lady."

"I'll let her know you were overjoyed on her behalf," Taya said, dryly.

"Yes. Delighted. This will make, what, the fifth little annoyance we'll have rampaging through the house whenever you invite your friends and family over?"

"The baby isn't even born yet," she pointed out. "Much less rampaging. And you shouldn't call children 'annoyances.'"

"I don't call them that to their faces."

"Yes, you do."

"Did Mitta put out any lemon?"

"Here." She handed him the plate, smiling to herself. Eventually, Cris would have to get over his aversion to perpetuating the family line. She wasn't in any hurry to have children, either, but she didn't expect them to beat the odds forever.

"Speaking of children, do you know about Amcathra's niece? The one who's sick?"

Cristof sobered and nodded.

"A respiratory illness. I found out about her a few years ago, when Janos took time off to watch her while his sister was sick."

"Rikard thought she'd be better off in Demicus. I think… I think that may have been why he did what he did. To earn the money to take her there."

"From what I understand, it wouldn't help. The damage to her lungs is irreversible. Poor Janos… I wonder what he told his sister? This can't be easy on him." Cristof raked a hand through his hair. "I told him there wasn't any blood debt between us. I understand you did the same."

"Of course."

"Good." He frowned. "Although I might have felt differently if Rikard had shot you."

Taya waved his words away. "Is there anything we can do for the girl?"

"I can talk to Janos about it, but he's a proud man. I don't think he'll accept our help."

Taya thought it might be better for the lieutenant if someone circumvented his pride for a change, but this wasn't the time for it. He and his family were going to need time to come to grips with their loss and the scandal, first.

"The newspapers have discovered that you're back in town," she said, drawing his attention to the paper and stack of mail by his arm. He settled back and began to read, frowning. Taya returned to her book, looking forward to visiting her sister Katerin and brother-in-law Tomas. She couldn't wait to be an aunt.

"The reporters are saying I was wounded in Mareaux," Cristof said at last, folding the paper and setting it aside. "The Council won't be happy about that."

"They'll probably leak the truth about the derailment by this evening's edition," Taya predicted.

"The reporters will stake out the sector gates," her husband muttered, picking up his mail and a butter knife. "I won't be able to leave Primus for days."

"Good. You need the rest. There's a letter opener on the tray."

"Redundant technology," he scoffed, using the butter knife to slit open an envelope. He favored his bandaged left hand. Taya hoped it would heal well.

He glanced at the page and then refolded it, sliding it back into the envelope and setting it to one side.

"Now you have grease on your letter," she observed.

He nodded absently and opened a black-bordered envelope.

"Macerain's cremation is in two days."

"We should both go."

He nodded and opened the third letter, glanced at it, and handed it across the table.

"This one's for you, love."

Taya took it. Professor Dautry had invited the exalted to take an aerostat ride with her. *I promise this trip will be uneventful*, she'd written on the bottom.

"Oh, no. It's definitely for you."

"I'm recovering. And avoiding reporters."

"You *are* recovering. But I don't think any reporters will be lurking around the sector gate at five in the morning."

"Five?"

"Best time for a flight." She tapped the invitation on the table, thinking.

"No."

"If the Council's that worried about our diplomatic relations with Mareaux, taking a balloon ride with Mareaux's newest representative would be good press."

"Taya. I'll get sick."

"We'll feed you a light dinner and make you skip breakfast. Just like the last time we flew."

"That—" he flushed. "That was an emergency."

"So is this, diplomatically speaking." She propped the invitation on the teapot, facing him. "Think about it, ambassador. The flight's tomorrow morning."

She left Cris at the breakfast table with his stack of correspondence and journals and flew down to visit her sister in Tertius, then the dispatch station on Secundus. All of her old colleagues had read the newspaper article, and she dutifully reassured them that Cristof's injuries hadn't been received at the hands of a Mareaux assassin. Knowing her friends, the news would be all over the city by the end of the day. Maybe she'd save the decaturs' press liaison some effort.

When she returned home, she found Cristof sitting in his workshop, leaning over a bright red cloth covered with gears and springs.

"Making another watch?"

He turned, flipping up a magnifying lens on a headpiece covered with lenses.

"Just killing time."

"That's a bad thing for a clockwright to do." She walked across the crowded room and kissed him. "And that's an extraordinarily ridiculous piece of equipment you're wearing."

"It's not ridiculous; it's useful. Look." He fanned the lenses over his head with obvious pleasure. "Five levels of magnification and an extra arm to hold any standard loupe."

"Oh. It's *new.*"

"An engineer I know on Tertius sent it to me. Mitta left the package on my bench." He took one of his watchmaker's loupes and screwed it into the headpiece's ring, then flipped it up and down to demonstrate. The magnifying lens made the cuts and bruises around his eye stand out. "Ingenious, isn't it? He even built in extra space allowance for my glasses."

"Uh-huh." Taya bit her tongue. *It's taking his mind off his injuries,* she counseled herself. *And you knew what you were getting into when you married him.* "Too bad there aren't any compartments on the head strap for all your little picks and screwdrivers."

"It's more useful to keep my tools on the bench," he said, seriously.

"Well, then." She looked down at the watch parts to hide her amusement. "It's nice to see you tinkering again."

"Given the way things are working out, I thought it might be expedient to brush off my old skills."

"The Council can't blame you for being attacked. Besides, there's plenty of diplomatic work you can do right here in the capital. Like being seen in public with a visiting scientist from Mareaux."

"Yes, yes," he said, flipping the loop back up over his head. "I've already accepted the professor's invitation."

"You have?"

"Given the choice between disagreeing with my wife or facing my most abject fear, I have, of course, chosen to face my fear."

"Oh." She feigned disappointment. "Then I guess I'll have to scrap my plan to wring a concession out of you in bed."

He glanced toward the door. "If I hurry, I can overtake the messenger, but you'll have to give me a shot of morphine before you begin wringing."

She leaned over and draped her arms around his neck.

"Tell you what. I'll wring gently. But only if you take off that silly headpiece."

Winter mornings were bitter and cold in Ondinium. Taya and Cristof were bundled up as they crossed the University quad to the inflating silk envelope of the Mareaux aerostat. It was a very small dirigible, compared to the queen's; little more than a balloon with an engine and propellers. Professor Dautry waved, and the man next to her turned.

"You're right." Cristof muttered as he lifted a hand. "Apparently this is business, after all."

The Mareaux ambassador to Ondinium, Lord Andrieu Courtenay, walked over, pulling off his hat and gloves. Silver-haired and tall, he fit Taya's conception of aristocracy much better than had the short and tubby Lord Pomeroy, or the motherly Queen Iancais. Of course, it was possible that Lord Courtenay's physical resemblance to an exalted was why he'd been assigned to Ondinium. He didn't wear robes, but he'd let his silver hair grow much longer than most men wore it in Mareaux, and his waistcoats were cut rather longer than the Mareaux norm.

"Exalted Forlore," he said, bowing in the Ondinium style. Taya saw him scan the stitches and bruises on Cristof's face, though he kept his expression politely neutral.

"Lord Courtenay." Cristof offered his uninjured right hand, Mareaux-style. They shook. "Are you interested in the professor's new anemometer, too?"

"It's always a pleasant surprise when Mareaux has technology to share with Ondinium, instead of the other way around," Courtenay replied amiably. He turned to Taya. "It's good to see you again, Taya Icarus."

"Likewise, ambassador." Since a Mareaux curtsey would look ridiculous in her winter-weight flight suit and armature, she held out her hand and shook, as well.

As Lord Courtenay and her husband chatted about inconsequentials, Taya slipped away to watch the aerostat crew — volunteers from the University — ready the dirigible.

"Did you invite the ambassador?" she asked Dautry, when the woman finally paused to greet her.

"I mentioned that you two might join me this morning, and he invited himself. I hope that's not a problem."

"No, it's probably for the best. If you don't mind, I'm going to free-fly, rather than join you in the basket."

"Gondola. That's fine. This is the smallest, safest aerostat I brought; I thought that after everything the exalted has been through, he might appreciate a gentle ride. We can take the big 'stat up another time. Lord Courtenay told me about the derailment, by the way."

"We were lucky."

"I'm glad." Dautry raised her eyes to the ondium wings that curved over Taya's head. "Tell me, is there any chance I could try one of your armatures?"

"The eyrie keeps a spare set of wings especially for guests. I'm sure I can arrange a flight for you, if you'd like."

"I would."

"I'll look into it." Taya looked around. "The weather seems good."

"I'm told we won't get any snow today, and I've been studying the local wind currents. My plan is to take the ambassadors on a short hop to Gryngoth Plaza."

Taya mentally reviewed the flight path. The route would avoid wireferry lines and most other obstacles.

"Good choice. The plaza's by the sector edge, though, and there's always an updraft from Tertius along the cliff. Try to land on the University side of the statue, if you can clear enough space."

Dautry nodded and moved off to talk to her assistants.

Soon the dirigible was ready, and half its ground crew headed to the plaza. Cristof joined Dautry and the ambassador in the gondola, looking resigned. She gave him a thumbs-up and a reassuring smile, then pulled on her flight cap and goggles. With a shudder, he turned to face the ambassador, keeping his back to the open air.

Deciding he'd manage, Taya headed off to climb the University flight tower.

The dirigible's ascent was slow. She waited until it had cleared the rooftops before she leaped from the metal dock and spread her wings. The wind was freezing, and as she kicked out the tailset and slid her ankles over the bar, she tilted toward the Science & Technology building. The updraft from its subbasement steam engines provided a welcome gust of warm air. She rode it in a circling glide before beating forward to join the balloon.

Taya made long, easy arcs around the aerostat as it flew over the University campus, rocking her wings in salute when Dautry and Courtenay waved to her. Cristof didn't wave. His hands were locked on the sides of the gondola.

The balloon's passage drew all kinds of attention, and the streets and windows were crowded with gawkers craning their necks to watch the vehicle's flight over their sector. The balloon slowly passed over the markets and gradually descended into Gryngoth Plaza, where young crewmembers grabbed its dangling ropes and hauled it to a bumping stop.

Taya made an awkward, swooping landing on the low wall that ringed the crowded Plaza. Onlookers backed out of range of her sweeping metal wings, providing enough space for her to hop down to the cobblestone plaza. She locked her wings, pushed up her goggles, and worked her way through the mob to the aerostat.

Cristof looked well as he stood by the balloon with the Mareaux ambassador. She slipped past Professor Dautry, who was answering questions from the crowd, and slipped her gloved hand into her husband's.

"Good flight?" she asked, as he turned.

"Not bad," he said, leaning over to kiss her. "It doesn't rock as much as a wireferry."

"That's because we move with the wind, instead of against it," Professor Dautry explained, turning. "Even people who are afraid of heights often find dirigible travel comfortable."

"How remarkable," Cristof replied, neutrally.

They stayed until the University crew broke down the dirigible, then walked back to the University together, surrounded by enthusiastic onlookers and persistent newspaper reporters. The ambassadors provided the press with reassuring statements about the mutual goodwill between Ondinium and Mareaux until chartered carriages arrived to take them home.

"I've set out a late breakfast," Mitta greeted them as Taya pulled off her armature and Cristof stripped out of his winter gear. "Pyke brought your mail this morning and said you had an important letter. I put it on top of the pile, if that suits you?"

"Thank you," Taya said, sliding her armature over its stand and hurrying to the breakfast room in her flight suit. Cristof reached the letter first, slitting the envelope open and shaking out the page inside. Taya pressed close to read it over his arm.

The unsigned sheet contained the same long list of account numbers that had been sent on the punch cards. But now each account number, deposit, and withdrawal was linked to a business name and a list of goods, and somebody had drawn a series of brackets and arrows connecting each of them. And at the top of them all— Allied Metals & Extraction.

"Patrice Corundel," Taya whispered, the name coming out with more vitriol than she'd intended.

Lieutenant Amcathra set the letter down on the low table between their chairs and leaned back. His black castemark looked like a shadow in the gaslit room. They'd sent him a note as soon as they'd read the letter, but he hadn't been able to join them until after dinner, showing up in full uniform, as always.

"This is suggestive," he said. "It is not conclusive."

"I know." Cristof leaned forward and tapped the abbreviations next to the lists of goods. "Most of these deliveries originate from AME's Hamet-Benoit storage yard in Engels. I want to take a look at its files. There should be documentation — inventories, bills of lading, receipts — that we can check against the record of deposits. If there's a reasonable match, we can open an inquiry."

"If Allied Metals & Extraction hired Rikard to kill you, then it already considers you a threat," Amcathra said. "Do you think you will find anything if you visit the facility?"

"Not if they know I'm coming."

"You disguised Cris once already," Taya said, trying to read the lieutenant's stony expression. "Can you do it again? Can you get us into the yard without anybody knowing?"

"I presume you are not ready to present your suspicions to the Council?"

"No, not yet," Taya replied. "For one thing, most of the decaturs have some kind of investment in the Big Three or their affiliates. If we tell the Council, AME might hear about it and start burning files."

Amcathra's pale eyebrows twitched, but he didn't try to defend the decaturs' integrity. They all knew far too well that Ondinium's loyalty program, Refinery, wasn't perfect.

"If you wish to travel unobserved, you should not go by train. However, I do not believe the exalted is fit to hike across the mountains or don an armature for another unauthorized flight."

"No," Cristof agreed. "But the exalted believes he can obtain permission for a cross-country dirigible flight in the interest of a joint Ondinium-Mareaux scientific experiment."

"You are prepared to fly in an aerostat across miles of wilderness in the middle of the winter, with a foreigner, in order to break into a Big Three storage yard unobserved?"

"The thought had occurred to me."

"With all due respect, Exalted, the idea is ludicrous."

"Ludicrous?" Cristof scowled and pushed up his glasses. "Why?"

"It's not that far," Taya added, grabbing the folded map that she and Cristof had been poring over earlier. She spread it on the table. Their proposed flight path was marked in graphite. "Only fourteen hours, if the wind's with us, and it should be."

"How will you return?"

"The train runs to Engel, here." She pointed. "And the yard's right about here." She pointed again. "So, Professor Dautry lands outside of Engel and we cut north to the yard while she goes into town, hires some operates to pack her aerostat back to the station, and catches the next train to the capital. Once we're done looking around, we'll do the same."

"You would need to present your papers once you arrived at the Safira station."

"Of course, but we wouldn't need any identification to catch the train at Engel. We can fake our castemarks to look like two operates heading to the city on break and then wipe them off before we get to Safira."

"Counterfeiting a castemark is illegal," Amcathra retorted. "And the storage yard will be fenced and guarded."

"It won't be the first time I've had to break and enter as part of an ongoing investigation," Cristof said.

"The last time you did so without a license, Exalted, you were nearly arrested."

"Granted." Taya's husband pulled off his glasses and began to polish them with his handkerchief. "But that was a long time ago. And this time I'll have Taya to watch my back."

"Is this the story you promised to tell me later, Lieutenant?" Taya asked.

"*Much* later," Cristof said, firmly.

"Moreover," Amcathra continued, "what if you are attacked? You are in no shape to run or fight, and while I am aware that your wife is adept with her knife, a blade is little defense against a firearm."

"We'll try to avoid men with guns," Cristof said, his voice starting to gain an edge.

"The idea is ludicrous," the lictor repeated. "You will need me to travel with you."

Taya's heart leaped, but Cristof shook his head.

"That's not why we invited you here, Janos."

"Perhaps not, but considering the flimsiness of your plan, it is the inevitable result. I must either stop you or accompany you, and an illegal trade agreement with Alzana is too important to dismiss without thorough investigation."

"But we're going to... it's likely we'll end up breaking some laws during the investigation," Taya protested. She dearly wanted Amcathra's company, but she understood why Cristof was protesting.

We're corrupting him, her husband had said.

"I am certain you will break fewer laws if I am there to supervise your actions." Amcathra glanced at the clock on the mantelpiece. "Have you spoken to the Mareaux professor about this yet?"

"No...."

"Then you have much preparation to do. I recommend you carry it out with the greatest possible discretion."

"We will, but we're going to have to get clearance for the flight," Taya said. "We don't want to get shot down by a patrol."

"Submit your flight request to me, and I will see that it remains secure." Lieutenant Amcathra stood. "Good evening, Exalted. Icarus."

"You don't have to do this, you know," Cristof said, standing with him. "We just wanted to keep you up to date on our plans, not make you an accessory."

"When the Council hears of your proposed flight, it will ask me to accompany you, anyway."

"The Council doesn't need to keep making you my nursemaid," Cristof grumbled.

"I am accustomed to the role. There is no reason to escort me out."

Taya waited until Lieutenant Amcathra's footsteps faded down the hall before giving her husband a speculative look.

"What do you think?" she asked.

"I think," Cristof said, sitting again, "that he likes the plan."

CHAPTER SIXTEEN

"ARE ONDINIUMS ALWAYS subject to a military invasion of their privacy?" Professor Dautry asked, her voice chilly, as they floated over the northeastern industrial sector of Tertius. She hadn't been pleased when Amcathra had announced his intention to search everything on the dirigible an hour before launch, even though he'd found nothing incriminating in her bags. Cristof's bag, however, had contained a needle pistol that Lieutenant Amcathra had sternly unloaded before returning.

"Innocent people have nothing to hide," Amcathra replied, holding his rifle muzzle-down as he gazed out over the city. "If I had searched my lictors' possessions more closely in Mareaux, much trouble might have been avoided."

"You could have confined your search to the bundles that were vulnerable to outside tampering. Or were you afraid my undergarments might be explosive?"

"I have assured myself they are not."

Taya shot the lictor a glance, wondering if he were deliberately provoking the professor. Dautry looked similarly uncertain, her eyes narrowing as she split her attention between the argument and the demands of navigation.

"And what about your own weapon? Are you an exception to Ondinium's law?"

"Not in this case." The lictor unloaded the magazine and released the compressed gas from the cylinder.

"Wait!" Taya protested. "I thought one of the reasons you were coming with us was because *we* couldn't use a gun."

"I can use a rifle," Professor Dautry objected. "I used to hunt quail with my brother."

"I mean, you and I are forbidden to use guns, and Cristof shouldn't use one until his arm heals."

"I understand why *I* might be forbidden to carry a rifle in Ondinium," Dautry said, puzzled, "but why are you?"

"Icarii aren't allowed to carry firearms. We're not even supposed to touch them."

"Ah... it's part of your infamous ban against airborne weapons," Dautry said with comprehension. "I thought all those papers I had to sign for this flight were because I'm from Mareaux, but it's really because Ondinium suffers from a deep, institutionalized fear of attack, isn't it?"

Taya bridled.

"Ondinium is not afraid of being attacked," Amcathra said before she could reply. "It is afraid of being defeated."

Cristof cleared his throat.

"It's afraid of being *destroyed*," he corrected. "As it nearly was in the Last War. I presume you know our history, Professor Dautry."

"Everybody knows about the fall of the Ondinium Empire, but those were ancient times, Exalted."

Cristof nodded. He'd stationed himself with his back to the open air and kept his eyes fixed on their faces.

"Ancient but not forgotten. The Empire was forced to retreat to the most defensible territory in its possession. Ondinium is completely landlocked here. No rivers run from one side of the country to the other or from the border to the capital, which protects us from a naval attack. And the capital is surrounded by steep mountains with narrow passes, so invading infantry or cavalry would have to be willing to suffer an extraordinarily high casualty rate before they could have any hope of defeating us."

"But an invading *aerial* force...." Dautry said, nodding.

"Exactly. It was an aerial force that nearly destroyed the capital despite all its other precautions. So one of the Council's first actions during the Virtuous Reclamation was to forbid the export of ondium and the manufacture of aircraft such as this. We believe combatants should face each other on equal terms; it's the only way to keep war from becoming slaughter. Attacking helpless victims from above is morally indefensible, so we prohibit the creation of aerostats and we forbid icarii to bear arms."

"And yet, here we are," the professor said, gesturing.

"And yet here we are," Cristof agreed, declining to glance in the direction of her hands. "The Council can control technological development within its own borders, but it can't control what happens in other countries. Hot air balloons didn't worry us, but load-carrying dirigibles are a significant threat."

Taya rested her forearms on the gondola's edge and gazed at the sooty, smoke-covered streets, factories, and wireferry towers that slowly passed below them. If a terrorist group like the Torn Cards were to drop its bombs on the city from this height....

It was a sobering thought.

"And what will Ondinium do if it decides Mareaux's dirigibles endanger its safety?" Dautry asked, sounding uneasy.

"Reconsider its defenses," Amcathra replied.

"It wouldn't start manufacturing dirigibles of its own?"

"Never," Cristof said, firmly. "The prohibition against airborne weaponry has existed for centuries. Airborne vehicles of war are abhorrent to our culture."

"I suspect, Exalted, that if Ondinium truly felt its safety were in danger, it would find some way to reconcile itself to its abhorrence," Dautry replied. "Human nature is very adaptable."

Taya decided the conversation was entering dangerous territory and touched the professor's arm, pointing over the side.

"Have you been to Oporphyr Tower, where the Council sits?" she asked. Of course Dautry hadn't been permitted there, but her reply gave Taya an opening to point out the city's major features. Cristof, still attempting to conceal his fear of heights, buried his nose in one of his new journals while Dautry and Amcathra listened to Taya's tour.

They passed the northern gates and the ring of factories, warehouses, and storage yards that covered the snow-laden foothills. The temperature plummeted, and all four pulled on hats and scarves. Dautry and Cristof amused themselves for some time checking the aerostat's instrumentation and comparing their results with those of other documented flights. Taya wondered how long it would take before Cristof thought to mount some of those dials and meters onto her armature, and whether she'd be able to stop him.

"There." Amcathra pointed a black-gloved finger toward a valley beyond the pass. A glittering blue-and-white lake filled most of it, its banks cluttered with sawmills and reservoirs. "That is Menoth Lake, Professor."

"It's very pretty," Dautry said, politely.

"It is named after the lictor who commanded a fort on that site. The fort stood on a cliff overlooking the surrounding hills before it was blown into a crater by an ondium-hulled aerostat."

"Did you study military history, Janos?" Cristof asked, gazing toward the lake as he pulled off his glasses one-handed and made a show of polishing them against his coat front. Taya smiled. He couldn't see a thing without them.

"I wrote a thesis about Captain Menoth in officer training."

Taya perked up. Amcathra revealed so little about himself that even this morsel seemed like a major revelation. "Why?"

"I wanted to develop a strategy that would have saved him and the fort. However, after I studied the battle, I realized that his situation was hopeless." Amcathra looked out at the lake. "The most effective defense against an attack from the air is a defense in the air."

"Which your country refuses to pursue," Dautry said, dryly.

"So you understand our concern, Professor," Cristof said, turning and sliding his glasses back on again. "Unfortunately, it's a very short technological leap from a research vessel like this to a war ship like the kind that nearly destroyed Ondinium."

The air grew even colder as the early winter night fell. Dautry brought the dirigible lower, hanging lanterns over the sides and keeping the maneuvering poles close to hand. They had planned to sleep in shifts, but the bitter chill made sleep impossible. Taya was glad she could press close to Cristof. She pitied Amcathra and the professor, neither of whom seemed inclined to share more than the most unavoidable physical contact with each other.

Hour after miserable hour passed, broken only by flurries of activity when they scraped too close to a tree or had to ease the dirigible around an unexpected outcrop of rock. Around midnight Amcathra passed around a thickly insulated container of lukewarm tea. Taya drank sparingly, preferring to avoid peeing over the side of an aerostat even in the relative privacy of darkness. She passed the container to her husband. Lucky men.

Finally, she spotted a glimmer of light against the horizon.

"There." Her voice sounded loud in the silence that had fallen over the small group. "Is that Engel?"

Everyone roused. Cristof pulled a spyglass from his bag. The eyepiece clinked against his glasses as he focused.

"It must be. I see a dark line running up to what looks like two or three lanterns, or maybe streetlights— probably the train tracks and platform."

Each of them studied the lights until they agreed that they were drawing close to the station. Taya checked her watch: 1:48 in the morning.

"Take us east," Amcathra ordered, extinguishing all but one of the lanterns. The last one he adjusted until only a narrow, focused beam of light streamed from between its shutters. Dautry steered the dirigible away from town and cut the engines.

They began their descent quietly and cautiously. Amcathra held the lantern and whispered terse instructions, a better aerial navigator than Taya would have expected, while she and Cristof leaned out the doors using their poles to guide the aerostat between the trees.

At last they reached a small clearing. Dautry eased the aerostat to a landing. Amcathra and Taya both leaped out, staggered, and hauled the vehicle closer to the trees.

"Thank the Lady." Cristof stepped down more cautiously and crouched, planting his hands firmly on the snowy ground. "Next time, I'll steer and the professor can hang out the door."

"Pretty good flying, Exalted," Taya said, crouching next to him and wrapping her arms around his neck. He looked up and kissed her, the cold rims of his spectacles making her shiver.

"Remember our first flight?" he asked, his forehead against hers. She grinned and kissed him again.

"Are we fogging up your glasses yet?"

"Naturally." He straightened them and squinted through the clouded lenses. "And just like last time, we have too much to do to sit here dawdling."

"Oh, is 'dawdling' what you call it now? You're getting complacent, married man."

"You are both dawdling," Amcathra grumbled. He'd spread out their map on a bush and was checking a compass while Professor Dautry sorted through their gear. "Do whatever needs to be done to officially terminate this scientific excursion, Exalted."

They jotted notes in the trip log and set up the professor's camp in short order. Dautry would, they'd agreed, remain there until morning. If they had returned by then, they would help her break camp and carry everything to the station; if for any reason they hadn't, she'd set out for Engel herself and hire laborers to carry everything back for her. Dautry confirmed that she was carrying her identification and flight clearance papers and enough money to cover any foreseeable problems.

"Just tell me again there aren't any wolves or bears out here," she said, looking around with a grimace.

"Wild animals seldom approach towns," Amcathra said as he pumped up and loaded his air rifle again. "Keep your food hanging in the tree until morning, however."

"I don't suppose you'd leave me your gun."

"No." He slung it over his shoulder. "You have nothing to fear, Professor."

"We should be back before morning, anyway," Taya assured her.

"Well, good hunting, or whatever you're up to." Dautry ducked into her canvas tent. Taya envied her, wishing she could curl up in a warm sleeping bag, too. Instead, she finished fastening the last buckles on her armature and picked up a lantern.

CHAPTER SEVENTEEN

LIEUTENANT AMCATHRA WAS, without a doubt, the quietest and fastest of them in the forest. Taya's short height and small build was ideal for an icarus but left her floundering in the snow and struggling to keep up with the two taller men, and Cristof would never be accused of being naturally athletic.

Taya had hoped that her armature and counterweights would help on the hike, but her wings kept snagging on underbrush and low-hanging tree branches, and stray twigs insinuated themselves with uncanny ease between the leather straps of her armature. Despite the night's bitter cold, it didn't take long before she was sweating.

The shipping yard fence seemed to rise up from nowhere, a tall, solid wooden wall with the name and logo of Allied Metals & Extraction stenciled every ten feet. The ground around it had been cleared of trees, but snow had blown up hard against the barrier.

"We should move to a side where the snow has not drifted," Amcathra advised. "Those mounds will not support our weight."

"I can fly over the wall and scout," Taya volunteered, ready to shake the snow off her boots. "I don't see much light coming over the fence."

"Which means you won't be able to see any cables or chimneys in your way, either," Cristof objected.

"You will scout soon, Icarus." Amcathra stood. "Come."

He led them around a corner of the fence to a side that was clearer and gestured for them to wait. His lantern was soon a small, flickering light in the woods paralleling the fence.

"How are you feeling?" Taya whispered, watching Cristof wince as he slid his pack off his right shoulder.

"I'd rather be in a warm bed."

"Maybe you should rest here while Amcathra and I look around."

"Tch." He pushed up his glasses. "You need me to figure out what's being shipped— the two of you wouldn't know a crank shaft from a cam stack."

"And that will undoubtedly be the key to the conspiracy."

"There's no use searching for prohibited trade goods if you don't know what they look like. Do we have any more tea?"

"We drank it all while we were setting up camp."

"Janos is a lousy quartermaster."

"I'm sure AME has a stove and kettle. Have him brew you up a fresh cup while you rummage through the filing cabinets."

"There is no gate on this side," Amcathra reported with satisfaction when he rejoined them. "I did not see any sign of a patrol, either."

"Then it's my turn to take a look around." Taya strode out to the cleared area before the fence. Amcathra and Cristof set their lanterns down along her path as she strapped on her cap and pulled down her goggles.

The air was dead, which meant she needed a running start. She pulled lead weights from her belt until the ondium counterweights were lifting her off her feet. Then she slid her arms into the armature and sprinted.

Unfolding her wings, Taya beat down and forward. Several steps and two hops later she was aloft, beating hard to gain altitude while she kicked down her tailset. She wobbled as she rose over the trees. *About three pounds too light*, she estimated, turning to ride the wind.

Behind her, the men hooded the lanterns, leaving only the smallest glimmer of light to mark their position. Ahead of her, most of the freight yard was dark, too. A light by the fenceline indicated a gate, and more light glowed from a door in a long, narrow building. It was the shed where the AME's freight cars were stored, she guessed from the line of tracks that led inside. The company spur would connect to the main railway line, which would be convenient for smugglers. The railway inspectors couldn't search cars stored in a private railyard.

She circled, looking for a guard. Another building off to the side was lit up, and she could smell the smoke and feel the heat rising from its chimney. Some kind of barracks, she guessed, or maybe the hut where the watchmen stayed warm at night.

Taya ascended high enough to spot her companions' glint of light. Using it as her beacon, she landed on the inside of the fence, her backbeating raising a small snowstorm that caked her goggles. She pushed them up onto her flight cap and pulled her rescue rope free, missing twice before she managed to get one end over the top of the tall fence.

Within minutes, Amcathra was dropping into the snow in front of her, taking the weight of the landing on his good leg. Cristof awkwardly straddled the top of the fence, holding the second lantern. The lictor reached up and took it, then stepped aside. Taya winced as her husband swung his other leg over the fence, teetered, and pushed off, his knees buckling when he landed.

She darted forward, but Amcathra was already there, grasping the exalted's backpack strap to steady him.

"My glasses...." Cristof's gloved hand patted the snow. Taya saw a glint of silver in the lamplight and grabbed it.

"I've got them."

"Are you all right?" Amcathra hauled the exalted to his feet.

"I'm fine," Cristof said, irritably. "Let me go. You're the one who sprained his ankle." He squinted. "Taya?"

"Here." She handed him his glasses. "We should have counterweighted you."

"I said I'm fine." He rubbed his lenses on the front of his coat, which did nothing to clear them. Frustration darkened his expression. "Scrap!"

"Allow me, Exalted." Amcathra took the spectacles and dried them on the end of his black, military-issue scarf. "Did you find the office, Icarus?"

"Yes, I think so." She pointed left. "There's a door over there, across from the warehouse. If we cut northwest through the train shed, it looks like the main office is at the front of the yard, not too far from the big gate on the tracks."

Cristof put his glasses back on and picked up his lantern. The narrow beam of light shined off the snow, a pale track between the two buildings on either side of them.

"How many guards are there?" he asked.

"I didn't see anyone walking around, but I heard voices in the little hut over there," she pointed southwest, "and there are lights in the train shed."

"Wait here." Amcathra left his lantern with them and walked to the train shed door, his dark uniform vanishing in the shadows.

Taya laid a hand on Cristof's forearm.

"I'm all right," he snapped, pulling away.

You're tired and cold and in pain, she thought, trying not to feel stung by his rejection. *And it's making you cranky*. But there was nothing either of them could do about it, and pointing it out wasn't going to improve matters.

She had a hypodermic needle and the leftover morphine tucked into one of her flight suit pockets. As soon as they were back at camp, she'd give him a shot and let him sleep through the train ride home.

Amcathra returned after what felt like a very long time.

"Is anyone in there?"

"Two men are playing cards by a stove. They are not paying attention to the yard."

They skirted around the train shed. The yard between them and the fence was filled with lifting and loading equipment, a series of dark silhouettes against the snow and moon. Amcathra led them through to a small building by the gate and stopped at the door.

"Exalted."

Cristof handed the lictor his lantern and shrugged off his backpack. Amcathra turned the lantern's narrow beam on the door lock as the exalted pulled off his gloves and rummaged through the pack. In a moment he'd removed his toolkit and the ridiculous headpiece.

"No wonder your pack is so heavy," Taya muttered.

Cristof ignored her, snapping one of the lenses down and starting to work on the door with his tiny tools. He breathed on his fingers once or twice to warm them as he manipulated the tumblers, but at last the lock clicked open. He stepped back and snapped up the lens with a look of satisfaction.

Amcathra opened the door and slid inside. Taya waited behind while her husband tucked everything back into his pack.

"Does he always make you pick the locks?" she whispered, handing him his gloves.

"Not *always*."

"And did your new ... tool ... make it easier?"

"Yes." He shot her a look that dared her to say anything. Taya forbore, although it took some effort.

Inside, Amcathra set the lantern on the table, its narrow beam turned on a row of wooden filing cabinets. The dark office was cold, but not as cold as the air outside.

"You search. I will guard," he said, waving Cristof forward. The exalted laid his backpack and gloves on the table and began skimming through the files. Taya pulled up a chair and straddled it wrong-way-forward to accommodate her wings as she read over his shoulder.

For a few minutes the only sound in the office was that of drawers opening and closing and pages being flipped. Taya wanted to help, but it was a one-man job, and Cristof knew his way around business records better than she did.

"Here," he said, laying a folder on the desk. "This is a new shipment to the shell company. Will you add it to our list?"

"Sure." She leaped up, grateful to have something to do, but was stymied when she realized the ink in the bottle on the front desk had frozen solid. A bit of searching unearthed a short, paper-wrapped graphite pencil. She began copying dates, order numbers, and business names onto a blank sheet of paper.

Cristof set another file in front of her and returned the first to the cabinet. Taya worked as fast as she could with cold fingers.

"What's being shipped?" she asked as she wrote.

"Nothing prohibited." Cristof opened another folder. "But what's listed on the bill of lading isn't necessarily what's in the crates."

"Can we check the crates?"

"I hope so." He closed the folder. Taya finished writing and handed him the file she'd been copying. He put it away and opened the next. His eyes lit up. "Perfect!"

"What?"

"The next shipment to the shell corporation is scheduled for tomorrow." He reached inside his coat to check his pocket watch. "Today. In a few hours, as a matter of fact."

Taya thought of the freight cars in the shed. "Do you think it's already been loaded?"

"Almost certainly." He copied out the last entry himself. Amcathra was already slinging his rifle over his shoulder and straightening up the chairs they'd moved.

"Do not forget that there are men in the train shed," the lictor cautioned. "You must search the cars very quietly. I will keep watch and subdue the watchmen if they investigate."

Cristof nodded, putting the last folder away and closing the file cabinet. Taya picked up the list she'd drawn up, hesitated, and handed it to the lictor. Lieutenant Amcathra was the least likely to be searched if they were caught by AME's security guards.

They left the office door unlocked and retraced their route to the train shed, Amcathra in the lead. He paused by the shed, listening. Taya heard desultory conversation and the riff of cards being shuffled. The lictor moved onward, taking them to the shed's back door. Taya held her breath as they sneaked inside, expecting to be caught any moment.

Holding his lantern low, Cristof checked the labels on the crates stacked up around the rear car, then shook his head.

Amcathra pointed to himself, then to the front of the shed, and vanished around the other side of the tracks. Taya and Cristof waited for a silent count to ten, then slowly, carefully slid the metal boxcar door open. Several times it rattled and grated on the tracks, and they froze, hearts pounding. Nobody noticed, though, and at last they'd opened a gap wide enough to slip through.

Cristof entered the boxcar first, taking the lantern with him. Taya shrugged her wings back up into high position and wiggled in after him, careful to keep the tips from scraping against the top of the doorframe.

Destinations were stenciled on the sides of each wooden crate. None matched the bill of lading. Disappointed, they slid out and moved to the next car. Amcathra was nowhere to be seen, but the voices from the front hadn't changed.

The second car held the payload. Cristof set his lantern on top of a crate as Taya slipped back out into the shed to pick up a crowbar.

"I'll do it," she whispered when she returned. Cristof stepped back without a word.

His wounds must really be hurting, she thought, jimmying the flat end of the crowbar between the wooden lid and the top of the case. She leaned on the steel bar and felt her boots leave the boxcar floor.

"Scrap!" She dropped back down, scowling. Cristof gave a muffled laugh and shrugged off his backpack. He pulled out the flat lead weights she'd removed from her belt earlier.

"You shouldn't be carrying those," she hissed. No wonder he'd fallen so heavily off the fence. She fumed at Amcathra for letting her husband be so stupid.

Cristof leaned over and kissed her forehead, oblivious to her pique. Reminding herself to scold the lictor later, Taya slid the lead ingots back into her belt. This time when she leaned against the crowbar, her feet stayed on the floor. The nails squealed as they tore out of the wood and she stopped, certain that the sound must have been heard across the entire shipping yard.

Her pulse slowed when nobody shouted or came to investigate. Working more carefully, she loosened the rest of the nails in the lid. Both she and Cristof lifted it up and leaned it against another crate.

Straw rustled as her husband rummaged through it. He pulled out a piece of paper, glanced at it, and handed it to her.

"This is it," he whispered, digging in the box again. The name on the bill of parcel matched the name on the bill of lading.

So now the question was whether the crate really contained innocuous steel pipes or something more sinister.

Cristof grunted as he tried to pull a long, oilcloth-wrapped object out from under the straw. Taya tucked the bill of parcel into a pocket and helped. The inner swathes of fabric were covered with oil that left their fingers sticky.

"It *is* a pipe," Taya whispered, disappointed.

"Bring the lantern over here." Cristof tilted the tube up while Taya held the light over his shoulder. "It's rifled."

"What does that mean?" The pipe was far too big for a rifle.

"That it's the barrel to a very big weapon," he whispered. He laid it down and began rummaging through the crate again. "There are more in here."

"So they *are* selling weapons to Alzana!"

"Let's put everything back and tell Janos."

"Why do we have to put everything back?"

"We don't have a warrant."

"Scrap."

They rewrapped the pipe and replaced it under the straw. Just as they were lifting the crate lid, a whistle blew.

They froze, staring across the lid at each other.

The whistle blew again, and someone started to shout. They set the lid on top of the crate. Taya eased the boxcar door shut as Cristof covered her with his needle gun. They crouched in the darkness, holding their breath.

The shouts didn't sound alarmed, but there were a lot of them. Taya heard sliding doors being pulled open and boots striding across the wooden floor.

"Are they looking for us?" she whispered.

Cristof lowered the gun and pulled out his watch, angling it toward the lantern's glimmer of light. "Quarter past four. Too early for morning shift."

Men were approaching, their voices growing louder. Cristof hooded the lantern, plunging them into darkness. Taya backed up, trying not to stumble over anything. Her wings brushed against crates and the roof. She found a narrow gap between the crates and the metal side of the car and wedged herself in, every nerve on edge. Cristof slipped in next to her and touched her hand. She grasped it.

"It's okay," he whispered, his lips against her ear. "They can't do anything to us."

She squeezed his hand. Of course not. They might be held for questioning, but ultimately Amcathra was a lictor favored by the Council and Cristof was an exalted, with all the privileges of his birth. They'd be fine.

But getting caught would wreak havoc with their investigation. AME would have enough time to destroy the incriminating evidence and they'd lose their chance to arrest whoever was behind the illegal trade.

Workers passed by the car, their voices muffled.

As the minutes ticked by, the noise in the shed grow louder. More people were coming in, moving things, opening and closing doors. Then someone opened their boxcar door. Lantern light glowed against the sides of the crates. Taya shrank backward, holding her breath.

"There's still room in here for a few more crates," someone said.

"Headquarters says no mixing freight in the last two cars."

"Headquarters is a pain in my ass," the first person grumbled. The door slammed shut, plunging them back into the darkness. Something metallic rasped and clanked, rattled a few times, then thumped against the door.

Taya breathed a sigh of relief. "Thank the Lady!"

"Don't thank Her too fast, love. They just locked us in."

Her relief evaporated.

"Really?"

They sat, listening to the preparations outside.

"Should we pound on the door?" she ventured at last. Her husband sighed.

"We could, but… maybe this isn't such a bad situation. If we stay here, we can keep searching the crates."

"But we'll be trapped all the way to Mareaux!" She felt a burst of panic. "That's days away!"

"No, no, calm down." Cristof reached out and took her hand again. "Janos knows where we are. As soon as he hikes back to Engels, he'll send a message to have the train stopped. We won't be in here for more than a few hours. We should be back in our own bed by nightfall."

Taya took a steadying breath. Of course. Amcathra had her notes in his coat pocket; he knew exactly which train they were on and where it was going. And he wouldn't rest until he knew Cristof was safe.

"I'm starting to hate trains," she muttered, embarrassed.

"Will you be all right?" Cristof asked. "If you want, I'll pound on the door and get us out right now. It doesn't make any difference to me."

"No, I'll stay." She steeled herself. Cristof might say he didn't mind, but she knew he'd be disappointed if he couldn't catch the traitor. "At least we're out of the wind."

She wasn't certain how much time had passed before the cars began to move, but it felt like forever, sitting in the darkness trying to interpret the noises from outside. At last they heard the small steam engine that moved the cars back and forth from station to supply yard and felt a series of jolts. Taya was relieved to see dim light filter through the cracks between the boxcar door and its frame. At least when the lantern's oil ran out, they wouldn't be in the dark.

The trip along the spur didn't last very long. They braced themselves as the car was transferred from one spur to another and put in line to hook up to one of the larger trains passing through Engels.

"Well, we might as well start searching," Cristof said when everything grew still again. "It'll be easier to open the crates while the car's not moving."

Enough light seeped through the cracks for them to see the breath in front of their faces and read the marks on the crates. They doused the lantern and picked up the crowbar.

The work went slowly. Each time they pulled out a new piece of equipment, Cristof sketched it on the back of one of his scientific journals, using the pencil Taya had taken from the AME office. Finally they opened the last crate. While Cristof puzzled over its contents, Taya pulled out her watch. Seven a.m. They'd been in the Engels station two hours. How long would it take for Amcathra to hike from the AME supply yard to town? He wasn't the kind of man who'd let a sprained ankle slow him down if he needed to move quickly.

But that assumed he could get out of the yard immediately, she reminded herself. If he decided to remain hidden, it could take him a long time to slip out and back over the fence.

"Don't worry," Cristof said, glancing up at her.

"I'm not worried," she said, tucking the watch back into her flight suit. It wasn't quite a lie. She wasn't *worried*; she just wanted to get out of the car. "But we have a problem."

"Other than being locked inside a boxcar?"

"Well, it's related. What do we do when we have to pee?"

He looked around at the walls, then down at the floor, with an expression of growing discomfort. "I wish you hadn't asked that."

"Sorry."

"We could pile some packing straw in a corner. It's dry and absorbent."

"It'll smell."

"We'll put it by the door so we can kick it through the cracks when we're done. They're wide enough for that. And once the train starts moving, I can widen them a little more with the crowbar."

"This is the kind of situation that takes all the romance out of a marriage," Taya observed.

"Is it an emergency?"

"Not yet."

"Good." He walked over to one of the crates and picked out a pipe. "Let's see if I can devise something better, then."

The car started moving about fifteen minutes later, jolting from track to track until Taya heard it being connected to cars in front and behind. Chains rattled and railroad workers shouted. By then Cristof had constructed a small, unwieldy funnel out of the pipes, tubes, and reservoirs he'd found in the crates, the pieces bound together with tightly knotted strips of oilcloth.

"The thin end goes through the crack between the door and the frame," he said, handing it to her. "Be careful of overflow."

Taya eyed it without enthusiasm. She supposed it was a step up from peeing on the floor, but only by the smallest of increments.

She set it down and started kicking straw next to the door.

"But—" her husband started to protest.

"In case of overflow," she said, darkly. "Now do me a favor and go as far away as you can and turn your back."

"Have I told you recently that I love you?"

"Go *away*, Cris."

"I need to use it when you're done."

Time passed. Taya pulled off her wings and set them floating in one corner, and Cristof worked on reconstructing the weapon on paper. She dozed fitfully. Each time she awoke, she checked her watch and then closed her eyes again. The boxcar had warmed up a little from the sun beating on its metal walls, although she still kept her gloves on as she napped.

By her husband's calculations, they would reach Safira by one in the afternoon. Taya hoped so. They were nursing the canteen of water in Cristof's backpack, neither of them keen to use the makeshift toilet-pipe a second time, so thirst gnawed at her throat. She was hungry, too. Her husband had crammed plenty of tools and scientific journals into his backpack, but nothing to eat.

"I think it's some kind of steam-powered air gun," Cristof declared at last.

"Like the lictors' rifles?"

"Larger, but it would operate on the same general principle. A steam engine compresses the air instead of a manual pump, that's all."

"Those barrels looked huge."

"I suppose it could be an air cannon. It would need to build up an immense amount of pressure to propel heavy shot any distance, though."

"And why would anyone use steam instead of powder for a cannon?"

Cristof ran a hand through his long black hair, considering the question.

"Well, generating steam requires somewhat less effort than manufacturing gunpowder. And you could build a watertight steam generator, whereas water ruins gunpowder. And steam's safer than powder around open flames. So steam might be the better choice in a wet climate, or when fire might be problematic."

"Then why do we use gunpowder?"

"For one thing, powder weapons are more portable and easier to get ready. If you were trying to sneak up on an enemy, you wouldn't want to have to power up a steam generator in order to use your weapons."

"So they'd work best in a fortress," Taya speculated.

"That would be a logical place for them," Cristof agreed. "Or mounted on horse-drawn chasses or a train."

"They wouldn't use the weapons against Mareaux, though. Or Demicus. We're the only enemy on their border."

"If we're lucky," Cristof said, "they'll use the weapons against each other."

Taya made a face. Alzana was a large country full of feuding aristocratic families loosely united under a king. It wasn't impossible to imagine some progressively minded Alzanan nobleman purchasing Ondinium weapons to use against an unwanted neighbor, although she didn't think Cristof needed to sound so cheery about it.

She leaned back in the straw, closing her eyes. If they ever visited Alzana, she'd have to make sure her husband wore his mask full-time. Keeping him mute would be the only way to prevent a war....

Later she awoke with a gasp. The train was slowing down to the sound of whistles and the shrieking of metal on metal. Brakemen's feet pounded on the roof over them.

"Cris!" She sat up and found him curled around her. "Wake up. We're here!"

He yawned and sat up, blinking like an owl and fishing for his glasses.

The boxcar began filling with sooty, choking smoke as the train stood still but the engine continued to puff and chug. Taya wondered if they'd arrived in Safira or if Amcathra had ordered the train stopped on the tracks. She and Cristof stood, brushing off straw and dirt.

"There might be a delay in the yard," Cristof suggested after ten minutes had passed. "We're a freight train, not a passenger train, so we don't have queuing priority."

After another twenty minutes passed, the train began moving again, picking up speed. Taya turned a questioning look on her husband.

"A fuel and water stop?" he suggested. He pulled out his watch and snapped it open. "Interesting."

"What?"

"It's three in the afternoon."

"I thought we'd be in Safira by one!"

"Well, I didn't bring a train schedule with me!" He took a calming breath and rummaged through his pack. "Let's look at the map."

Taya nodded, trying to figure out which side of the car the sun was on. It wasn't shining through the door. Engel was northeast of Ondinium, so if they were heading into Safira, the afternoon sun should be on their... right.

Shining through the door.

No— wait. She rummaged through her flight suit pockets for her compass. She'd never needed it in Ondinium, but it was standard safety equipment. Her fingers closed on the small metal case and she pulled it out.

"Perfect," Cristof said, taking it and laying it next to the map. They stared at the needle, and then at each other.

The train was heading north. Away from Safira and Mareaux.

"Tracks don't go in a straight line," he ventured, the crease between his eyebrows deepening. "Maybe we're just going around an obstacle."

"Then we'll change directions in a few minutes."

"Almost certainly."

But they kept watching, and although the needle shifted a few times as the train went around curves, their overall trajectory remained unchanged.

The train was headed north, not south.

"Cris," Taya asked, frightened. "Where are we going?"

He leaned over his map and began scribbling calculations on the parts of his journal cover that weren't covered with sketches of machinery. At last he shook his head.

"Well?" she pressed.

He measured off the scale with the graphite pencil and began plotting alternate courses. "Eight hours is a long time, even including stops. The question is, have we been going north the whole time?"

Taya dug in her pockets until she found the bill of parcel. She tilted it toward the light, searching for the scrawl in the box labeled *Destination*. Her stomach sank.

"This says Kovolo, Cris. Not Mareaux. Where's Kovolo?"

He frowned, running an ink-stained finger over the map's folds.

"Kovolo, Kovolo… it sounds Demican." His finger stopped, high on the page. "It's one of the border towns. We're heading to Demicus, not Mareaux."

"Oh, Lady. We just *assumed*…."

"That goods ordered by a Mareaux shell company would be delivered to Mareaux." He looked grim. "But the Mareaux are strict about import/export inspections, whereas the Demican border is only minimally supervised. Illegal weapons would be much easier to smuggle through Demicus."

Taya licked lips that suddenly felt very dry.

"How far away is Kovolo?"

Cristof was already measuring off the distance. "This map doesn't show rail routes, but I'd say a day, if the line's fairly direct. Two, if it isn't."

Two days without heat, food, or water? In this crowded, rocking, confined little space? Taya sank down and wrapped her arms around her knees.

Cristof folded the map and slid it into his pack, then sat next to her.

"It's just a guess," he said, quietly. "But at some point the train will need fresh fuel and water again. We can pound on the boxcar walls."

"Amcathra probably thought we were headed to Mareaux, too," she said, after a moment. "He won't be happy when he can't find us."

"He'll figure out what happened."

"I'll bet he orders every train in Ondinium stopped and searched."

Cristof put an arm around her shoulder and pulled her close.

"That wouldn't surprise me at all," he said. "And when we get back, he'll tell us exactly how stupid we were to get locked in a boxcar and shipped to the border."

Chapter Eighteen

THE CAR WAS getting dark when Taya stood and began to pace. Cristof put down the journal he'd been squinting over. Neither of them had suggested lighting the lantern again. They both knew that they had to conserve its fuel.

"What's wrong?"

"I'm hungry."

Cristof held out a hand and Taya took it, letting him pull her down and wrap his arms around her. She rested her cheek on his chest, staring into the encroaching darkness, and felt a little better.

"So am I. But we'll be out of here tomorrow."

"How much water do you have left?"

"Not enough." He straightened up, and Taya reluctantly moved back. "If we could scrape up snow from outside, somehow...."

"Is the car watertight? Maybe it'll ice up tonight and we can catch the melting water."

"That might work, around the door." He reached over and rubbed a corner of the oilcloth wrapped around the gun barrels. "Not very absorbent— it'd sluice condensation, but it wouldn't absorb it well enough to be wrung out into the canteen."

"What about our clothes?"

"I think it's more important for us to stay warm." He stood and began shaking out the oilcloth sheets. "Let's stretch these out by the walls and door, just to see if we can collect any drips. It can't hurt to try."

Sleep came poorly to both of them, although they turned two of the crates into straw-packed nests, pulling on their hats and gloves and covering themselves with oilcloth. Eventually

Taya felt warm, but hunger, thirst, and fear made her toss and turn all night.

She'd never been in a situation like this before. She felt helpless. Of course Cristof was right— they'd be able to raise a racket at the next refueling stop, and somebody would come investigate. But what then?

Nobody would drag them out and shoot them, would they? She'd convinced herself that there wasn't any danger back in the AME supply yard, or in Engels, but way out here? They were a long way from the capital.

Of course, Lieutenant Amcathra's and Professor Dautry's testimony would point investigators toward AME, but what if Amcathra and Dautry vanished, too? If AME caught Amcathra in the supply yard, how hard would it be for them to figure out that the foreign balloonist at the train station had been with him?

And if all four of them vanished? The Council might never figure out what had happened. Their loss would be chalked up to a flight accident.

Taya curled up into a ball.

Allied Metals & Extraction is a corporation, not a group of terrorists, she told herself fiercely. *So what if it's smuggling weapons? Carrying out a little illegal trade on the side is a lot different from committing murder.*

Except that somebody had convinced Rikard to kill them, and it could have been Patrice Corundel as easily as the Mazzolettis.

The next morning Taya pushed off her oilcloth blanket to see Cristof coiling one of the lengths of fabric into a cone and laying it over a stack of crates.

"Did we get any water?" she asked, through dry lips.

"A little." He moved one of the metal parts that he'd tentatively dubbed a water reservoir under the end of the tarp. "There's some ice build-up on the metal walls and around the door, too. Help me scrape it off?"

The end result didn't fill his canteen, but collecting the ice killed an hour of the journey, and they both enjoyed a sip of metallic-tasting water at the end of it.

Taya's night fears seemed ridiculous in the light of the day, so she refrained from mentioning them. She and Cristof sat side-by-side, leaning against a crate with an oilcloth tarp draped over their laps. The air had grown colder, and the morning sun shined through the cracks around the boxcar door.

"At least we've confirmed Alister's suspicions," Cristof said. "AME might have been able to squirm its way out of an accusation that it sold prohibited material to Alzana by pointing to the shell corporation, but it can't deny shipping material under false bills of lading."

"If it's shipping to Demicus, shouldn't it have set up a Demican shell corporation?"

"I don't think Demicus has any corporations, shell or otherwise. It barely has any cities."

"Well, since we know AME is breaking the law, can we do something about it when they let us out? You could force the train to stop at a watering station until lictors come, couldn't you?"

Cristof hesitated.

"Maybe, if the engineer is a law-abiding man and there's some way to signal from the watering station, but… scrap, we'd lose so *much*! I don't want to just stop one shipment— I want to find out where the shipment is going and who's involved and how far the conspiracy extends. Right now, if we confront AME, it'll deny everything. Someone will be fired and the account with the shell corporation will be closed, and a few weeks later, the mastermind behind the operation will set up another one, and everything we've done — all the information Alister sent me, all those people who died — will count for nothing."

Taya was taken aback by the frustration in her husband's voice. She'd been so caught up in her own worries that she hadn't stopped to think about Cristof's reaction.

"I thought I was a better investigator than I was an ambassador," he continued, bitterly. "But it looks like I should just stick to making clocks."

"It's not your fault we're trapped."

"I insisted we search the crates."

"We both agreed to investigate the boxcar." She took a deep breath. *I can do this.* "If you want to ride with the cargo to its destination, let's do it."

"How?"

"We can live without food for a few more days."

"No. I'm not going to sit here and watch my wife starve."

"Neither of us is going to starve in three days," she pointed out, ignoring the hollowness that clawed at her stomach. But her husband was already shaking his head.

"Even if we stayed here, we'd get caught as soon as they opened the door to unload the cargo."

"We could hide."

"It's obvious someone's been in here." He waved a hand at the mess they'd made opening and rummaging through the crates.

"We can straighten up today. Besides, if they notice anything wrong, they'll step inside to look and we'll cold-cock them and run outside."

He stared at her as if he were looking at a stranger.

"The hunger's going to your head."

"I distinctly remember you telling me you were good at fisti-cuffs."

"You said 'cold-cock,' not 'punch in the face.'"

"Well, whatever it takes. I'm not choosy."

He exhaled loudly, then leaned back against the crates.

"And after we subdue the inspectors and leap out into the middle of the freight yard, what next?"

"We hide and find out where the crates are being taken, of course."

"In metropolitan Kovolo."

"We're grubby enough now. It wouldn't be that hard to dis-guise ourselves as famulates." She tugged on a long lock of his hair that hung over one shoulder. "Although you'd have to tuck this up under a cap."

"I could cut it again."

"Don't you dare. I like it long."

"I know, love. That's the only reason I put up with it."

"You're a very obliging husband."

His expression lightened, and Taya felt a moment's satisfac-tion. She'd forgotten how hard Cristof could be on himself. She should have realized that he'd blame himself for their troubles.

"It won't work, though," he said after a moment. "You can't abandon your wings."

"Oh. You're right." She'd forgotten, for a moment, but of course she'd have to escape in her armature. "Then you'll definitely have to cold-cock the freight yard workers before they see me."

"I wish you would stop using that phrase."

"Do you need to use the funnel again?"

"Not as long as you keep reminding me about the temperature."

"We could hide inside one of the crates. Then they'd lift us out and take us straight to our goal."

"We can't hammer the lid back on if we're inside."

"Then we just have to hide and sneak out. All we need is a moment when everyone's outside, or only one person is inside and he turns his back on us."

"You seem very intent on my hitting someone."

"It's less fatal than shooting someone. And *I'm* no good at hitting people."

"I beg to differ."

"That was ages ago, and I was mad at you."

He smiled, pulling off his glasses and inspecting them in the morning light that trickled around the door.

"Don't underestimate yourself," he said, sliding them back on again. He finally looked at her, his smile fading. "Are you serious about riding all the way to Kovolo? It won't be comfortable."

Taya shoved away her misgivings.

"It's important. You're right— Alister put his life on the line to send you that information, and a lot of other people were killed to keep you from investigating it. We can't stop now."

He reached over and pulled her close.

That night, the train began to slow again. Taya sat up and stared into the blackness.

"Cris? What time is it?"

"I don't know. Just a minute." She heard him climbing out of his crate and moving around in the rocking boxcar. A moment later a match flared, illuminating his hands and the face of his watch. "About two."

"Do you think we're in Kovolo?"

They listened. The train jolted, its whistle shrieking and its brakes screeching. Soot-filled clouds of smoke drifted down on the cars instead of being swept past by wind and speed. Taya coughed, covering her mouth as she heard the brakemen calling out. Cristof waved out his match as light shined through the cracks around the boxcar door.

"It's a station," Taya exclaimed, climbing out of her crate and reaching for her armature.

"It might just be another refueling stop," he cautioned.

"With lights? At night?"

Cristof stood and listened while she snapped her armature's metal keel around her chest. Then, nodding, he began straightening up their sleeping crates.

The smoke in the boxcar increased, and the volume of the engine rose. Was it just a refueling stop, after all? Determined not to believe it, Taya stuffed the map and journals back into Cristof's pack and, reluctantly, slid a few of her flat lead weights into it, as well. She hated to make him carry more weight, but they couldn't leave the weights in the car, and if she had to launch herself from the ground, she'd need to be as lightweight as possible.

The brakeman descended the side of the boxcar. Voices rose. People passed by the door, their shadows darkening the car's interior as they moved. Taya heard loud scraping sounds by the side of the car, and the boxcar bobbed. Cristof did his best to nail down the lids of the two crates they'd left open. Then he moved forward, taking his pack and leaning close.

"They're uncoupling the cars," he whispered. "We might not be getting out yet."

They waited, breathlessly. Shouts, a whistle, and the locomotive's engine began to chug. Wheels clattered on the tracks, but they didn't move.

More shouts, whistles. Another engine, growing louder. The brakeman shouted to someone and the boxcar shuddered. Taya looked up at her husband.

"It's a transfer. We're being hooked up to a new train."

"From Kovolo?"

"I don't know," he said, helplessly.

Her spirits sank. For a brief moment, excitement at the thought of getting out had made her forget about her aching stomach and dry mouth, but now all the discomforts of two days with no food and little water returned.

They waited. The boxcar began to move, slowly. Taya could tell they were being switched from track to track by the voices around them as brakemen jogged beside the car, shouting to each other.

With nothing else to do, they cleaned up the remaining traces of their presence.

After about ten minutes, the car stopped again. They waited until the voices began to gather outside their car.

Taya locked her wings in close and climbed up on the crates, crouching in a dark corner. Her hands shook from a combination of excitement and nerves.

On the other side of the car, Cristof checked his pistol and holstered it. He, too, crouched on top of a stack of crates, keeping as close to the wall as he could.

Metal clanked as the padlock on their boxcar door was removed. With a thunderous boom, it was rolled to one side and fresh cold air filled the car. Taya shivered, startled to realize how comparatively warm their little enclosed space had been. Light played over the sides of the crates. Every loose wisp of straw and crooked nail stood out to her eyes, but whoever was checking them didn't seem to notice.

"You got the delivery order?" somebody asked.

"D/O's right here."

"We need everything unloaded before five."

"No problem. It'll be off by four."

The speakers and the light moved away, and Taya heard them unlocking the next car. She edged forward, blinking to readjust her eyes to the dark. Cristof slid down the stack of crates, edged up to the open door, and peered out. He held up a hand. She heard the men talking again. Then a third door rolled open.

He waved her down and she dropped to the boxcar floor.

"Out and to the left," he whispered, his breath hanging like a cloud in the chilly night air. He reached for his needle gun. "You first."

Taya glanced outside. The railway workers were looking inside a freight car further down the track. She slipped out of the boxcar onto a platform bristling with block-and-tackle arrangements and scrambled to the left, away from the workers. A gap between the boxcar and the switcher locomotive offered a hiding place, although the tips of her wings scraped its sides. Snow crunched under her feet. She crouched and scooped up a handful to eat. The sensation of cold water trickling down her throat was exquisite, despite the snow's ashen, chemical flavor.

This part of the freight yard was dark, except for the lanterns held by the workers. Farther away, she saw brighter lights— the front of the yard or the main terminal. The moon gave off a dim glow through the thick clouds that hung overhead. Dirty black snow was piled everywhere, rutted by wagon tracks and footsteps. An icy breeze blew across the yard, carrying the scent of smoke, oil, and hot metal.

Cristof emerged from under the car, brushing snow off the front of his coat, and looked around. Taya pointed to a line of freight cars on the next track over, dark and abandoned-looking beneath the horizontal arm of a goods-yard crane. They dashed across the open space, keeping the AME cars between themselves and the workers.

Then, with two sets of cars between them and the yard crew, they huddled down.

"Wait here and keep an eye on the crates," Cristof whispered, putting his pack on the ground and massaging his left arm. "I'll figure out where we are."

"Are you all right?" she asked. He dropped his hand.

"Slept badly."

"I can—"

"I'm fine."

"Buy us some dinner while you're out," she said, trying to keep her voice light.

"I will." He touched her wings with a strained smile and headed off toward the brighter lights.

Taya frowned at his back. The last couple of days couldn't have been good for him— exertion, cold, hunger, sleeping in the rough. As soon as she had a chance, she would insist he pull off his shirt and let her see what was under his bandages. Maybe Kovolo had a hospital.

White flakes drifted down from the sky. She broke an icicle off the freight car and sucked on it, pretending it was food.

The freight handlers arrived, pulling hand trucks and laughing at something one of them had said. Their voices sounded oddly flattened, as if absorbed by the snowy night. They were mostly big men, although Taya spotted two women among them, nearly as muscular and tall as the men. Most of the workers had light-colored hair and square features; Demican or Demican-descended.

Taya waited tensely as the workers started unloading the boxcar they'd been in. Maybe it was the darkness or the late hour, but none of them noticed anything, and soon the once-opened crates were at the bottom of the stack.

Half an hour later, Cristof rejoined her, his hat and coat powdered with fresh snow. He held three small, covered tin pails.

"The workers' lunches," he whispered. "I didn't dare go into the main station, so I stole them from a bench on the other side of the yard."

Taya pulled open one of the lids and dug inside. Bread, a chunk of hard cheese, a pickled pig's foot. Her mouth watered as she broke the bread and handed half to her husband. For a moment they forgot all about watching the freight, tearing the cheese into chunks and sharing bites of the pig's foot.

The food was gone in a matter of minutes. Taya's stomach growled for more, but Cristof was already tucking the contents of the other two pails into his backpack. She supposed he was being wise, even though she'd happily devour it all right now.

"I hope they aren't taking those crates very far," she breathed, dropping the bone and gristle back into the stolen pail. "I'm dying for a cup of tea."

"They're probably taking them to the nearest AME warehouse." Cristof pulled out his leather wallet, fished out three coins, and dropped one into each empty pail.

"That's going to raise some questions."

"I'm only a thief by necessity."

"Well, you've just paid for a month's worth of pigs' feet."

He nodded, unconcerned.

The workers left the cargo stacked on the platforms, and the AME freight cars were hauled away. Taya checked her watch. They'd finished before four as promised. The Kovolo freight yard was nothing if not efficient.

Several minutes later, another set of cars pulled in on the opposite side of the platform. They had enclosed steel sides but no roof. A new set of workers began loading the crates into the wagons.

"That's going to be a cold ride," Taya muttered unhappily.

"Why don't I ride, and you follow in the air?" Cristof suggested, packing snow into his canteen. "They can't be going far."

"We don't know that, and I'm not going to take the chance of losing you."

"But—"

"I'm not strong enough for a long flight," she said, cutting him off. "If they go more than a few miles, I'll fall behind."

"Just trying to spare you another ride," he murmured. She nodded, squeezing his arm to show that she wasn't angry. But there was no way she'd be able to stay aloft for very long, not as tired and weak as she felt.

Moving the freight to the new cars took another hour. Fearing another uncomfortable journey, Taya took the time to empty her bladder in a dark corner of the yard— a complicated operation that involved removing her armature and flight suit. By the time she rejoined Cristof, the top of each car was covered by a canvas tarpaulin, metal grommets secured to hooks built into the sides of the cars. The workers went on break, complaining in advance about the station's weak tea as they walked up the platform.

Taya and Cristof abandoned the lunch pails by the tracks and crept across the yard like burglars. Cristof unhooked the corner of a tarp over the last car and helped Taya inside. After a few tense moments of trying to squeeze through the narrow gap with her armature on, she hastily stripped it off. Together they crammed her wings into the gap between the top of the crates and the taut length of tarp. Taya slipped in, pulling the armature down as close to her as she could and trying to keep the wings from poking the tarp. Cristof joined her, then reached out to fasten the loose tarp back over the hooks.

"Lieutenant Amcathra will never find us now," Taya whispered. Cristof squeezed her hand.

"He'd do the same thing, if he were here."

I wish he were *here*, Taya thought, with a touch of guilt. She loved her husband dearly, but she'd feel much safer if the quietly competent and deadly lieutenant were by their side.

The workers eventually returned, or maybe a new crew arrived. Taya and Cristof remained silent as the tarps were checked one last time and the engine started. A whistle sounded, the brakes were disengaged and the new train began to move.

CHAPTER NINETEEN

NO LIGHT TRICKLED into the car, but the scent of roast chicken filled the tiny space.

"That smells delicious," Taya groaned, her stomach growling. Cristof wriggled around next to her, digging into his pack.

"Take off your gloves." She yanked them off and reached out, taking the chunk of meat he was holding out for her. "Careful of the ribs."

She couldn't answer— her mouth was full, and it stayed that way until she had sucked all the meat off the bones and licked her fingers clean.

"Should we just drop the bones, or....?"

"I'll throw them outside." He took hers and she felt a sliver of icy air slip under the tarp as he slid a hand out to discard them.

"Is there anything else?"

"Not now. The rest of the food will be all right if it freezes. I didn't want to eat icy chicken, though."

"I'm still hungry."

"We need to be careful. We don't know how long it'll be until we stop," Cristof warned.

"Then pass the canteen," she said, sighing.

Afterward, she laid her head down on one of her arms. The crates were hard, her armature was poking her, and the air was freezing. Nevertheless, the steady rocking and rhythmic clattering eventually lulled her to sleep.

Cristof shook her awake. She sat up, hit her head on the canvas tarp, and ducked flat again, gathering her wits. They'd stopped, although the engine was still rumbling. It was still dark.

"Should we get out?" she whispered.

Voices— somebody who sounded authoritative, and two others replying. Taya's fingers tightened around her armature. If they had to leave quickly, it would be almost impossible for her to carry it in her arms, but she couldn't leave her wings behind.

But the train began to move again, making a turn and heading downhill. Taya and the armature slid forward. She threw out a hand to keep from banging against the car wall. The descent continued for a long time before the tracks flattened out and made another turn. Minutes later, the wheels scraped and rattled over something, sending the car shuddering from side to side.

Beside her, Cristof exclaimed and scrambled to the side, trying in vain to peer out from beneath the tarp without unhooking it.

"Cris!" she protested. "What's wrong?"

"They're using an automated gauge changer! That's brilliant— why don't we have one in Terminal?"

"A what?"

"The car has variable-gauge axles. When we passed through the border, the gauge changer forced the wheels to move wider to accommodate the wider Demican tracks. I've seen models, but I never realized we'd actually *built* one."

"Doesn't a gauge changer defeat the whole purpose of having differently gauged tracks? The whole goal is to keep foreign trains from entering Ondinium, isn't it?"

"Well… yes. But I think all the tracks along the Demican border are owned by Ondinium corporations, anyway."

"It's still a security breach, isn't it?"

"I suppose they thought efficiency was more important than security." He looked at her and sighed. "I'll report it, I promise."

"If you don't, I will," Taya warned him. "Does that mean we're in Demicus now?"

"We must be."

"I can't believe I'm stuck in here where I can't see anything!"

"I'm sure you'll have a chance to sightsee later. By the way, what do Demicans eat? Bear?"

Taya smiled. She could only see his silhouette, but she could imagine his expression.

"They eat what we eat, mostly. Chicken, goat, pig. The northern clans keep reindeer, but I don't know if they eat them or not. Do we have to talk about food? I'm still hungry."

"Sorry."

She wished she could see where they were going. But logic told her that, this close to the border, the countryside wouldn't look much different from Ondinium, anyway.

"Does your map show anything past the Demican border?" she asked.

"No."

"How far do corporate trains run into Demicus?"

"It can't be more than a couple of miles. I suppose some lines might go several miles in to accommodate logging, but most wouldn't need to do more than parallel the border."

Taya tried to relax. With luck, they'd be out soon.

By the time the train slowed, however, they had traveled close to four hours. Dim light filtered through the canvas tarpaulin, and the air was still cold enough for their breath to make little white clouds. Cristof pulled off a glove and checked his watch.

"Eleven-forty-five."

"Broad daylight," she said, dismayed.

The train jolted and rolled forward. They were plunged into relative darkness, and the sound of the engine changed. When the train stopped again, she heard a loud hissing of released steam as the engine was shut down. Voices rose around them, then faded. Taya heard a thundering, rolling sound and the crash of metal on metal. Then, silence.

She twisted and looked at her husband, barely able to make out his face in the dim light. He laid a finger on his lips. They waited. All they could hear was the ticking of cooling metal.

Cristof slid a hand out and unhooked a corner of the tarp, looking out.

"Clear," he breathed. In moments, both of them were on the platform. Taya hastily stepped into her armature and locked her wings high while Cristof fastened the tarp. They ran across a wooden floor covered with piles of melting snow and ducked behind a long row of barrels by the wall.

Only then did they stop to look around.

The wooden train shed was covered by a steeply angled metal roof. The track ran through both ends of the building, each blocked by wide, rolling metal doors to protect the locomotive and its cargo from inclement weather. The battered wooden platform on either side of the track was covered with machinery designed to move freight. Doors on the opposite side of the shed were sized to accommodate either human passage or the movement of large loads. Dim sunlight filtered through long, narrow windows set high in the wooden wall. Wind rattled the glass in their panes. The bottom half of each window was covered by packed snow that had collected on the exterior, and the interior glass was darkened by soot. The result was a gray, unfriendly illumination.

Cristof pointed and they crept over to one of the human-sized doors opposite. He inched it open, his free hand clutching his needle gun.

The door revealed another, much larger building, so large that it took Taya's breath away.

The first thing she saw were the aerostats— giant dirigibles so tall and vast that they looked like some artist's manic hallucination. A galvanic jolt of fear made her skin crawl. The dirigibles' inflated envelopes were forbiddingly long, cylindrical metallic balloons that resembled silver thunderclouds bound to the earth by heavy cables and iron rings. Each of the monstrous machines was at least five times as long as the little Mareaux aerostat they'd crashed in Echelles.

When at last Taya was able to drag her eyes away from the giant aerostats, she marveled at the bizarrely constructed wooden walls of the building, each criss-crossed by metal support beams that arched up in a gentle curve to a series of catwalks high above. But then her gaze moved inexorably back down from the catwalks to the incredible, frightening aerostats again.

At last she registered the sky-blue, rampant Alzanan gryphons painted on each silver envelope's side, right above a big black number.

Her fingers tightened on Cristof's shoulder. He flinched, then blinked and eased the door shut.

"Lady help us," he whispered, reaching up to clasp her hand.

"We need to get out of here." Taya tugged him to one side, toward the stacks of crates by one of the larger freight doors. They ducked in the narrow gap, Taya lowering her wings to keep them hidden. "We need to warn the Council."

"You'll have to fly back to Kovolo."

"I don't even know where Kovolo *is*!"

"Follow the tracks." He pointed to one of the doors. "We entered there. The rails will lead you back to the border."

"What about you?"

"I'll hide in the forest."

Taya was loathe to leave him in enemy territory. Still, with luck, she could reach Kovolo before nightfall. Then, she promised herself, she'd return with food and equipment.

"All right. Wait here." The train shed was still empty, so she jogged to the small door beside the great sliding metal entrance. She cracked it open and looked outside.

Icy snow stung her cheek. She didn't see anyone, so she opened it a little wider, squinting as she looked up.

"The wind's too strong to fly," she reported when she rejoined Cristof. "I can't leave until the storm's over."

"Then we need someplace safe to hide before they come back to unload."

"We could go outside and look around," she suggested. Cristof nodded, still gripping his needle gun.

They emerged outside next to the train tracks, which continued forward into the camp. The massive hangar loomed to their right, taller and longer than the train shed. Taya squinted through the wind-driven snow to their left, peering past the next two buildings. The train shed was on the end of a small narrow encampment nestled in a high valley. She could make out a mass of dark, wooded mountainsides in the distance, their timberlines swiftly giving way to sheer cliff faces.

Somewhere beyond those cliffs lay Ondinium, placidly unaware of the threat on its doorstep.

Cristof touched her arm. She followed him to the next building, stumbling as she left the wall's protection and felt the full force of the wind. It yanked on her metal wings and threatened to toss her into the air. She wrapped her fingers around the straps on Cristof's leather pack. He turned and grasped her arm, pulling her close. Huddling together, they ran across the open space and pressed against the wall of the next building.

"Around the side," Cristof whispered, still gripping her arm. Taya let him lead while she focused on keeping the erratic gusts from catching her wings and pulling her away.

They reached the lee of the building. Taya crouched, glad to be out of the icy, dangerous blast. Voices and laughter sounded from inside.

Cristof pointed to the next building over. They struggled through the storm to it, ducking out of the wind again.

"Where are we?" Taya asked. With the exception of the tall hangar, all the buildings looked alike— wooden-framed boxes with corrugated metal sides and narrow slits of windows that were clearly there to let in the light rather than offer a view.

"That last building was a mess hall, I think. It must be lunchtime."

"Lunch might be worth surrendering for." Taya's stomach clenched at the thought of hot food.

"We'll eat as soon as we find someplace to hide."

"How about in here?" She looked hopefully at the building beside them.

"I'll look." He slipped around the side. Taya shivered, hopping from foot to foot until he returned.

"Barracks. Latrines beyond. We'll have to look on the other side of the hangar."

"Give me your pack. I need some extra weight."

She wrapped one of the straps around her left arm and clutched the pack close to her chest with her right.

They dashed across the open space, pausing long enough in the lee of the train shed to catch their breath before following the tracks around the front of the hangar. Taya barely had a chance to register its astounding height before they ducked around a smaller, shorter attached building. Its human-sized door was painted with warnings in Alzanan and Demican:

Inflammable Gas Processing Station. Danger.

Cristof yanked the door open and pulled her inside. Taya winced, half-expecting something to blow up, as he closed the door behind them.

Narrow windows let in thin rays of light that revealed machinery that didn't look at all like the buoyant gas generator Taya had seen in Mareaux. The assembly was larger, for one thing, and more industrial-looking, a confusing labyrinth of metal cylinders, pipes, boxes, valves, and levers that loomed over their heads. A large coal hopper and several crates filled the rest of the space.

Taya edged around the machines, moving as quietly as she could. The room was empty.

"Nobody here," she reported. "There's a door that leads to the hangar. I hope nobody comes in."

"They're not going to launch a dirigible in this weather."

"What *is* all of this?" Taya asked, gesturing to the equipment around them. Cristof took off his glasses, cleared them with his scarf, and put them back on again to peer around. He indicated the tallest cylinder.

"That's probably a fuel tank. It pipes something over there," he pointed to a large metal box, "but that's all I can tell you. Professor Dautry would know."

"Maybe. Those aerostats are *years* ahead of the ones we saw in Mareaux."

"That doesn't mean they didn't originate in Mareaux. Alzanans are good at industrial espionage."

"I don't think you give them enough credit," Taya objected, picking up the backpacks they'd left on the floor.

"They're good at criminology and behavioral studies, and they're reasonably clever at metallurgy and chemical experimentation, but they fight among themselves far too much to develop the kind of large-scale industry they'd need to challenge Ondinium." Cristof frowned, his eyes drifting to the equipment around them. "And they're usually no good at keeping secrets, either. How in the world could they have built this so close to our borders without somebody turning coat and selling us the information?"

"It must be a military operation."

"Yes, but it still would have involved hundreds of people...."

"Maybe they hired Demicans?" She dug through his pack and unearthed two hard rolls, one dry sausage, and a canteen of half-frozen water.

"Maybe." Cristof frowned. "Janos said something about a nationalist movement. Those bear people."

"The *sheytatangri*," Taya supplied. She pulled out her utility knife and divided the food. "Let's eat while we talk."

They pulled off their gloves. The bread was dry and cold, and even though Taya chewed each bite until it turned to mush to make it last longer, it vanished too quickly.

Cristof's eyes were turned toward the generator, but his gaze was a million miles away.

"What is it?" she asked.

"Those ships use explosive gas."

"It's cheaper than the alternative, isn't it?"

"Yes, and easier to manufacture. But it's much more dangerous."

"Professor Dautry said the Alzanans have developed a new engine. Maybe that makes it safer."

"What kind of engine?"

"Something eclectic. Eletric?"

"Electromagnetic?"

"That's it. She said they were working on... aeronave?"

"Nobody's ever managed to build an electromagnetic engine powerful enough to propel a dirigible. The engines add more weight than buoyant gas can lift."

"Well, Professor Dautry said she was looking forward to trying one of the new Alzanan engines on her dirigible in Echelles."

Her husband's frown grew.

"Then why didn't the Council know about them?"

Taya took a bite out of the sausage and forced herself to chew it thoroughly. *Make it last longer than the roll*, she counseled herself.

"Maybe it does. Maybe that's why it suddenly got so interested in Mareaux's aerostat experiments," she ventured. "Mareaux would let us in and show us around; Alzana wouldn't."

"Maybe. But still...."

Taya sucked the last bit of grease off her fingers. Cristof must have eaten his sausage as quickly as she'd eaten her roll; it was already gone.

"So, what do you want to do?" she asked.

"I'd like to take another look at those aerostats," he said. "The more information you can take to Kovolo, the better. We'll do it tonight. For now, we should try to get some rest. The Alzanans can't take their dirigibles out in these winds, and there's no reason for them to come in here until they do."

"I feel like all we've done for the last two days is sit and wait," she muttered.

Cristof leaned over and kissed her cold cheek.

"Take off your armature and get some sleep, love. You're going to need all your strength to fly back to Kovolo."

"I don't like the idea of leaving you here, either," she added as he sat by the door with his back to the wall and his gun on his lap.

"Just bring me some hot tea when you return," he said, smiling up at her.

She sighed and pulled off her armature, tucking a strap under the backpack to keep it in place. Then she curled up with her head in her husband's lap and waited for nightfall.

Chapter Twenty

THE SIX GIANT dirigibles were lined up in two rows of three each. One floated almost directly in front of them, the long, sleek horizontal ridges on its silver envelope a marked contrast to the bulging, bulbous envelope of Professor Dautry's ungainly aerostat. Two gondolas were fastened beneath the gargantuan envelope. The closest looked like a ship's cabin, while the farthest contained the ship's engines, each connected to a giant steel propeller.

On this side of the dirigibles, the sky-blue Alzanan gryphons had been replaced by a snarling white bear's head.

The Alzanans *were* allied with the Demican *sheytatangri*. That was bad news for Ondinium, which had blithely trusted its "backwards" northern neighbors for centuries.

Her husband was considering the guard sitting between the two rows of aerostats. The guard wore a blue-and-red military uniform and was engrossed in a book. He was alone, his rifle slung carelessly over the back of his chair.

Cristof looked up, and Taya followed his gaze to a second guard leaning on the catwalk, his rifle slung over his shoulder.

She touched his arm and gestured to the door behind them. He shook his head, put a finger against his lips, and began sneaking up to the nearest aerostat's gondola.

Silently cursing his insatiable curiosity, Taya followed, ducking the thick ropes that tethered the giant ship to metal rings bolted to the wooden floor.

The vehicle's painted envelope loomed over her like an exalted's mansion, putting Taya's little metal wings to shame. She wondered how fast the engines could propel the gargantuan vehicle. When the wind was right, icarii could reach a horizontal speed of about

40 miles an hour, but they couldn't maintain it for very long. She didn't think that such a massive vehicle could move that quickly, but it would have the advantage of never tiring.

Cristof opened the gondola door and waved to her. She slid her arms into her wings to pull them close to her body — her husband had left his backpack in the gas processing room, but she'd refused to leave her armature — and stepped inside.

The gondola's interior was deeply shadowed, although one of the hangar's lamps cast a dim beam of light through a window. A narrow passage ran down the center, lined with long metal lockers. Metal platforms by the windows held large swivel-mounted guns. The barrels were the same size as the parts they'd found on the train.

Allied Metals & Extraction *had* been betraying its country.

Taya walked down the middle of the gondola, counting the big, swivel-mounted cannon. Two on each side, staggered. When she reached the front of the gondola, she paused. The front opened onto a curved bay of glass windows and steel wheels, levers, and dials. If Taya craned her neck, she could see the Alzanan guard through the window. He turned a page, oblivious to their presence. She backed up, feeling nervous.

Cristof, on the other hand, was caressing the instrument board. He adjusted his silver-rimmed glasses as he examined the shadowed dials. His long, dark hair tumbled around his shoulders, and his expression was rapt.

Taya spotted a rolled-up map in a rack. Locking her wings over her head with the greatest of care — the struts supporting the cabin roof were low — she picked it up and opened it.

The map depicted Ondinium, with the names of each major city neatly labeled in Alzanan. She searched for their location and found it marked in red in the middle of the mountains, a few hours from the Demicus-Ondinium border and far from any clan settlements. An Ondinium signal station was indicated along the border almost directly south of them.

It would be faster for her to fly to that station than to follow the railway tracks back to Kovolo. If the wind was with her — and judging from what she'd felt in her brief walk outside earlier that day, it was blowing north to south — she would have little trouble getting there. The lictors at the station could send an emergency signal back to the capital at once, giving her more time to return and make sure Cristof was safe.

Satisfied, she rolled up the map and tucked it beneath one of her armature struts. Cristof abandoned the controls to rejoin her, carrying a firearm that he'd picked up from a cabinet in the front.

"Flare gun," he whispered, tucking it into the courier's pouch on her leg. She recoiled, but he caught her hand before she could pluck it out again. "Just in case."

Taya squirmed. It was against the law and every code of behavior she'd grown up with for an icarus to carry a weapon. Maybe, just maybe, a flare gun wasn't the same thing as a pistol, but it *looked* the same.

He tilted his head toward the door. She followed him out of the control room and back through the gondola. Instead of going out, though, he climbed up the stairs in back. Taya waited, certain that her wings would never fit through the tight passageway without making noise.

"Storage," he whispered when he returned. Taya opened the gondola door, looked out, and crept to the shadowed hangar wall.

She turned around to discover that Cristof wasn't with her. He had stopped next to the gondola, leaning back to study its connection to the dirigible's taut envelope. Then he stepped back to examine the separate engine gondola.

This is no time to be a gearhead! she raged silently, glaring at him.

One of the small hangar doors opened and two new guards strolled inside, laughing and shaking snow off their coats. Taya shrank back against the wall, and Cristof froze in the dirigible's shadow.

"Reading on duty, Tazio?" one of the newcomers bellowed in Alzanan. The guard on the chair closed his book. "Haven't you been reprimanded often enough?"

"I have to do something useful with my time. Even the Demicans are smart enough to stay home in this weather." Tazio jerked a thumb over his shoulder at the guard on the catwalk. "And Durante's still brooding."

"Up yours," Durante shouted across the hangar. "Just wait until *your* fiancée breaks up with you because you've been sent out to some damn icy wasteland."

"Lucco doesn't have to worry about that," said the guard who'd been silent so far. "*His* girls don't even wait until he's out the door before they call in their next customer."

Lucco's amiable retort was cut off by Durante's cold voice.

"Did you just call Marianna a whore?" He swung his rifle around.

"Hey, hey." Tazio set down his book. "Easy, now. Foscatti was talking about Lucco, not you!"

"Marianna's an angel," Foscatti hastened to add. "Come on, Durante, don't be so upset. She just wants to hear that you love her. If you send a letter out with the train tomorrow, she'll forgive you in no time."

"That's right," Lucco chimed in. "And when you go home a hero, she'll wish she'd never doubted you."

The guard slowly lowered his rifle.

"It's just… she imagines these crazy things…."

"So write her back, tell her how much you love her, and ask her to give you a month before she makes any decisions," Tazio urged. "Look, let's go get dinner and write the letter together."

"That's right, Tazi will help you," Foscatti agreed. "He's good with words."

"Well…" Durante lowered his head to gaze at his boots, then nodded and looked up. "You're right. I'm sorry. I'm just—" He broke off his sentence with an oath and yanked his rifle back to his shoulder. "Tazi! To your right!"

Tazio spun. Taya gasped and started forward.

"Don't move!" Cristof snapped, aiming his pistol at Tazio's face. Taya froze.

Ondinan. Her husband had shouted in Ondinan.

Tazio, who had left his rifle slung over the back of his chair, raised his hands.

"Wait! Don't shoot!" he pleaded, speaking Ondinan with a heavy accent.

"Back up!" Cristof shouted, still in the same language.

Taya knew her husband read and spoke Alzanan. He wasn't talking to the soldiers. He was talking to her.

She clenched her fists. Two against four, and her without anything more threatening than a flare gun? Would they believe it was a real weapon if she kept it close when she threatened them?

"Drop your gun or I'll shoot!" Durante shouted from the catwalk. "Drop it!"

"Drop it!" Lucco echoed, swinging his own rifle around. Next to him, Foscatti had his firearm up and against his shoulder, as well.

"Are those percussion rifles?" Cristof asked, switching to Alzanan. "Do you really want to start shooting around envelopes filled with inflammable gas?"

Taya stepped deeper into the shadows as the guards' eyes flickered to the inflated envelope that loomed over Cristof's head. He was right— she couldn't use a flare gun here. There'd be nothing left of any of them except cinders.

"Foscatti, raise the alarm," Lucco snapped. The young soldier turned and shoved open the door, shouting for help.

"There's nothing you can do," Durante blustered, squinting down the barrel of his rifle. "Surrender and we won't shoot you."

"Shooting me would be a very bad idea," Cristof said. He took several steps to his left, moving away from Taya and closer to the middle of the hangar. The barrel of his needle gun was centered on Tazio's face. "I am much more valuable to you alive."

Taya knew what he was doing, and she hated him for it. He was distracting them, leading their eyes away from her. He was sacrificing himself to give her time to escape and warn Ondinium.

"Who are you?" Tazio demanded. His hands were still up and his voice quavered, but he faced Cristof squarely. "That castemark— that can't be real."

"It's real," Cristof said, taking a few more steps away from the dirigible. "Trust me, Tazio. Your commanders will want me alive."

The soldier started at the use of his name. "But... but you can't be an exalted. You aren't blind."

Up on the catwalk, Durante exclaimed with surprise at the word "exalted," and by the door, Lucco let the barrel of his rifle sag as he stared at Cristof's face.

Before either could say anything, more soldiers began pouring inside, barking at Cristof to drop his weapon.

Hating herself, Taya crept back. Step by step, while everyone's attention was focused on her husband, she narrowed the distance between herself and the door to the gas processing plant.

In the middle of the hangar, Cristof raised his hands, his needle gun held high. Tazio lunged forward and snatched the weapon from him. At the door, Lucco spoke rapidly to the newcomers, warning them not to shoot. The soldiers included Alzanans in uniform and Demicans in traditional felt coats and fur boots.

"What is this?" somebody roared over the commotion. "You found a spy?"

"Yes, sir!" Lucco said, snapping to attention. The other soldiers kept their weapons trained on Cristof, but the straightening of backs and pulling in of elbows indicated that the encampment's commander had arrived.

The officer strode forward, his military coat swinging open over a rumpled uniform. It revealed an ornate sword swinging from one hip and a gun holstered on the other. Snow powdered his shoulders and graying hair. Taya studied his face. She'd never seen him before.

"General," Cristof said, politely, in Alzanan.

The general's eyes flickered to Cristof's face. He raised an eyebrow. "Exalted?"

"Exalted?" echoed another, familiar voice. "My goodness, is that you, Ambassador? I'd heard you were dead."

Taya clapped a gloved hand over her mouth to stifle an involuntary gasp.

The newest speaker was Gaio Mazzoletti, resplendent in an Alzanan captain's uniform. But the figure that had made her gasp stood behind him, one hand on his arm— a tall, copper-skinned Ondinium wearing a tightly buttoned Alzanan military longcoat and an exalted's blank white mask. He wasn't wearing traditional robes, but his hands were gloved, and his long black hair hung in thin braids carefully woven back from his masked face.

Alister?

Had Alister been meeting the Mazzolettis, that rainy day in Echelles?

"Gaio Mazzoletti." Cristof gave the Alzanan a disgusted look. "You're a long way from Mareaux."

"After all the fuss there, I was recalled from the pleasures of diplomacy to the trials of military service. And what brings *you* so far north, Ambassador?"

"Be quiet, Captain," the general snapped. "Decatur, what do you know about this exalted?"

Silence.

"General..." Lord Gaio glanced at the assembled troops. "I expect the decatur would appreciate it if you could make this conference private. Not *all* Ondinium exalteds are as shameless as Forlore."

The general gave a disgusted snort. "Caste games." His eyes fixed on Tazio. "You, sublieutenant. Get your rifle. You and

everyone else who found the spy, stay here. The rest of you, search
the complex and the surrounding area for other intruders. Go."

The soldiers raised their rifles, saluted, and ran out.

"Very well," the general continued, his displeasure clear. "This
is as private as you're going to get, Decatur."

The Ondinium pulled off his mask, revealing a handsome,
older face marred by sunken eyelids over closed eyes. Dark,
deeply tattooed slashes broke the wave-shaped castemarks on
his cheekbones.

He wasn't Alister. He wasn't anyone Taya had ever seen before.

"Neuillan," Cristof said, his tone as disapproving as the general's. "Still a traitor, even in exile. Don't honor him with the
title 'Decatur,' General. He's outcaste, and he's certainly not a
member of Council anymore."

A thin, unpleasant smile twisted the blind exalted's lips as
he pulled off his gloves.

"You sound older, Cristof. But it seems you're still poking your
sharp little nose where it doesn't belong." He stepped forward
and touched Cristof's face. "How is your little brother? I hear
you had him outcaste, too."

"As far as I know, Alister isn't betraying his nation to the
enemy."

Neuillan dropped his hand.

"I expect he would have gotten around to it eventually, if I
weren't going to save him the effort. Where is he?"

"I don't know. I don't care."

"You should. I don't suppose he appreciated being blinded,
scarred, and exiled any more than I did." Neuillan's voice hardened, losing its false pleasantness. "And I'm sure he spends as
much time thinking about revenge as I do."

Taya tensed, touching the flare gun. Maybe if she threatened
to blow up the hangar, they'd let her escape with Cristof. Or
would they call her bluff? Blowing up the hangar would certainly
send a warning to Ondinium, but Taya wasn't suicidal, and the
Lady's Forge would grow cold and dark before she killed the
man she loved.

"So this is Cristof Forlore, Ondinium's new ambassador." The
general looked at Lord Gaio. "I thought he was dead."

"I thought he was, too," Gaio admitted. "He looks a little the
worse for wear, though, doesn't he? He must be a remarkably
lucky man."

"Not lucky enough." The general turned to address Cristof. "Why shouldn't I execute you right now?"

"I'm here to negotiate."

"Really, Ambassador?" The general looked amused. "I would have expected more diplomatic fanfare."

"I've never cared for fanfare. Ask Neuillan."

"If Forlore is here, that pet lictor of his is probably here, too," Mazzoletti warned.

"Don't be ridiculous," Cristof retorted. "Rikard is dead and Janos is halfway to Kovolo already."

"You executed the boy? Not that I regret his loss— he was a terrible assassin. I don't think his heart was in it."

"Janos shot him. Rikard was his nephew."

"How very tragic," Lord Gaio murmured, unsympathetically.

"If there are any lictors hiding here," the general said, turning and raising his voice, "I suggest you come out while you still can. We'll treat you leniently now. If we find you later, we'll shoot to kill."

"What an excellent idea." Neuillan held out a hand, palm up. "Give me your gun, Captain."

"I suggest you use Forlore's," Lord Gaio demurred. "Compressed air is so much safer, this close to the dirigibles."

Tazio placed the needle gun into Neuillan's palm. The blind man grasped it with an unpleasant smile.

Taya stepped forward, pulling out the flare gun. Her heart hammered as she raised it.

"You may not kill him, Decatur," the general snapped. "Forlore will be more useful as a hostage."

A flash of anger crossed Neuillan's face.

"No he won't," he spat. "Ondinium isn't Alzana, General. Ondinium is a *machine*. This man is no more important to the Council than a broken gear to an engineer. They would rather discard him than allow him to be used against them."

"Nevertheless, his knowledge of Ondinium's defenses will be more current than yours."

"He owes me a life, General. I was his guardian when his parents died, and he thanked me by arresting me and sending me off to be blinded and exiled."

"Well, as I understand it, you *were* betraying your country," the general observed.

"I was working for your king!"

"A traitor is a traitor. I doubt you're any more loyal to King Agosti than you were to your Council."

"But you trust him to lead your invasion, General?" Cristof inquired.

"*I* am leading this invasion," the general corrected. "The decatur is only an advisor. Would you like to be an advisor, as well? Perhaps with your assistance we could reduce the amount of collateral damage that will be inflicted upon your country. I should hate to mistake a farming village for a military outpost."

"No!" Neuillan shouted, turning and pulling the trigger. Cristof collapsed with a cry of pain.

The general, Lord Gaio, and Tazio lunged at the decatur as Taya aimed the flare gun at the group. Lucco, Foscatti, and Durante converged on her husband, grabbing his hands as he tore at the long steel needles that pierced his side. Bright crimson blood covered his hands and heavy coat.

Tears stung her eyes and her finger trembled.

If she fired, she'd kill everyone in the hangar. And Cristof was still alive— his screams were proof of that.

"Oh, Lady…." she groaned, jamming the flare gun into her leg pocket. She turned and ran through the door, grabbing Cristof's backpack. Someone behind her shouted for a medic.

She raced past the crates and machinery and yanked open the outer door.

The camp was abuzz with activity. The wind wasn't as strong anymore, but snow was falling, thick and cold, and icy air stung her tear-filled eyes. She shot one last look behind her, but the gas processing machinery stood between her and her husband. For a fleeting moment she considered firing her flare gun into it, instead, but no, she didn't dare, not if there was any chance that Cristof would be harmed by the explosion.

Hugging the pack close to her chest, she ran past the tracks, past wooden buildings, past a startled guard who shouted out, and through a rutted, frozen dirt road that dragged at her feet. Somebody fired, then fired again. Terrified, she veered away from the gates. More shots. A fence. For a split-second she crouched next to it, panting, while soldiers ran toward her. Then she threw Cristof's pack over the top of the fence, then fumbled with her weight belt, tossing her lead weights after it. When she was almost light enough to be blown away by a hard breeze, she leaped and scrambled over the barrier.

On the other side, she found some of the weights and jammed them back onto place, then snatched up Cristof's pack and continued into the darkness.

At long last she staggered to a halt, scratched and bleeding. She leaned against the nearest tree, tears running down her face, and vomited, continuing to heave long after her stomach was empty.

The chasm that had beckoned after the train wreck opened before her once more; a Cristof-shaped hole in her life that left her speechless and sick with horror.

He was alive. She clung to that, to the terrible memory of his screams. He'd been wounded by a needle gun fired in haste by a blind man. The needles might tear him up, but they probably wouldn't kill him, not through his coat and clothes. Needle guns weren't *designed* to kill.

She ground her forehead against the cold, sharp bark of the tree, welcoming the pain.

He'd be fine; they'd take care of him, they needed him as a hostage.

But he'd been shot in the arm and side— the same arm and side that had been injured in the derailment. Bile burned in the back of her throat. What if something went wrong? What if some half-healed injury re-opened? What if his pain was too much for his heart?

What if he died while she was standing here feeling sorry for herself?

She shoved herself away from the tree. Distant shouts indicated that the soldiers were still on alert.

Taya picked up the pack and waded deeper into the underbrush, her metal wings catching in branches and her booted feet sinking knee-deep into snow. She couldn't see a thing, and more than once she stumbled and fell. Each time she thought about not getting up, and then she forced herself back to her feet.

When she couldn't hear or see the camp anymore, she stopped, panting, and huddled in a gap between two large pines.

What could she do now?

Blow up the gas processing plant and smuggle Cristof out of the camp. Hijack the train and drive it back to Kovolo. Steal a dirigible and fly it back to Ondinium.

Except Cristof would be too injured to move, she didn't know how to drive a train or fly a dirigible, and a camp full of Alzanan soldiers and Demican clansmen would be shooting at her all the while.

Lady, please, please, keep him safe, she prayed. *He's already weak — he's already been wounded — please, you didn't forge him to die like this!*

Unless, of course, She had. But that thought was no comfort at all, so Taya thrust it away. Whatever purpose the Lady had for her tools, she never used them carelessly. Each soul was reborn to fulfill a distinct purpose in life, and as long as they worked toward that purpose, the Lady would keep them safe.

Taya couldn't guess what plans the Lady had made for Cristof, but she knew what the Lady had intended for *her*. She'd been born to carry messages. And now she had to carry the most important message in her life.

She lifted the lantern from Cristof's pack and shook it. A little oil left. She lit it, keeping the beam low. Its glow steadied her. She rummaged through the pack and pulled out half a sausage.

Half a sausage? It was Cristof's half from lunch, tucked back into his pack when she hadn't been paying attention. For a moment she didn't understand why he'd kept it, and then she did.

He'd been planning to give it to her for her flight. Because he'd known she'd need the extra energy to reach Kovolo.

Tears burned her eyes as she jammed it into a pocket and dug into the pack again. His map of Ondinium. His slim leather toolkit. Four scientific journals, rumpled, dog-eared, and covered with scribbles. His cherished, ridiculous-looking headpiece full of magnifying lenses. An empty canteen. A bundle of ammunition for the needle pistol. The pencil she'd taken from the AME freight yard. Her extra lead weights.

Exactly the kind of useless miscellany she'd expect a gearhead like Cristof to pack, she thought, blinking back fresh tears. She turned out her own pockets.

The Alzanan map. The morphine needle and a bottle— she wished she'd given them to Cristof to carry in his coat pocket. The watch that he had made her, with a wing engraved on the cover.

Her wings and compass and safety rope and utility knife.

What did she need?

How much could she carry?

She stared at the stack of goods, her mind blank. Then she picked up the Alzanan map and unfolded it, laying it next to Cristof's map of Ondinium. The Alzanan map wasn't as detailed, but it included Demican territory around the border. She located the same spot on Cristof's map and began to measure.

They were about forty miles from the border, as the icarus flew; about fifty-five if she angled southwest to Kovolo. The signal station along the border still seemed like her best bet. The strong winds through the mountain pass would slow her down, and she wasn't at her strongest or most energetic, but if she flew carefully, she could be there in two to two-and-a-half hours.

She checked the time. Just a little after eleven.

The heart-shaped ruby her husband had embedded in the face of her watch glittered and made her gasp with a sudden surge of grief. She snapped the case shut and slid the watch back into its pocket, swallowing the lump in her throat.

The sooner I get to the signal station, the sooner I can come back.

She took another look at her inventory.

She needed the canteen, which she filled with snow. Sausage. Maps. Tool case. Flare gun. She stored them all in the courier's pockets that covered her suit, trying to balance the weight. The lantern was too bulky to carry, although she'd need it on the walk back, but she tucked the matches into a pocket.

She held the headpiece full of lenses, turning it over and over in her hands.

Useless. Utterly and completely useless.

She put it back with the rest of the discards, stood, and tucked the pack high in the branches of one of the pines.

All right. She picked up the lantern and narrowed the hood, leaving herself only the smallest glimmer of light. She'd hike back to camp to orient herself, and then she'd take off.

She walked about ten steps before turning back. She found the tree again, pulled down the pack, fished out the headpiece, and crammed it into one of her larger pockets.

She didn't have Cristof's watch, so his ridiculous headpiece would have to keep him safe.

The lantern helped her avoid the bushes and branches, and the snow had stopped falling at last, but Taya still felt like she was walking in circles until she finally heard the low thrum of engines rumbling through the forest. As soon as she saw the glow of bright lights through the trees, she snuffed out the lantern and advanced more cautiously.

The camp was flooded with spotlights powered by a noisy generator. To Taya's dismay, two of the gigantic dirigibles had been moved outside and were floating close to the ground, Alzanan and Demican soldiers swarming around them. One ship's engine was rumbling, and the flaps on its tail fins moved back and forth as if being tested. A large lamp mounted on the front of its gondola snapped on, its bright beam piercing the darkness a minute before it was extinguished.

She bit her lip.

A searchlight meant that the dirigible could fly at night, which she couldn't unless she had a well-illuminated destination in sight.

A small signal station forty miles away in the mountains wasn't a well-illuminated destination.

She'd planned to take off at the first light of dawn, but it seemed that the general was taking Cristof's presence as a sign that he needed to attack at once. Scrap! How fast could he get his ship ready? She fished out her watch and checked it. Almost midnight. She wasn't sure how quickly the Alzanan vessel moved, but if it left before dawn, it could easily reach the Ondinium border before she could.

That left her with only one choice.

She'd have to follow the dirigibles until the sun came up.

CHAPTER TWENTY·ONE

TAYA EXPECTED THE entire fleet to launch at once, but only Number Six was being readied for immediate departure. She walked back and forth along the edge of the woods, stamping down the snow in a long track as she ate the last half of the sausage. She kept checking camp for some sign of Cristof, but there was nothing.

He's in their hospital, she told herself, fretfully. He's safe. The temptation to search for him was almost overwhelming, but the milling mass of soldiers and engineers in the encampment deterred her. She'd never be able to sneak into camp unobserved.

At last the loading was finished. A group of soldiers marched aboard the vessel— ten or twelve, by her uncertain count, which seemed like a small number for an invasion. Then again, the gondolas were compact. With all the crates they'd brought aboard, those twelve men would be packed together inside.

The gondola doors closed, workers coiled ropes and stored them away, and the giant aerostat's lights snapped on.

Taya walked up and down her crude little path, kicking away stones and making sure it hadn't iced up. She was underweight, which would facilitate a running take-off but make maintaining control in the air more difficult.

The ship began to move. A ragged cheer went up from the encampment, quickly stilled by a sharp command. Taya gazed with awe as the nose of the great, building-sized vehicle tipped upward for the ascent.

The dirigible didn't move very quickly. She hopped up and down and stretched her arms, loosening her cold muscles while the Alzanan ship ponderously rose out of the valley. At last, when all she could see was its searchlight, she buckled on her flight cap, pulled down her goggles, slid her arms into her wings, and ran.

Running take-offs were always ungainly, and this one was no exception. Fortunately, there was nobody to see her struggling-duck ascent. At last her wings caught the wind and she rode it high enough to kick down her tailset. Her heart was already laboring from the exertion. Two days spent locked in a train without enough food or rest was taking its toll. Freezing air knifed through the buttonholes and cuffs of her flight suit as she searched the horizon for the dirigible's searchlight. At last she found it and followed.

After ten minutes it became clear that outflying the ship would be a challenge. It wasn't moving quickly, but unlike her, it moved steadily, without the constant back-and-forth she had to engage in to negotiate unsteady thermals and winds.

Taya flew higher. The clouds were starting to break. The moon's pale illumination was both blessing and a risk; it allowed her to study the vehicle more closely, but she'd be silhouetted against the stars and moon. Military icarii used black-enameled wings, but a courier's wings were bright, shiny silver, easy to spot and recognize.

To reduce the risk, Taya beat forward until she was over the ship's long, vast envelope, her ears filled with the roar of its engines. The Alzanan dirigible's design was very different from Dautry's, in size and in construction. It seemed more solid, metallic, and sharp-edged. She dropped closer, spotting something that had been invisible from the ground. On the very top of the envelope stood a small wooden platform with railings and two large, swivel-mounted guns.

Taya veered away, searching for a gunner. Nobody was in sight. That made sense; why would Alzanans station a gunner on top of their dirigible at night, in the cold, so far away from a military target?

But the platform gave her an idea.

She kicked up her tailset and dropped onto the platform feet-first, backbeating to maintain her balance. The soles of her boots hit the wood, skidded, and gripped. She swiftly folded her wings against her body and crouched next to the gun tripods, listening for any sign she'd been heard.

Hearing nothing but the roar of the engines and the creaking of the gun tripods, she straightened and locked her wings close.

Gripping the platform's front rail, she leaned forward and gazed into the star-studded night.

The view from the top of the dirigible was breathtaking— an endless panorama of stars above and night-covered peaks below, their shapes revealed in momentary flashes as the dirigible's searchlight moved back and forth.

Ondinium's peacetime flag depicted five silver stars on a field of black. Stars were sparks from the Lady's forge, the old legends declared, each falling star a newly hammered soul plummeting to Ondinium to be reborn. Of course Ondinium's astronomers had long since proved that stars were natural phenomena, but here, on top of a gigantic, rumbling weapon of war, Taya felt a touch of the night sky's eternal magic.

She closed her eyes and prayed for Cristof.

After a while she sat with her back to the prow. Her mind drifted as she listened to the ship's engines, their roar louder or softer depending on how hard they labored to fight the wind. Several times she nodded off, awakening with a start as she started to slump. Next to her, the tripods creaked as the ship continued its implacable progress.

It's strange for a dirigible to have guns on top, she thought, sleepily. What could a gunner hit from such a high vantage point? Another dirigible? But nobody else had anything powerful enough to attack this one. Mareaux's little dirigibles couldn't carry much more than a few soldiers with rifles.

The only other thing that could fly high enough to come within the guns' range would be an icarus.

An icarus!

A flash of outrage dispelled Taya's sleepiness. She stood, pulled off her gloves, and ran her hands over the gun to see if she could snap something off, but it was too solid.

All right, she thought. *If I can't break you, I can dismantle you.* She pulled her husband's leather tool kit out of her pocket. *You never know when you might need a screwdriver*, he'd told her once, not long after they'd met. Sure enough, he was right.

She couldn't wait to tell him.

Taking the gun itself apart, she soon realized, wouldn't be easy. But slipping it off the tripod was possible, although she had to pound a few metal pins out of the frame. She paused after each strike, listening. Nobody came to investigate, and at last both heavy guns laid on the platform floor.

Taya slid her gloves back over her frozen hands.

They'd been flying over an hour, by her best guess. If she was going to get to the border before the Alzanan ship, she'd better get moving. The outpost would keep a lamp lit outside as a matter of course, for use by military icarii and lost travelers. All she needed to do was forge straight ahead and keep her eyes open.

She scowled at the guns by her feet. No point leaving them here. She shoved one off the edge of the platform and gave it a strong push. The weapon slid down the envelope's slope, picking up speed as it descended, and plummeted over the side.

Pleased, she launched the other gun over the other side of the ship.

Too bad she couldn't destroy the tripods, too, but that would take better tools than she had. Shrugging, she climbed over the platform railing and unlocked her wings, sliding her arms into place.

This hasn't happened since the Last War, she thought, staring at the point on the side of the envelope where the gun had vanished. An icarus launched from a flying ship. Before she could think about it long enough to be intimidated, she threw herself forward, kicking hard against the taut material of the envelope.

For a moment the huge, gryphon-painted side of the envelope whipped past her. She spread her wings. The air currents were choppy from the vessel's passage and she fought for control as she descended.

A bright light swept up and skewered her. She flinched, instinctively closing her eyes against the blinding glare.

Gunfire opened her eyes again in a hurry. She'd been spotted!

Still dazzled, Taya twisted into a dive, hoping she wasn't close to the forest canopy yet. The searchlight lost her, but she couldn't see anything, spots dancing before her eyes. She threw her wings out, blinking rapidly, and felt a gear catch in her left wing.

Light engulfed her again. She dodged, but the light followed, moving jerkily as whoever was guiding it sought to keep her spotlighted. She felt sharp vibrations through her wing feathers and heard something whine past her ear.

Stupid! She should have dropped under the gondola, hiding in its blind spot. Too late now. Her eyesight had adjusted. The cliffs, forest, and valley below looked black and white in the harsh glare of the dirigible's bright spotlight.

The grind in her left wing was getting worse. She was losing air through her feathers, which weren't closing all the way. A bullet hit her tailset. She cringed, remembering the last time she'd been shot.

Her left wing froze. Taya yanked her arm backward and felt both relief and sickness as, with a grate that shuddered through her entire armature, it moved again. She forced the wing into a spread and began a long, despairing dive to the valley floor.

Her landing was hard and painful, taken on her knees but throwing her sideways as her recalcitrant wing refused to backbeat. She staggered to her feet, looking up, and saw the searchlight move on.

Furious, she yanked her arms out of the wings, grabbed the flaregun Cristof had given her, and fired at the ship.

Smoke surrounded her. The missile rose and exploded far overhead in a bright cascade of red light.

She'd missed.

She threw the useless gun away, swearing. Then, in the dying light from the flare, she pulled her floating left wing close, searching for the damage.

There— a line of gears wasn't meshing anymore, knocked out of alignment by a bullet. She pushed on them, hoping to snap them back into place with her thumbs.

The flare blinked out, plunging her into darkness.

She swore again, frustrated tears burning her eyes.

At last she took a long, deep breath. She locked her good wing up, used her safety line to clip her armature to one of the leather loops on her flight suit, and climbed out.

The light from the stars wasn't much, but it was enough for her to see the bent and chipped feathers that had been hit by Alzanan bullets. A fresh gouge on the keel cage that had been snapped over her chest made her wince.

She'd gotten lucky.

But, as the Alzanan general had said, not lucky enough. She looked up at the sky, frustrated. There was no way she'd be able to beat the ship to the signal station now.

For a moment she was consumed by an urge to drop down into the snow and give up.

Cristof was captured. She was grounded.

The Alzanans had won.

She took a deep, shuddering breath, clenching her fists.

Not yet.

She wouldn't give up. The dirigible might beat her to the border, but there were five more ships in that hangar. One ship wasn't going to attack Ondinium by itself; it must be a scout of some sort, maybe checking to be sure Cristof hadn't been leading a military operation.

She might, possibly, be able to beat the other ships to the border. *If* she was close enough, and *if* she didn't waste any time feeling sorry for herself.

Filled with grim resolve, Taya bound her broken wing to the rest of the armature and slid herself back into its metal framework. She checked her compass, making a mental note of the direction the ship had been going, and began to walk.

CHAPTER TWENTY-TWO

TIME STRETCHES IN infinite directions in the forest, in the cold, in the dark. Taya's progress became a mechanical repetition of movements broken only by her occasional stumble over a snow-covered branch or stagger when a gust of wind threw her off-balance. She became preternaturally aware of the crunching of the snow under her boots, the sound of her strained breathing, and the creak of her armature. Noises in the darkness made her freeze, her gloved hand gripping her utility knife. Wolves lived in the Demican woods, and bears, and both had been known to attack lone travelers.

If she hadn't wasted her flare firing at the Alzanan ship, she could have used it against a predator.

Too late, now.

Taya was concentrating so hard on the sounds around her that even though she saw the lights moving in her direction, she didn't understand what they meant. Then, abruptly, she realized that they indicated the presence of humans.

She stopped.

"Hello?" she ventured, her voice cracking and barely above a whisper. She cleared her throat and called out more strongly. "Hello? Hello?"

Somebody shouted. The lights changed direction, moving toward her. With belated caution, Taya brandished her knife. The newcomers were approaching from the wrong direction to be from the Alzanan encampment, and they were moving faster than a man could walk.

Then they appeared— three large, bearded men on skis. They skidded to a halt about ten feet away from her in a spraying plume of snow. Two carried rifles over their shoulders and held lanterns; the third carried some kind of long stick. They wore long, embroidered felt coats and bright hats with ear flaps. Their boots and gloves were trimmed with fur, and their faces looked stern.

Taya stood as tall as she could.

"Well met in peacetime," she said, in Demican. "I am Taya Icarus."

One of the figures cocked his head.

"Well met in peacetime," he replied, in the same language. "I am Juha Pasanen."

"Mika Talus."

"Edvin Talus."

They fell silent, inspecting each other. Taya was suddenly, self-consciously aware that she was a very small, poorly armed woman facing three large foreign men with no reason to respect her caste.

"You are Ondinium," Edvin observed.

"I am." She hastened to add, "I came here to find out what the Alzanans were doing. Did you see their, their aerostat?" She used the Ondinan word. "The flying ship?"

"We saw it," Juha said. "And we saw a flare. Was it yours?"

"Yes. The ship is Alzanan. It's the scout for an invasion. I need to get to Ondinium to warn my people."

"Why did you signal it, then?"

"I was trying to shoot it."

"You missed."

"It was the first time I have ever fired a gun."

Mika and Edvin chuckled.

"You are an Ondinium flyer?" Juha continued.

"An icarus, yes," she said, cautiously.

"You are missing a wing."

"It was damaged by an Alzanan bullet."

"It will be difficult for you to warn your country, then, will it not?"

"There is a signal station not far from here, on the border. If I can get to it, I can send an alert." She took a breath and hoped they weren't *sheytatangri*. "Will you help me?"

Juha turned to the other men.

"It is your time."

"We are hunting," Edvin explained to her, leaning on one of his poles. "We were curious when we saw the big ... *aerostat* ... and the flare, so we came out to see what had happened. But a war between Alzana and Ondinium is none of our business."

Taya debated with herself over how much to say. These three didn't seem very politically inclined; maybe they didn't know what was going on.

"Those ships have a white bear's head painted on them, as well as an Alzanan gryphon. When Ondinium sees that bear, this fight is quickly going to become every Demican's business."

The hunters looked at each other. Juha scratched his beard, his eyes narrowing.

"*Sheytatangri?*"

"The *sheytatangri* will drag Demicus into the Alzanan-Ondinium conflict," Taya agreed. Juha glanced at her, then back at his companions.

"Clan Vost."

"Of course; they always forge ahead on their own." Edvin sounded annoyed. "Elder Helka will have to call an assembly."

"Please— I know you need to warn your leaders, but I need to warn mine, too. Could one of you take me to the border?"

"Why?" asked the third man, Mika, who'd been silent until now.

"I—" Taya hesitated. "I have no money with me, but I will tell the Council that your clan is not involved in the attack. And my husband is an exalted; we could arrange to send a reward to you later, or offer you favored trading status at one of the border towns...."

"Is it true that exalted men wear dresses and masks?" Mika asked. Edvin and Juha laughed.

"Yes," she said, irritated that they were mocking Ondinium customs. But Cristof mocked them, too, so she supposed she couldn't be too sensitive about it.

Cristof....

"I have no patience for empty promises from Ondinium," Mika said after the laughing died down. He turned to the other two. "If the *sheytatangri* and the Alzanans want to wipe them out, let them."

"No, not without calling an *ating* first," Edvin objected. "The *sheyta* don't speak for all *tangri*. Now we will have Alzanans and Ondiniums fighting their war on our land, and who will suffer? Not Vost! It will be our clans, the ones closest to the border."

"You said that Clan Vost was behind this?" Taya asked, biting back her impatience. "I will tell that to Ondinium's Council, our elders."

"Vost is on the northern coast. They trade with the Alzanans." Juha shrugged. "I have heard that the Alzanans pay some of them to speak against Ondinium in the *tangri*."

"That sounds like a typical Alzanan strategy. Which clan do you belong to?"

"Malo."

"Clan Malo knew there was a foreign encampment in the mountains," Edvin added, "but we assumed it was another Ondinium mine."

"On your land?"

"That is Clan Alta land. They allow foreigners to take their metal and wood."

"Short-sighted," Juha muttered.

"I will tell the Council that Clan Malo objects to the invasion and that the Council should talk to Clan Alta about the encampment," Taya promised.

"Listen to her," Mika grunted. "She does not know one clan from another, and neither do her elders. Her promises are as worthless as her broken wings."

"All the more reason to explain it to the girl, Mika," Edvin countered. "I think it would be useful to have an Ondinium exalted in debt to us. Eliina trades in Kovolo."

"We should keep our heads down and stay out of it."

"Then what would we do with this girl? Leave her here to feed the wolves?"

"She wants help and I want more than promises." Mika turned and looked her up and down. "What about sex?"

Taya flushed, her hand tightening on her knife.

"No."

"Your wings?"

"I'm not permitted to give them away."

"We could kill you and take them."

"You could try," she countered, taking a nervous step backward.

"Oh, shut up, Mika," Edvin said, sounding exasperated. "Nobody is going to kill you, girl. We can take you to Pekka Lake, at least."

"I am not helping an Ondinium," Mika objected.

"Eliina would skin me alive if I passed up a chance to make a trade alliance with the wife of an exalted." Edvin looked at Taya. "Ondinium has a station at the lake. A flyer like you lives there."

Taya didn't think Edvin was referring to the station she wanted, but she didn't care to be abandoned in the middle of nowhere again, either. Especially around Mika.

"Thank you. I appreciate it, and I will remember."

"I will go, too," Juha decided. He turned to Edvin. "Which one of us will carry her?"

"*Carry* me?"

"She does not look very heavy," Edvin said, grinning through his icy beard.

Taya wasn't enthusiastic about being carried, but Edvin convinced her that it would be fastest if she clung to his back as he skied. With many misgivings, she folded her operational wing to minimize the drag. Then she hopped up, wrapping her arms around his broad neck and tucking her legs around his waist.

"You weigh as much as my seven-year-old daughter," he laughed. She didn't try to explain about ondium; she just nodded and promised herself that Cristof would never, ever learn about this particular leg of her trip.

Lady, just give me a chance to tell him about this trip at all, she prayed.

Edvin and Juha bade goodbye to Mika, and in moments they were skimming across the snow.

The Demicans seemed comfortable traveling in silence. It reminded her of traveling with Lieutenant Amcathra. She wondered where he was and what he was doing. Then she wondered how her husband was doing. Then she tried not to think at all, because all of her thoughts were depressing.

The Demicans sped down a series of slopes, finding paths in the forest that Taya knew she would have missed on her own and taking them as carelessly as she might turn down a street in her own neighborhood. If the route to the lake was marked in any way, she didn't see it. At one point they stopped and Juha turned to look at Edvin, who just shrugged Taya up higher on his back and waved him forward. Taya felt ridiculous.

The two Demicans finally slid to a stop upon reaching a flat, snowy expanse. Taya dropped down, her legs and arms aching, and stretched. Edvin did the same, grinning as he rolled his shoulders back and forth.

"You are a little heavier than my seven-year-old," he admitted.

"Is this Pekka Lake?" she asked, looking around for some sign of a border station. She saw nothing but wilderness on either side. Dawn was still far away, but the stars were fading and the pines were dark silhouettes against a lightening sky.

Juha ignored her, working at the buckles on his skis.

"The Ondinium border is over there," Edvin said, pointing.

"Do you have a boat?"

"Of course. Sailing is much faster than skiing, and it is easier to bring game home on a boat." He crouched and began taking off his skis, as well.

"What were you hunting?"

"Deer."

Taya felt a moment's disappointment. She'd been hoping he'd say bear.

"Is the hunting good out here?"

He nodded.

"And it is also good to get out of the house for a few days," he added, amiably. Taya smiled.

"How many children do you have?"

"Four. Two sons and a daughter, and a nephew. You?"

"No children, not yet. I have a niece or a nephew on the way, though."

A rustling noise made her turn. Juha was pulling loose branches away from three odd-looking boats.

"I have never seen a boat with skis before," she said, staring.

Edvin jabbed his skis straight up in the snow and trudged over to help his companion. "How else would we cross the lake? The water is frozen."

Fascinated, she watched as the men set up two long, narrow boats — one painted bright yellow and the other bright red, and both bearing wide painted eyes on either side of their sharp prows — and raised their sails.

"Do you know how to ride an ice craft?" Edvin asked, as they finished.

"No."

"Then sit in the back and avoid moving," he said.

"My wings might cause some problems," she warned him.

He nodded, inspecting them.

"Keep them low, away from the sail."

As the Demicans pulled the boats out onto the ice, Taya heard a mechanical noise in the distance. She looked up with a sinking heart. Another of the giant Alzanan ships was flying toward them, its painted beasts looking eager to sink their claws and teeth into Ondinium.

Juha and Edvin looked up with her. One dirigible passed overhead, and then another, and then another, and then a fourth. Taya waited, but the fifth ship never came. She wondered if it had been delayed or incapacitated.

"It is the *sheytatangri*," Juha observed.

"Did they think the clans would ignore this?" Edvin asked, scowling.

"What will the clans do about it?" Taya felt sick as she watched the dirigibles vanish toward the horizon.

"We will discuss that at the *ating*." Edvin turned back to his ship. "Are you ready to leave?"

"Yes. Please." She pulled off her armature, securing it to her flight suit with the safety rope, then embraced the awkward mass as she settled into the narrow seat. She hoped Edvin was a good sailor.

He sat in front of her, perched on the yellow-painted hull, one foot resting on the ice. He tugged his blue-and-yellow hat closer around his ears and grasped the ropes that controlled the two sails.

"Ready?"

"Ready."

Edvin lifted his foot and swung into his seat as the ice boat began to move. The wind puffed the sails, sending the two craft skimming along the icy surface of the lake.

Under any other circumstances, Taya would be ecstatic to speed across a frozen lake at such high speeds. But now she hugged her armature close, the nausea of helpless worry filling her empty stomach with bile as she watched the shoreline flash past.

The trip didn't take long; the sun hadn't quite risen over the mountains when they reached the wood-and-stone building standing next to a wooden dock. Juha and Edvin deftly steered their boats to the dock, bringing them to slow, sliding halts. Taya climbed out onto the icy lake, clutching her armature.

"Go up," Edvin said, tilting his head toward a set of wooden steps. "Juha and I will be there in a minute."

"Thank you," she said, picking her away across the slippery ice. She clambered up to the dock while the Demican hunters furled their sails and secured their craft. A slatboard walkway led to the house's front porch. A sign over the door declared it to be the *Pekka Border Station* in Ondinan and Demican. Taya didn't see any signaling apparatus.

She knocked.

No answer. She shifted her armature to one arm and pounded harder.

"Hey!" she shouted, in Ondinan. "Wake up! Is anyone in there?" She rattled the door handle, but it was latched. She pounded again.

"All right, hold on, I'm coming," somebody said, faintly, inside. A lock clicked and the door swung open, revealing a skinny, haggard-looking young man who inspected her with bloodshot eyes. "Oh, scrap," he groaned, closing his eyes. "Who are you?"

"Taya Icarus, and I need to send a message to Ondinium immediately." She pushed past him, smelling cheap liquor, and began untying her armature. The main room of the station was cluttered, musty, and dark. Her foot hit a bottle that rolled to one side. "Who's the icarus here?"

"Uh." The man swayed a moment, swallowing. "Me."

She gave him a sharp look. He was in no shape to fly.

"Can you send a 'graph from here?"

He turned, groping for the nearest chair, and sank into it. "No."

She released her bundled armature, not bothering to watch as it floated up and thudded against the ceiling.

"Then where's your armature?"

He stared at her, pale and uncomprehending.

"Your armature?"

He lifted a shaking hand and pointed to a set of wings floating in a dark corner.

The door slammed open, letting in light and a gust of cold air. The young man cringed as Edvin and Juha walked in, stomping snow off their boots and loosening their snow-dusted jackets.

"It is as dark as a cave in here." Edvin pulled open a window and unfastened the shutters.

"Please...." The icarus shrank back, looking ill as he protested in Demican. "Shut the door."

Juha closed it as Edvin threw open the shutters. Grateful for the light, Taya inspected the other icarus's armature, pulling out Cristof's toolkit. She'd need to adjust the strut lengths to accommodate her smaller size.

Juha built up the fire in the large stove in one corner as Edvin opened two more windows. The morning light did nothing to improve the room, which seemed to combine a cluttered general store with somebody's personal living space.

"So, Nayan," Edvin said as he looked around, "what happened to Hari?"

"He was transferred," Nayan said, letting his head sink into his hands. "A week ago. Do I know you?"

"We met twice last spring, but you were drunk then, too." Edvin seemed amused. Taya began adjusting Nayan's armature as Juha set a pot of water on the stove. "This girl says the Alzanans are invading Ondinium."

Nayan lifted his head an inch.

"What?"

"They just flew five giant, heavily armed dirigibles across the border," Taya snapped in Ondinan. "Shouldn't you be on the lookout for something like that?"

"I monitor water travel." Nayan dropped his head again. "North Peak Six monitors the rest."

"Do you have anything to eat?" she asked, disgusted. He groaned.

"He has food," Juha reported, checking the cupboards.

"Is there anything I can make quickly? I'm starving, but I can't waste any time."

"I apologize," Edvin said, his eyes widening. "I should have offered you food."

"Yes," Juha agreed, although whether he was agreeing with the apology or the observation, Taya couldn't tell. She tried on Nayan's armature, then pulled it off to adjust the tailset. Juha began slicing cheese and sausage. Her stomach growled.

"Tell me about the clans," she said. "How many are likely to support the *sheytatangri*?"

"The clan elders do not endorse the *sheytatangri*. The *sheytatangri* demand unity, but our elders prefer independence. They do not want to elect a king or queen of Demicus."

"*Sheytatangri* are terrorists," Nayan muttered in Ondinan from beneath his arm.

"They've teamed up with the Alzanans," she replied, in the same language.

Nayan groaned again.

"The elders will call an *ating* to censure the *tangri*," Juha said, from the kitchen, "but there is little we can do to stop a flying ship."

"Well, if the *ating* would stop the clans from cooperating with the Alzanans, even for a little while, that might help," Taya said.

Remembering Mika's criticism, she pulled out the map she'd taken from the Alzanan aerostat. "Where are the clans located?"

Edvin looked curiously at her. Taya wondered if he'd ever seen a map of Demicus before.

"This is where we are now," she said, finding Pekka Lake. "Where's your clan?"

Assisted by Juha and the extremely reluctant Nayan, Taya marked the location of a number of Demican clans, along with their political, personal, and *tangri* affiliations. Some of the names were familiar from her diplomatic corps studies, but the books had done little to prepare her for the complexity of clan structures and relationships.

"Thank you," she said when they were finished. "That will help. How long will it take to call the *ating*?"

"Elder Helka can summon our closest neighbors within a few days," Edvin said. "But for a full *ating*, messengers must be sent weeks away. It is not a quick process."

"Can you have the neighboring clans meet yours here at the station? If " she glanced at the map, "Malo, Alta, and Teje decide not to support the invasion, we will want to let the Council know as soon as possible."

"Here?" Nayan sat up, wincing.

"Here," Taya said, firmly. "Which means you'll have to repair my wings and fly the clans' decision up to North Peak Six so they can 'graph it back to Oporphyr Tower. This is important, Nayan— you'll be the diplomatic liaison between Demicus and Ondinium."

"Me?" Nayan stared at her through bloodshot eyes. Edvin and Juha looked equally unconvinced.

"You're the only person available. Ondinium is counting on you." She hoped he was up to the responsibility. "Edvin, Juha, do you think you can convince your clans to work with Nayan?"

"We can try," Edvin said, dubiously. "I understand that it will be necessary to contact your Council, but...."

"He can do it," she said, with more confidence than she felt. "Thank you. Is there anything I can do for you? As I said, I have no money now, but—?"

"My wife Eliina trades furs in Kovolo with an Ondinium woman with a circle on her forehead," Edvin said. "Rupa. Rupa... Aelius? A name like that. If you can help her with her trade, or bring her something to take back to the clan, you could leave it there."

Taya jotted down the names, waved the note a moment to dry the ink, and tucked it into her flight suit pocket next to her watch.

"I will do whatever I can," she promised. "Juha? What about you?"

The hunter pushed the sliced cheese and sausage toward her.

"Give Eliina money for me. She knows what supplies I need."

"I will." Taya bolted down half the food and then jammed the rest into her flight suit pockets without a moment's hesitation. Nayan didn't look like he'd be eating any time soon. Juha handed her a mug. She wrinkled her nose at the steaming combination of hot water and the same herb-flavored liquor she smelled on the icarus.

"I need to be able to fly," she objected.

"It will keep you warm," Juha said. "You have far to go."

I suppose a little diluted alcohol probably won't kill me, she decided, taking a hesitant sip. The heat *was* welcome. Taya had forgotten what it felt like to stop shivering.

She finished the drink and turned back to the map.

"Show me the best route to the station, Nayan."

The icarus dragged himself over to her. This close, Taya could see stains on his clothes, a careless combination of Demican fur and felt and Ondinium silk and cotton. His hair had a brownish tint to it, and dark stubble covered his cheeks and chin. Like her, he wasn't a pureblood.

"Here." He pointed with a trembling hand. "And here." His finger moved north. "Fifteen minutes most days. Wind's good to here." He pointed beyond the station. "Then it's dangerous." He glanced at her bundled armature. "How bad is the damage?"

"The Alzanans shot at me and knocked some gears out of alignment. I'm sure you'll be able to fix it with a manual and a good set of tools, but I don't have the time." She pulled out her compass, checked the route, and folded the map. "Edvin, Juha, thank you very much for helping me. This is very important to all of us."

"What is your name again?" Edvin asked.

"Taya. My husband is Exalted Cristof Forlore; whatever I send your wife will have the Forlore name on it."

"I will tell Eliina," Edvin promised.

"Taya. Tell your elders there are many Alzanans in the north," Juha said. Taya looked at him, confused. He met her eyes. "The Alzanans sell the northern clans guns and generators; things Ondiniums will not sell to the southern clans."

"Then ... if there were a war ... do you think the northern clans will side with the Alzanans?"

"The clan elders will not approve of a *tangri* making an alliance without consulting them, but if they feel they must choose sides, it is likely that they will choose the side that does not treat them like children."

"Thank you," she said, unhappily. "I'll warn the Council."

With her hasty meal sitting uneasily in her stomach, Taya strapped herself into Nayan's armature and walked outside to climb the ladder to the roof.

The sun had finally risen over the surrounding peaks and crags. The sky was a brilliant pale blue dotted with fluffy white clouds. With her breath condensing before her, Taya stretched her muscles, tested the borrowed armature's gears, and then threw herself into the air.

Nayan, like all icarii, was smaller than average, but he was still taller and heavier than Taya. She'd adjusted the armature's struts, straps, and tailset to accommodate her height, but there was nothing she could do about its overall mass, which had been designed to lift a heavier body than hers. She swooped up into the sky and struggled to keep herself aligned. Nayan's broader wings would have been perfect if she'd wanted to skydance, but for straightforward travel, they weren't as accommodating as her own, smaller wings.

On the other hand, she didn't have to work as hard to gain altitude. Soon she soared over peaks washed in light from the sunrise. There— a glimmer of silver. She angled toward it. It was the train track that circled Ondinium, supplying the nation's border stations and ensuring that troops could be transported to any place in the country.

Not that infantry would be much good against dirigibles.

A bright gleam caught her eye. The signal station. But to her alarm, its signal mirror tilted out toward Demicus instead of toward the other peaks along the border.

Taya let the warmer currents flowing over the peaks lift her higher as she searched the skyline. Her eyes caught another flash farther away. The ships had crossed the border and were working their way through the difficult passes toward their first targets. They hadn't gotten as far as she'd feared; maybe the Alzanans hadn't realized how bad the wind conditions could be in Ondinium's high passes.

North Peak Six had once been one of imperial Ondinium's ancient stone forts, although most of the original fortress had been abandoned to the elements. She circled and landed on the station's flight dock. The snow around the station was trampled and bloodstained. Taya grimly locked up her wings, loosened her utility knife, and climbed down the metal ladder.

The signaling engine was still rumbling, but the snow around the station's entrance had been churned up and bullet holes riddled the open doors. Taya pushed them aside and flinched at the sight of a dead lictor slumped over a table, covered in blood.

Two more lictors, one male and one female, sprawled in blood-stained heaps by the wall closest to the punch-card engine. Bullet holes in both walls indicated a two-sided firefight, although Taya didn't see any rifles in the lictors' hands. The Alzanans must have looted them.

"I'm sorry," she whispered, sickened. If only she'd gotten there sooner…. She walked around the building to the engine room door. Inside, the large steam engine's firebox door was hanging open and the flame was low.

Taya grabbed the shovel by the coal box and added more fuel to the fire until it burned hot enough to drive her back. She prodded the firebox door closed with the shovel's handle, then backed out of the engine room with relief. *Hard to imagine I'd ever feel too hot again*, she thought.

A grubby dedicate stood next to the door, pointing a rifle at her. Next to him, leaning on the wall, a heavily bandaged lictor sat holding a pistol.

They lowered their weapons as soon as they saw her wings. "Icarus?"

"Who are you?" she demanded. Dried blood and dirt had been ground into the dedicate's coat and trousers and ran down his face, and brambles were snagged in his hair. His left hand was bandaged. The lictor beside him looked worse, with half his face swathed in bloody rags.

"I'm Karl," the dedicate said, looking relieved. "This is Corporal Sapur. We were attacked by Alzanans in a huge flying ship. Everyone else was killed."

"Does Ondinium know yet?"

"No. The Alzanans disabled the mirror before we knew what was happening."

"Can you fix it?"

"I think so. If you'll help. It's heavy, and the corporal's not in any condition to lend a hand."

"Let's do it, then."

Leaving Sapur by the foot of the stairs, Karl led her up to the top of the signal station. The storm panes that protected the giant lamp were cracked, and the lamp and its mirrored reflector had been tilted up and out of their support frame.

"I think they turned it to signal the other ships," Taya said. "There are five of them now."

"I heard the others arrive this morning." Karl picked up a long metal pole and inspected the bent end, frowning. "They stayed here a while and left when it got a little lighter. Sapur and I were hiding. Here, we need to roll the mirror back on the tracks."

Taya glanced at his bandages. "Can you use your hand?"

The dedicate gave her a humorless smile.

"I'll use it, one way or the other."

They hoisted the mechanism back into its support frame-work, squinting against the bright light, and manually turned it around to point in the correct direction.

"It won't rotate until I fix it," Karl said, "but at least we can 'graph the capital."

Downstairs, they helped the wounded corporal into the build-ing. Karl paused at the door, just as she had, but then moved in, averting his eyes from the dead bodies. They put Sapur into a chair. He closed his one good eye, wincing.

"Signal that there are five, maybe six Alzanan dirigibles in Ondinium airspace," Taya directed as Karl pulled out a punch machine and an unperforated card. "Ten to twelve guns each. They're being guided by Decatur Neuillan."

"A decatur!" Karl gave her a shocked look, then swallowed and began punching. She pulled out her invasion map and unfolded it, checking the route.

"What's south of here?" she asked.

"On the way to the capital? Glasgar Base, Patimbrium and Quadrapur."

The names roused the corporal, who straightened and looked at the map.

"I'll tell them the ships are probably headed to Glasgar," Karl said.

"And," she added in a tight voice, "Exalted Cristof Forlore may be aboard one of the ships as a hostage."

"The ambassador?" The dedicate blinked and then gave her a second look. "Wait, are you that icarus he married?"

"Yes."

"I'm sorry — I mean — is he all right?" Copper cheeks flushing, he turned back to the punchcard.

"He was shot. Don't bother putting that down; keep the message short."

"But he's alive?"

She swallowed.

Of course he's alive.

"He was when I left."

"Lady keep him," Karl murmured, devoutly. He finished, filling two cards. "This is crude work, Icarus, and it's not encoded."

"That's all right. Can you send it now?"

He nodded, skirting the bodies of the two dead lictors to flip a series of switches. He slid the cards into the feeder tray.

"I'll set it to repeat until it's manually stopped," he said, turning and heading toward the door. "Come on. I want to make sure it's working."

It wasn't, at first, but to Taya's relief the dedicate located the belt that had been knocked out of place and hooked it back up. The signal began flashing its message.

Taya hoped they were in time.

"Are there going to be any more of those ships?" Karl asked. "This fort has cannon, although they've only been used in drills. Still, if we'd known...."

"There were six ships in the hangar. The guns might be useful if the last one shows up late."

"I'll talk to the corporal, then."

They returned to the signal room. Taya leaned over the map, finding North Peak Six and tracing the flight route to Glasgar.

"The dirigibles were just about here when I flew in," she said, pointing. "They don't have as much of a head start as I thought, since they stopped here to regroup, but I don't think I can beat them to Glasgar Base." She studied the map. "I guess all I can do is try."

"The winds through those passes are treacherous," Karl objected. "Sometimes we don't even let the trains through, and a train weighs a lot more than you do."

"There's a railway," Corporal Sapur said, weakly. "Under the fort."

Karl looked puzzled, but Taya understood at once.

"The atmospheric railway?"

The lictor nodded.

"Can you take me there?"

He shook his head.

"Start the pumps. Emergency setting. Get in fast. Seal the doors."

"Are you sure? The last time, we had to get permission from the Council."

"This is war."

War. Taya looked around at the blood and corpses. He was right. This was war.

"All right," she said, folding the map. "Tell me where to go."

"Key's on the sergeant."

Karl walked over to one of the dead bodies and fished out a ring of keys, wiping his hands on his pants when he was done. He brought the ring back to Sapur, who sorted it and showed two keys to Taya.

"Follow me." He lurched to his feet and Karl slid a shoulder under his arms. "I'll take you to the stairs. Bring two lanterns."

Their route took them out of the station and into the abandoned part of the stone fortress. Sapur instructed them through its massive, arched hallways and past thousand-year-old bas reliefs that still retained flecks of their original gilding.

"This place is beautiful," Taya said as they half-carried the corporal down a flight of broad, shallow stairs. Mythical beasts cavorted on the walls to either side of them. "It's like being in a museum. Does anybody ever come here?"

"The lictors carry out exercises about once a month," Karl said, looking around with curiosity. "But the rest of the staff isn't allowed in. We were told it wasn't safe."

"These forts were carved out of solid rock. They're as safe as the mountain."

"It's not safe," Sapur gasped, "because it contains a state secret."

Taya remembered what the stationmaster at South Alpha Incline had said about the death penalty. "Maybe Karl shouldn't go any farther."

"No choice."

"I won't tell anyone you came with us," Taya promised the suddenly queasy-looking dedicate.

"Thanks," he said, swallowing hard. He knew what keeping a state secret implied, too.

They passed through several more halls and stopped at a giant, locked door. Taya unlocked it with one of the keys. A long, steep stairwell descended into the darkness.

"Tracks lead to the pump room," Sapur said.

"Am I going to know how to turn everything on?"

"Switches are labeled. Set them to emergency."

She looked at the corporal's pale, sweating face.

"Do you want to come with me? There'll be a hospital at Glasgar Base."

"No time to help me down."

Taya knew better than to argue. She took the lantern.

"Good luck," Karl said.

"Strap in," Sapur advised.

Taya jogged down the stairs, one hand on the stone wall and the other holding the lantern. The air was musty and smelled like rock, and by the time she reached the bottom, she felt like the whole mountain was bearing down on her. The sensation made her throat and chest tight.

As the corporal had promised, tracks ran from the stairs into a pitch-black tunnel. She found a small service handcar and pulled it onto the rails, set the lantern by her feet, and began pumping the car down the tracks.

As before, the tunnel opened up into a larger chamber, its walls giant sheets of bedrock intricately carved with imperial-era designs. The lantern light didn't reach the other side of the chamber. Taya unlocked the pump room door and paused to study the confusion of steel levers and glass dials that covered one wall. A large sign over one panel said "Start Here." An arrow pointed down.

She dutifully lifted the levers marked "Pump Room On" in the order in which they were numbered. A loud clicking and a series of metallic bangs echoed through the room. Something started to chug.

Did the lictors keep the railway's engines stoked twenty-four hours a day? Impossible, she decided. The engines must have some kind of automatic ignition mechanism.

Cristof would love this.

Arrows engraved into the wooden face of the control panel led her eyes to three more levers. She lifted the lever labeled

"Emergency Operation" and ignored the other two, "Manual Operation" and "Automatic Operation."

The arrow from the "Emergency Operation" lever pointed to a small sign at the end of the panel.

1. Enter train immediately.
2. Seal doors.
3. Secure luggage. Unsecured items may cause injury.
4. Secure harness. Do not unfasten until train has come to a complete stop.
5. Remove masks and spectacles. Avoid holding objects that may be jarred from your hands during transit.

Taya took a deep breath. Leaving the keys on the control panel, she ran out to the tubular-looking train car and climbed inside as fast as she could, leaving the lantern on the tracks. In the darkness, she closed the door and pulled herself out of her armature. Holding it in one hand, she sat down and buckled herself in. The sign hadn't said how much time she had, and she wasn't about to sit in the vehicle without being strapped in.

Then she reached over and buckled the armature in, two seats away, blindly running the straps through its struts and doing her best to secure it by touch.

Good enough. She sat back and tugged on the buckles and straps to make sure they were tight. The engine's roar grew louder and louder around her.

At last, just when Taya was starting to wonder if she'd done something wrong and the whole station was going to explode around her, the train leaped forward, slamming her sideways against her harness. The side of her head hit the curved head protection and she bit the edge of her tongue. Blood filled her mouth as the car hurtled forward into the heart of the mountain and then plunged straight down.

Chapter Twenty-Three

BY THE TIME the car stopped, Taya's hands were shaking so much that she could barely manage to unfasten the buckles. She finally worked them open and lurched across the darkness, fumbling for the door. She pulled the metal bar down and tumbled forward as it opened, her knees collapsing under her weight.

She laid on the wooden platform, heedless of the grit grinding into her cheek. Her gloved fingers curled as she tried to stop the world from moving.

Somebody shouted. Footsteps vibrated the wood beneath her ear.

She didn't care. As long as the ground didn't drop out from beneath her, she didn't care.

Voices rose around her. Someone touched her shoulder.

"…injured? I need to move you."

"No," she rasped. Her throat was sore from screaming.

"Are you in pain? Is anything broken?"

She opened her eyes and saw a black knee next to her face.

"There's a pair of wings in here, Captain. Nothing else."

Captain. A lictor.

Taya started to raise her head and felt her stomach lurch. She paused.

"Icarus?" The lictor laid his hand on her shoulder. "Are you ill? Have you been injured?"

"Sick," she breathed.

"Emergency transit would make anyone sick," somebody muttered.

"At least we know the brakes still work," another person replied, cheerfully.

"Are you wounded?" pressed the captain.

"No." She didn't think her sore throat counted, and as far as she could tell all her bones were intact, although the last few minutes of the trip had been full of terrible, jarring jerks that had ground her against the safety harness.

She pushed herself up. Darkness swam before her eyes as she rode out another wave of nausea.

"Icarus, you were on an emergency transport from North Peak Six Signal Station," the captain said crisply. "Are you responsible for the invasion warning we received from that station?"

"Yes." She licked her lips, tasting blood. "I saw the ships."

"Then we need to get you to the base." The captain stood. "If you need to vomit, go ahead."

She didn't want to vomit. Although, when she staggered to her feet, clutching his hand, she wasn't sure she would have any choice in the matter.

She stood doubled over and motionless a long minute. When she thought she would be all right, she straightened, feeling like an old woman.

"Captain, her wings?"

"Bring them."

Concentrating on a point just in front of her eyes to minimize her nausea, Taya paid no attention as they left the platform and climbed into a small, engine-powered railcar. The lurch as it started moving nearly undid her.

She huddled in her seat with her arms folded over her knees and her head sunk between them. The captain left her in peace.

By the time she climbed out, Taya was starting to feel like she might survive. She peered around, finding herself in the middle of a very active military base. Armed lictors in full uniform were hauling crates and duffel bags and leading heavily loaded pack mules. Military icarii hurried through camp in their distinctive gray uniforms and black-enameled wings.

"This way, Icarus," the captain ordered. She followed.

"Have you seen the ships yet?" she asked.

"We sent out scouts as soon as we received the warning. They left about half an hour ago. We're still waiting for their report."

Half an hour?

The atmospheric railway had taken her to Glasgar much faster than she could have flown; much faster than they'd traveled from South Alpha Incline to Overlook, too. Although, to be fair, this route had seemed to be mostly straight down.

She hated to think about what would have happened if the emergency brakes *hadn't* worked.

The captain led her through a two-storey stone building to a room full of black-uniformed men and women standing around a large table. They turned as she walked in.

"An icarus from North Peak Six," the captain reported, saluting. "She said she sent the warning."

"Taya Icarus, sirs." Taya pulled off her flight cap and goggles. She could tell by the number of stars on the sleeves around her that she'd just walked into a command meeting. She searched the room for a familiar face but recognized nobody.

"Icarus." One of the officers stepped forward, a middle-aged woman with a strong, stocky build and short salt-and-pepper hair. "I'm General Kammel. The Alzanans have Exalted Forlore?"

"Yes, General. He's… he was shot by Decatur Neuillan, but he was alive when I left. The Alzanans wanted him as a hostage, so they're probably bringing him with them."

A low murmur of outrage filled the room.

"Sit down. Captain, get her food and drink. Icarus, we need a full report."

Taya took the chair but shakily declined the offer of anything to eat or drink. The lictors quickly spread out the map she'd taken from the Alzanans and studied it as she described the hangar's location and then, with more confidence, the dirigibles' guns and structure. Kammel didn't like her news about the Demicans and the *sheytatangri*, or about Gaio Mazzoletti's presence among the soldiers.

"The Mazzolettis are a powerful Family with a strong military background," one of the lictors volunteered. "But their relationship with the Agostis is shaky."

"What did the uniforms look like?" Kammel asked.

"Red pants, dark blue jacket top," Taya replied, uncertainly. "Most of the soldiers were wearing dark blue overcoats with the Alzanan gryphon on the breast."

"Piping? Buttons? Frogging? Epaulets? Braid?" Seeing her blank look, a lictor pushed a pen and paper in front of her. "Can you draw the uniform for us?"

She tried, identifying the colors as well as she could under their questioning.

"Sounds like the Abandanza Family," someone guessed. "Now *they're* an old military family. Lots of investments in armaments."

"And closely tied to the king," someone confirmed. "What's their relationship with the Mazzolettis?"

"Doesn't the whole army belong to the king?" Taya asked, confused.

"Each Family governs its own territory and maintains its own military force," General Kammel explained tersely. "The king's army is composed of the combined private militias of every Family. It isn't logical, it isn't well-unified, and it isn't efficient."

"The Families often operate autonomously, too," a lictor added. "Or at least, that's what Agosti is going to tell us."

"'Graph this information to the Council," General Kammel ordered. She turned back to Taya. "How many—"

A train whistle pierced the air. Everyone in the room glanced at the case clock standing in a corner.

"Three hours to Kovolo," someone murmured.

"Lady speed them," someone else said. A murmured response filled the room.

"Lictors?" Taya asked, and received a nod in response.

"The 6th Regiment. They'll find that outpost, and if the exalted is still there, they'll get him out," Kammel assured her.

"Thank you." Taya didn't know whether she should hope Cristof had been left behind, too badly injured to be moved, or taken aloft, where he might be killed if Ondinium began to fire at the Alzanan ships. Both possibilities made her ill.

The interrogation went on another fifteen minutes before Kammel was satisfied.

"Thank you, Icarus," she said at last. "I think that's all we need. Captain, return her armature and show her to the mess. Icarus, you look like you could use some rest. Get something to eat and find a place to nap, but don't go too far. We may need to consult you again."

"Thank you, General."

The captain gave her directions and returned to the meeting. Feeling oddly alone despite the noise and bustle around her, Taya walked toward the long stone building. Her stomach had settled down from the nightmarish ride, at least enough for her gnawing hunger to override any lingering sense of disequilibrium.

She'd never been to Glasgar before. It was one of the old, sprawling fortified cities that dotted the high mountains throughout the nation. Like the fortress she'd just left, it was an imperial-era feat of solid stone architecture.

Ondinium's capital was older than Glasgar, but it had been in a state of constant development since its near-destruction in the Last War. Its skyline was full of wireferry cables and factory chimneys and its shops boasted contemporary facades, cheerful glass windows, and brightly painted metal signs. Even in conservative Primus, the exalteds' estates reflected a variety of post-war architectural innovations.

Glasgar, on the other hand, was pure empire, full of blocky, weathered stone. The military base didn't boast any wireferries or factories, although some of the taller buildings had poles on their roofs that flew large, geometrically patterned signal flags.

A military icarus landed a few yards away and, seeing her silver wings, gave her a short nod as he locked up his own. For a moment Taya was tempted to ask if there was anything she could do to help, but then her stomach growled and she changed her mind. She would be in no shape to do any long-term flying until she'd eaten.

The harried staff in the mess hall didn't bother asking for her papers when she joined the queue. A mixed group of men and women sat at the long tables eating together— some wore uniforms and some didn't, and a variety of castemarks were in evidence, although the lictor's stripe was most prevalent. A group of flight-suited but wingless icarii had gathered around one table. She considered joining them, but they wore military corps insignia and seemed deeply engrossed in their conversation.

Instead, she chose a single seat by herself and began to eat. The buzz around her was all about the invasion. She detected a combination of shock and outrage in the discussion, as well as a certain level of anticipation. Speculation ran rampant— how fast could the dirigibles move? How well were they armed? How many more were on the way? Why were the Alzanans invading in the middle of winter? How many more lictors were being mobilized? How did you fight a flying vessel? Several dedicate military engineers were saying with obvious delight that the attack would force the Council to increase the budget for heavy artillery, while others were wondering if the ships could be defeated with something as simple as incendiary arrows shot down from the peaks through which they passed.

Nobody said anything about Exalted Forlore. Taya wondered if the information about his capture had been withheld or if nobody in the room cared.

She was halfway through her second bowl of stew when the door to the mess hall slammed.

"They sighted the ships!"

A roar of excitement met the declaration. The dedicate carrying the news jumped on a table, raising his voice to talk over it.

"Five dirigibles in Dayaduar Pass. Recon says the wind's giving them trouble."

Cheers rose. Taya nodded to herself. Whatever intelligence the Alzanans had gathered from Exalted Neuillan, it hadn't included the kind of flight data that only an icarus could provide. She moved her soup bowl aside and unfolded Cristof's map, locating Glasgar and searching for Dayaduar Pass. The dedicate on the table was saying something about the size of the ships, but she ignored him, scrutinizing the tiny print on the map for some indication of the Alzanans' location.

"About here," said a familiar voice. A black-gloved finger landed on Dayaduar Pass.

"Lieutenant!" Taya leaped to her feet. The Demican lictor stepped backward with an air of alarm as she threw her arms around his neck. "How did you get here?"

"Icarus. Your armature is gouging me," he said, his voice strained.

Taya dropped back to her heels, still clutching his uniform sleeves. She could tell from the stiff way he was standing that she was making him uncomfortable, but she didn't care. She felt like the earth had suddenly steadied beneath her feet.

"I'm sorry. It's just so good to see you."

"I was told you would be here." He looked down at her hands. "We can talk while you eat."

Taya reluctantly released him and sat down, ignoring her stew.

"How did you get here?" she repeated.

"I was on the train to Kovolo when it was diverted to pick up the 6th Regiment. When I heard that an icarus had reported the dirigibles' presence, I thought it might be you. Where is the exalted?"

Taya's fear and dismay returned like a surge of nausea.

"The Alzanans have him. Exalted Neuillan shot Cris. He was alive, but..." Taya reached out, grasping Amcathra's arm again. "It was the same side that was hurt in the train crash. I don't know how bad it was. There was nothing I could do for him, so I turned and ran."

"That was the appropriate choice."

"But I don't know if he's all right," she said, agonized.

"Was he shot with an Alzanan pistol?"

"No. His own needle gun."

"Needle guns are seldom fatal."

"I know, but...."

"You made the correct choice to leave your husband and alert your country."

"I don't think that'll be any comfort if— if he dies."

"The Alzanans will treat his wounds. He is more useful to them alive than dead. Is he on one of the dirigibles?"

"I don't know. Maybe. Why?"

Amcathra hesitated. Taya's hand tightened on his arm.

"They're going to burn them, aren't they? The ships."

"It is the most efficient form of counterattack, assuming the ships are using the Alzanans' usual inflammable gas for buoyancy."

"But they'll kill Cris, too."

"The Council considers Exalted Forlore to be expendable."

"No!" Taya stood, furious. After all Cristof had done for Ondinium? She would go straight to the general and—

"*I* do not consider him expendable, Icarus."

She froze and forced herself to sink back down into her seat, fixing her eyes on him. Of course not. Cristof was his friend. And so, she assumed, was she.

He had killed his nephew to save her, after all.

"How do we rescue him?"

The lieutenant glanced down at the map.

"I cannot counter a command to destroy the ships," he said, his voice so low that he might have been talking to himself. "If the exalted is aboard one of them, he must be extracted before we attack."

"I can do that."

"You must. There is a pump on the side of this building. Wash. Requisition a new flight suit. Wait for me."

"Wash...." She looked down at her leather suit, registering how filthy it had become in the last few days. "That sounds like a good idea."

"We will both appreciate it." He stood. "I will meet you here in an hour. Try to rest. You must be able to think clearly."

"Thank you, Lieutenant." She reached out to grasp his arm again, knowing he didn't like it but needing to emphasize her words. "Really."

He nodded and left, avoiding the crowd around the table where the dedicate was still answering questions. Taya bolted down the rest of her stew, folded her map, and went outside to find the supply depot.

Between the noise in the mess hall and her worries about Cristof, she hadn't expected to fall asleep after she'd washed and changed. But she must have, because she woke to somebody shaking her armature and calling her name.

"Taya? Taya Icarus?"

"Huh? What?" She batted the stranger's hand away and sat up, groggy. Her entire upper body ached. When she'd stripped off her flight suit to wash, she'd found long, dark bruises criss-crossing her chest and arms, souvenirs of her rough ride to Glasgar. Now she felt every aching inch of them.

"Lieutenant Amcathra told me to fetch you," the young lictor said, self-importantly.

"Then let's go," she said, running her hands through her short hair. "Where are the Alzanans?"

"About forty minutes away, at their current rate of progress," the lictor said, leading her outside and through the streets. He sounded enthusiastic. "We have a relay line set up to report their progress. Some lictors from one of the outlook stations tried firing at them, but their rifles didn't have enough range."

"What about cannon?"

"Dayaduar Pass is so sheer, nobody thought it needed to be defended from invaders." The lictor shook his head, turning down another of Glasgar's narrow stone streets. "Can you believe those bastards? Challenging *us* in the air!"

"What else are we doing?"

"The army's being rallied and the signal stations are on high alert in case this is a distraction. Every train has been diverted to military use and I hear the most probable targets are being evacuated. Including all nonessential personnel here." He waved a hand, and Taya saw that within the last hour, the number of people in Glasgar's streets had noticeably diminished.

"What about the capital?"

"They'll never get that far." He led her up a long, narrow set of stairs cut into Glasgar's defensive wall, which zig-zagged up the mountain slope. At the top, he pointed higher.

"The lieutenant is up there, on that watchtower. Can you fly there?"

"If I'm cleared."

"You're fine. Fly safely."

She raised a hand and climbed up on the wall, wincing as Nayan's armature dug into the bruises left by the railway harness. The new flight suit helped. It had been designed for military use, so it had more fleece padding than her old courier's suit, and boiled leather plates had been added wherever they wouldn't restrict her movement. She'd transferred all of her personal belongings to the suit's pockets, even the cheese and sausage she'd taken from Nayan's house. She wasn't hungry anymore, but she'd learned her lesson: never fly without food.

Lieutenant Amcathra was overseeing a small group of lictors and dedicates who were hard at work preparing the fort's artillery. One group was setting up two heavy guns that faced out into the air. Long ribbons of very large brass cartridges were piled up next to them. Nearby, another lictor was setting up a mortar. The dedicates were arranging signal flags and monitoring the other watchtowers through field glasses.

Amcathra, too, had a set of field glasses around his neck and a large rifle slung across his back. To Taya's surprise, he held out a hand to steady her as she landed on the crenellated parapet.

"What's happening?" she asked, hopping down off the wall.

"I have spoken to General Kammel." He walked away, and she followed. "She is sympathetic but refuses to release any of her icarii for a rescue attempt. She says she cannot divert valuable human resources to search for an exalted who may or may not be aboard any of the ships."

"What about me?" Taya asked, anxiously.

"She was significantly silent regarding your deployment during the battle." Amcathra stopped next to a pile of equipment. "If you succeed in rescuing your husband, I do not expect the Council will be so ungrateful as to reprimand you. If you fail, it is likely you will die and it will not need to issue a reprimand."

"So, you're advising me not to fail and survive," Taya said, grimly.

"It would not be the most salutary course of action." He picked up a narrow canvas pack dangling with straps. "This is an ondium rescue harness. Have you ever used one?"

"No, but I've heard of them." Taya took it, startled to find it all but weightless.

"The carrying case is lined with lead to counterweight the harness. The case rips apart here and here, with these red straps. Let the case fall; it is unimportant. The harness is vest-shaped with hook-and-eye closures, and it can be attached to an armature with the vest facing forward or backward. It is sized for an adult and zeroes at approximately 170 pounds."

"That's about how much Cristof weighs."

"The exalted does not weigh enough for his height."

"That's what he says, too."

Amcathra strapped the case to her armature, centered and low on her keel. "Are you certain he is being held hostage?"

"I'm pretty sure that was the plan."

"Then he is likely to be with the commanding officer."

She nodded. "I'll bet the general, Neuillan, and Cristof are all on the same ship. Neuillan's supposed to be an advisor, and the general wanted Cristof's knowledge, too."

"How many people can a ship carry?"

"I'm not sure. The one I saw being loaded carried twelve soldiers and a lot of cargo."

"They will be armed and alert." Amcathra jerked on the last strap, tightening it, and stepped back. "You are unlikely to succeed."

Taya looked askance at him. "It wouldn't hurt to be reassuring, Lieutenant."

He grunted, reaching down to pick up a holster.

"This contains a signal gun with an extra flare cartridge. We have established a line of recon icarii; when you land with the exalted, fire it and someone will find you. Remember that the gas inside the envelopes is inflammable."

She took it. Amcathra held out a second holster.

"This is a needle pistol. I hope you will not need to use it, Icarus, but it is better to kill than to be killed."

Taya's mouth was dry as she eyed the weapon. "I'm not even supposed to touch that."

He slid the weapon out and showed it to her.

"This is the safety. If it is here, the gun will not fire. If it is here, it will. I will leave the safety on." He clicked it. "Remember to take the safety off when you enter the vessel. This is the magazine that holds the ammunition. It can be removed and replaced like this. And this is the canister for compressed air. I will give you a spare magazine and compressed-air canister."

"The Council could take my wings for this."

"We will address that problem if you survive."

"I'd really rather not carry a gun."

A flash of irritation crossed the lieutenant's face.

"Then give it to Exalted Forlore," he barked. "He is not afraid to kill."

Taya snatched the gun from his hands, startled. *He's worried about Cristof, too,* she realized.

"Where do I put it?" she asked, meekly. Amcathra helped her loop the two holsters onto her belt and secure the ends to her legs. He snapped straps over the top to keep the guns from sliding out. She bounced on her toes. The rescue harness weighed nothing, but the guns were heavy.

"Well?" Amcathra asked, watching her. His face was expressionless again.

"I'm fine. Is there anything else?"

He looked down at the pile and selected a long, thick tube.

"This is an observation ladder. I do not know if you will need it, but it could be useful."

She nodded. Another ondium tool in a counterweighted case. It would add to her drag, but it wouldn't add to her weight. He slid it into a long pocket down one leg of her suit. She twisted to look at the matching pocket on her other leg.

"What's that one for?" she asked.

"A map case. You will not need a map."

"No. What else do you have for me?"

He picked up a flat, wide belt with two bulging pockets, saying nothing. Taya looked at it, then up at his face.

"Another weapon?"

"Yes."

She bit her lip. "I'm sorry, Lieutenant. You're right. The only thing I should be worrying about is rescuing Cristof. If I have to kill someone to do it...." she suddenly felt weary. "Well, it won't be the first time."

He handed her the belt. It, too, was heavy. *The military doesn't counterweight its weapons*, she thought, hefting it. Of course, icarii weren't supposed carry any.

"Two pockets; two bombs. They are small, but I do not think you will need a large bomb to ignite an envelope. Each bomb has a twenty-second fuse. You will need that time to drop it and fly out of the range of the explosion."

"One should be enough."

"I believe in redundancy. One of the fuses could fail, or the Alzanans could throw one of the bombs overboard in time to save themselves."

Taya blew out a breath, finding it difficult to discuss slaughter so casually.

"So, is this what happens in war?" she asked. "All our laws and taboos get set aside? Professor Dautry was right."

"With luck Glasgar will take down the ships, so that Professor Dautry's worst fears will not be realized."

"What do you mean?"

"I would prefer to avoid resurrecting the abhorrent. But it is my duty to protect Ondinium, and I will do whatever is necessary to achieve that goal." He gestured. "The belt straps around your waist. I know that it is heavy; you may wish to abandon it once you have the exalted. I advise you to attempt the rescue as soon as possible. Once the ships are in range, Glasgar will begin firing with rifles, cannon, and mortars. You will not want to be in the same airspace as the dirigibles."

"When will they start firing?" she asked, nervously, as she buckled the belt of bombs over her stomach.

"When the ships are approximately a mile away."

"Anything else I should know?"

"An aerostat's blind spots are directly beneath, behind, or overhead it, like an icarus's. If you cannot fly in a blind spot, keep the sun at your back to force the Alzanans to squint when they aim at you."

Taya nodded grimly.

"However, it would be better to avoid being seen at all."

"I'll try to stay hidden."

"If the exalted is not on a ship but you have the opportunity to distract and delay the Alzanans, please do. Not all of the — of our defenses — are prepared yet."

"I'll do what I can."

"I wish I could go with you, Icarus, to spare you these decisions."

"I wish you could, too." She wanted to hug him again, but mindful of his pride and the sharp edges of her armature, she restrained herself. "Thank you, Lieutenant."

"Fly safely." He turned and walked back to the stairs, heading back down. "I will see you again as soon as I am able."

Taya wished she could affect such a cool demeanor. Instead, she touched all her new equipment, reassuring herself that it was secure, strapped on her flight cap, and pulled down her goggles. Feeling unusually bulky, she trudged back to the wall.

"Joining the observation team?" asked one of the signalmen cheerfully. She waved, letting him think what he wanted, and climbed into an embrasure. The lictors shouted a ragged send-off of good wishes as she slipped her arms into her wings and launched herself off the steep fortress wall.

Chapter Twenty-Four

TAYA SPOTTED THE five Alzanan dirigibles when she flew around a tall, bare peak too sheer to hold snow. They flew in a loose, spread-out line that shifted back and forth as they compensated for the winds through the pass.

She promptly followed Amcathra's advice and rose as high as she could, keeping her back to the sun. Nobody was standing on the top gunnery platforms, nor were the dirigibles flying any flags. The only visible difference between the ships were the big black numbers painted on their prows.

Guessing that No. 1, in the lead, was most likely to be the command ship, Taya headed for its platform, overshot, and had to do some fierce backbeating. The platform rail caught her under the ankle and she jerked both feet up as the dirigible moved forward beneath her. She managed to kick herself backward and land, jarring one of the mounted guns with her hip. The cold mountain wind tore at her wings, trying to drag her off the ship.

The Alzanans were traveling much faster than they had been the night before.

This wasn't the same ship she'd landed on the night before, either, she saw, eying the mounted guns with distaste. Sabotaging them was one thing she was sure she could do without risking the Council's censure.

Too bad she didn't have time to visit each ship and remove them all.

She knelt by the tripods, dismounting the guns more quickly than she had the first time. She left them loose on the wooden platform, loathe to risk raising an alarm if someone saw them fall. Satisfied that she'd accomplished at least one worthwhile goal, she tucked her husband's tools away and eyed the expanse of envelope around her.

Was it safe to walk on? She'd stood on it briefly during her take-off the night before, but she hadn't put all her weight on it. The surface was slippery, covered with condensation, and gave a little when she pushed down with her fingers. Now that it was daylight, Taya noticed several bulging, hooded protuberances running along the top of the ship's envelope. She couldn't begin to guess at their purpose. More important, though, were the metal eye bolts fastened along the length of the hull as if specifically designed for a climber.

Well, she thought, *that makes sense, if the crew has to repair the envelope in flight.* But the other thing she noticed in the daylight was the access panel in the envelope immediately behind the wooden gunnery platform. Did crew members actually climb through the envelope? How did they breathe?

One thing was certain; she wasn't going to use it. Let the Alzanans risk their life in a gas-filled balloon; she'd rappel safely down the side.

Taya stared at the mountains, gathering her courage. If she was right about how many people were in each ship, it was going to be difficult to rescue Cristof without killing somebody in the process.

Her hand crept to the needle gun.

She'd stabbed a man once, but he'd lived. And she'd kicked another man into an abyss; he'd died. She wasn't proud of either incident, but each had been self-defense: kill or be killed.

Jumping into the control center of a military gondola and shooting people wasn't exactly self-defense, although she expected it would quickly turn into a kill-or-be-killed situation.

She pulled out the gun with one gloved hand, studied it, and clicked off the safety.

On the other hand, if that's what it took to rescue her husband....

She could wrestle with her conscience *after* he was safe.

She slid the gun back into its holster and checked to make sure the bombs and matches were within easy reach.

Off in the distance, she spotted Glasgar's defensive walls clinging to the steep mountain face like a climbing vine.

Lieutenant Amcathra had said that the weapons' firing range was one mile. She was running out of time.

She tied one end of her safety line to the front of the gunnery platform and crept out along the spine of the hull, feeling a hard frame beneath the silver fabric envelope. She stopped at the first eyelet and ran her rope through it, and then the next. The wind dragged on her wings and she locked them close to avoid straining their gear locks.

Taya wrapped the line around one wrist, glad that her military-issue gloves had boiled-leather reinforcing, and coiled the remainder in her other hand. Then she stepped backward, walking down the side of the dirigible's envelope as the line slipped over her glove.

With luck, all the Alzanan soldiers would be watching Glasgar and wouldn't notice her silhouetted against the side of the command ship.

Her boots strode over the head of the painted Alzanan gryphon. Plenty of rope left. She kept moving until she reached the envelope's longitudinal midpoint. There, she grabbed the rope with both arms and jumped. Her legs dangled as the underside of the envelope recessed.

This half of the descent was more difficult. Taya fought to keep her grip on the rope as she was blown diagonally by the wind flowing around the dirigible's streamlined shape. She wasn't afraid of falling; there was plenty of room between the dirigible and the ground. But if she fell, she'd be seen, and her rescue attempt would be worthless.

A distant boom made her start. A puff of smoke rose up ahead of the dirigible, floating in midair.

Glasgar was firing.

Heart pounding, Taya let herself down hand-over-hand until she saw the top of the control gondola. A wooden ladder rose from a hatch in the gondola's roof up to a matching hatch in the bottom of the envelope. Access to the gunnery platform, she surmised. She swung, stretching out a hand to catch the ladder. She missed and tried again. This time, her gloved fingers closed on the ladder's rail. She pulled herself forward and looped the rope around one of the rungs.

Down here, the roar of the engines was deafening. She looked behind her, along the underbelly of the dirigible, to the second gondola. She could be seen if any of the engineers looked forward. She hurried down the ladder and crouched close to the gondola's hatch, trying to keep herself small.

Two more booming explosions sounded, and the tenor of the engine changed. The dirigible was rising.

All right, she thought, bracing herself. She pulled off her gloves and jammed them into the front of her flight suit, then unholstered the needlegun. *It's now or never.*

Lady help me.

She grabbed the hatch's lifting ring and yanked it open, thrusting the gun straight down.

Nobody was standing on the ladder. She squirmed through the hatch door, using her free hand to pull her wings in and then twisted, pistol out.

She was in a low-ceilinged second floor built over the main gondola. Narrow stairs led down, the same kind of stairs Cristof had investigated during their reconnaissance in the hangar. Racks of ammunition and machine parts surrounded her. And there, barely an arm's length away, was her husband, sitting on a blanket on the floor, one thin wrist handcuffed to a metal support girder. He was wearing an Alzanan military coat, and his gray eyes were wide behind his silver-rimmed glasses as he stared at her.

Relief and gratitude nearly buckled her knees. She forced herself to look away and search the rest of the small chamber.

Nobody was guarding him. Of course not. Why should they? Where would he go if he slipped his restraints?

Taya grabbed the hatch door and pulled it shut. Between the roar of the engines and the ever-increasing number of explosions outside, she doubted anybody could hear her walking overhead, but even so she stepped across the floor as softly as she could before kneeling next to Cristof and pulling up her goggles.

"I—"

Cristof leaned forward, grabbed her armature's ondium keel with his free hand, and kissed her with hungry desperation.

Taya dropped the needle pistol. With a surge of joy so strong that it brought tears to her eyes, she cupped his face and kissed him back. The world settled back into its proper pattern again.

Her husband was alive.

Another explosion boomed outside. She reluctantly released him.

"Taya—" he started.

"Take this," she said, handing him the needle pistol. She grabbed his handcuff, rattling it against the metal pole, and scowled. Amcathra hadn't given her a hacksaw.

"Taya," Cristof repeated, leaning forward to put his mouth next to her ear as she pulled his case of tools out of her suit pocket, "I think I've been delinquent in telling you how much I love you."

She grinned, opening the toolkit.

"I love you, too." She put the kit in his lap. "But I don't know how to pick locks."

He raised an eyebrow and returned the gun. Taya gingerly held it aimed at the stairs.

Very faint voices sounded, hardly discernible over the engines and the explosions. Something exploded so close that the gondola rocked.

The Ondinium military was finding its range.

Then voices rose below, cheering and whooping about a hit. Taya's hand tightened on the pistol. She hadn't heard any gunfire. And if the dirigible was flying high enough to avoid Glasgar's artillery, that meant that the only way it could hit anything was by dropping bombs.

They had just shattered one of Ondinium's most sacred moral prohibitions.

She forced herself to take a deep breath and ease her finger off the pistol's trigger.

The handcuff fell open. Cristof replaced his picks, wincing as he slid the toolkit into his coat pocket.

"How badly are you hurt?" Taya eased the front of his coat open.

The Alzanans had given Cristof a new shirt. It hung half-open, revealing bandages swathed around his side. She felt a moment's burst of anger. The gondola was freezing, this high in the winter sky. They could have at least buttoned up his shirt. She glanced at his left wrist and saw more bandages peeking out from beneath his sleeve.

"Does it hurt?" she asked, setting the gun down. She buttoned his shirt and coat all the way up to his neck.

"Would you still respect me if I said yes?" The gray hue under his normally copper skin belied his light tone. Taya touched his cheek as another explosion rocked the gondola.

"Let's get you out of here." She unstrapped the rescue harness case and tore it open. The ondium harness, a long vest made of heavy ondium plates covered with straps and latches, bobbed up.

"Put this on."

Cristof's adam's apple bobbed as he recognized it.

"I'll need help."

Taya did her best to work the ondium vest over her husband's arms without jarring him, but by the time she'd strapped it around the front of his coat, he was breathing hard and sweat had broken out on his brow. She dug into her suit, pulling out the bottle of morphine.

"No." He shook his head. "I need a clear head."

"You need to not faint when I move you." She measured a half-dose into the hypodermic needle. He didn't object a second time, which told her all she needed to know about how much his wounds were hurting him. She pushed up his left sleeve and administered the drug between his bandages just as the Alzanans began to cheer again.

Cristof abruptly grabbed the needlegun with his right hand. Taya yanked out the hypodermic needle, startled, as he raised the gun next to her head and pulled the trigger.

She spun.

Exalted Neuillan stood poised at the top of the stairs, one gloved hand falling to the long metal needles that pierced his chest.

Taya lunged to her feet and grabbed the exile's coat before he could collapse down the stairs and warn the enthusiastic Alzanans of their presence. Neuillan staggered and fell to one knee, groaning. Taya tore off his mask and clamped her hand over his mouth. The scarred holes where his eyes had been were crinkled with pain. She wondered if he had any idea what had just happened to him.

"I'm sorry," Cristof whispered in her ear. He reached over her shoulder and pulled the trigger a second time.

Steel needles drove through Neuillan's blind eyes and into his brain.

Taya gave a low, horrified gasp and jerked her hand away. Neuillan collapsed, blood streaking his face.

Cristof dropped back into a seated position, using the back of his gun hand to wipe sweat from his forehead. His pale gray eyes were cold behind their glass lenses.

"I'm sorry," he repeated.

Taya swallowed as explosions thundered around them.

Sometimes she forgot that her husband wasn't just the self-deprecating clockwright-turned-ambassador that he sometimes wore like another mask.

Lieutenant Amcathra had remembered, though.

"Taya?"

She looked down at Neuillan and hardened her heart. Trying not to think too hard about what she was doing, she stripped off the dead man's gloves and scarf, then turned to her husband. She would deal with this later, when shells and bombs weren't exploding around them.

Cristof let her help him up. She wrapped the scarf around his neck and held the gun while he pulled on Neuillan's gloves.

"We'd better go," she said, handing it back. He nodded.

Pulling down her goggles and pulling on her gloves, Taya climbed up the ladder and opened the hatch. The wind threw it back with a bang she barely heard over the roar of the engines and the fighting. She squirmed up to the top of the gondola. Her line was still tied around the rung.

"Come on," she said, holding out a hand. Cristof hesitated, gesturing down the stairs with his gun. She shook her head. With an air of regret, he thrust the pistol into his overcoat pocket and began to climb one-handed.

When he reached the gondola he froze, staring at the emptiness around them. The wind whipped his long black hair around his face.

"Don't look," Taya shouted. Then, remembering his solution on their flight to Engels, she slid his glasses off his nose. He reached for them, then gulped as the ladder shifted beneath him. Taya tucked his glasses in a pocket high on her left arm, buttoned it, and pointed to her own eyes.

He swallowed hard and fixed his nearsighted gaze on her face.

Wrapping one leg around a rung, she untied her safety line and fastened its steel ring to one of the twist-lock carabineers on her husband's rescue harness. If he panicked and started to fall, she wanted to make sure he didn't go far.

"Up," she urged, tugging on his coat. Keeping his eyes on her, he crept the rest of the way out of the hatch, hugging the ladder. He was still favoring his left arm, she noted. She hoped the morphine kicked in soon.

She reached down and closed the hatch just as something dark hurtled down in her peripheral vision.

Spinning, Taya gaped as three more bombs tumbled out of the hatch in the middle of the ship's belly. She leaned over the gondola's side, one hand on the ladder, and watched as the bombs aligned themselves, nose down, and sped toward Glasgar. The dirigibles were flying so high that the ancient city appeared to be laid out below them like a map. She could clearly discern the destruction the bombing had wrought— entire buildings and lengths of wall had been destroyed, and fires were spreading across the surrounding forest, sending long lines of smoke drifting over the rubble.

A missile whistled past and exploded in midair. Taya felt the concussion and a blast of heat against her face, but it barely rocked the ship, its smoke dissipating behind them. She looked up. The envelope looked unscathed.

"Taya!"

She pulled herself back, leaning close to her husband. His eyes were screwed shut, so she touched his gloved hand to indicate she was listening. She didn't know if his shivering was from his fear of heights or the freezing air.

"I'd rather. Not. Fly into a bomb."

She patted his hand and looked out again, evaluating their chances of getting away safely.

The Alzanans seemed intent on turning Glasgar into a pile of burning rubble. One of the dirigibles was flying higher than they were, its bombs systematically destroying the walls on which she'd seen the artillery corps lined up. Pretty soon, the fort wouldn't have any weapons left.

Flying into that fiery devastation didn't make any sense. Better, she decided, to wait until the bombing stopped.

"Taya?" Cristof opened his eyes, looking at her.

"We'll wait," she shouted.

His shoulders slumped with relief.

"But not here." She pointed behind them, to the engine gondola, and then up. "We need to climb to the gunnery platform on top."

He looked ill as he gazed at the bulging expanse of fabric that curved over them.

"You can do it." Her mind raced as she tried to figure out how. "I need you to hold on very tight and keep your eyes shut." She wrapped her safety line around his gloved wrist several times and closed his fingers over it. They were shaking.

"Ready?" she asked. He nodded. She lifted his other hand, closing it around the line. A strangled gasp rose from his throat as his feet slid from the ladder rungs and he dangled in midair, as light as a leaf blown by the wind.

Taya grabbed the safety line above him, wrapped one end around her glove, and pulled both of them up, hand-over-hand, to the bulging midpoint of the envelope's swell.

Her husband's weight was zeroed out by the rescue harness, but hers wasn't, and by the time she reached the longitudinal swell, she was panting. Taya dragged them both over the curve and up a little higher, until Cristof got his feet braced on the envelope underneath him. He opened his eyes and took in the long silver field that stretched out to either side.

A mortar shell exploded close to the front of the ship. Taya felt the wind shift as the pilot compensated and changed course. She shook one hand loose and gave her husband a thumbs-up. His nod was barely perceptible, but at least he wasn't paralyzed with fear.

The rest of their ascent was slow and careful. Taya reached back to help whenever the wind buffeted her husband to his knees. While her military-issue flight boots had thick leather soles that had been ridged to help her land on slick surfaces, Cristof's expensive winter boots had smooth leather soles that made his footing precarious.

When they reached the flat top of the envelope, Taya led him along its hard spine to the gunnery platform. He sat down hard, leaning against the railing.

Taya unclipped the line between them and handed him his glasses. His ears and nose were blue with cold. She pulled off her gray army scarf and wrapped it around his head, covering his ears.

"Thank you." He slid his glasses on and looked around, fear surrendering to curiosity. Taya coiled the safety line while he reassured himself that he was on a more or less stable surface. Only the roar of the dirigible's engines and the cliff faces sliding past them indicated that they were in motion.

"I'm going to look," she said.

"Wait." He reached out and grabbed her arm. "Don't leave yet."

She sat by his right side, as close as her armature would permit.

"What happened?" he asked, moving his gloved hand over to take hers. "I was terrified they'd catch you."

"*You* were terrified? I wasn't the one who got shot!"

"I hoped you hadn't seen that."

"I didn't know what to do. As soon as I was sure you were alive, I ran."

He squeezed her hand.

"Good."

"It didn't work out that well." She looked around. "I still have to get you off this ship. It sounds like the bombing's slowing down, so—"

"We can't leave." He twisted to look at her, his expression earnest. "You saw what they did to Glasgar. We're the only ones left who can stop this fleet."

"Scrap." Taya leaned her head against the guardrail. "You and Lieutenant Amcathra."

"Is he all right?"

"He was down there. In Glasgar."

They both fell silent, listening to the engines and bombs. Taya closed her eyes. The lieutenant would be fine. He'd studied aerial attacks. He'd know exactly what to do to defend himself.

"He gave me some bombs," she added, thrusting away her doubts. "Just in case." She unbuckled her belt and pulled it off. Cristof inspected the metal orbs.

"He must have known the Alzanans would raze Glasgar. That's the only reason he'd arm an icarus. He must have known you'd be Ondinium's last chance."

"But he only gave me two."

"Maybe that's all he could get his hands on. He couldn't possibly have requisitioned them legally." Cristof gestured to one of the guns she'd dismantled. It had slid halfway off the platform before getting caught between the rails. "Do those work?"

"I suppose so. They were mounted on the tripods. I assumed they were going to be used against icarii, so I took them down."

He pulled the weapon closer, examining it.

"How do the gunners get up here?"

"I think they climb through there." She pointed to the hatch door.

Cristof gave her an incredulous look.

"We could have climbed *through* the ship?"

"I'm not going in there. It's full of gas!"

"It can't be full of gas if the Alzanans use it." He pulled up the hatch. Taya flinched, holding her breath, but her husband was already peering inside. "It's an access shaft. It must lead down to the control gondola. I wonder how this thing was built?"

"We don't need to go back down there."

"I think the ammunition for these guns was being stored in the same place I was."

"So?" She didn't like where this conversation was going.

He turned and looked at her over the rims of his glasses.

"If we blew up two of the ships and captured this one...."

"Do you have any idea how to drive a dirigible?"

"We'll hold the crew at gunpoint."

"And then what? There are still two other ships."

"They wouldn't shoot the command ship."

"They might, if we took it over!"

"Then we'll kill the crew, aim the dirigible at the mountain, and jump."

Taya stared.

"That's insane."

"Taya." Cristof laid a hand on her shoulder, looking serious. "These Alzanans just slaughtered hundreds of men and women in the most cowardly fashion possible— by dropping bombs on them from the safety of the sky. And unless we do something about it, it'll happen over and over until the ships run out of bombs or land to refuel. We can't let that happen. *I* can't let that happen."

"But you won't be the one planting the bombs," she said, flatly.

He leaned backward, pinching the bridge of his nose under his glasses.

"No. You're right."

"If I plant bombs on these ships, how am I any better than them?"

"At least you're fighting them face-to-face," he retorted. "You're risking your own life, not killing from a distance."

"Cris, I know you hate Alzana, but—"

"How can you *not* hate it? After what it just did to Glasgar?"

"The king of Alzana might not even know what's going on here."

"You don't believe ships like this could be built and tested without the king's consent, do you? Do you have any idea how much they must have *cost*?"

She didn't, but she guessed it was a lot.

Cristof took a deep breath. "I could borrow your wings."

"No." She didn't even have to think about it. "Not in these winds. You'd get yourself killed."

He looked out at the passing terrain, sharp lines furrowed down his brow.

Taya's stomach churned. She hated arguing with her husband. She especially hated arguing with him so soon after getting him back.

"I know you still have nightmares about the Great Engine and Alister," Cristof said at last. "And I know you don't want to be responsible for the lives of these soldiers. If there were any way in the world I could place the bombs myself, I would. Could you carry me there?"

"I don't know." She rubbed her forehead on her knees, feeling her goggles press against her nose and brow. "It's not the weight. It's the drag. And… it wouldn't make any difference, would it?"

"The next target is Patimbrium," he said. "I heard them talking about it yesterday. Do you know how many families live in Patrimbrium?"

Taya averted her gaze, hating him for asking that.

Glasgar was, primarily, a military outpost. Patimbrium was a small city. Its primary industry was mining and smelting, and it was home to a mid-sized railway junction. Taya wondered which of the Big Three owned most of the mines there.

Not Allied Metals & Extraction, she was willing to bet.

She'd forgotten to ask Amcathra what he'd done about AME. She wondered if she'd ever have a chance to ask him, or whether he was sprawled somewhere in Glasgar's rubble, staring up at the sky like his nephew.

Tears burned her eyes.

All right. She would plant the bombs. She would kill dozens of people in order to save hundreds, maybe even thousands.

But how heavily would the act weigh on her soul? Cristof was right— sometimes she still woke up in the middle of the night, sweating from nightmares about killing the lictor beneath Oporphyr Tower, or watching Alister blinded and outcaste. How many more nightmares would she suffer if she sent these Alzanan soldiers back to the Lady?

How many more would she suffer if she *didn't*, and helpless cities were bombed to rubble?

She pushed up her goggles and rubbed her eyes with the cold, hard leather of her flight suit cuff.

"All right," she said, defiantly. She pulled her goggles down. "I'll do it."

"I'm sorry," Cristof said, for the third time. He seemed genuinely anguished. "I wish I could do it, instead. But I can't fly."

"I know." She picked up the belt and stood. "Which ship?"

He climbed to his feet, squinting into the wind.

"One that isn't very close." He pointed. "Four and Five are behind the rest."

"I'll have to dive," she said, calculating how far she could fly in twenty seconds. "It'll be the fastest way to leave the ship."

He turned toward her, looking troubled. "Am I going to lose you over this?"

She started to reassure him that she'd get away in time, but then she saw the look in his eyes and realized, with an internal jolt, what he really meant.

She opened her mouth to deny it, and then hesitated.

"We'll figure it out afterward," she said, instead.

He closed his eyes and nodded.

"I do love you, Taya. More than anything."

She forced a smile as she cinched the belt around her waist again. Her husband hunched his shoulders, watching as she climbed over the railing, slid her arms into her wings, and gauged the wind.

Lady, she prayed, *give me strength.*

Chapter Twenty-Five

THE WIND WASN'T as strong as it had been in Dayadaur Pass, and it blew in the right direction. Taya didn't have to work to stabilize and circle over her target.

The fleet had moved past Glasgar, dropping altitude but staying clear of the mountains around it. The valleys below looked desolate— no smoke indicated the presence of villages or camps. Taya was grateful for that. It would be bad enough to send an dirigible hurtling down in flames; dropping it on a village would be horrifying.

Her landing on the unoccupied gunner's platform on top of Number Four was flawless. She knelt and opened the hatch, still wary of escaping gas. When she was certain she was safe, she cradled the bomb between her knees and pulled out the matches. With another suspicious look at the open hatch, she struck a flame.

It promptly blew out.

Oh, Lady, is that an omen?

She crouched closer to the bomb, curling herself around it and hoping Lieutenant Amcathra had been right about the fuse giving her twenty seconds to escape. If it blew up while she was leaning over it...

Then she wouldn't have to worry anymore, would she?

She struck a second match and immediately touched the flame to the fuse.

It sparked, then ignited.

Taya dropped match and bomb down the access hatch and leaped to her feet, thrusting her arms into her wings. *One thousand, two thousand*— expecting to be engulfed in flame at any moment, she ran across the top of the dirigible and hurled herself up and out into the sky, keeping her wings open only long enough to clear the ship before folding them against her sides.

She hurtled past the sky-blue gryphons, past the wooden gondolas, the air screaming in her ears.

—*six thousand, seven thousand, eight thousand, nine thousand*—

She stretched out her wings and kicked down her tailset, thrusting herself down against the natural buoyancy of her ondium.

—*fourteen thousand, fifteen thousand, sixteen thousand, seventeen thousand*—

The explosion was deafening, and the heat from the blast sent her spinning. Taya tumbled a long moment before fighting to stabilize herself on the suddenly tumultuous currents.

By the time she regained her bearings, Number Four was nothing but a fiery missile plummeting to earth.

She drew in a sharp breath, appalled by the scale of the destruction. The whole ship was on fire, its strange, spiky framework standing out like a dark skeleton against the flames before it also ignited. Another sharp series of blasts echoed between the mountains as new fireballs arose from the envelope's depths. Taya swept herself up with a surge of sheer, primal terror, riding the explosion-heated thermals up past the remaining four dirigibles.

Cristof.

Shaken and panting for breath, she wheeled around to look for him.

The surviving ships were struggling to maintain an even keel as they were battered by the rising heat waves. Number Four left a thick column of black smoke and crimson sparks behind as it fell. It hit a cliff face and tumbled, collapsing on itself, flames leaping up afresh as its twisted, blackened framework bounced down the cliff, scattering sparks and debris.

Cristof stood on top of Number One, gripping the gunnery platform's railing and staring at the destruction.

Taya flew to him, stumbling as she hit the spine of the balloon several feet from the platform. To her surprise, he scrambled over the railing and ran to her.

"What happened?" He grabbed her armature. "Are you all right?"

She nodded and turned. From the broad back of the envelope, all she could see was the column of black smoke rising behind them.

"It burned so fast...." she gasped, hardly able to hear herself. Her heart was pounding against her chest and her muscles were twitching with nervous energy.

"Did anyone see you?" Cristof demanded. She shook her head.

"Good." He wrapped an arm around her metal-protected shoulders, walking her back to the platform. "Lock your wings."

She automatically complied, slipping her arms free. He tugged her down to sit next to him again. Then he rested his forehead against hers, wool against leather. The rims of his glasses and her goggles touched.

She tried to explain. "I don't— I can't—"

"Never mind. It's all right. We'll think of something else."

Relieved, she closed her eyes, seeing flames shooting into the air behind her eyelids. A minute passed.

"I'll capture the ship," he said, matter-of-factly.

"How?" She straightened.

"I have the needler. It's not much, but it's close quarters down there, and I'm a good shot. Once I've secured it… we'll see how the other dirigibles do in a firefight with one of their own."

"What good are guns against something this big?"

"All we have to do is tear open the envelopes. Even if the ships don't explode, they'll be forced to land."

"Wait." Taya felt a stirring of hope. "If that's all it takes— I don't mind tearing holes in the envelopes. The ships wouldn't crash at once, would they?"

"No, not from a leak. But Taya, cutting through this fabric won't be easy." He ran a hand over the taut, silver-painted envelope. "It covers a wooden frame. The gas balloons are inside the frame. Bullets may get through to them, but not knives."

"What if we were inside?" She still didn't want to go inside the envelope, but if it meant she didn't have to drop another bomb….

"If you cut through to the gas in an enclosed space, you'd poison yourself."

"Could we use the guns?" Taya glanced at the two she'd pulled from their tripods. "If we shot through—"

An Alzanan oath startled them. She started to turn, but Cristof shoved her aside. She caught herself on the platform rail and saw an Alzanan soldier halfway out of the access hatch, tugging a revolver from his holster.

Cristof grabbed one of the dismounted weapons and swung it across the soldier's face. Bone crunched and blood spattered over the silver envelope. The soldier reeled. Her husband dropped the firearm and grabbed the man's uniform, but the Alzanan seized Cristof's leg and yanked, sending her husband sprawling on his counterweighted back. The scarf around his forehead slipped over one eye and he clawed it off, letting the wind snatch it from his gloved fingers.

Taya jumped forward, clutching the soldier's gun arm. His gun fired into the air. Cristof rolled over and wrapped a hand around the weapon's cylinder. The soldier jerked, and both of them skidded across the silver envelope.

Cristof twisted, forcing the revolver from the young man's grasp. It came loose, and the soldier barely had time to swear before the exalted pointed the gun at the Alzanan's face and fired.

Taya scrambled backward, sickened by the bloody mess.

"Help me," Cristof gasped, trying to wrestle the soldier's body out of the hatch with one arm. Taya edged around the gore and grabbed the young man's jacket. Together they hauled the corpse onto the top of the envelope, smearing blood and brains everywhere.

Taya looked away, nauseous.

Cristof pointed the revolver down the access hatch, then cautiously peered inside. His long black hair blew into his eyes and he impatiently raked it aside.

"I think he was alone. Either someone *did* see you, or they sent him up to scout."

"Do you think they heard the shot?"

"Probably not. The engines are louder down there than they are up here."

"How many soldiers are there?"

"Eight in the front gondola, counting Neuillan and me. Five, now. Another six in the rear gondola — engineers, mostly — but there won't be much they can do to us." He cocked his head, considering the ship's expanse. "Even if there's a crawlway through the envelope to the front gondola, they'd be easy targets coming down the stairs."

"Then you're going down?"

"I have to, now."

"I can't climb down that hatch. Even if I folded my wings—"

"I know." He pushed up his glasses with the back of his gloved wrist. "Why don't you stay up here and fly down in twenty minutes? I'll leave the hatchway open for you."

"So you can do all the killing before I get there."

"I'm trying to spare you, Taya. You've already done enough. Too much." He popped open the cylinder. "Five rounds left.

I'll have to kill the two remaining gunners. Maybe not the pilot and the bombardier. I don't know what General Credero will do. Alzanans take their honor seriously. He may prefer to die than be captured."

"Was— was Mazzoletti with you?"

"No." Cristof glanced at her. "He's the captain of one of the other ships."

"Which one?"

"I don't know."

She took a deep breath, wondering if it had been Number Four. Not that it mattered. Cristof was right. They couldn't let the Alzanans reach Patimbrium.

"You're right. I don't like killing. But I don't want you going down there alone, either, so I'll watch your back and try to shoot the other ships' gas envelopes."

"Are you sure?"

She held out a hand. "Give me the needler. I'll give it back to you down below."

He dug the pistol out of his pocket and handed it to her, his gray eyes studying her face.

"I'll have to go slowly," he said, "so give me ten minutes or so."

"Be careful."

He touched a feather on her wing and descended into the access hatch.

Taya crouched next to the bloodstained hatch door and pulled out her watch. She didn't want to close the door; it would be dark down there, even if the air was safe. Instead, she dug out the spare compressed-air cartridge and extra magazine and reloaded the needle gun. Then she checked to make certain the safety was off and reholstered it.

After five minutes, she slipped her arms into her wings and walked across the top of the ship. The Alzanan soldier was still sprawled next to the gunnery platform. There didn't seem any reason to move him.

She kicked off.

The first thing she noticed on her descent were the signal flags hanging from the gondolas on the ships. They said something about the explosion, she guessed— and maybe about her.

She flew forward, keeping the envelope between herself and any lookouts on the other ships.

The Alzanans were flying through a steep-sided, narrow mountain pass that showed no signs of habitation. Taya looked for the gleaming lines of a railway but didn't see any indication that the area was ever traveled. A flash of light on one of the peaks caught her attention. She squinted through her goggles but couldn't make out what had caused it.

Ice? A signal station? An icarus on reconnaissance?

She rocked her wings back and forth.

Another icarus would know an ally was with the ships.

She hoped it was an icarus and not a patch of ice.

Hitting the struts that supported the control gondola was tricky. Her feet struck a horizontal strut sideways, halting her forward motion with a jar, but unlike a wireferry tower, this strut moved. She dropped her feet to the vertical crossbar, tottered, her tailset scraping the supports, and threw her weight forward. Yanking an arm out of its wing, she steadied herself.

Close. If she hadn't had plenty of experience weaving through Ondinium's wireferry lines, she didn't think she'd have made it. She locked her wings and kicked up her tailset, then clambered through the support framework to the ladder. Securing her safety line, she pulled out the needle gun and opened the hatch at the bottom of the envelope.

Nobody was in there, either. She stepped back and waited, deafened by the sound of the engines.

At last a boot emerged, and the hem of a coat, and Cristof climbed down. Taya grabbed his arm as the wind caught him. He shot her a grateful look.

Something pinged against the support girder closest to them. Taya frowned as she saw a fresh scar in the paint. Her eyes rose past Cristof's shoulder to the gondola behind them.

An Alzanan soldier was leaning out the window, aiming his rifle.

With an inaudible shout, she pulled Cristof down to the roof of the gondola. A muffled zipping sound passed close to her ear. Her husband twisted around, reaching into his pocket for the pistol. Taya yanked on his arm, getting his attention, and pointed down the open hatch.

Another bullet whined past. A small hole appeared in the flapping tail of Cristof's borrowed military coat.

He gave up reaching for the pistol, thrust his legs through the hatch, and dropped inside.

Chapter Twenty-Six

TAYA SQUEEZED INTO the gondola after him, her metal wings catching in the narrow hatch. Gripping the ladder with one hand, she yanked on her wings with the other, pulling them inside with a grating she felt all the way through her armature.

Two sharp, dull bangs punctuated the roar of the engines. Cristof was halfway down the next set of stairs, his back pressed against the wall, firing the revolver he'd taken from the young soldier.

Someone inside the lower level of the gondola fired back.

Taya backpedaled, nearly tripping over Neuillan's extended arm. His body was still on the floor. She supposed that if the Alzanans hadn't looked for him during the assault on Glasgar, Number Four's explosion would have driven his absence from their minds.

Cristof fired two more shots in rapid succession, then backed up the stairs and dropped the revolver.

"Gun!" he shouted, holding out his hand.

Taya dug out the needler and slapped it into his palm. He ducked back down the stairs, shooting a short, hissing burst, then darted out of her sight.

She pushed up her goggles and edged down the stairs after him, tensely anticipating a bullet.

Two soldiers had fallen over the big guns. Cristof crouched next to the foremost gun on the right side of the gondola, using one of the metal weapon locker doors as cover while he shot a burst of needles over the top.

One of the dead soldiers was only a couple of yards away, beside the rear left gun. Taya steeled herself and darted into the gondola, throwing herself down next to the corpse. Bullets tore into the stairwell wall where she'd been standing.

She tugged the revolver out of the soldier's holster.

"Do you need another gun?" she shouted over the roar of the engines.

"Yes, please!"

She sent the revolver spinning across the gondola floor. Cristof grabbed it and snapped off a shot at the doorway.

"Exalted Forlore!"

The general's voice was louder then either of theirs and seemed to come from all around them. Taya spotted the flared cone of a speaking tube tucked into one corner of the gondola.

"General Credero!" her husband shouted back.

"You've shot our pilot," the general said in Alzanan.

Taya grimaced. That wasn't good.

"Are you ready to surrender?" Cristof asked in the same language as he rummaged through the locker, pulling out ammunition and filling his pockets. The cartridges were the wrong size for his pistol; he was weighing himself down, trying to compensate for the zeroing-out of the ondium safety harness.

"I was going to ask you the same thing," the general said.

"I'm the one with the big guns, General."

Reminded, Taya turned her attention to the big gun nearest her. Like the weapons on top of the ship, it was swivel-mounted. Unlike the guns on top, it was also set on rails that could be slid forward to thrust the barrel out the window. In addition, it had a belt of ammunition running out of one side.

Carefully nudging the dead soldier out of the way, Taya swiveled the gun toward the control room door. It rotated 45 degrees before stopping. Not quite far enough.

Another shot made her duck and press against the cabin wall.

"You won't find those guns much use inside, Exalted."

"Then it seems we're at a stalemate, General." Cristof fumbled in his weighed-down pockets and unearthed his toolkit.

"I have the advantage."

"But I have you pinned down. Let's see which one of us gets tired first." Cristof studied the tripod mount, pushing his glasses high on his forehead as he squinted.

With a sense of inevitability, Taya fished into her flight suit until her fingers closed on his clockwright's headpiece.

"Cris! Here."

She tossed it to him.

He stared at it a moment, then dropped his glasses back down on his nose and transferred his stare to her. She shrugged.

Blowing her a kiss, he slid the headpiece on and flipped down the lenses. In seconds he was leaning over the tripod again and pulling out his tools.

Taya checked the soldier next to her. Dead. Her gaze rose to the soldier farther forward, sprawled across from Cristof. He was dead, too.

Three soldiers, the general, the pilot, the bombardier. And six more soldiers in back.

Her eyes widened as she remembered Cristof's comment about them climbing through the envelope. No wonder the general was biding his time. All he had to do was wait for reinforcements.

She grabbed one of the handles on the back of the gun and rotated the weapon in the opposite direction. Again, the barrel didn't quite point all the way back. It could send bullets into the wall next to the stairs, but not up the stairs.

Good enough. She didn't want to kill anybody— just keep them away. She looked for the trigger. It wasn't in the conventional place, but when she tested another lever, the gun went off with a deafening burst, shaking on its tripod and throwing brass shells everywhere.

Taya yelped and jerked her hand back and the gun stopped firing. It was like a needler, then— it fired more than one shot if you kept the trigger pulled.

The empty brass bounced on the gondola floor a few times and fell still. She looked over her shoulder. Cristof was staring at her again.

"Sorry," she shouted, her ears still ringing.

"Please be careful, Exalted," the general said through the speaking tube. "Those are powder-burning weapons."

"Dangerous choice for a ship like this," Cristof called back, returning to his work. "I thought you were buying steam-powered cannon."

"We were," the general replied. "Unfortunately, our departure time was unexpectedly pushed up."

The wood wall by the stairwell was riddled with holes, revealing open sky beyond. Taya scowled. They were going to use these guns against *icarii*?

Cristof groaned as he lifted his gun off its tripod and dropped it with a thump. He pulled off the headpiece and wiped his forehead, his face pale and covered with sweat. Taya wondered if the morphine was wearing off.

"General," he shouted. "I now have one of the guns pointed directly at the control cabin. It won't serve either of us if I have to use it."

Silence. Taya shot a glance back at the stairs, making sure nobody was descending.

"Very well, Exalted," the general said at last. "Hold your fire."

The Alzanan general appeared in the doorway. Fresh blood spattered one side of his military coat and trickled down the side of his face. He held his ornate sword in one gloved hand, and his gun holster was empty.

Taya stood. "I'll do it."

"I have you covered."

The general studied her with interest as she walked through the cabin past her husband.

"Number Five reported seeing an icarus," he said. "Are you the one who destroyed Number Four?"

"Yes. I'm sorry about that." She held out her hand. "Do you surrender, General?"

His gaze flickered past her to Cristof.

"Shouldn't I surrender to him?"

"Business with an exalted is traditionally carried out through an icarus."

"But this exalted speaks. Surely he can also take my sword."

"I'd rather he keep his hands on the gun. He's a better shot than I am."

The general bowed and handed her his sword. She lifted his coat, checking for any other weapons he might be carrying, and found none.

"Thank you. What should we do with him?" she asked, stepping away and glancing over her shoulder. Cristof had released the big gun but was keeping the soldier's revolver trained on the general. "Please don't say kill him."

"If you'll go upstairs, General, my cuffs are still locked to the pole there."

The Alzanan opened his mouth to protest and Cristof cocked the gun.

"If it was good enough for an exalted, it should be good enough for a general."

The general shrugged. Cristof fell in behind him. They were halfway up the stairs when a burst of gunfire met them.

Cristof tumbled down the stairs and hit the ground with the lightness of someone who weighed only as much as the contents of his coat pockets. Taya's heart was in her mouth as he rolled to his right. His face was spattered with blood.

"Shoot! Shoot!" he shouted, flattening himself next to the cabin wall.

Taya dropped the sword and ran to the big gun. The weapon began its staccato firing, brass spraying out one side and clattering everywhere. Bullets tore up the gondola's wall.

She released the lever, deafened. Cristof shouted something, but she couldn't make it out.

An Alzanan soldier stormed down the stairs, firing a rifle. Bullets whined through the cabin. Taya only got a glimpse of his pale, frightened-looking face before Cristof shot him twice in the chest. The soldier staggered and slumped, his rifle sliding down the stairs.

Taya made an involuntary noise. The soldier was Durante, the one with an upset fiancée back home.

Cristof scrambled back to her.

"There are three more up there!" he shouted. "They killed the general!"

Taya was glad Cristof hadn't gone up the stairs first.

"I'll get the loose gun," she said. A minute later, she had propped it on an overturned chair and aimed it up the stairs. Cristof fired a short burst up into the stairwell and through the gondola roof. The gun shook itself off the chair. He grimaced as he tried to pick it up.

"I'll fire it," she volunteered, replacing it on the chair for him.

"No. Go check on the pilot. Make sure someone's still driving."

"Oh, scrap," she muttered. She ran to the front cabin, half-expecting to see a cliff face looming before them through the windows. The sky was clear, but a body lay on the floor, and another was slumped in a chair next to a wheel. The seated Alzanan rolled his head to one side, looking at her, and raised a trembling hand. His face was colorless, and blood had pooled beneath his chair.

"I surrender," he said, in Alzanan.

"Are you still in control of the ship?"

"For a while," he said, bleakly. She lifted the lapel of his heavy coat. Blood stained the front of his uniform.

"Got me in the stomach," he said, his voice strained. "Lucky for you. Slow way to die."

"Do you have any medical supplies on board?"

"Up top."

"I'll be back in a minute. Keep the ship in the air. Some of your men are still alive."

"Don't worry. Who knows? Might not be my time yet."

Another burst of gunfire exploded from behind them. Taya glanced out and saw Cristof getting to his feet, holding his side.

Another body was sprawled on the stairs, and a third young Alzanan was descending, his hands raised high over his head.

"I surrender!" he cried out in a quavering voice. "Please don't shoot!"

She recognized him, too. Tazio, the bookworm.

"Keep us on course," she ordered, and walked back out to her husband. "Is he the last one?"

"I think so." He wiped his face with his sleeve, smearing sweat and the general's blood. "How are we doing?"

"The pilot's bleeding to death but holding the wheel. I'm going to get bandages so I can patch both of you up." She turned to Tazio. "Is anyone left up there?"

"No, ma'am. There are two soldiers in back, the engineer and another gunner for protection, but otherwise...." the youth scanned the bloodstained, bullet-riddled gondola with a shocked expression. "This is all of us."

"You'd better be right." She turned him around and marched him back up the stairs in front of her. Nobody was waiting for them. She cuffed his wrist to the pole next to Neuillan's and General Credero's corpses, found a box of medical supplies, and took it back downstairs.

An explosion rocked the ship.

Chapter Twenty-Seven

TAYA RAN INTO the control room. The pilot was swearing as he worked the controls. Cristof was standing by the front window, shouting for field glasses.

"Gunner's lenses," the pilot snapped in Alzanan, pointing. Taya grabbed the strange-looking heavy goggles and handed them to her husband. Cristof eased them over his glasses and turned to the windows, adjusting the focus.

Another explosion boomed around them, and a distant rattle of gunfire. Something moved at the bottom of the window. Taya looked down. One of the Alzanan ships appeared at a lower altitude, ponderously swinging about.

"We're being fired on from the mountainside," Cristof reported, his voice tense. "Sounds like mortars."

Heavy guns rattled. The dirigibles were firing back, maneuvering so the gunners could fire from the gondola windows.

"Lictors," her husband added, pulling back from the window when his goggles' lenses hit the glass. "They must have moved fast to get to this pass."

"Maybe they used one of those pneumatic trains."

"Do you want me to take us out of range?" their pilot asked in Alzanan.

"Move us so we can fire on that dirigible," Taya directed, pointing.

"You want me to help you fire on my people?"

"I'm going to aim at the envelope. I swear on the Lady, all I want to do is force them down. The sooner this ends, the sooner we can get you to a hospital." *And Cristof, too,* she thought, shooting her husband a concerned glance.

The Alzanan snarled but complied.

"The lictors have rifles, but I don't think any of their shots are coming close," Cristof added.

"I'm going to try to stop a dirigible," Taya said. Rushing into the gondola's main room, she yanked down the windows in front of the three still-mounted guns. The noise level in the cabin rose as wind whistled inside, buffeting her wings. Their pilot was easing them into a slow, turning descent, and the other dirigibles appeared to be hanging sideways in the air.

Taya shoved the rear-mounted starboard gun forward on its rails, found the locking mechanism, and kicked it closed. Another set of hands-free gunner's lenses hung off one of the locker handles. She pulled her flight goggles down around her neck and replaced them with the Alzanan set. Everything was fuzzy. She fumbled with the focus wheel until the enemy ships leaped into view. Number Two was directly ahead.

Perfect. She aimed at the snarling bear's head and fired.

Dark holes tore into the silver fabric as hot brass flew around her, some of the shells ricocheting and hitting her. She shifted the heavy, rattling gun, watching bullets trace a line in the envelope, and then eased back on the firing lever.

Her arms ached and her ears rang. She pushed the gunner's lenses up and wiped her face, smelling gunpowder.

Number Two fired back.

Taya hit the ground as bullets burst through the wooden gondola walls in a shower of splinters. Her wings rattled as broken wood struck them.

She'd been firing to disable. The other ship was firing to kill.

Rays of sunlight streamed through the new holes in the gondola.

"They should have made these things out of metal," she said, shakily, to nobody in particular. She faintly heard Cristof shouting. She waved a hand to reassure him that she was all right, then wiped her face to make sure she *was*. A thin streak of blood smeared her hand.

She pulled down the lenses again. Number Two didn't show any signs of spinning downward. She remembered what Cristof had said about penetrating to the gas balloons.

She aimed and fired once more. This time, as soon as she lifted her thumbs, she rolled to one side and flattened herself.

Several seconds later — a long time, by her count — the Alzanans returned fire.

When they stopped, she looked outside. She'd done more damage to Number Two's envelope, but either their ship or her own had moved. She didn't have a good shot anymore.

Running in a low crouch, she returned to the control cabin. Cristof was steadying the pilot, who'd slumped over the wheel.

"Was he shot?"

"He fainted."

She straightened the pilot in his chair and checked his wound. The bullet had entered the left side of his stomach.

Cristof handed her the bandages from the medical supplies.

"Can you wake him up?" he asked.

She pressed the fabric to the man's side.

"Are there any smelling salts in there?"

Two loud explosions made them both look up. Trails of smoke wisped past the window.

Cristof unearthed a small brass container labeled *sal volatile*. Taya uncapped it, waving the damp wire loop embedded in its cork under the Alzanan's nose.

The pilot groaned, his eyes opening.

"Hold this," she ordered, putting the man's hand over the bandage. She pulled out the bottle of morphine and rapidly fixed a dose.

"We need him awake," Cristof warned.

Taya ignored him, plunging the needle into the Alzanan's arm. She only had a half-dose; at best it might dull the pain.

Her rough bandaging job wasn't going to help the pilot much, either, but it was the best she could do. She'd only been trained in emergency first aid.

A bullet pinged off the window next to them, cracking it. All three looked out and saw dirigibles Two and Three lining up in front of their ship. Alzanan soldiers were manning the guns.

The pilot grabbed the wheel. "Time to go."

They began a slow, heavy turn. The thick windows in front of them made snapping sounds as the cracks and stars left by enemy gunfire began to spiderweb across the glass panes. Taya grabbed Cristof's arm and tugged him toward the cabin doorway.

Seconds later, bright bursts of light flashed from the enemy ships, and the weakened window glass sprayed backward out of its frame. The pilot turned and threw his arms over his face. Taya and Cristof were knocked off their feet as the wind that shrieked through the broken windows slammed their counterweighted masses into the back wall. The ship shuddered. Somebody began shouting incoherently through the speaking tubes.

Taya grasped her husband's coat. Even with his pockets full of lead and brass, the rescue vest made him too light for safety. He struggled to his feet, wrapping his gloved fingers around the struts of her armature. The pilot laid prone in a puddle of blood and broken glass. Taya only had to glance at his bullet-riddled body to know he was dead. She felt an irrational surge of grief for the man.

"Taya!" Cristof shook her. "We have to go! The engines have been hit!"

The shouting abruptly made sense— one of the engineers in back was warning the control room that the engines had been struck and were on fire. Taya let Cristof pull her out of the cabin and back to the gondola door.

"What about—" she looked up the stairs, where Tazio was handcuffed.

"No time!" Cristof threw open the doors. "Out! Before we blow up!"

"But—"

He grabbed the keel of her armature, screwed his eyes shut, and threw himself backward out the door.

Wind whistled past her ears as they fell. Shocked, Taya grabbed her husband's arms, afraid he might lose his grip.

"I — hate — falling," he said in a strangled voice. His face was pale, the wave castemarks on his cheekbones standing out like brands. His gray eyes opened and locked onto hers, as though he were afraid that if he looked away, she'd vanish and leave him alone in midair.

"It's okay." Her heart pounded as she gathered her wits. He'd forced them out to save them. The ship was going to explode.

She let go of one of his arms and caught a strap from his rescue harness that was whipping against her side. First things first. She snapped it to her armature.

"Even if you let go of me, you'll float," she reminded him.

"I'm *not* letting go of you." He closed his eyes again. "You can start flying any time, please."

She found the strap on the other side of his harness, digging it out from between them and snapping it into place. Then she scooped out the ammunition in his coat pockets, letting it fall in a glittering stream of lead and brass.

"We're linked. Loosen your grip."

"Taya...."

Well, he didn't *have* to loosen his grip. She twisted her arms into her wings. They were in no immediate danger; the cliffs and hills were still a long way away. Number One was getting smaller above them, bright orange flames licking out of its aft gondola as the engine burned. The two vessels in front were rising to avoid it, and a third, behind, was turning to increase the distance between them.

Taya spread her arms, shifting them into horizontal flight. At once she realized that even though Cristof's weight was all but zeroed out, he had no way to support himself on the horizontal. Some of the straps on his harness were probably meant to help, but she didn't have time to sort them out, and she was getting tired.

Up or down? Back to the ships or down to the cliffs? The cliffs beckoned, even though she knew they should keep harassing the ships.

Number One exploded with a deafening boom.

The sudden burst of air and thermals buffeted them to one side. Taya's weariness was swept away in a surge of adrenaline.

"Look out!" Cristof shouted. Taya shot a quick glance up and saw burning detritus soaring through the air. The whole ship was coming down on them in bits and pieces.

Up. She needed to go *up*, above the burning wreckage.

"Don't move!" she shouted, straining to ride the chaotic thermals. Ash and embers swirled around her like snow as she propelled them up through the periphery of the explosion, avoiding the burning skeleton of the ship that was breaking into fiery pieces as it fell. She headed for the nearest dirigible, remembering Lieutenant Amcathra's advice— one of its blind spots was directly below it.

But she'd forgotten about Number Five. As she pulled above the fireball, she heard distant gunfire over the growl of ship engines.

"Scrap!" They were a small target, but if someone got lucky, Cristof was between her and their bullets. She twisted around, fighting to put her back to the dirigible, even as she felt him ripping open a pocket on her leg.

"What are you doing?"

"Shooting back!" he shouted, pulling out her flare gun and the extra cartridge. He pulled himself higher on her keel and threw an arm around her neck. "Before they hit you."

"Don't— watch my wings!"

"Just hold me here a minute, love." He raised his other hand, which was gripping the weapon, to enclose her in an awkward embrace. "...never pierce an envelope from here...."

The flare gun spat next to her ear and she heard the missile whistle away. She continued bearing upward, even though it was impossible to see anything with Cristof's hair and coat collar flapping in her face. The straps of his rescue harness tugged on her armature as he shifted, his hands moving behind her head.

"Would you stop that?" She gauged their distance to Number Four. She wasn't sure what they were going to do when they reached it, but at least it would provide some cover.

"Give me a minute." He paused. "Damn!"

He shifted, and she heard another spit and trailing whistle.

"Barely deserve the name 'gun'...." her husband grumbled, opening his hand. The empty flare gun gleamed in the sunlight as it fell.

"I hope the army didn't want that back. Could you move your shoulder out of my face?"

"I— yes!" He slid down and gave her a triumphant grin, his glasses askew as he clung to her keel. "It went right through the gondola window. That'll keep them busy."

She didn't know whether to laugh or cry. How could her husband be so enthusiastic about hurting people?

"We still have to get above Number Four," she said.

"I have an idea." One of his hands tightened on her armature as the other straightened his glasses. Then he dropped his hand to her belt, twisting her second bomb free. "How fast can you fly us up?"

"You'll never be able to light that while we're flying."

He looked at it, then her, crestfallen.

She craned her neck up and saw the signal flags flapping below Number Four's gondola. Inspired, she shifted direction, angling toward them.

"If I hold us under the gondola and act as a windbreak, could you light a match?" she asked.

"I could try."

"You'll have to let go of me."

He swallowed, his eyes flickering to the narrow leather straps that bound them together.

"I— all right."

"When I get near the flags, grab the lines or the support poles. It doesn't matter which, but hold us in place until I can slide my arms out of my wings."

"How counterweighted are you?"

"To about ten pounds."

"Good." He carefully slid the bomb into his coat pocket and tugged on the security straps. "I can manage that."

It was like maneuvering through the wireferries in Tertius, except her courier's pack had never been as long and ungainly as Cristof. She twisted once and overshot, Cristof's gloved fingertips brushing against the edge of a crimson flag. Gritting her teeth, Taya backbeat and tried again, worried that even though they were below the gondola's windows, Numbers Five or Three might spot them.

With a jar, she was caught short. Her wingtips scraped against the bottom of the wooden gondola. Cristof winced as she pulled her wings in with a jerk. He grabbed a flag and pulled them up to one of the lines, closing his right hand tightly over it. She locked her wings in close and wriggled her arms free to grab the line with him.

For a moment they rested chest-to-chest, panting. Sweat ran down his face and his pulse pounded in his neck.

"How are you feeling?" she asked.

"If my nerves ever settle, I'll let you know." He mustered an unsteady smile. "Did the other ship blow up?"

She bobbed up to look past him.

"It's descending. There's smoke coming from the rear gondola. You must have damaged the engines." She was relieved. At least one ship had been defeated without killing everyone on board.

"Good." He took a breath, looking up. "We need to move backward, under the hatch."

Awkwardly, moving hand over hand as they were buffeted by the strong air currents that swept under the gondola, they drew themselves beneath it.

"Where did you put the matches?" he asked.

"Left waist pocket. No, *my* left."

He fished the tin box out one-handed and scrutinized her for a moment, his gray eyes wandering over her armature. Then he released the line, tensing as he bobbed against the straps that connected them.

"You're zeroed out," she reminded him. "You're doing fine. You must be getting over your fear of heights."

"Not in this lifetime." He pulled out a match and struck it against the locking mechanism that sealed her armature keel. Flame burst up for a second before being blown out. Pungently scented smoke tickled her nose. He tossed the match away. "Could you shift a little to the right?"

She angled around. He pulled out several matches and put them between his teeth. Then, bomb in one hand, he struck a second match and thrust the fuse into its flame. No luck. A third. Failure. A fourth. The cord crackled and caught.

Cristof dropped the match and grabbed her shoulder, pulling himself up and throwing his elbow into the trap door. Taya risked a glance as it slammed open. She caught a glimpse of someone's started face and then Cristof bobbed over her again, lobbing the bomb as far back into the gondola as he could.

She released the flag line and thrust her arms into her wings as they dropped. Cristof grabbed his glasses with a yelp, his free hand locking around her keel. She spread her arms and beat down as hard as she could, angling them up and away. Twenty seconds, moving slower this time because she was ascending and fighting the drag of a second body... but up was safer than down. She threw everything she had into lifting them higher.

Then she heard the explosion, first one and then a second.

She knew what to do this time. She had a sense of how long the thermals would buffet her, and for once she wasn't worried about being scalded by falling rubbish. She kept them as steady as she could and rode out the percussion.

I'm getting used this, she thought, fleetingly and with regret.

"Drop your legs," she shouted as she took them into another ascent. After a heartbeat or two, Cristof complied. "Are you all right?"

"Can we land now?"

She spotted Number Three a little below and behind her.

"Get ready," she said, swinging them around toward the empty gun platform on top.

It was a mess, but at least she kept her wings high as they stumbled and fell together. She landed with her knees on either side of her husband's waist, straining to keep her weight off his bandaged ribs and arm. He sagged, dropping his hands to the wooden platform and letting his head fall back. The noise of the dirigible's engine throbbed around them, regular and reassuring.

"Thank you," he said, closing his eyes. "That was utterly terrifying."

She slid her arms free and braced one gloved hand on the platform, unsnapping the clips that bound them. Then she unhooked his vest.

"Wait." He grabbed it, opening his eyes again. "We're not on the ground yet."

"I know. I want to see your injuries." Brushing his hands aside, she unbuttoned his coat and pulled it open. "Oh, Cris...."

Fresh blood stained his shirt, seeping through the bandages. She started to lift his collar when he grabbed her hand.

"Don't." He brought her hand to his lips and kissed the flesh between her glove and sleeve cuff. "There's nothing we can do about it now."

"Does it hurt?"

"Excruciatingly."

"You're always so stoic," she joked, fighting back a lump in her throat. She needed to get him someplace safe.

"I'm afraid you married a clockwright, not a hero."

"Not true." She slid off and helped him sit up. "You disabled two ships. This is the last one."

He looked up from re-fastening his harness, blinking.

The sky around them was empty.

They stood and leaned on the platform rail. Number Five was still descending, trailing black smoke, and burning trees in the valley behind them spoke to the fates of Numbers One and Two. Number Four, of course, was far behind them.

Cristof put his hand in his pocket and withdrew it, empty.

"Do you have any weapons left?"

"My utility knife."

"My needler went down on the first ship." He scowled. "And so did my new loupe-piece."

"I'm sorry."

"I should have put it into my pocket."

"You were distracted."

"Especially after you went through so much effort to bring it to me." He sounded chagrined.

"You still have your watch, don't you?"

"No— the Alzanans took it."

Taya felt a superstitious chill. "I hope we can get it back."

"It's probably down there someplace, in pieces."

Metal hinges creaked and Taya froze.

"You are really the most frightfully irritating people," Gaio Mazzoletti said from behind them. "Just how often do you have to be killed before you stay dead, Ambassador?"

Cristof looked at her, his lips tightening, and slowly turned.

"So, Lord Mazzoletti," he said, his voice steady. "Have you finally decided to get your own hands dirty?"

Taya turned with him, frantically weighing and discarding escape possibilities as she watched Gaio Mazzoletti climb out of the access hatch. His eyes were on Cristof but his pistol was trained on her. He brushed some nonexistent dust off his captain's coat and stepped onto the platform, pressing his gun barrel against her temple.

"Well, your own people have certainly proven inept," he replied. "But you'll notice I'm not threatening *your* life."

"I noticed." Cristof's voice was tight with anger. Taya fought to keep her own expression neutral, for his sake.

"Then you'll be so kind as to take three steps back. Where's the rest of your team? Or are you all that's left?"

Cristof gave him a withering look.

"Not going to answer? Then I'll assume you're alone, since my crew hasn't reported seeing any other icarii. What a loyal little wife you have, Ambassador, coming to rescue you all by herself."

Taya's hand twitched toward her counterweight belt.

"No moving, please, or I will paint the ship with your brains." She froze.

"Don't." Cristof's voice was tight. Taya wasn't sure if he was talking to her or to Gaio.

"You have put me in a difficult situation, Ambassador. I have a choice between continuing on by myself or turning back to face a court martial."

"You might survive a court martial."

"I might survive a visit to your capital. We already know that my ship can stay out of the range of your mortars and cannon, and I have enough ammunition to make short work of any icarii who might attack."

"You missed *us*."

"I must say, we hadn't realized Ondinium's taboo against icarii bearing weapons was so flexible. Or is your wife a renegade, like you? What's the punishment for an icarus who drops a bomb? Death?"

Taya felt sick to her stomach as she saw Cristof look away, his fists clenching.

"Now," Lord Gaio continued, "the real question is whether it's worth keeping you two alive anymore. I confess that I'm inclined against it."

"I'll do anything you want to keep her safe," Cristof said, tautly. He raised his head and drew in a sharp, startled breath.

Gaio shoved the barrel harder against Taya's skull.

"Don't try anything, Ambassador."

"No—" Cristof lifted his hands, his voice shaking. "Sorry. It's just — my side — don't hurt her."

"Cris...." Taya wanted to comfort him, but she didn't dare move.

"I suggest you avoid any abrupt moves if you want to keep your wife alive."

"All right. All right." Her husband slowly reached up and pulled off his glasses. His hands trembled as he cleaned them on his scarf and slid them back over his nose. He looked directly at Taya. "Tell me what you want, Lord Mazzoletti. Just don't hurt her."

"Are you begging me?"

"Yes. I'm begging you."

Lord Gaio grunted. "You could have made that a little more satisfying, Ambassador. Where's that infamous exalted pride I've heard so much about?"

Cristof shook his head, still looking shaken. Light flashed from his lenses.

"I don't have any pride. Ask anyone."

"Your husband isn't impressing me, Icarus."

"He doesn't need to, Lord Gaio." Something was wrong, but Taya wasn't sure what. Cristof's first reaction, controlled fury, she'd expected. But this sudden trepidation was something different, and she didn't believe it had anything to do with his wounds.

"What do you want me to do?" Cristof asked, still gazing at Taya. His intense focus reminded her of the times he'd refused to look away from her face in midair. Was that it? Was he suffering an attack of vertigo? Not on top of a dirigible's broad envelope, surely.

Something flashed in his glasses again. Taya's eyes widened.

Something was out there, behind them. Something that terrified him.

"Let's start with the capital's air defenses," Gaio said. "Neuillan has already told us everything he knows, so don't try to lie to me. For each discrepancy between his testimony and yours, your wife will lose a part of her body usually considered important to an icarus."

"Neuillan was exiled from the capital years ago." Cristof's voice was unsteady. "If our descriptions disagree, it won't be because I've lied to you."

"Well, you'll just have to be convincing, then, won't you?"

Taya braced herself. She was going to be shot. It didn't matter whether or not Cristof told the truth. Maiming her would be the fastest way for Lord Gaio to prove he was serious and to break down any residual resistance Cristof might be feeling.

She'd try her hardest not to scream, for Cristof's sake.

"There—" Cristof faltered. The bright dot in his glasses was growing larger. Taya focused on it, trying to stay calm. "The mountains around the capital are all fortified. I can mark the locations on a map. They're armed with cannon and mortars. I've heard rumors of gas weapons, too, but I don't think they'd be effective against your ships. I expect the fortresses have been mined to prevent them from falling into enemy hands."

"You *expect*?" Lord Gaio moved the barrel of the gun and Taya drew in a sharp breath, waiting for it to touch her elbow.

A shot cracked, and then a second and a third. Cristof tackled her, bearing her backward and throwing an arm over her head. Taya gasped as she hit the platform, her wings rattling and the struts of her armature digging into her back and sides. Was she dead? Her eyes rose over his shoulder, and she saw a giant silver raptor flying through a pale mist of smoke and vapor. Was it a heavenly messenger from the Lady? She stared and waited for the pain and the darkness.

Two more shots rang out, and she saw black-clad shapes on top of the bird, holding rifles.

Lord Gaio crumpled, his chest a mass of blood.

Chapter Twenty-Eight

THE BIRD-SHAPED vessel was crafted out of priceless ondium plates, with motionless wings that extended horizontally on either side of the hull. It wasn't a dirigible— no balloons of any sort held it up. *Nothing* held it up. It simply floated in the sky, slender and deadly, its gleaming metal hull engraved with curling, geometric patterns that looked like stylized feathers, or waves, or perhaps wind currents made visible. The ship's streamlined prow was a featureless silver oval broken only by two curving glass windows, not unlike a raked-back exalted's mask. Its giant metal wings resembled an icarus', connected to the hull by a complicated system of gears and flywheels and pistons.

As Taya watched, the ship continued its stately glide forward, revealing gunnery ports hanging open in its metal underbelly and a crimson flag streaming beneath its sharp prow. The flag displayed gold stars against a blood-red field.

"Cris...."

"Don't." He raised a hand and placed it over her eyes. "Don't look."

"What is it?"

"An ornithopter. An imperial ornithopter."

"I thought Ondinium destroyed all its ornithopters in the Virtuous Reclamation."

"So did I."

"But—"

"Don't look at it. We shouldn't be seeing it."

She reached up and gently lifted his wrist.

"Cris." She met his eyes, seeing the fear in them and knowing that it was for her. "We can't pretend it's not there."

"I think it would be better for us if we did."

The ancient ship's shadow fell over them, and she finally heard its engines over Number Three's. The great silver wings moved, ondium feathers rasping shut with a spinning of giant gear trains. Pistons shifted and the wings swept backward, slowing the vehicle.

"They know we've seen them."

"Taya...." Cristof helped her up and grabbed Gaio Mazzoletti's gun, keeping his eyes averted from the ship. His jaw was tight. "Neither of us are cleared to see that ship. And you *know* what the Oporphyr Council must have done to keep a secret this big for so long."

She took his free hand and gently squeezed it.

"I didn't go through all this just to lose you to a bunch of paranoid bureaucrats," she said, firmly. "We'll deal with the Council together."

His fingers tightened around hers, but he still looked apprehensive.

The mist surrounding the ancient ship thickened, vaporous tendrils curling around the stern like the designs etched into its ondium hull. Taya guessed that effect was caused by a combination of smoke, steam, and condensation rising from hot metal at a freezing altitude. It gave the ship an unearthly appearance.

A rope arced over the raptor's silver rail and uncoiled. Taya released Cristof to grab it and lash the end around the gunnery platform rail. Seconds later, a lictor slid through the vapor and landed next to them. He adjusted the rifle slung over his shoulder and shot Lord Gaio's corpse a cursory glance before turning to them.

"Exalted. I am pleased that you still live."

"Janos—" Cristof's astonished greeting was interrupted as Taya threw her arms around the lictor, not caring if her armature bruised him or her welcome embarrassed him.

"I thought you were dead!" she exclaimed, finally voicing the fear that had been haunting her ever since she'd seen Glasgar reduced to rubble. "Oh, Lady, I was so afraid you were dead!"

"As you can see, Icarus," the lictor said with effort, attempting to extricate himself, "I am quite alive."

"How did you get away from the bombs? Why are you on an ornithopter? What happened?"

"Exalted..."

"Taya, give him a chance to breathe." Cristof laid a hand on her arm, even though he looked as delighted to see his old friend as she was. "You're making me jealous."

"Hush." She let her husband tug her away, although she clung to Amcathra's sleeve. "Are we going to be all right, Lieutenant?"

"If you will allow us to secure this ship, I will do what I can to ensure your well-being." Slipping his arm out of her grasp, he turned and waved to the crew. More lines fell.

A small platoon of lictors landed on the ship, each armed to the teeth. Cristof pointed out the access hatch and the rungs on the side of the envelope. The boarding party split up and began its descent.

"Exalted." An ensign bowed to him, her eyes flickering with embarrassment from Cristof's bare face. "Captain Amcathra ordered me to take you aboard to our physician. Do you need a bosun's chair?"

"A what?"

"Do you need to be lifted to the ship, Exalted, or should we raise a ladder for you?"

"Chair," Taya said, but Cristof gave her a withering look.

"I can climb to the ship, thank you. Did you say *Captain* Amcathra?"

"Acting captain, Exalted."

"He's in charge of that thing?"

The ensign hesitated. "Yes, Exalted. The *Firebrand*. It isn't standard protocol for the captain to leave his ship, but he insisted on being the first to board. He said you would expect no less."

"Of course," Cristof said, nonplussed. He looked at Taya and gathered himself. "Uh, of course. I entirely support … Captain … Amcathra's actions."

The lictor bowed again, uncertainly, and hurried off.

"Do you think he knew Ondinium had these ships all along?" Taya asked.

"He must have, if he's the acting captain. He must have flown them before." Cristof looked around. "I suppose there are enough remote passes out here for secret military maneuvers."

"Then he's been keeping secrets from you."

"Apparently." Cristof gave her a crooked smile. "At least now I'm not so worried about our fate. If he were under orders to kill us, he could have done it before he boarded."

Taya gave a pensive nod. She didn't want to doubt Lieutenant — Captain — Amcathra. But he was the same man who'd killed his nephew in the line of duty. If he were forced to make a choice, which would be more important to him: his orders or his friends?

"It looks like they're emptying the ship and preparing to march," she reported to Amcathra, pulling off her goggles. As tired as she was, she hadn't been able to refuse the lictor's request to locate the grounded Number Five while he secured Number Three. She walked over the *Firebrand*'s ondium deck to the navigation chart and pointed. "It's right about here. Be careful, though; they've still got a lot of guns."

"Thank you, Icarus." Amcathra marked the spot with a pencil. "I will report it."

"You're not going after them yourself?"

"No." He turned. "Mr. Cadra, we are returning to base with the captured ship."

"Yes, sir." The lictor saluted and turned, shouting orders.

"Wait. I know you're busy, but— what's going to happen to us?" Taya asked as Amcathra rolled the chart. He handed it to one of several young lictors who dogged his footsteps, nodded to Taya, and led her down a short flight of stairs to the cabins.

Cristof was sitting in the mess hall in the prow, looking through the window. He'd been freshly bandaged and given a lictor's uniform, the coat hanging loosely over his shoulders.

"I don't feel so nervous on an ornithopter," he said, turning. Taya tucked an arm into his and kissed his cheek. He'd been dosed with so many painkillers that his pulse probably wouldn't rise if they threw him overboard. She was glad he was still on his feet, though. "So, are you going to execute us, Janos?"

Amcathra pulled up two light wooden chairs. "We should discuss the matter before we return to base."

"That's not the 'no, of course not' I was hoping to hear."

"'No, of course not,'" Amcathra repeated, dryly. "It is the Oporphyr Council's job to execute you, not mine."

"Ah, good. I told Taya we'd be safe in your hands." Cristof sat, and Taya perched on the chair next to him, hoping the two men were joking. "You're far too pragmatic to waste medicine and bandages on a man you were about to kill."

"Yes." Amcathra's gaze was steady. "And if it is any comfort to you, I believe your statuses as Ondinium's only exalted ambassador and his official representative will clear you to this security level, assuming you pass another loyalty examination when you return. However, from now on you will be under a considerably higher level of scrutiny than you have been in the past."

"I don't know how much higher the Council's scrutiny can go unless you come to live with us." Cristof sighed. "I refuse to wear a mask, my brother's a traitor, and I married out of caste. Do they really think I'm any more of a security risk now than before?"

"In the past, the Council considered your wife a positive, if caste-inappropriate, influence on you." Amcathra met Taya's eyes. "However, now that she has carried and used weapons, I fear that evaluation will change."

"You gave me those weapons!" Taya protested.

"*I* do not disapprove of your actions."

"But you knew the Council would disapprove?"

"Could you have rescued the exalted without them?"

Taya scowled. Amcathra waited a moment, then turned back to her husband.

"It is, however, my sincere hope that their increased security will not require me to live with you, as your wife exhibits an inexplicable penchant for spontaneously hugging me."

"What?" Taya gave the lictor a startled look. Amcathra and Cristof stared at each other a long moment, and then Cristof's lips started to twitch. Captain Amcathra tilted his head and Cristof exploded into laughter.

"That is *not* funny," Taya scolded, blushing. "What in the Lady's name are you laughing about?"

"I'm sorry." Cristof tilted up his glasses and wiped his eyes. "Nothing. Ouch, Janos, that hurts." He touched his side and made a face.

Taya scowled. "You aren't laughing at me, are you?"

"No, no— at us. I mean, which one of us is worst-suited for marriage. Janos or me. When you and I got married, I told Janos he won."

"I apologize for your husband's sense of humor," Amcathra said. "He is under the influence of painkillers."

"I think you both have a rotten sense of humor," she muttered, giving them a dark look. "And there's nothing wrong with hugging a friend!"

"Setting aside the question of our future living arrangements," Amcathra said mildly, "it is important that you understand that everyone who knows of these ships is under a suspended death sentence. A slip of the tongue or the wrong word at the wrong time will result in summary execution."

"How long have *you* known about them?" Taya asked.

"I was recruited into aerial service after I finished my thesis on Captain Menoth."

"Longer than I've known you, then," Cristof observed. "So that's why you were sent with us to Mareaux— to study their aerostats."

"My familiarity with airborne vehicles of war was one reason for my transfer to your delegation. My familiarity with you was another. The Council is under the impression that you are more likely to reveal any disloyal sentiments to me than to a stranger."

"I'm discontented, not disloyal."

"I want to know more about these ships," Taya demanded. "How often do you fly them? How many people know about them?"

"Members of the aerial service have regular military duties in Ondinium but are excused for a two-week training course each year, which is when we refresh our flight skills. Until yesterday we have never been called out for active duty. I do not know how many of us there are in Ondinium, and I prefer not to speculate."

"How did you get this command?"

"I was in Glasgar and my senior officers were not."

"Did you know you were going to command one of these ships before or after you sent me to rescue Cris?"

"Before." He met her narrowed gaze, his blue eyes candid. "I was ordered to abandon my mission to Kovolo and report to the nearest ornithopter hangar as soon as my train stopped in Glasgar. However, when I learned of your presence and the exalted's capture, I knew I would have to help you rescue him before I could report with a clear conscience."

"So you armed me and sent me away, knowing you'd be coming after me."

"I *hoped* to come after you, Icarus. I still had to travel to the hangar, bring the ship aloft, and locate the invaders. I am pleased to have arrived in time to be of assistance."

"I wish I'd known you were coming. Maybe things would have worked out differently." She wondered if she'd have dropped the bomb, if she'd known help was on the way. Or let Cristof take the ship single-handed. "And in the end you ended up rescuing me, instead. This is the second time you've saved my life."

"Several of us shot Lord Mazzoletti. I do not know whose bullet killed him."

Taya had no doubt that Amcathra's was among those that had found their target.

"Moreover," the lictor continued, "you must not assume that the *Firebrand* could have defeated the invaders by itself. We would have been outnumbered and outgunned had you not disabled most of the ships first. Your efforts — yours and the exalted's — made our victory possible. I will inform the Council of your exemplary work."

"But we had to kill so many people...."

"They would have died in either case. Moreover, if it had come to a ship-to-ship firefight, it is likely that many of my crew would have died, too. Your actions saved Ondinium lives."

"I still don't like it."

"That is as it should be. The Council would feel uneasy if an icarus were not only willing to carry weapons but also happy to take lives. It is already uncomfortable with your husband's enthusiasm for violence. Exalteds are supposed to guide military strategy, not participate in it."

"Seems to me like rules are being broken all around us," Cristof remarked. "You said this ship would be outgunned — does that mean it carries weapons?"

"Ship-to-ship weapons, Exalted. Not bombs."

"The Council's splitting hairs. It's still an airborne, weapons-carrying vehicle. We preach to everyone about how enlightened we are because we shun aerial warfare, and yet here we are, building our own aerial army...."

"We did not build these vehicles, Exalted. These ornithopters are imperial artefacts, manufactured before the Reclamation."

"Hairs."

"I will not argue the point. I suggest you do not, either." Amcathra's gaze strayed out the window, where the mountain peaks were growing larger. "The Council is not in the mood for arguments. You saw our red flag."

"The flag of war," Taya said.

"Yes. The Council considers this invasion an act of war and is preparing for military action against Alzana. It is likely that these ships will be kept secret and called out again only in the event of another aerial invasion. However— I can imagine alternate scenarios."

Cristof frowned.

"The Council wouldn't be bold enough to respond with an aerial attack of its own," he said. "That would be a diplomatic disaster."

"It has been two thousand years since the Last War," Amcathra said. "This invasion makes it clear that Ondinium's restrictive policies have caused it to fall behind the rest of the world in military innovation. If the Council does not strike back at once, other countries may sense its weakness and ally with Alzana against us."

"Demicus is already split," Taya said, troubled. "They're going to call an assembly of clans, but I was warned that the vote might go against us."

"The *sheytatangri* can be very influential. And Alzana will offer the clans weapons that Ondinium will not."

"But... the Great Engine has always promoted an isolationist policy."

"Its advice is only as good as the data it receives. The Council has not been keeping close track of events beyond Ondinium's borders."

"I won't support taking this war beyond our borders," Cristof said, scowling. "Especially not into another country's airspace."

"You are not a decatur and you have very little influence over your peers," Amcathra said, flatly. "You remain in caste at the convenience of the Council, which has thus far considered you to be slightly more of an asset than a liability. If you oppose the Council, that opinion will shift, and you and the icarus will suffer the consequences."

Taya took Cristof's hand, daunted by the grim picture the lictor was painting.

"So you're advising me to shut up and do whatever the Council says," Cristof said, bitterly.

"Yes."

"Maybe it won't be that bad," Taya ventured.

"We can hope not." Amcathra stood. "I am required on deck. Please behave circumspectly when we land and score well on your loyalty examinations. I would not wish to have wasted my medicine and bandages, Exalted."

"Go." Cristof scowled at him. Amcathra hesitated, looking at them.

"My intention is only to keep you safe."

"We know. It's all right." Taya gave him a sad smile, her hand tightening over Cristof's. "Thank you."

The lictor nodded and shut the door behind him.

Seven days later, Taya sat in a small office in Oporphyr Tower. She and Cristof had been separated and debriefed, then subjected to a battery of written and verbal loyalty examinations. She hadn't been sure until the bitter end whether she'd pass; for the first time in her life, she'd marked the answers she thought were safe, rather than true.

Taya's faith in Ondinium's moral superiority had been shaken. She'd seen too many of its secrets and learned too much about its disregard for human life to trust it anymore. But she made an effort to conceal her new, bitter wisdom in her interviews and test answers, and she must have succeeded, because at last she'd been permitted to sign the Official Secrets Act and rejoin her husband.

A lictor entered the room, looked around, and stepped aside. Decatur Constante walked in.

Taya stood and bowed, her palm on her forehead. Cristof gave the decatur a cool nod.

"Are you letting us go now?" he inquired, without any pretense of friendship.

"Soon." Constante brushed her robes aside and sat down. The wrinkles in her face were deeper than they'd been when Taya had seen her last. "We have a few final issues to clear up. Your Refinery scores were not as high as the Council would like—"

"That's the same program that allowed Neuillan, Alister, *and* Rikard through," Cristof scoffed. "I'd stop trusting it, if I were you."

"Its parameters have been adjusted," the decatur said, her voice hard. "The fact is, neither of you have a reputation for minding your caste, and you, especially, Forlore, have a criminally tainted bloodline."

Cristof looked away.

"I've never claimed otherwise," he muttered. "You're the one who insisted I come back to Primus and play your little ambassadorial games."

"It was tit for tat, Forlore; don't pretend otherwise. I know about the bank account you set up for your brother in Mareaux."

Taya held her breath, but her husband simply stared at the floor, his jaw clenched.

"The Council has voted to send you to Alzana. *Il Re* Quintilio Agosti claims the invasion was an unauthorized use of force by rogue Families and is suing for peace. We don't believe the invasion was unauthorized, but we do believe Agosti would like to avoid a war now that we've been alerted. Your job will be to listen to his lies, demand the most advantageous terms possible, and try to discover how many more ships he has hidden."

"But they'll kill us!" Taya protested.

"You two seem to be quite capable of defending yourselves, Icarus. We will, of course, send lictors with you. Lieutenant Amcathra has already requested command of your security arrangements, if you are willing to trust him after the incidents in Mareaux."

"He's a lieutenant again?" Cristof asked, raising his eyes to her face.

"His promotion to captain was temporary, and his behavior in this last affair was only marginally more satisfactory than your own. We did not authorize him to arm an icarus with firearms and explosives." Constante waved a hand to cut off Taya's protest. "At any rate, King Agosti is unlikely to condone your assassination if he is genuinely trying to avoid a war."

Taya fumed, but she didn't think there was anything she could say that would change the decatur's mind. The Council had the upper hand, and short of leaving Ondinium entirely, there was nothing she could do to defy it.

"What about Demicus?" she asked. "Has there been any news from Nayan about the *ating*?"

"We are in the process of sorting out the clan alliances in Demicus," Constante said, shortly. "The process you set in motion has been placed under others' guidance. You need not concern yourself with it. Alzana is more important."

"But what about Nayan?"

Constante gave her a stern look.

"Nayan is who you will become if you do not follow orders, Icarus— an example to others."

Taya's eyes widened. She wondered what the hapless young man had done to deserve his fate.

"When do we leave?" Cristof asked, quickly.

"Another week; perhaps two." Constante glanced at her paper-strewn desk. "We are still running scenarios through the Engine and studying the captured dirigibles. In the interim, you are not to speak to the press or anyone else about what happened."

Cristof gave a short nod. "Under penalty of death. Yes, I noticed that paragraph in the Act."

"We are releasing you back to your estate. I suggest you brush up on your Alzanan." Constante rose.

"Thank you, Exalted," Taya said stiffly, standing and bowing again. The decatur left, and a lictor led them out.

Oporphyr Tower's halls were empty and echoing as they headed toward the wireferry station. Amcathra waited for them at the wireferry. He stood as they walked in.

"Exalted. Icarus."

"You look as tired as I feel," Cristof said. "So— Alzana?"

"Unfortunately."

Their escort ushered them inside the wireferry car and closed the door.

"You know, I'm almost not afraid of these anymore," Cristof said, sliding to the center of the seat.

"You shouldn't be, after everything you've been through." Taya sat next to him. The car jolted and swung as the cables began to move, and Cristof's scarred cheek twitched. She smiled and took his hand, feeling his cold fingers wrap around hers as he lifted his eyes to contemplate the wireferry's plain metal roof.

Taya twisted to take one last look at the government complex behind them, washed crimson in the sunset. Her smile faded as her eyes reached the topmost tower, where Ondinium's flag snapped in the wind.

Gold stars on a red field.

She turned forward, her good mood lost.

"I have something for you, Exalted," Amcathra said, shifting in the seat behind them. He held his hand over the seat back. "This was among Gaio Mazzoletti's possessions."

Cristof reached up and the lieutenant dropped a heavy gold watch into his hand.

"Your watch!" Taya felt a burst of relief. "It's back!"

"I am afraid it has been broken."

Cristof opened the front and inspected the cracked glass, then turned it and opened the back. His fear of the wireferry was forgotten as he tilted up his glasses and scrutinized the workings.

"It looks like a problem with the mainspring and a few of the gears. I can fix it at home." He closed it, beaming. "Thank you, Janos. I'm glad to have it back."

"I am pleased to know that the damage can be repaired."

Taya took Cristof's hand again as she gazed out the window at the steep sprawl of the city below. Lights glimmered from windows and shop fronts, street lamps and factory yards. The wireferry hummed above them, and an icarus swept by, one last courier hurrying back to the central office before nightfall.

Ondinium operated like clockwork, she thought, feeling the weight of Cristof's watch in their clasped hands. But no matter what Neuillan had said, its citizens weren't gears to be discarded once they were broken. They were the engineers who kept the vital machine ticking and who fixed it when it broke.

"The city's beautiful at night," she mused. "All those lights in the dark, like our peacetime flag."

Cristof risked a quick glance out the window.

"Enjoy it while you can. We won't see it again for a while."

"The view?"

"Of course."

"We *shall* see it again, Icarus," Amcathra said, firmly.

"You know, I'd prefer it if you called me Taya," she said. "And may I call you Janos?"

The lictor folded his arms over his chest.

"The use of given names too often suggests an inappropriately close relationship."

"You let Cris use your name."

"Exalteds may do as they wish."

"The other Demicans I know use first names with me."

"They do not have my responsibilities."

"Janos isn't comfortable with intimacy," Cristof said. He nudged up his glasses with his free hand. "Of course, I wasn't, either, until I met you. In fact, given your affectionate habits, maybe you'd better stick to 'Lieutenant' and let him stick to 'Icarus.' I *am* a jealous man."

Taya rolled her eyes. "So if I find him a girlfriend, you wouldn't have any reason to be jealous, and he'd feel free to use my name, right?"

Cristof cocked an eyebrow, then shot an amused glance at the lictor.

"That seems like a reasonable solution," he agreed.

The wireferry clattered to a stop at the Primus station. Taya stood and followed her husband out. Then she turned and leaned on the doorway.

"So, Lieutenant, is a bubbly Cassi more your style, or a serious Professor Dautry?"

"Good night, Icarus. Please do not forget that we have a war to fight." Amcathra leaned forward and slid the wireferry door shut in her face.

Taya grinned at him through the bars and, with a lighter heart, hurried to catch up to Cristof.

"It'll be easier to defeat the Alzanans," her husband predicted.

She linked her arm through his. "Maybe. But defeating Lieutenant Amcathra will be much more fun."

~ Preview of Book Three ~
Chapter One

THE RIFLES' PERCUSSION rang in Taya's ears and a cloud of acrid gunpowder drifted through the air. Blood trickled over the snow-powdered courtyard.

She wished she were home.

"There, Ambassador." *Il Re* Quintilio Agosti waved a hand toward the bodies. "I trust you will assure your decaturs that Alzana has brought its traitorous officers to justice."

Cristof's silk-covered fingers tightened on Taya's arm.

A year ago, watching men being executed would have made Taya sick. Now what made her sick was its pointlessness. Nobody in the small prison courtyard believed that the dead men had masterminded the invasion, and nobody believed their deaths would prevent a war between Alzana and Ondinium. The two nations enacted their thousand-year-old script like creaking automata in a traveling stage show, each line and gesture predetermined.

"Are we finished here, Your Majesty?" she asked, her words tasting like ash.

A small smile played beneath Agosti's well-groomed beard. He knew she was disgusted, and he took pleasure from the knowledge. It was the only pleasure he'd get from their assembly. Cristof's emotions were unreadable beneath his ivory mask, and Lieutenant Amcathra and his lictors would be content to stand in the snow for hours if it meant watching more Alzanans die.

"Would the ambassador like to see more?" Agosti countered. "I could arrange to have other criminals brought before the firing squad, if it would amuse him."

Taya tensed. Cristof tapped her forearm.

Enough.

"The ambassador has seen enough," she said, her voice tight. "These executions *weren't* among our demands."

"But they were necessary, nevertheless." The king's expression remained complacent. "A lesson, if you will."

For whom? Taya wondered. She glanced past the king toward the sullen-looking group of aristocrats who'd accompanied them, her gaze inexorably drawn to the cold, hostile glare of Lady Fosca Mazzoletti.

Mazzoletti noted Taya's inspection and her lips pulled back in a grim, humorless smile. There was no way she could know that Lieutenant Amcathra had killed her twin brother, Gaio, to save Taya and Cristof, but she suspected something. Taya looked away, pulling her heavy fur cloak closer around her shoulders. The other nobles' cold, flat expressions offered no relief. Even the soldiers in the execution squad seemed resentful as they shouldered their rifles.

King Agosti's middle-aged daughter and adolescent granddaughter huddled a little apart from the rest of the group while his thirteen-year-old grandson studied the corpses with morbid fascination. The young *principe* was still in school, but the brass buttons and military cut of his coat indicated that he'd eventually follow his oldest sister into the army. Major Pietra Agosti hadn't attended the execution; she was away with her company, and the king's youngest grandson laid in bed with a cold.

Il Re Agosti glanced at the sky. "It's starting to snow again. If the ambassador doesn't wish to see more, we should return to the palace."

Cristof's fingers moved. *King meet me after.*

"Thank you, Your Majesty." Taya said. "The ambassador hopes to resume our talks this evening. We have much left to discuss."

"Yes, we do, but surely we wouldn't want to disturb our digestion with business." The king patted her arm with careless intimacy. "We'll resume our talks tomorrow."

Say Council end talk soon.

"As you wish," she said, hiding her distaste. "However, the ambassador wishes to remind you that the Council will grow impatient if we don't reach an agreement soon. The decaturs acquiesced to this truce at your request, Your Majesty, but their deadline is almost upon us."

"Indeed, indeed." The king laughed, but no amusement reached his eyes. He leaned closer. "Now that my enemies know where I stand, we should be able to proceed more expeditiously."

Taya reviewed his words twice before deciding that they weren't a threat. Not to her, anyway. She reassessed the hostile expressions on the Family leaders' faces.

What? Cristof inquired.

"The ambassador is pleased to hear that, Your Majesty," she said, shooting her husband a neutral look. "We look forward to discussing the situation with you tomorrow morning."

"Splendid." The king's expression collapsed into a sneer as he turned and regarded his entourage. "Sergeant! We are finished."

The sergeant barked orders. His men saluted the king and marched off, leaving the corpses behind.

"Ambassador." *Il Re* Agosti gestured to the line of towering steam-powered carriages waiting on the parkway before turning to his family.

Taya repeated the king's comment to Cristof as they began their slow walk across the snow-covered cobblestones. Lieutenant Amcathra remained beside them as his seven lictors ran ahead.

You trust him? Cristof tapped as they reached the carriages. The lictors were scrutinizing the steam engine's dials and checking their readouts against a chart. *Il Re* Agosti considered the tall, smoke-bellowing carriages standout symbols of Alzanan's modernity, but Amcathra monitored their operation with open suspicion.

"No, not really," Taya said, waiting for the lictors to let them enter. The Alzanans were already climbing ladders up to their Family carriages. The royal carriage was particularly tall and ornate, painted silver and sky-blue and surrounded by flamboyantly uniformed Alzanan soldiers standing at attention.

"Today's demonstration may have been intended to intimidate dissenters," Amcathra speculated, his rifle cradled in the crook of one arm. "Several of the executed officers belonged to Families in attendance."

Cristof's fingers moved. *Dangerous.*

"He says that sounds dangerous."

"Indeed." Amcathra inspected the chart and allowed his lictors to lean a ladder against the coach's towering eight-foot-tall wheels. "Exalted."

Taya helped Cristof climb and slid into the coach beside him. Amcathra closed the door as his lictors secured the ladder beneath the vehicle.

Taya drew the carriage curtains and untied Cristof's blank-featured ivory mask. She smiled at her husband's thin, careworn features and pale gray eyes and brushed a wayward strand of black hair away from his forehead. When he wasn't wearing his glasses, the new scars around his left eye were clearly visible.

"How are you feeling?"

"Less pleased than I ought to be, considering there are five fewer Alzanan officers in the world." He rubbed his face against a silk-covered shoulder. The coach jerked into motion, shaking and rumbling over the cobblestones. "What about you?"

"I'm all right." Her smile faded. "I must be getting used to violence."

"I'm sorry."

"I hope the king is finally planning to settle down to our negotiations," she said, avoiding the compassion in her husband's eyes. "I'm ready to leave Alzana."

"One way or the other, we'll be gone soon." He rested a fabric-draped hand over his ivory mask as she set it in his lap. "It's late winter, and the Council will want to attack by spring. We need to be back in Ondinium before that."

"You're assuming we'll fail."

"Did you think we'd succeed?" His crooked smile was humorless. "These negotiations are just a delaying tactic, love. Alzana is rushing to outfit whatever other dirigibles it has in hiding and the Council is rushing to pull more… more *machines* out of storage. This war's inevitable; you and I are just the intermission entertainment."

"Well, our work wasn't entirely in vain," Taya said, trying to cheer them both up. "The other nations have agreed to remain neutral, and I don't think they would have if their ambassadors hadn't met you in Mareaux. Showing them a face instead of a mask made a difference; they aren't as intimidated by Ondinium as they used to be."

"No, nobody would call me intimidating," Cristof agreed. She made a face at him. "Anyway, you—"

The coach swayed as something struck the front panel with a sharp report.

"Ambush!" Amcathra roared.

CLOCKWORK SECRETS: HEAVY FIRE
**IS THE THIRD AND FINAL BOOK IN
THE CLOCKWORK TRILOGY
~AVAILABLE FALL 2014~**

Our titles are available at major book stores and local independent resellers who support Science Fiction and Fantasy readers like you.

EDGE Science Fiction
and Fantasy Publishing

www.edgewebsite.com

Our titles are available at major book stores and local independent resellers who support Science Fiction and Fantasy readers like you.

Alphanauts by J. Brian Clarke (tp) - ISBN: 978-1-894063-14-2
Apparition Trail, The by Lisa Smedman (tp) - ISBN: 978-1-894063-22-7
As Fate Decrees by Denysé Bridger (tp) - ISBN: 978-1-894063-41-8

Black Chalice, The by Marie Jakober (hb) - ISBN: 978-1-894063-00-7
Blue Apes by Phyllis Gotlieb (pb) - ISBN: 978-1-895836-13-4
Blue Apes by Phyllis Gotlieb (hb) - ISBN: 978-1-895836-14-1
Braided Path, The by Donna Glee Williams (tp) - ISBN: 978-1-77053-058-4

Captives by Barbara Galler-Smith and Josh Langston (tp)
    - ISBN: 978-1-894063-53-1
Children of Atwar, The by Heather Spears (pb) - ISBN: 978-0-88878-335-6
Chilling Tales: Evil Did I Dwell; Lewd I Did Live edited by Michael Kelly (tp)
    - ISBN: 978-1-894063-52-4
Chilling Tales: In Words, Alas, Drown I edited by Michael Kelly (tp)
    - ISBN: 978-1-77053-024-9
Cinco de Mayo by Michael J. Martineck (tp) - ISBN: 978-1-894063-39-5
Cinkarion - The Heart of Fire (Part Two of The Chronicles of the Karionin)
    by J. A. Cullum - (tp) - ISBN: 978-1-894063-21-0
Circle Tide by Rebecca K. Rowe (tp) - ISBN: 978-1-894063-59-3
Clan of the Dung-Sniffers by Lee Danielle Hubbard (tp) - ISBN: 978-1-894063-05-0
Claus Effect, The by David Nickle & Karl Schroeder (pb) - ISBN: 978-1-895836-34-9
Claus Effect, The by David Nickle & Karl Schroeder (hb) - ISBN: 978-1-895836-35-6
Clockwork Heart by Dru Pagliassotti (tp) - ISBN: 978-1-77053-026-3
Clockwork Lies: Iron Wind by Dru Pagliassotti (tp) - ISBN: 978-1-77053-050-8

Danse Macabre: Close Encounters With the Reaper edited by Nancy Kilpatrick (tp)
    - ISBN: 978-1-894063-96-8
Dark Earth Dreams by Candas Dorsey & Roger Deegan (Audio CD with Booklet)
    - ISBN: 978-1-895836-05-9
Darkness of the God (Children of the Panther Part Two)
    by Amber Hayward (tp) - ISBN: 978-1-894063-44-9
Demon Left Behind, The by Marie Jakober (tp)   ISBN: 978 1 894063 49 4
Distant Signals by Andrew Weiner (tp) - ISBN: 978-0-88878-284-7
Dreams of an Unseen Planet by Teresa Plowright (tp) - ISBN: 978-0-88878-282-3
Dreams of the Sea (Part 1 of Tyranaël) by Élisabeth Vonarburg (tp)
    - ISBN: 978-1-895836-96-7
Dreams of the Sea (Part 1 of Tyranaël) by Élisabeth Vonarburg (hb)
    - ISBN: 978-1-895836-98-1
Druids by Barbara Galler-Smith and Josh Langston (tp)
    - ISBN: 978-1-894063-29-6

Eclipse by K. A. Bedford (tp) - ISBN: 978-1-894063-30-2
Elements by Suzanne Church (tp) - ISBN: 978-1-77053-042-3
Even The Stones by Marie Jakober (tp) - ISBN: 978-1-894063-18-0
Evolve: Vampire Stories of the New Undead edited by Nancy Kilpatrick (tp)
    - ISBN: 978-1-894063-33-3

Evolve Two: Vampire Stories of the Future Undead edited by Nancy Kilpatrick (tp)
-ISBN: 978-1-894063-62-3
Expiration Date edited by Nancy Kilpatrick (tp) - ISBN: 978-1-77053-062-1

Fires of the Kindred by Robin Skelton (tp) - ISBN: 978-0-88878-271-7
Forbidden Cargo by Rebecca Rowe (tp) - ISBN: 978-1-894063-16-6

Game of Perfection, A (Part 2 of Tyranaël) by Élisabeth Vonarburg (tp)
- ISBN: 978-1-894063-32-6
Gaslight Arcanum: Uncanny Tales of Sherlock Holmes
edited by Jeff Campbell & Charles Prepolec (tp)
- ISBN: 978-1-8964063-60-9
Gaslight Grimoire: Fantastic Tales of Sherlock Holmes
edited by Jeff Campbell & Charles Prepolec (tp)
- ISBN: 978-1-8964063-17-3
Gaslight Grotesque: Nightmare Tales of Sherlock Holmes
edited by Jeff Campbell & Charles Prepolec (tp)
- ISBN: 978-1-8964063-31-9

Green Music by Ursula Pflug (tp) - ISBN: 978-1-895836-75-2
Green Music by Ursula Pflug (hb) - ISBN: 978-1-895836-77-6

Healer, The (Children of the Panther Part One) by Amber Hayward (tp)
- ISBN: 978-1-895836-89-9
Healer, The (Children of the Panther Part One) by Amber Hayward (hb)
- ISBN: 978-1-895836-91-2
Hell Can Wait by Theodore Judson (tp) - ISBN: 978-1-978-1-894063-23-4
Hounds of Ash and other tales of Fool Wolf, The by Greg Keyes (tp)
- ISBN: 978-1-894063-09-8
Hydrogen Steel by K. A. Bedford (tp) - ISBN: 978-1-894063-20-3

i-ROBOT Poetry by Jason Christie (tp) - ISBN: 978-1-894063-24-1
Immortal Quest by Alexandra MacKenzie (pb) - ISBN: 978-1-894063-46-3

Jackal Bird by Michael Barley (pb) - ISBN: 978-1-895836-07-3
Jackal Bird by Michael Barley (hb) - ISBN: 978-1-895836-11-0
JEMMA7729 by Phoebe Wray (tp) - ISBN: 978-1-894063-40-1

Keaen by Till Noever (tp) - ISBN: 978-1-894063-08-1
Keeper's Child by Leslie Davis (tp) - ISBN: 978-1-894063-01-2

Land/Space edited by Candas Jane Dorsey and Judy McCrosky (tp)
- ISBN: 978-1-895836-90-5
Land/Space edited by Candas Jane Dorsey and Judy McCrosky (hb)
- ISBN: 978-1-895836-92-9
Lyskarion: The Song of the Wind (Part One of The Chronicles of the Karionin)
by J.A. Cullum (tp) - ISBN: 978-1-894063-02-9

Machine Sex and other stories by Candas Jane Dorsey (tp)
- ISBN: 978-0-88878-278-6
Maërlande Chronicles, The by Élisabeth Vonarburg (pb)
- ISBN: 978-0-88878-294-6

Milkman, The by Michael J. Martineck (tp) - ISBN: 978-0-77053-060-7
Moonfall by Heather Spears (pb) - ISBN: 978-0-88878-306-6

Of Wind and Sand by Sylvie Bérard (translated by Sheryl Curtis) (tp)
- ISBN: 978-1-894063-19-7
On Spec: The First Five Years edited by On Spec (pb)
- ISBN: 978-1-895836-08-0
On Spec: The First Five Years edited by On Spec (hb)
- ISBN: 978-1-895836-12-7
Orbital Burn by K. A. Bedford (tp) - ISBN: 978-1-894063-10-4
Orbital Burn by K. A. Bedford (hb) - ISBN: 978-1-894063-12-8

Pallahaxi Tide by Michael Coney (pb) - ISBN: 978-0-88878-293-9
Paradox Resolution by K. A. Bedford (tp) - ISBN:978-1-894063-88-3
Passion Play by Sean Stewart (pb) - ISBN: 978-0-88878-314-1
Petrified World (Determine Your Destiny #1) by Piotr Brynczka (pb)
- ISBN: 978-1-894063-11-1
Plague Saint, The by Rita Donovan (tp) - ISBN: 978-1-895836-28-8
Plague Saint, The by Rita Donovan (hb) - ISBN: 978-1-895836-29-5
Pock's World by Dave Duncan (tp) - ISBN: 978-1-894063-47-0
Puzzle Box, The by Randy McCharles, Billie Millholland, Eileen Bell, and Ryan
    McFadden (tp) - ISBN: 978-1-77053-040-9

Reluctant Voyagers by Élisabeth Vonarburg (pb) - ISBN: 978-1-895836-09-7
Reluctant Voyagers by Élisabeth Vonarburg (hb) - ISBN: 978-1-895836-15-8
Resisting Adonis by Timothy J. Anderson (tp) - ISBN: 978-1-895836-84-4
Resisting Adonis by Timothy J. Anderson (hb) - ISBN: 978-1-895836-83-7
Rigor Amortis edited by Jaym Gates and Erika Holt (tp)
- ISBN: 978-1-894063-63-0

Silent City, The by Élisabeth Vonarburg (tp) - ISBN: 978-1-894063-07-4
Slow Engines of Time, The by Élisabeth Vonarburg (tp)
- ISBN: 978-1-895836-30-1
Slow Engines of Time, The by Élisabeth Vonarburg (hb)
- ISBN: 978-1-895836-31-8
Stealing Magic by Tanya Huff (tp) - ISBN: 978-1-894063-34-0
Stolen Children (Children of the Panther Part Three)
    by Amber Hayward (tp) - ISBN: 978-1-894063-66-1
Strange Attractors by Tom Henighan (pb) - ISBN: 978-0-88878-312-7

Taming, The by Heather Spears (pb) - ISBN: 978-1-895836-23-3
Taming, The by Heather Spears (hb) - ISBN: 978-1-895836-24-0
Technicolor Ultra Mall by Ryan Oakley (tp) - ISBN: 978-1-894063-54-8
Ten Monkeys, Ten Minutes by Peter Watts (tp) - ISBN: 978-1-895836-74-5
Ten Monkeys, Ten Minutes by Peter Watts (hb) - ISBN: 978-1-895836-76-9
Tesseracts 1 edited by Judith Merril (pb) - ISBN: 978-0-88878-279-3
Tesseracts 2 edited by Phyllis Gotlieb & Douglas Barbour (pb)
- ISBN: 978-0-88878-270-0
Tesseracts 3 edited by Candas Jane Dorsey & Gerry Truscott (pb)
- ISBN: 978-0-88878-290-8
Tesseracts 4 edited by Lorna Toolis & Michael Skeet (pb)
- ISBN: 978-0-88878-322-6
Tesseracts 5 edited by Robert Runté & Yves Maynard (pb)
- ISBN: 978-1-895836-25-7

Warriors by Barbara Galler-Smith and Josh Langston (tp)
  -ISBN: 978-1-77053-030-0
Wildcatter by Dave Duncan (tp) - ISBN: 978-1-894063-90-6